WORLDS BEYOND THE HORIZON

WORLDS BEYOND
THE
HORIZON

by JOACHIM G. LEITHÄUSER

Translated from the German
by HUGH MERRICK

NEW YORK   ALFRED A. KNOPF   1955

L.C. catalog card number: 55-9288

© Alfred A. Knopf, Inc., 1955

THIS IS A BORZOI BOOK
PUBLISHED BY ALFRED A. KNOPF, INC.

FIRST AMERICAN EDITION

Originally published in German as UFER HINTER DEM HORIZONT: Die Grossen Entdecker Der Erde Von Kolumbus Bis Zur Weltraumfahrt. *Copyright 1953 by Safari-Verlag Carl Boldt und Reinhard Jaspert, Berlin.*

PREFACE

THIS IS NO BOOK OF HEROES. It could easily have become one, for seldom has so small a band of men contributed so much to the transformation of the world as did the great seafarers, conquerors, and explorers from Europe during the Age of Discovery. They were so bold—or so foolhardy—as to press on to the ends of the world and then beyond. They tore wide open the narrow horizon that fettered the medieval West, set themselves goals from which their contemporaries recoiled in terror, entrusted themselves to seas whose farther limit might be the abyss of hell itself, feared not the elements nor legendary monsters nor the secret terror of the unknown, bestrode shores whose existence had not even been conjectured, and endured hardships and exertions that we today can hardly envisage. They gave the world a new countenance; they found followers possessed of the same urge, men willing, like themselves, to hazard all if only they might set foot on ground unseen before of man's eyes and wring from the earth her secret mysteries.

Even so, this is no book of heroes. For the story it unfolds is so adventurous and dramatic, so thrilling and revelatory, that glorification would only falsify it. I have therefore tried to present it (always allowing for the omissions inherent in the compression of such a mighty mass of material) in such a way that the events are pictured exactly as they occurred, revealing the magnificence, the baseness or even the haphazard nature of the motives and actions, and that combination of fantastic courage, energy, unscrupulousness, endurance, and devotion which alone made success possible and so enlarged and changed the known boundaries of the world.

The great ventures of the men who were the first to sail beyond the horizon of the continent of Europe, and of their followers who penetrated undisturbed tropical wildernesses or the icy polar oceans, unfold in tales of error, failure, and blind strokes of fortune, in examples of human passion and insufficiency, of self-sacrifice and steadfastness of spirit, constituting one of the most important chapters in the history of mankind.

A chapter as impressive as it is tragic, for just as the discovery of the world was the fulfillment of a mission whose true significance the people of the day were not yet ready to grasp, so the occupation of its unknown regions imposed new duties, again beyond the mental grasp of contemporary humanity, charged suddenly with the full responsibility for the weal or woe of those newly discovered, newly uncovered tracts. A chapter of history which shows that, however stupendous a feat it was to reach the shores beyond the horizon, mere achievement is not the end of the story; for on the successful discoverer in the very moment of his triumph falls the heavy burden of creating for his feats of discovery a definite meaning and character.

CONTENTS

[xi]

LIST OF PLATES

LIST OF DRAWINGS

IN THE TEXT

LIST OF MAPS AND CHARTS

Part I

Out into the Ocean

INTO THE UNKNOWN

I T P L E A S E D the Carthaginians to permit Hanno to go seafaring beyond the Pillars of Hercules and there to found Libyo-Phœnician settlements."

So begins the oldest traveler's report that has survived to reach us today. In a few simple words it tells the story of one of the finest and bravest undertakings of the early ages. It tells how in about 530 B.C. a huge Carthaginian fleet (reputedly manned by thirty thousand men and women, though it is a fair presumption that at some stage in the lapse of time one scribe or another introduced a naught too many) sailed out into the ocean through the Strait of Gibraltar, scattered colonies on the African shores, and then followed the coast southward along the fringes of the "desert land." The Carthaginian sailors gazed on a new, unknown world—huge jungles, wild men of the forests, an immense river housing hippopotamuses and crocodiles—and even dared to go ashore on several occasions. It is difficult to say whose was the greater fear when first discoverer and discovered met face to face. The natives promptly fled, but the Carthaginian report also records their own terror: "We heard the sound of flutes and cymbals, the beating of drums and a ghastly shrieking. Thereat we were affrighted and the seers bade us leave the island. Sailing instantly onward, we passed along a burning region, filled with sweet scents, from which fiery streams poured in spate into the sea. The land was not to be trodden for very heat. And from it too we hastened on our way, seized with a great terror."

Yet their fear does them no discredit, for they had amply

proved their courage in setting in motion and pursuing this great
adventure in spite of all its terrors, among them a volcanic eruption, probably of the great Cameroon volcano. At the southernmost point of their voyage the Carthaginians came upon an island,
where they once more landed. They relate how the island was
"peopled by forest-dwellers. There were however a great multitude of women with shaggy bodies whom our interpreters named
gorillas. The men we pursued, could however catch none, for they
fled one and all, climbing steep precipices and defending themselves with rocks. Of the women we captured three, who however
bit and tore with their nails our leaders and were loath to follow
them. These we slew and brought their skins to Carthage. And
further we sailed not, for there was a scarcity of provender."

Readers of later days have often racked their brains over the
odd story of the women. For the most part, it was held to be a fig-
ment of imagination, till the discovery of the great anthropoids of
Africa seemed to lend credence to the ancient Carthaginian account. But it will never be resolved who or what did the biting.
Were the Carthaginians not able to distinguish between beast and
human being? Or were these really aborigines clad in skins—for
the Carthaginians were hardly likely to have flayed human beings
and certainly could not have cured their skins on the spot?

The outstanding thing about this ancient report is not so much
its content, but the fact that it was ever written. For the bold and
adventurous types that risk their lives in ships and embark on expeditions into inhospitable seas and the far unexplored corners of
the earth have rarely been endowed with literary talent, above all
in an age when reading and writing were the province of the few.
The report rendered by the Carthaginian General Hanno thus
marks a level of culture not touched again till we come upon records left by the leaders of great expeditions of discovery in more
recent times. And another remarkable thing is that this text ever
survived. For it was certainly not by any set intention that old
Carthaginian manuscripts were handed down to us, in face of the
thorough destruction and utter devastation meted out by history
to the important trading-city of Carthage at the hands of the re-
lentless Romans.

It is the Greeks whom we have to thank for the preservation of Hanno's report in spite of everything. For this ancient race, which has showered upon mankind unforgettable works of art and poetry, of philosophy and mathematics, was also a race of mariners, trading to the farthest known bounds, founding colonies and settlements on the way, and piecing together a complete picture of the accessible world of their day. At Delphi, the seat of the world-famous oracle, and also in the Greek cities of Asia Minor men were busy gathering greedily and recording every scrap of information about the lands and peoples of the Mediterranean basin, of Africa and the approaches to Asia. Nor were the Greeks satisfied with knowledge drawn from secondhand accounts—the old reports of earlier voyages by Phœnicians, Egyptians, Cretans, Carthaginians, or the more recent observations of their own traders—but began to undertake journeys that served no other purpose than to explore and obtain information about distant lands. And so the science of geography was born.

AN ANCIENT SHIP

The historian Hecatæus (*c.* 500 B.C.) was probably the first of Western learned men to undertake purely scientific travels. The most famous of all was Herodotus (*c.* 495–425 B.C.), whose approach to a historical work of wider scope was so thorough that he first paid a personal visit to each of the districts to be covered by his work—mainland Greece, the Ægean Islands, the Black Sea coasts, the Persian Empire, Arabia, Egypt up to Assouan, Cyrenaica, the Syrtes as far afield as Carthage, Sicily, and Italy to the Apennines. The outstanding weight of Herodotus' repute is perhaps best illustrated by the effects of his mistakes: as late as the nineteenth century his error about the source of the Nile was still confusing the savants, who were still left propounding a confluence of the Nile and the Niger.

Hardly had the Greek geographers tidied the world roughly into three regions—the Orient (Asia), the Occident (Europe), and Libya (Africa)—when the orbit of the world began to expand mightily: Alexander's campaigns broadened the horizon and at the same time introduced a new era of exploration, because he had en-

SAXON SHIPS

couraged the company of distance-measurers, naturalists, historians, and philosophers.

Under Alexander and his successors, Greek soldiers and explorers found their way to the extreme bounds of India and into the heart of Africa to the headwaters of the Nile. Eager traders found their way overland and by sea to China, the silk land: sea traffic to the East increased beyond all dreams when, in about 100 B.C., the law of the monsoons (those seasonal varying winds that blow between the coasts of Africa and India) was established.

Meanwhile, the mighty Roman Empire had succeeded that of Greece. Its legions tramped the desert sands and primeval German forests, its triremes plowed not only the blue Mediterranean but the rough North Sea up to far Scandinavia and northward beyond the Orkneys. When the learned Ptolemæus of Alexandria collected all the accumulated knowledge about the world in the second century after Christ, he was able to survey far more than the highly organized territories of the wide empire of Rome, with its wonderful traffic lanes from England to the Persian Gulf, from the Danube basin to Africa: he could also write of areas far beyond its confines, such as the Caspian Sea, Central Asia, and even the Malay Archipelago.

This marvelous fund of knowledge faded into tragic oblivion in the West. Sadder still seems this effect of the shrinking horizons when one recalls how intelligently the earth's stature was understood by even the ancient Greeks.

The Pythagoreans had already drawn the inference, from the force of attraction that everywhere exerts its earthward pull, and from the laws of harmony, that the world must be a globe. In his *Phædo* Plato hinted at the globular shape of the earth and tentatively linked up with discoveries made by Archytas of Tarentum (*c.* 379 B.C.) or one of his pupils. Aristotle and Eudoxus (d. 355 B.C.) went further in their search for clear scientific proofs: the earth's shadow on the moon is circular, the horizon is everywhere a curve, ships on the horizon reveal first their masts and then their hulls, different constellations are visible in the southern and in the northern skies. Aristarchus of Samos (280 B.C.), Hipparchus, and Anaxagoras even taught the theory of the earth's movement round the sun. The first measurements of the earth's area were attempted by Dicharchus (*c.* 320 B.C.) and carried on by Poseidonius and Eratosthenes (276–196 B.C.); the last-named, though he knew nothing of America or the expanses of the Atlantic or Pacific, reckoned the earth's circumference to be 40,000 kilometers—a fantastic result, for the correct figure is 40,003.423. A century and a half before Christ, Crates of Mallus, though naturally with incorrect details, constructed the first globe. And in Europe's early Middle Ages what conception was left of these miraculous flights of the spirit and of these discoveries of the earth's true shape? A miserable flat plate as the center of the universe.

Once the barbarian Germanic hordes had swept down upon Italy, annihilating all culture with might and main, not a trace survived of the priceless writings of the geographers, nor of the handbooks designed for the use of navigators, with their descriptions of every seacoast, island, roadstead, and foreign land, nor of the comprehensive notes of the roads and cities of the Roman Empire ("Itineraries"). Under the narrow dominion of the Christian church the teaching of the earth's globular form and of the antipodes was resisted and forbidden. The universal low level of culture led, in the geographic sphere, not only to a sad clouding of the established facts, but to the wildest flights of bizarre fancy. Instead of occupying themselves with the Roman geographers, men preferred to follow the cult of late Roman sensation-mongers like Macrobius and enthusiastically pictured on their maps as inhabitants of distant regions horrific monsters and human abortions, some with only one eye, some with twin heads, no heads at all, or

A DARK-AGES VIEW OF THE RACES OF UNEXPLORED REGIONS

the heads of dogs, and others that sheltered from the burning heat of the sun beneath monstrous lips or gigantic feet.

The geographic image of the world had to conform exactly to the Bible. Jerusalem was regarded as the center of the flat earth. "Thus saith the Lord God; This is Jerusalem: I have set it in the midst of the nations and countries that are round about her" (Ezekiel v, 5). A typical example of the spirit of the age is that of Saint Cosmas Indicopleustes, who accomplished a notable voyage to India, but testified: "Of what use is this or that knowledge of this earth, if by it our Faith be not enhanced?" This traveler over the earth's surface fashioned for his time a picture of the world that conformed in every detail to the Bible: its shape and measurements correspond precisely with the Ark of the Covenant, whose dimensions God himself had laid down. The universe is a longish box, arched on top, transparent as glass. On its floor is the earth, with its three continents of Europe, Africa, and Asia; above the last-named and greatest continent rises Mount Ararat, where Noah's ark came to rest. And round this mountain circle the sun, moon, and stars, now visible, now obscured.

Even on the maps of the world which the monks of the Middle Ages fashioned, the earth followed the dictates of the Bible: it was a slab, at whose eastern end lay Paradise. Out of it flowed the four streams described in the first Book of Moses (Genesis), which were sometimes identified with the Ganges, Nile, Tigris, and Euphrates, at other times as the Nile, the Danube, or as other rivers issuing from beneath the ocean. True, even then there were fine navigators, especially the Normans, who, thanks to their splendid skill in building ships with keels and stern rudders, ventured the world's high seas and pushed far beyond its known boundaries; but all their achievements proved utterly sterile.

SHIPBUILDING IN THE ELEVENTH CENTURY.
FROM THE BAYEUX TAPESTRY

In vain did a learned man like Adam of Bremen collate and record what he could about their deeds—his reports received too little recognition and distribution, and were soon forgotten. It is hard to hazard a guess as to how the West would ever have emerged from its narrow confinement had not an impulse from outside set spiritual development into motion once again.

The man to whom the West owes its greatest debt of gratitude was Mohammed. Obviously, Islam's prophet had no intention of waking Europe out of its spiritual coma; his object was to stir the Arab tribes to religious ecstasy and warlike fanaticism. Under the prophet's green banners the mounted armies of Arabia swept far across Egypt, North Africa, Syria, Palestine, and Asia Minor to the Indus and the Caucasus; forced their way into Rhodes, Sicily, Sardinia, Corsica, the Balearic Isles, southern Italy, Spain, and the south of France. There they met, at Tours and Poitiers, their first rebuff, and came to a halt only when they had mastered for Islam an area greater than Alexander's empire, stretching over all northern Africa, half the Mediterranean, and western and central Asia. The Christian world struck back and attempted to recapture the Holy Sepulcher in Jerusalem by successive Crusades.

These religious campaigns, in which each side regarded those on the other as heretics of hell and sought to annihilate them in the name of the true God, had for the Western world the great advantage that they at least brought its inhabitants into contact with a definite culture and taught them in the course of time to draw profit from the treasury of knowledge which the Arabs had safeguarded. The meetings of Christian with "Saracen" or "Moor" were not exclusively warlike clashes. The Hohenstaufen Emperor Frederick II, who, under a Papal ban and with little support from the crusading knights, yet won greater successes than any of his predecessors because he was on good terms with the Sultan of Arabia, popularized at his court Arabian philosophy, algebra, chemistry, medicine, and astronomy; cultural stimuli spread outward from the Moorish Empire, situated in Spain; and through their sojourn in the Orient, European crusaders learned to improve their taste and their knowledge; and in the end, trade with the Near and Far East, traversing the Arabic world, brought closer relationships into being.

In geography, as in many another scientific field, the Arabs had preserved the heritage of the ancients; for example, besides the works of Aristotle, those of Ptolemæus, unknown in the West, had been translated into Arabic and had proved to be of the first importance to mapmakers and astronomers. But the Arabs also enriched their knowledge of the world by voyages of exploration astonishing in their scope, such as those of the geographers ibn-Batuta and al-Idrisi.

The impulses and traditions, which gradually found their way into the West, received a further impetus when, after the capture of Constantinople by the Turks in 1453, the expelled Byzantine

AN ELEVENTH-CENTURY SHIP. FROM THE BAYEUX TAPESTRY

sages came to Europe, bringing with them the ancient sources of knowledge, which they too had preserved. The fall of Constantinople marked, in varied aspects, a turning-point in history and, indeed, provided the motive for the discovery of America.

The great Mongol whirlwind of Genghis Khan and his followers had swept away all other Asiatic empires, constituting a dire menace to Arabic as well as European communities and driving before it hordes of refugees of diverse racial origin. Among these were the Turks, who, having settled somewhere in Persia, first conquered their host country by their ferocity and bravery, then assumed the leadership of the whole Mohammedan world and, six hundred years after the Prophet's death, fanned afresh the flames of the ancient religious frenzy. The resulting campaigns against the West, which later reached even Vienna, were not the only outcome: more important was the barrier placed across the trade routes between Europe and the Far East. Because the Turks sealed off the Orient, the West was forced to seek communications with

India, China, and Japan by other routes, and this proved the end of an era during which ships had mainly plied back and forth across the Mediterranean between Constantinople, Alexandria, Venice, and Genoa on their peaceful trade missions. It became essential to break through the known boundaries of the world—and from the moment when Europe began its eruption into the wider spaces and shattered the existing bounds of science and geography, a sharp upward surge soon carried the old but comparatively unimportant continent forward to transform it in a very short space of time into the center of the world.

With the broadening of knowledge and of its sphere of influence it enjoyed an undreamed-of enrichment of its spiritual, political, and economic forces; the world picture that was to take shape in Europe in the course of two centuries was the first complete and scientifically correct mirror of the planet on which we live.

Underlying the great adventures now launched by European navigators were two compelling causes, one political and religious, the other commercial. The first was the desire to gain a powerful ally in the rear of the Mohammedan lands. According to the legend, Prester John was still alive and had founded a great Christian empire deep in Asia; to find a way to it was essential. True, it was by no means clear where these Christians lived—in Greater or Lesser India, Upper, Middle, or Lower India, names and notions all confused and descriptive of China, Japan, and India and, indeed, of parts of Africa. Further preoccupation with this problem resulted in a fusion of myth and truth and the identification of the realm of the prophet-king as Habesh (Abyssinia). There the missionaries Frumentius and Ædisius had introduced Christianity in the fourth century; later the Mohammedans had cut the country off from the other Christian lands, but in 1123 an Abyssinian mission again succeeded in reaching Rome. From then regular communication was maintained between Abyssinia and the Frankish Empire until in 1429 the Sultan of the Mamelukes had the Abyssinian ambassadors, on their return from the Frankish court, arrested and beheaded in Cairo. So now Europeans were seeking a sea lane around the African deserts to Habesh, the "Third India," in the hope of finding there an ally who would not only be politically valuable but would be able to restore and protect the lost commerce with Asia.

This second commercial reason meant much more than the mere rehabilitation of general trade relations. The valued silk and other costly products of Asia were of course highly prized, but they were not indispensable. Europe's urgent need, ever scarcer owing to the Turkish strangle hold on trade routes, was spices.

Spices had come to be beyond price in Europe—a nutmeg, as the price of spices now rose to dizzy heights, was weighed against gold. The wealth of Constantinople, of Alexandria, and of Venice arose entirely from the fact that they were exchange ports for the spice trade to Europe. And even later when, at the beginning of the sixteenth century, the direct route was opened up, the vast profit continued to beckon seafarers to the land of spices: for a bushel of cloves cost two ducats in the Molucca Islands, in Malacca the price had risen to fourteen, in the port of Calicut it commanded fifty, and in London it could be sold for two hundred and thirteen.

So spices came to have a decisive influence on world history. Not so much because European palates, once they made their acquaintance, were so spoiled that they were reluctant to do without them, as on account of the definite famine that had come into being. The demand, as they grew ever scarcer, became so heavy that it worked as a force potent to lever aside the weightiest obstacle in the way.

This tremendous hunger for spices is best explained by the conditions under which men lived in the Middle Ages. Every kitchen depended on the plentiful use of spices, as there were no potatoes, few vegetables or hors d'œuvres, but only a monotonous round of preserved meat. In northern Europe, before the modern system of crop-rotation and the cultivation of root crops provided winter fodder, all the cattle had to be slaughtered and pickled in the autumn. In order to make the dreary taste of this diet more bearable over a period, pepper and cloves were added. Nor had the ordinary mortal anything varied to enjoy: no tea, no coffee, no cocoa. Exceptionally wealthy people could get hold of sugar or wine; everyone else had to lend taste to his thin beer or acrid wine with spices. These were also plentifully used medicinally; only strongly scented brews of medicine encouraged belief in their healing properties; and the inhabitants of the medieval towns needed quantities of strong perfumes, not only as a reputed safeguard against the frequent pestilences and the plague, but also to protect them from the prevalent stench that robbed them of their breath.

So Europe had long been seeking pepper, cloves, cinnamon, nutmeg, ginger, benzoin, galangal, cardamoms, cassia, frankincense, sandalwood, and other aromatic products from southeast Asia. The Turkish barrier on the old trade route had, of course, not entirely cut communications, but the prices of the available spices rose phenomenally because the Arab traders sailed from India to the Persian Gulf or Suez and the cargo had then to be brought overland on camels and re-embarked in ships in the Mediterranean ports.

So the age of the great European discoveries of the world did not begin with a search for unknown shores, but as searches for the way to a goal that had long been known. Christian zeal had led devoted missionaries into Asia, that great continent teeming with races, cultures, and religions, some hundreds of years before. It was in 1246 that the first Papal mission under Giovanni de Piano Carpini reached Mongolia and paid court to its ruler, the Great Khan. The Franciscan Rubruk and other fearless holy men followed later. Johannes of Montecorvino, with the energetic aid of Brother Arnold of Cologne, founded Christian communities in Peking and elsewhere in China: the chronicles of the Missionary Oderich of Portenau's travels between 1325 and 1330, and of the Papal Legate Johannes of Marignola between 1338 and 1353, furnished a true picture of China before its doors were closed to the rest of the world by the nationalistic Ming dynasty.

It was, however, a Venetian merchant, Marco Polo (1254–1324), whose pen produced the most truthful, interest-awakening, and pregnant chronicle—indeed, one of the most important books in the world's history—while suffering enforced leisure as a Genoese prisoner of war. His contemporaries regarded him as a complete romancer, being unwilling to believe that the Far East

Phœnician Ships. As Early as 595 B.C. the Phœnicians Rounded the Cape of Good Hope

Loading an Ancient Greek Cargo Vessel

Reconstruction of the Viking Oseberg Ship

A Roman Bireme of Classical Times

r. Marco Polo at the Court of
ai Khan in 1275.
ature from Marco Polo's
unt of His Travels

w. The Empire of Prester John.
 Ortelius'
trum Orbis Terrarum, 1573

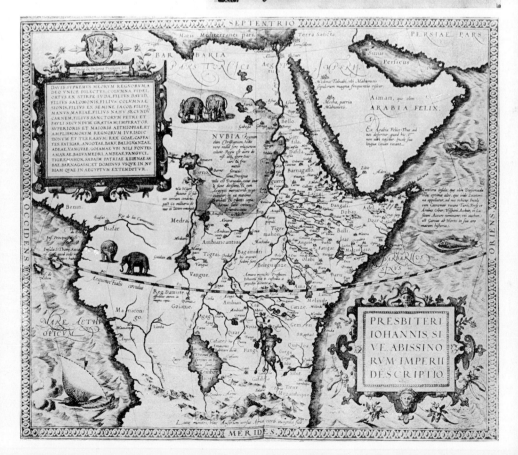

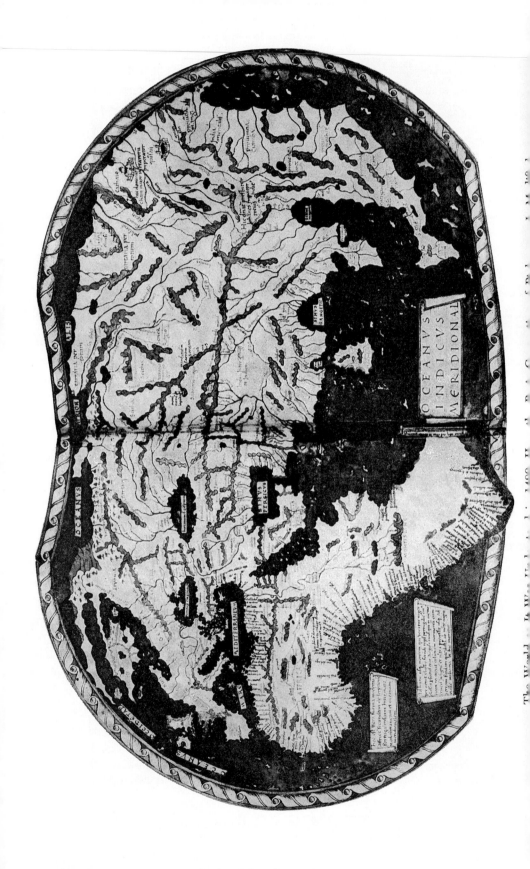

The World as Henry the Navigator knew it in 1490. Henry died in 1460. But the map of Fra Mauro, on which he based his explorations, was not completed until 1490.

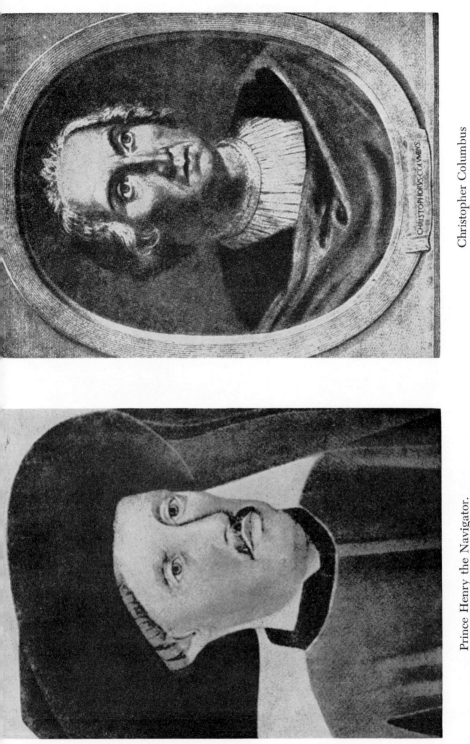

Prince Henry the Navigator.
From a Late Fifteenth-Century Miniature

Christopher Columbus

Sebastian Cabot. From a Contemporary Portrait

Amerigo Vespucci. From a Facsimile in Montanus

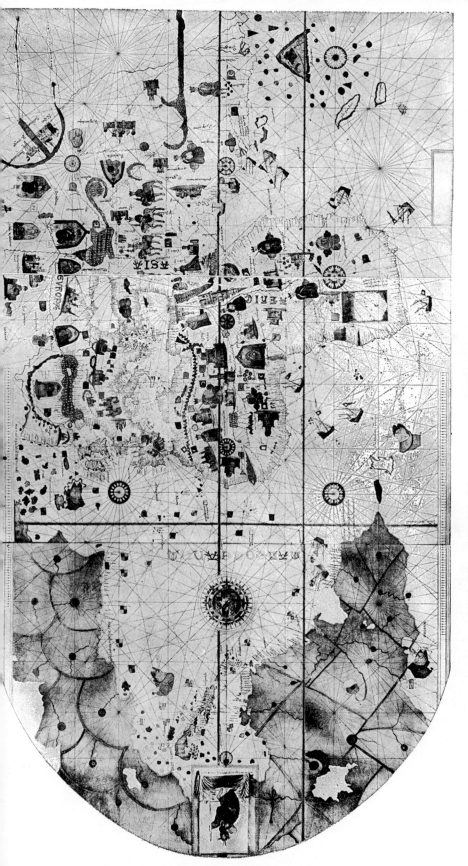

A Spanish Map of the World in 1500, Prepared by Juan de la Cosa, Columbus's Pilot. This Is the First Dated Map to Show the Western Hemisphere

Waldseemüller's Map of the World in 1507, Showing North and South America as Separate Continents

was ahead of the West in matters of cultural, technical, political, administrative, and economic development; yet Marco Polo's descriptions of his travels were not without their influence, exciting men's imaginations and—however much opposition they invoked—shaping the ideas that men formed of Asia.

In spite of the errors it contained, Marco Polo's chronicle was a picture that only an exact observer, possessed of deep knowledge

MARCO POLO, VENETIAN TRAVELER TO THE ORIENT (1254–1324?)

of conditions, could have painted. As a young man he accompanied his father and his uncle (who had already visited the court of the Great Kublai Khan, the emperor of Mongolia and China, on a voyage they undertook in 1271 as merchants and Papal ambas-

sadors) to visit that great ruler, the peaceful, highly cultured successor of Genghis Khan. When Marco Polo returned to his native
city with his father and his uncle, he was forty-one. He was then
to have his first taste of the world's suspicion: how could these
three grubby companions be the respectable Messers Polo whom
men had long ago declared to be dead? These beggars ought first
of all to produce their credentials! So the returned wanderers arranged a great feast, arrayed themselves in fine clothes, and produced from the linings of their tattered, travel-stained garments
their costly treasure of rubies, emeralds, sapphires, gold plate, and
pearls.

So Marco Polo was able to convert the first doubters; but he
could not allay the disbelief in what he was later to set forth in his
book. It all sounded too much like a fairy story. The Polos, having
been kindly received in Cathay (China), had carried on their
trade there and undertaken journeys far afield through all the
provinces of the empire, in the service of the Great Khan; Marco
had even become governor of a province, Kiangnan. He was thus
able to describe faithfully not only the many lands and peoples of
Asia, their way of life, their marvelous ports and capitals, but also
their fabulous networks of legendary canals and highways, their
highly organized system of administration, and such unlikely
things as paper money and black stones that you could burn—
coal. They begged him on his deathbed, in the face of his approaching end, to sort out truth from romance in his narration;
he is said to have answered that he had not related the half of
what he had seen.

Marco Polo visited the whole of China and was the first European since Alexander's campaigns to see India. When the spice
famine afflicted Europe, people began to pay attention to his reports of the Malayan Islands where pepper, nutmeg, and other
spices were to be found in abundance. In addition, the other
riches of which he had spoken—the precious stones of Ceylon, the
pearls of Malabar, the gold- and silver-studded temple buildings
of Siam and Tonkin—were powerful magnets, drawing men toward the Indies. The tales he had heard about the Island of Zi-
pangu (Japan) excited particular interest, for here one could re-

putedly find all the treasures of the earth. "The wealth of the land is utterly inexhaustible and the glory of the King's palace is indescribable. The whole roof is of golden tiles; so are the panels of all the chambers and the small tables which stand in its innumerable rooms. And the priceless red pearls are said to be found there in plenty." No wonder the mariners of Europe, braving the tumultuous seas to the rim of the world, dreamed of reaching this

KUBLAI KHAN (1216?–1294), FOUNDER OF THE MONGOL DYNASTY. FROM A CHINESE ENGRAVING

miraculous land and seeing with their own eyes this Isle of Gold, storied by Marco Polo.

The man whose energy was responsible for the first European voyages of discovery and whom men rightly nicknamed "The Navigator"—the Infante Henry of Portugal (1394–1460)—never sailed the seas. He was the Grand Master of the Christian Order for combatting the Moors, an unremitting employer of the Portuguese captains whose duty it was ever and again to sail the oceans, to collect information, and to press fearlessly out into the unknown.

It was in 1415 that the Portuguese captured Ceuta on the Moroccan coast, that most important of Moorish bases. This was the first irruption into the very world of Islam; the Infante gave his thoughts to the best use of the new strategic position and hit upon the idea of taking the enemy in the rear and establishing communications with Prester John in that way. To do this, the Portuguese had to learn seamanship; at Sagres, Henry founded an observatory and the first navigation school the world had known. He employed Italian tutors, for they lived in flourishing trading-centers and had had rich opportunities of acquiring experience with sails and rigging. Their Portuguese pupils began by cruising cautiously along the western coast of Morocco. The Infante urged them on. Every year they had to sail a little farther along the coast of Africa till, in 1434, they reached the farthest possible point, Cape Bojador, which also bore the name of "Cape No," for here there was no farther progress to be made, as the salt content of the sea became so dense that all ships remained fast in its waters.

"Sail on!" commanded the Infante. For he had an idea that by sailing along Africa one would come to Habesh or, indeed, India. So on they went, ever onward, with new expeditions, new ships, new captains.

In the course of time this policy produced mounting results, and the extreme point of the known world was soon only a point of passage. In 1441 the sea captains Nuno Tristão and Antão Goncealvez reached Cape Blanco and saw the first Negroes; in 1445 Lancarote discovered the mouth of the Senegal River; in 1446 Diniz Fernandez reached Cape Verde; and in 1447 Nuno Tristão penetrated the neighborhood of the Gambia. A few years later, in 1455–6, that river was discovered and navigated by Aloise Cadamosto; in 1456 Antonio de Noli placed the Cape Verde Islands on the map; and shortly after Henry's death an expedition planned by him and commanded by Pedro de Sinzia reached the coast of what is today Liberia.

On his bare rock at Sagres, surrounded by his staff of scientists, Henry studied in their minutest detail the results and reports of his seagoing captains. Navigation, till then a chancy venture, was now established as an art or science; the sea was purged of the innumerable monsters with which the fear and boastfulness of seafaring men had peopled it; the mainland was explored and made known to all men. Henry's tenacity and energy were responsible for maps of Africa's hitherto unknown coastal areas and for heightening the knowledge that the West was then absorbing

A FOURTEENTH-CENTURY SHIP

from its new acquaintance with Aristotle and Ptolemæus, whose works were not translated into Latin till 1450! Those two writers had taught that there could be only desert land between the tropics, because the burning heat of the sun's vertical rays must destroy all vegetation. Henry was able to spread the news that far to the south lush herbs and tall palms were being encountered. "All this I write with due respect to his honor Ptolemæus," he commented with an ironic sense of superiority, "who noised abroad full many good things about the continents of the world, but whose thoughts about these parts were far astray. For innumerable black races live about the equator, and the trees rise to an unbelievable height: indeed, it is just in the south that the plants grow to their full strength and stature."

By the time the Infante died, he had laid the foundations not only of Portugal's sea supremacy, but also of the wonderful economic development to come: for the opening up of the new African tracts brought with it the start of a most lucrative trade, which cost the white men mere baubles and tinsel in return for gold, iron, musk, sugar, and, in addition to those valuable commodities, slaves too.

Henry the Navigator was responsible for the necessary preliminaries that in the end enabled the Portuguese actually to reach India. But the value of his work was not confined to Portugal; it was of benefit to the navigators of every European country because it gradually stimulated the urge to explore the world. The knowledge that the earth is a globe, which the ancients had already possessed, had gradually found its way into Europe again, thanks to communications by the Arabs; the spread of the art of printing increased the general interest in geographical works and, by popularizing the new discoveries, spurred on the interest in new voyages. The technique of shipbuilding made timely advances, as did the navigator's art, which could now rely on astronomic tables and on a practical instrument for taking reckonings, the quadrant. The magnetic needle—with which the Chinese had already been familiar in ancient times—was rediscovered in the twelfth century; but it was only now, at last, that men dared to trust absolutely in the compass and sail out across the open sea, far from the friendly protection of the coastline. That moment was the true dawn of the Age of Discovery.

2

COLUMBUS

WHEN the early seafarers ventured on the sea in their little wooden ships with neither chart nor compass, they were at the mercy not only of the winds but of the great ocean currents. That is the main reason why the great American continent was discovered so late: for there was no kindly current to bear English, French, Spanish, or Portuguese mariners across the Atlantic. If they ever ventured far out, they sailed aimlessly on an unknown, seemingly endless sheet of water, eventually to return to their homeland without accomplishing anything; if they strayed from their course, they either fell victims to the monstrous width of the ocean or were washed back to Europe by the Gulf Stream.

It was for this reason that the first discovery of America fell to the wild, red-bearded Vikings, not so much because their Nordic race had endowed them with any outstanding superiority over other peoples, but because when they sailed around Iceland, the Denmark Current and the Labrador Current carried them in the direction of North America's east coast. We know very little about the details of the voyages of the Norsemen, entangled as they are in legend, except that in A.D. 982 Eric the Red founded the first European settlement in Greenland, that in about A.D. 1000 Bjørne Herjulfson lost his way on a voyage to Greenland and sighted the American continent, and that not much later Leif Ericson landed on it and "Vinland" became the first short-lived colony on American ground. The voyages of the Vikings between Greenland, Newfoundland, Nova Scotia, and Vinland (probably somewhere in the region of Cape Cod) continued for a century or two; the last known journey from Greenland to America took place in 1347. But no echo reached the cities of Europe of the discoveries and battles fought with Indians by a handful of intrepid Norsemen who went wandering about in a direction where nobody in his senses could have anything to look for. The discoverers from western Europe had to shatter more than the bounds and fetters of nature: they had also to break down the preconceived ideas men had imposed. Tradition and hidebound

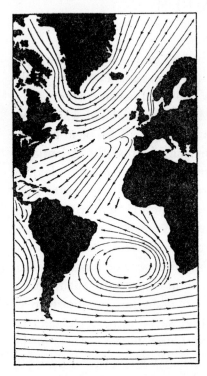 

ONLY THOSE WINDS BLOWING IN A SOUTHERLY DIRECTION FROM SPAIN HELPED THE EARLY VOYAGERS ON THEIR WAY TO THE NEW WORLD.

FAVORABLE OCEAN CURRENTS EXIST ONLY IN THE UPPER NORTH ATLANTIC AND BELOW THE GULF OF GUINEA.

lines of thought forbade any attempt to venture westward on the great ocean. The Strait of Gibraltar, the Pillars of Hercules, were the visible signs of world's end. Wondrous treasures might be won by sailing eastward to India or even China; to voyage westward was a waste of time. *Mare Tenebrosum,* the "Dark Sea," was the Romans' name for the Atlantic Ocean. Plato had already told how this ocean had swallowed up the Isle of Atlantis; mariners of all ages had brought tales of terrible monsters peopling these waters of hell, where eternal darkness brooded and a giant hand stretched up from the deeps to claw ships down into the abyss. Only those who had to seek absolution for a mountain of sin, like Saint Brendan (c. A.D. 587), were doomed to long years of wandering across that ocean, where devils lived in distant places and the water was so glutinous that all progress became impossible.

It is against such a background that we must visualize Columbus, the first man to sail straight out into the west across the ocean —Columbus, who, because he had a definite objective, broke out across a frontier that, to all intents and purposes, constituted in men's eyes the outer boundary of the world.

And before we take stock of Columbus in all his venturesome courage, his unbendable toughness, and his unswerving confidence of purpose, we should steep ourselves in the attitude of mind which ruled among his contemporaries and recall the tremendous and universal error that it fell to this one man to purge. The famous Nuremberg Chronicle of 1493 explains how at that time men believed that they had laid behind them six ages and that only the seventh and last awaited them in the future; and the Chronicle only left six blank pages, with whose completion the Last Judgment would irrefutably be at hand. Mankind believed itself to be in its old age; all that remained was this seventh and last age, in which the ruling forces would be want, sickness, and wickedness.

To quote from the Chronicle: "Conditions will be so terrible that no man will be able to lead a decent life. Then will all the sorrows of the Apocalypse pour down upon mankind: Flood, Earthquake, Pestilence, and Famine; neither shall the crops grow nor the fruits ripen; the wells will dry up and the waters will bear upon them blood and bitterness, so that the birds of the air, the beasts in the field, and the fishes in the sea will all perish."

But the surmises of the apostle of world disintegration were soon discredited. What followed was no blotting out of the world. Instead there came—with the discovery of America—a new impetus, a new urge to activity, a strong surge of the pulse of life, a new blossoming of culture destined to set immemorial landmarks along the road of a new age of knowledge. Moreover, it was within a few decades that the West was to experience this rebirth of the spirit. And if our present age lies under the cloud of imminent self-destruction, of dark prophecies and a general sense of inability to see the way out of its difficulties, perhaps it is fair to ask whether someday soon a new Columbus of space may not herald a new age of progress.

On August 13, 1476, a convoy of Genoese vessels carrying cargoes to Lisbon, England, and Flanders stood off the upper coast of Portugal, near Cape Saint Vincent, when it was suddenly attacked by a superior Franco-Portuguese fleet under the famous sea captain and hero William of Casanova. A fierce battle ensued. By nightfall three Genoese ships and four of the attackers' had gone down. While hundreds of sailors were drowning, a wounded Genoese, clinging to a wooden spar, managed to reach the Portuguese coast six miles away. He was Christopher Columbus.

It was a great landmark in the young sailor's life. Cast ashore here, he was able to reach Lisbon, which was at that time the hub of all sea enterprise and in particular the starting-point of the voyages of exploration out to the Azores and along the west coast of Africa. This was the great turning-point in the life of the young mariner. During the years he lived in Lisbon as a cartographer and bookseller he had the opportunity of learning everything in the realms of geography, mathematics, and astronomy which was essential to a master mariner; he had already sufficiently steeped himself in the stern practice of his craft.

In those years Lisbon's fine harbor was the mirror of the mounting commerce with newly discovered lands. In the spring the fleets sailed in laden with Negro slaves, elephants' tusks, Malagueta peppers, and coffers full of gold dust; in the autumn they set out again crammed with cheap trash like red caps, beads of glass, and falconry bells, for which the black men of West Africa paid immense rewards. In the city's narrow streets lounged sailors of every nationality, while traders and bankers turned the wheels of the new age of riches.

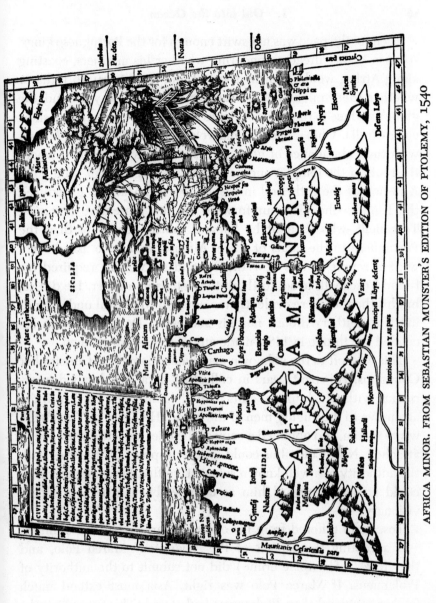

AFRICA MINOR. FROM SEBASTIAN MUNSTER'S EDITION OF PTOLEMY, 1540

Even so, the pace was not swift enough for the Portuguese kings. Alfonso V was already wondering whether his mariners, coasting along Africa, would find the shortest and easiest way to India or whether there might not be some more direct way around the globe's surface to the lands of riches in a westerly direction: a short cut to India, China, and the marvelous Isle of Cipangu (Japan) with their abundance of gold, pearls, and precious stones, where the roofs of the temples and palaces were said to be of solid gold. A bishop of the cathedral in Lisbon, Fernão Martins, introduced the King to the idea put forward by the Florentine humanist Toscanelli, who thought he knew a shorter sea route than the Portuguese to the lands of spice. Alfonso V at once asked for a written report of this new theory, and so Martins required his friend Toscanelli to set forth all the details in a letter. He did so, but his theories were evidently too novel for the royal understanding; for neither Alfonso nor his successor, Dom João, who ascended the throne in 1481, made any practical use of them.

This was left to the unknown man whose name was Christopher Columbus. He spent years in collecting data and detailed information with which to make his plan of sailing westward to India attractive to the mighty men of the world. He heard of Toscanelli, wrote to him, and obtained a copy of the rejected letter with a map attached. Now Columbus could at least support his theories with the authority of a well-known scientist, so that his contemporaries could no longer regard him as completely mad or as a lonely visionary.

Toscanelli differed from his contemporaries—as did Columbus—in accepting the reports of the "charlatan" Marco Polo, and therefore (a far worse crime) did not submit to the authority of Ptolemæus. If Marco Polo was right, Asia must extend much farther eastward than Ptolemæus had stated. This was not to be tolerated, for the repute in which the ancients were held at that time was enormous, and even fifty years after Columbus correct and faithful cartographers were still busy trying to reconcile the newly discovered continent with the Asia that Ptolemæus had established for all time.

Toscanelli, on the other hand, was irreverent enough to develop a new theory. He suggested that the eastern rim of Asia lay much nearer on the earth's surface to Portugal than had previously been allowed, and on his map he sketched a course for a ship sailing westward which would reach China after a voyage of only 5,000 nautical miles, or another course, passing the island of Antilia, which would reach Japan another 2,000 miles farther on.

The true distance from the Canary Islands to Japan as the crow flies is 10,600 nautical miles. Toscanelli reckoned it as 3,000, Columbus—the man who was in fact to master the gap—as only 2,400; for he based the earth's circumference (and so the extent of a degree) on three quarters of its actual dimensions and also made some errors of calculation which the learned men of his time were able to lay at his door—a circumstance by no means helpful to the critical examination of his fantastic plan.

So Columbus's discovery of America was actually the result of a considerable miscalculation, and his adventure would have foundered badly had not the American continent, as it happened, lain between Europe and the distant objective of his voyage.

Even if Columbus was wrong in his reckoning of the size of the world, even if he had no correct notion of what land he was to discover, there are factors that distinguish him from all his contemporaries and give him a true right to his eventual triumph. They are the unflinching energy, the inexhaustible patience, the unbreakable confidence with which he pursued his plan. Columbus was an ardent Catholic and felt himself a man chosen for a great deed; the riches of India which he hoped to reach by a short sea route were earmarked for the Christian battle to win back the Holy Sepulcher from the dominion of the infidel—an object for which so many Crusades had worked and failed in the Middle Ages.

It was in 1484 that Columbus first made known his plan for a voyage to India to João II of Portugal, whose activities during that year had included, on the one hand, the foundation of a faculty of navigation and, on the other, the murder, personally executed, of his brother-in-law, who was intriguing against him. Columbus's proposal was that the King should place at his disposal some ships in which to sail to Cipangu. João listened attentively and formed the opinion that he was dealing with a boaster and an exaggerator. Against the King's mistrust Columbus set his whole iron resistance and did succeed in gaining permission to have his plan checked by the Scientific Committee of Navigation. Those gentlemen, however, came to the sad conclusion that Columbus's submissions were nothing but empty verbiage, born partly of his imagination, partly of Marco Polo's false reports. All the same, Columbus and the King parted on friendly terms, for the latter left open the possibility of his support at a later time. But first he sent out two ships to discover the island of Antilia and, if possible, sail on to Japan. Nothing came of it, however, because they, like others who set out on a similar mission from the Portuguese possessions in the Azores, missed the favorable following winds that were later responsible for the success of Columbus because he held to the right latitude at the right time of year.

It is the lot of people who hold fixed ideas to lose much money. In 1485 Columbus fled from Lisbon on a foggy night in fear of arrest for the debts he owed. He now hoped to win support for his plans from Their Catholic Majesties Ferdinand of Aragon and Isabella of Castile, whose marriage had resulted in a United Kingdom of Spain.

But first he had to surmount a serious obstacle: how was he, an unknown stranger, to invade the royal court and explain his ideas to its royal heads? And even then there would be the difficult task of convincing them that his fantastic plan could be put into practice and persuading them to risk money and ships in its pursuit.

Fortunately he got to know a man of some repute as an astronomer, whose energetic support he managed to enlist; this was the Franciscan, Antonio de Marchenas. With his assistance Columbus made contacts with personages of importance, through whom he eventually succeeded in interesting the Queen.

On May 1, 1486, he was introduced in the audience chamber of the Alcazar at Córdoba to the Queen, a beautiful woman with blue eyes and dark-brown hair. She listened kindly to his impassioned explanations and encouraged him to translate his plans into fact. Unfortunately even she handed over the study of the matter to a council of fusty savants, and, in spite of the royal favor, Columbus had to endure several years of scorn and disbelief from those about him. He had continually to try to convince people who looked down on him with an air of intellectual arrogance, continually to guard against their enmity and slander, continually to hold his own against the bad jokes of ill-disposed busybodies. And the learned men who tested his plan at Salamanca shook their wise heads and came to the conclusion that his claims could not possibly be true—the ocean was not so narrow as the obstinate foreigner, who would not let himself be disconcerted by any objections, kept on insisting. But the character of this man from Genoa had some quality that influenced the scientists to postpone their decision, so that Columbus still had a faint chance of realizing his intentions. He was even placed on the royal payroll and, doubtless in earnest of future performances, received an award of honor—equal, it is true, only to the pay of an able seaman and thus a clear indication of the keen commercial instincts developed by high personages, of which Columbus was later to encounter so many bitter experiences.

During those days the rulers of Spain were engaged in a task that swayed their interest sharply away from navigation and voyages of discovery. This was the war against the Moors, who were now being driven step by step from the Spanish mainland, where for some hundreds of years they had maintained in their sphere of influence a notable standard of culture. These were heathens and it was therefore a good thing to drive them out; and once this crusading spirit was roused, a start was made by uprooting the Jews, regardless of the harm that accrued to Spain from this step.

In June 1488 the judgment of the savants was still not achieved, but something else happened: Columbus's pension suddenly ceased without his having received a definite yes or no. So he decided on another approach to the King of Portugal and wrote to João II saying that he wished to renew his offer and would be glad to return to Portugal if given a safe-conduct (to ward off his creditors). The King, whose other expeditions had all come to a bad end, at once gave his permission. It was not till December that Columbus reached Lisbon—only to suffer a fresh disappointment, for just before his arrival three ships made landfall bringing news of a discovery of great importance.

They were the caravels of Bartholomeu Dias, who had set out in the summer of 1487 to find a sea route to India. Sailing along the African coast, he left behind the farthest point yet reached (latitude 22 south, by Diogo Cão). The ships pressed ever southward and were driven so far south by a tempest that they lost sight of land altogether. After altering course several times, Dias sailed around the Cape of Good Hope and so discovered the southern point of Africa. This was the first time the direct sea route to India had been found by anyone, and the King of Portugal, on receiving the news, felt no desire to seek additional sea routes. So he sent Columbus away again, and Columbus's long, dreary waiting in Spain was prolonged once more.

Only a man of his toughness and endurance could have stood the struggle, year in, year out, to see his ideas put into practice. In May 1489 he was once again received by Isabella, who was conducting the siege of the Moorish city of Baza. Columbus seized the opportunity to fight, not only for his own personal cause, but also to wield the sword as a volunteer in the ranks of the besiegers on behalf of Christendom against the infidels.

During this time delegates from the Sultan of Egypt arrived and warned Isabella that if the war against the Moslems was continued, the Holy Sepulcher in Jerusalem would be laid waste. This gave Columbus the opportunity of pointing out emphatically how much better a Crusade to gain possession of the Sepulcher could be financed if he could first bring back the treasures of India by his short sea route. But Isabella's first preoccupation was her war in Spain; so when Baza capitulated at the beginning of December, she sent the volunteer, and with him Columbus the Discoverer, packing again.

He now endured a period of extreme want and for a time sought refuge in a Franciscan monastery. And when, after four and a half years—for officialdom in those days worked slowly indeed—the report of the learned panel was at last completed and laid before the royal pair, he touched the nadir of all his hopes. The scientists declared roundly that Columbus's proposals were impracticable and should be rejected. Of the reasons on which this judgment was based, the first two—that the journey to Asia would take two years and that the western ocean was boundless and probably impossible to cross—were more correct than Columbus's theory of a narrow ocean. But that made the other grounds adduced by the Spanish savants all the more untenable and reactionary. They stated that Columbus would be unable, if he reached the land of the antipodes, to return by way of this half of the globe (perhaps because the force of gravity had drawn him thither?). In any case, he would not discover any land at all, because there was none there to discover; had not Saint Augustine laid it down that the greater part of the earth's surface is covered by water? And finally they pontificated: "It is quite unthinkable that anyone could discover unknown lands of any worth, so many years after the Creation!"

Even on this advice Their Spanish Majesties came to no definite decision, but bade Columbus wait awhile longer till the war should be at an end. Columbus did in fact wait, but only for eight months. Then he had had enough of waiting and left for France to lay his plans before Charles VIII.

Farsighted friends made a last-minute attempt to reverse matters. Among them was the Queen's father confessor, thanks to whose influence another audience was granted. Isabella again listened sympathetically to Columbus's contentions and charged a fresh scientific commission with their examination. When this proved favorable, the Royal Council had only to decide on the financial considerations. Treasurers are often more difficult to convince than scientists; at all events, the conclusion was that Columbus's requisitions were too high.

On January 2, 1492, Granada, the Moorish capital and the last fortress of the Moslems on Spanish soil, gave in. Columbus had the pleasure of entering the city in the triumphal procession, then, a few days later at a gracious audience granted by the royal pair, was informed that his proposals had been finally rejected and he was free to go where he pleased.

So at the end of six years of hard work and bitter disappointment Columbus set forth to leave Spain forever. He rode away on a mule; all that remained was his vague hope that he might perhaps interest the King of France. At the village of Pinos-Puente, ten miles beyond Granada, a horseman overtook him. That was the moment from which a new era in the world's history should be dated, for he bore an urgent dispatch from Queen Isabella commanding Columbus to return to court.

Columbus had found an influential friend in a financial officer at court, Luis de Santagel, the Keeper of King Ferdinand's Privy Purse. On the very day of Columbus's departure Santagel had hurried to Isabella and energetically persuaded her to lend support to an undertaking that might produce at such small risk such great gains for Spain and Christendom. Santagel even offered to bear the expense of the small fleet himself. He succeeded in persuading the Queen to change her mind, and from that moment things began to move rapidly.

In April Columbus received his charter, by which the King and Queen of Spain ennobled him and appointed him Admiral of the Ocean, Viceroy and Governor of all islands and mainlands that he might discover; of the gold and silver, pearls, precious stones and spices, commercial and mineral products he was to retain one tenth and—here the envy of the world today will be roused—all free of taxes.

The preparations for the expedition proved onerous and took several months to complete. Columbus's fleet consisted of three vessels: the flagship, *Santa María,* of a little over a hundred tons, and two caravels, the *Pinta* and the *Niña,* each of about fifty-five to sixty tons. In spite of their small size, these ships were by no means fragile nutshells; they were thoroughly seaworthy, well built, well found, and performed wonders under sail, especially Columbus's favorite, the reliable little *Niña.* Probably the most famous ship ever to sail the ocean, she had an adventurous career: she helped Columbus to discover America, shared in his second voyage, survived a catastrophic hurricane in West Indian waters in 1495 when sailing alone, was later captured by pirates in Mediterranean waters, was then recaptured by her crew, and arrived home just in time to accompany Columbus on a third voyage to America.

The crew of the *Santa María* mustered forty men, the *Pinta's* twenty-five, and the *Niña's* twenty-four. Provisions for at least a year were shipped; there were no arms or armed men, as this was to be a pure voyage of discovery and Columbus, who carried with

THE *Santa María*. AFTER A WOODCUT FROM THE FIRST ACCOUNT OF COLUMBUS'S VOYAGE (BASEL, 1494)

him letters of introduction from the Spanish royal house to the Great Khan and various Indian and Japanese kings, envisaged only a friendly reception. Scientists and kings alike of those days cherished the naïve belief that every Oriental ruler would immediately fall at the feet of the first Christian from Europe who landed on his shores.

Early on Friday, August 3, Columbus gave the command to weigh anchor. The spirit that inspired him as he set out on his great venture is well illustrated by the Introduction that begins the most noteworthy and complete ship's log the world has ever seen—the log in which Columbus set down for the information of the Spanish King every detail of his voyage:

In the name of our Lord Jesus Christ
INASMUCH *as ye, the Christian, high and mighty Princes, King and Queen of Spain and of the Isles of the sea, our master and his lady, in this year 1492 after Your Majesties had concluded the war against the Moors, who had ruled in Europe, and after you brought it to an end in the great city of Granada, where, on the second day of January of that year I saw the Royal standard planted by force of arms on the towers of the Alhambra (the which is the citadel of that city) and where I saw the King of the Moors march to the city gates to kiss the royal hands of Your Majesties and of the Prince, my master, and whereas soon thereafter in the same month I did render report to Your Majesties of the lands of India and of a Prince whom men call the Great Khan, which being interpreted means "King of Kings," who like his ancestors did many times send ambassadors to Rome, seeking teachers in our holy faith, who might instruct him therein, but the Holy Father never did send the same, so that the souls of many men were lost through worship of idols and through the pursuit of false doctrines:*

AND WHEREAS *Your Majesties, as Catholic Christians and Princes, in the true faith of our Lord Christ, his defenders and enemies of the followers of Mohammed and of his false doctrines, decided to send me, Christopher Columbus, into the Regions of India, where I should visit certain Princes, peoples and countries, to obtain tidings of all their dispositions, and to establish how best to convert them to our holy faith and whereas ye did ordain me not to voyage by the land route (that commonly followed) to the Orient, but on a westward route which until this day no human being has pursued:—*

FURTHERMORE *after all Jews had been driven out of your Realms and Possessions, Your Majesties did in the same month instruct me, to betake myself to the said Regions of India with a sufficient fleet, for which purpose ye did endow me with much regard and did honor me in such manner that I may grace myself with a title of nobility and am appointed Admiral in Command of the Ocean as well as Viceroy and Governor, during my lifetime of all Islands and Mainlands which I may discover and occupy, or which shall in the future be discovered and occupied in the Ocean, and have further allowed that my eldest son shall succeed me and inherit my state for evermore,* I THEREFORE *did on the twelfth day of May of the year 1492 being a Sunday depart from the city of Granada and betook me to the city of Palos, a seaport, where I did fit out for the sea three ships well suited for such an undertaking, and did then sail forth from that harbor, well furnished with provisions and with sufficient mariners aboard on the third day of August of the said year, being a Friday, half an hour before sunrise, and set forth on the way to the Canary Islands, which form part of Your Majesties' dominions and which lie in the Ocean already named, in order thence to set course for India, till I shall reach it and deliver to the Princes there your Majesties' dispatches and so fulfill the commands laid upon me.*

Columbus had chosen the Canary Islands as the starting-point of his voyage because the standard of the art of navigation was at that time such as to leave him only the choice between sailing along the coast or holding on a straight course out across the high seas. According to the geographic knowledge of the day, the Canary Islands lay on the same line of latitude as Cipangu (Japan), which he believed he would reach by merely holding his course—another geographical error. But this mistake proved just as favorable to Columbus as his error about the breadth of the ocean, for on this erroneous longitude he picked up the northeast winds, which bore him across to America.

In order to appreciate fully the tremendous achievement of Columbus the Mariner, it must be recalled that until the discovery of America all voyaging had been carried out close to some coast or other. A direct voyage across the ocean with a definite objective, the discovery of new lands, and the safe return to a home base could be accomplished only by a man whose sure instincts made him feel at home on the broad seas. Columbus had no charts of the Atlantic with him, for he was himself the first to produce a reliable one; he had, however, the means of establishing the exact latitude of a given place, for this science was known to the navigators of his time.

It was much more difficult to compute the geographic longitude. This is possible only by comparing the actual time in a given place (obtainable from the sun's position) with some kind of permanent standard time taken along (from Greenwich or some other place) or acquired by reading the position of some heavenly body other than the sun. Columbus could do neither: his clock was a sandglass, which had to be reversed every half-hour—a duty occasionally overlooked by the cabin boy—and which was easily

THE NEW RACE DISCOVERED BY COLUMBUS.
FROM A DRAWING OF THE PERIOD

overturned or broken in heavy weather. Moreover, the science of astronomic observation was not sufficiently advanced, and when Columbus resorted to it he frequently took sights on the wrong star. The problem of establishing longitude was not satisfactorily solved till the eighteenth century, and then by two different methods: one was the construction of an accurate clock that could maintain a standard time in spite of the ship's motion; the other, the provision of exact mathematical tables of the moon's movements, which likewise enabled navigators to keep standard time.

But there were other difficulties in the way of accurate navigation. In Columbus's day there was as yet no means of measuring the speed of a ship. Later this was done by the simple method of dropping into the water a small board, which remained upright; a long line (the "log") was attached to this board, with knots at regular intervals along it; the speed with which these knots ran outboard gave the ship's speed. Columbus and his captains had to rely on judging their speed visually, by observing the bubbles that surfaced in the seaweed as they passed along the ship's side.

It should also be explained how the only instrument at Columbus's disposal for navigation by the stars was constructed: it was a wooden quadrant for sighting the stars, and from it hung a perpendicular pendulum that was supposed to record the degrees of height on a scale. This pendulum was nothing more than a silk cord weighted with lead, and it is easy to imagine the difficulties in using such an instrument on a pitching, rolling ship.

The quadrant and mariner's compass, the plumb line, a ruler and compasses, an incomplete chart, course-reckoning tables and the usual multiplication table—these were the only means Columbus had with which to find his way on the ocean, and though his reckonings could never be quite correct, he knew so well how to find it that he did not make a false maneuver on the whole voyage. Surely no navigator of our own day could have reckoned so correctly with the means at his command!

The little flotilla reached the Canaries in good condition, was refitted and re-tackled there, replenished with water, wine, provender, and fuel. On September 9, 1492, it set out into the unknown after avoiding a serious risk of further delay. This risk was provided by Doña Beatriz de Peraza, the ruler of the Island of Gomera, an exceedingly beautiful and voluptuous young widow, not yet thirty years old. As a young lady of the court she had turned King Ferdinand's head; then, at the instigation of the Queen, she had been married off to the Duke of Gomera, and had lost her husband, an unruly and grim man, when he was killed in a brawl. Columbus, too, fell for the charms of this lady—a matter all the more serious because he was a widower and would have made a most eligible husband for her. His own wife, Doña Felipa, had been a member of one of the most prominent Portuguese families and he had thereby been able to form valuable connections. She had died about ten years before; Diego, born in 1480, was the son of this union. Later, during his miserable years of waiting in Spain, Columbus had entered into relations with a young lady in Córdoba, Beatriz Enriquez de Harana, but she never married him—probably owing to their difference in rank—though she bore him another son, Ferdinand.

But in spite of all attractions, Columbus did not cast a marital anchor in the harbor of the Canary Islands, but parted from Doña Beatriz after a pleasant interlude and—now in his forty-first year—set course for his life's objective.

The first days of the voyage passed favorably indeed. A friendly trade wind drove the ships steadily on their proper course westward, and they covered a considerable distance in perfect weather conditions. Not till September 16 when they entered the sea-wrack of the Sargasso Sea did the crew have any misgivings. The strange aspect of the greenish-yellow seaweed, covering the whole surface of the sea, awoke all their memories of horrific tales; the sailors seriously feared that they would be held fast in this unusual conglomeration, though they could see for themselves that the ships were sailing freely and unhampered, day by day, for the weeds float on the surface and are only a few inches thick.

The favorable wind dropped on September 18, but everyone was more cheerful because, in spite of much slower progress, they all felt that they were nearing the land they had come to find. Passing stormbirds, the landing of a tunny fish, crabs in the seaweed—all these looked like signs of near-by land. The two smaller caravels sailed ahead of the flagship; everyone wanted to be the first to sight land and so win the money prize that had been offered. But when no coast appeared in the following days, the general mood changed completely. The steady blast of the favorable winds had given rise to the thought that there might be no winds in this area capable of carrying them back to Spain. All the fears they had put behind them woke again. Perhaps they had really reached the end of the world, perhaps there were really those ghastly monsters lurking hereabout to devour them, perhaps the learned gentlemen were quite wrong in their wonderful theory of a globe and ships did, after all, fall from the rim of a flat world into a bottomless abyss. . . .

On the evening of September 25 there rang out a sudden hail: "Land ahoy!" The general elation was soon turned to depression when it was established next morning that the hail had been a mistake. For many days now they made only slow progress over a calm sea; there was no task to occupy the crews but keeping the ships clean. Morale deteriorated, and the men began to turn against Columbus, the foreigner from Genoa, who was driving them on to destruction. Hadn't they known from the outset that the whole enterprise was sheer folly? Plenty of Portuguese navigators had pushed out into the west without ever discovering anything.

Columbus had foreseen that his crews would become discouraged if the voyage proved a long one, and he had devised a trick to deal with the situation. In addition to his own "true" reckoning he produced a "cooked" one showing greatly reduced progress, so that he could argue: "See, we are not so very far from home yet. Surely you have made longer voyages before?"

But after three weeks, during which not a yard of land had been sighted, this contrivance ceased to work. Not a man on board had ever taken part in so risky an enterprise, and now they had reached the limit. Some of the officers demanded of the Admiral that he turn back forthwith. But Columbus remained adamant, saying he would sooner be slain than return home empty-handed. With irrepressible confidence he tried to smother their smoldering flame of fear, doubt, weariness, and boredom which threatened at any moment to flare up into open mutiny.

During the week from October 2 to the 6th they made good progress again, but the Admiral's secret fears increased steadily as the land that, according to his reckonings, they should by now have reached resolutely refused to appear. He was afraid that he had bypassed Japan and that he would now have to sail on to the Chinese mainland. Another false cry of "Land ahoy!" on Sunday, October 7, did nothing to raise the general morale.

But on the evening of that day an event of tremendous importance for the history of America—and of Europe—occurred. It was nothing more than the passage of great flights of migrant birds over the ships; yet Columbus, remembering that the Portuguese had discovered the Azores by studying the flight of birds, immediately altered course southwestward to follow the direction of their flight. If he had held straight on his westerly course, it would have been much longer before he sighted land; and it is highly questionable whether he could have staved off the threatened mutiny long enough. Still worse, if they had continued in a westerly direction, the little fleet would have been caught in the Gulf Stream and carried away northward; it would probably have been driven onto the shores of Florida or, with a little better luck, borne away along the coasts of Georgia and Carolina and, in the end, homeward on a northerly course. They might have brought back a few gold nuggets, but nothing to encourage the King of Spain to support a further voyage of discovery. There would have been no settlements in the New World, no colonies—at least, not for many decades to come—no money for the wars waged by Catholic Spain. It is impossible to guess which way world history would have turned.

Throughout the night of October 10 the beating of wings was audible above the ships as the migrants flew overhead, but in spite of so heartening a sign this turned out to be the most critical day of all. The flotilla had now been at sea twice as long as any fleet that had ever sailed out before; they had passed the point at which Columbus had foretold they would make a landfall. How much longer could he go on at random? The captains of both caravels had already bidden Columbus on the previous day to give up this search for land. The Admiral had persuaded them to endure for three more days. But on the 10th the wind strengthened considerably and drove the ships so merrily westward that the crew of the *Santa María* fell into a fresh panic lest it should prove impossible ever to sail home again in the opposite direction. A heated argument with Columbus ensued; in the end, he promised his men to sail on for only two more days and then to turn back.

The stern wind increased to gale force, as if it wanted to come to Columbus's rescue in his determined race between success and failure. October 11 produced obvious signs that land was close at hand—branches, canes, a plank, plants floating past. If they had known how far these objects had been borne on the water—probably from South America—their cheerful mood would have been somewhat tempered.

Forsaking his normal caution, Columbus, who in face of his promise to the crews must have felt that every minute counted, gave orders to sail on throughout the night. The storm drove the ships on through these strange waters toward America: with an inexplicable instinct, he ordered a change of the westward course and so avoided the dangerous coast of Long Island, onto which he would otherwise have been borne.

Everyone watched eagerly for a sight of land, so as to win fame and the money prize. Then began a breakneck race between the ships through the dark, a race that could have come to a violent end on a reef or in the shallows.

Suddenly Columbus noticed the flare of a small light flickering in the distance like a candle. Immediately a sailor cried: "A light! Land ahoy!" Columbus chimed in: "I saw the light burning ashore some time ago." It was a case of hallucination—and who can wonder, in the state of nervous tension that reigned? Although Columbus had to admit it freely the next day, he had reserved for himself the prize offered for the first sight of land; his ambition as an explorer would not allow him to admit that another man had first glimpsed the land to whose discovery he had dedicated his own life.

About 2:00 a.m. (it was now October 12) the hail rang out again, this time from the *Pinta's* lookout: "Land ahoy! Land ahoy!"

This time there could be absolutely no doubt about it.

In the moonlight ahead lay a shimmering white sand dune; behind it stretched a long strip of land, the first they had seen for thirty-three days. It was the east coast of one of the islands of the Bahamas. Today it is called San Salvador or Watlings Island.

As daylight broke it became possible to distinguish excited, naked, brown-skinned people on the shore. Columbus had himself rowed ashore in the ship's boat, over which floated the Spanish royal standard; the captains of the two caravels followed. They had decked themselves out in their best for this ceremonial occasion. Columbus wore a dark velvet costume with a narrow Flanders ruff, purple silk stockings, and the cape that Spanish cavaliers affected on their appearances at court. The cord of his hat was decorated with a golden amulet; in his left hand he carried his sword, in his right the royal banner. Each of the captains bore a standard with a green cross and the royal initials *F* and *I* on it.

They all knelt on the firm ground, feeling it with their hands and thanking God, while their eyes filled with tears. Then Columbus arose and christened the island in the name of salvation: San Salvador. In an inspired speech, listened to alike by his sea captains, by his storm-hardened mariners, and by astonished natives, who of course did not understand a word of it, he took possession in the name of His Catholic Majesty. The mariners then hailed Columbus as Admiral and swore allegiance to him as the representative of Their Highnesses. Now that they felt complete masters of the situation, they asked forgiveness for their fearfulness and instability of purpose.

Seeing that the inhabitants were showing a peaceful and friendly disposition, Columbus loaded them with unexpected gifts: glass beads, red caps, and falcon bells. The innocent natives were delighted, having no idea of everything they were to lose through these strange white men. Columbus immediately wrote a dispatch about them, which was printed as soon as he returned to Barcelona and published throughout Europe.

"They are guileless creatures," it ran, "and their willingness to give away everything they possess could not be believed by anyone who has not seen it. They never say no about anything they own, if one asks for it; on the contrary, they offer it up to be shared, and show thereby so much affection as if they were making a gift of their hearts, and they are satisfied with any trifle one gives them in return, be it of value or of none. I gave orders that no worthless things like potsherds, pieces of glass or string be given to them, though they seemed to think they had acquired the loveliest jewels in the world, could they but possess these things."

There could hardly have been a better or more attractive proposition for rapacious men, greedy of gain and adventure. Future developments were soon to show how well equipped were the inhabitants of the highly cultured medieval West to exploit their fortune at the expense of poor, harmless savages.

Columbus, contrary to the practice of later explorers and conquerors, took pains to ensure that his men should not incur blame for any excesses against the natives. He was deeply religious: the visible success of his enterprise strengthened his conviction that he had a special mission. Seeing in all things the guiding hand of God, he insisted on the strict observance by his crews as well as by himself of innumerable rules of prayer and devotion; he never allowed himself to put to sea on a Sunday, and he made it his first duty to erect a cross and give a religious name to every newly discovered island. He immediately envisaged the possibilities of an enormous addition to the strength of Christendom. This is what he wrote soon afterward about the natives of Puerto Gibara:

"I am convinced, Illustrious Princes, that they would all become Christians had they religious instructors who knew their language, and so set I my hope in the Lord that it will please your Graces to interest yourselves in bringing so numerous a people into the Christian fold and to convert them, just as you have destroyed those who would not recognize the Trinity of the Father, the Son, and the Holy Ghost. And after your days are run, so will you leave your Empires in a state of peace and tranquillity, free of all heresy and ungodliness, and will with a serene conscience be able to stand before the throne of the Almighty Creator."

Unfortunately, alongside such radical and evangelistic ideas Columbus harbored another plan for dealing with these aborigines. Only two days after his arrival he was writing in his diary: "These men are totally unversed in the art of arms. . . . A force of fifty men would be sufficient to subdue them with complete ease and compel them to do whatsoever we like with them." In plainer words: this is a wonderful opportunity to make slaves of them.

Columbus immediately began to put this idea into practice by taking on board, without much ceremony, six natives as guides and future interpreters, before he sailed southwestward on the afternoon of October 14—for it was in that direction that the savages pointed, naming, if they could rightly be understood, more than a hundred other islands. Their language was totally unknown, and no traveler had ever described a race of men anything like them.

Columbus's voyage was a unique enterprise not only because of its course straight across the Atlantic, but also for its discovery of a whole world, which rightly became known later as the "New." Everything was new and unexpected: the natives, trees, plants, the islands, and the mainland, which was discovered soon afterward. The whole picture of the world was to be completely altered, now that the Spanish discoverers had crossed the divisible frontier that joined the Euro-Asian and African land masses, of which the world, as previously known, had consisted.

Of course Columbus could not yet know where he was or what it was he had discovered. His thoughts were wholly centered on reporting that he had reached India—he even called the natives "Indians." In the ensuing weeks he cruised around, looking in perplexity for the coast of Japan or China, looking for gold, for the Great Khan, for jewels and spices, and again—above all—for gold.

His course lay through the Bahamas, from island to island. The natives continually advised the white man that they would find what they were seeking on the next island—an obvious misunderstanding, for the simple Indians thought the Spaniards were seeking vegetable butter, crockery, and hammocks in their poverty-stricken huts. But when they at last understood properly what the white supermen were after, they pointed out the way to the great islands of Cuba and Haiti.

On Sunday, October 28, Columbus arrived in Cuba, which, according to the descriptions given by the Indians, possessed great stores of gold and pearls. At last he thought he had found one of Marco Polo's legendary discoveries. In vain did he search for roofs of gold or cities of ivory and alabaster: once again he found only a few poor, palm-roofed fishermen's huts and primitive savages in place of elegant Chinese clad in silks and brocades. All the same, Columbus encountered several things in these islands which could perhaps prove useful: native creole-pepper and a plant rather like cinnamon argued the possibility of a lucrative trade in spice; sweet potatoes tasting like chestnuts, wild beans, maize, and cotton grew here, and also a plant that Columbus could not guess would one day bring a greater profit than all the gold in South America—tobacco. The Indians rolled the leaves into cigars, inserted them in one nostril and inhaled the smoke several times, then gave or threw the glowing stumps away. Very soon the sailors had become addicts to "tobacco-drinking," which they later brought back as a new art to Europe, where, in spite of the strongest opposition by the Church and kings, the habit spread steadily.

THE PLEASURES OF TOBACCO

But the Spanish sailors also brought something much more uncomfortable back to Europe with them. Hailed by the natives as gods descending straight from heaven—women and girls everywhere kissed their hands and feet in reverent submission—and starved by the long voyage, they displayed very human desires in face of so much beauty unadorned, and the Indian women felt no compunction in surrendering their charms to the white visitors. It was only later when the invaders indulged themselves excessively in this respect that problems arose. The results of this intimate intercourse with Indian women in their natural state were fateful indeed for the Europeans. Syphilis, which was apparently indigenous in a mild form among the natives, flared up in the West into a ghastly running sore; it raged particularly in the following century, to such an extent that its miseries spared neither rich nor poor, philosopher nor king.

Columbus had to go on seeking for what he had set out to find; there was still no gold, still no confirmation that he was in Japan or India. Enthusiasm had long since died down; however lovely and overpoweringly beautiful these landscapes that he was the first European to behold, closer acquaintance with them remained bitterly disappointing. He had been sailing along the coast of Cuba for five weeks and it was now December; what was he to report to Their Highnesses at home? Of course there was the possibility of spreading Christianity among the savages. But what was to pay the costs of the expedition? Where were the fabulous treasures he had promised to find? His enterprise would have been a complete failure, and the rulers of Spain would no doubt have looked askance at this kind of harebrained venture, had not Columbus, in the second half of December, come upon a great island that, according to the Indians, was said to consist entirely of gold.

On December 20 Columbus sailed into a bay of fairylike loveliness such as he had never yet seen: it was Acul Bay in Haiti. Here the Indians lived in an almost more primitive state than elsewhere; the women were more beautifully shaped and did not wear even the usual loincloth of respectability, nor were they hidden by their jealous menfolk from the white men, as among many other tribes. The natives prepared the friendliest welcome for Columbus, dragging along everything they owned, from bread baked of yams to small nuggets of gold, and made presents of it to the Spaniards. Their ruler, the Cazique Guacanagari, sent an envoy to invite Columbus to visit him in his home, which lay on the other side of Cap Haitien. As there was every indication that the long-sought gold was to be found here, Columbus set out at dawn on the 24th, so as to celebrate Christmas with the Cazique.

Soon after midnight on Christmas night the sleep-befuddled ship's boy of the *Santa María,* whom, in defiance of Columbus's orders, the steersman had placed at the helm, noticed that the craft was aground. Terrified, he gave the alarm. Columbus, among the first to rush up, had to admit that the ship was firmly ashore on a reef. Immediately chaos reigned; swearing sailors, heavy with sleep, ran hither and thither as Columbus issued orders to save the vessel. Juan de la Cosa, the ship's captain and officer of the watch, with some of his Basque countrymen, who were on bad terms with the Castilians and particularly with the Genoese leader, made ready the ship's only lifeboat for their own escape. At the most dangerous moment they pushed off and left the others to their fate. The captain of the *Niña*, to which they rowed, sent them back on the spot; he had already sent his own boat to Columbus's aid. It was high time that both boats arrived. In spite of desperate exertions, the *Santa María* was past saving and Columbus had to let the crew row over to the *Niña*.

Luckily the end of their voyage was close at hand, so that the cargo could be safely brought ashore next day, the Indians helping stoutly with all their boats under Guacanagari's supervision. The eager natives did not steal so much as a nail, though everything they were carrying was to them of incalculable worth. Once ashore, they began an active barter trade with the sailors, exchanging lumps of pure gold for worthless gewgaws.

In a very short time the anxiety about the loss of the *Santa María* was assuaged. Columbus could rest assured that there was gold here and, according to what the Cazique said, great quantities of it. He decided, making an entry in his diary to that effect, that God had purposely driven the ship ashore so that here he might find the gold and settle a colony. The task of the colonists whom Columbus intended to leave here would be to collect enough gold and spices for the rulers of Spain to be able by their sale to fulfill this object—"to free the Holy Sepulcher within three years. For I did advise Your Majesties that the whole profit of my enterprise should be devoted to the capture of Jerusalem, and Your Majesties did graciously agree, since this was without any proposal from me your hearts' dearest wish." Even if Their Majesties found other ways of using the money, there is no doubt that this was Columbus's honest intention. In the moment when the European first set foot firmly on the new continent, he did so in all true thought and feeling of the Middle Ages—those Middle Ages that were to be swept away more swiftly by this very discovery of America than by any other single factor.

They built a fort out of the beams and deep planking of the *Santa María,* and thirty-nine men were left behind in it. Their

De Insulis nuper in mari Indico repertis

DISCOVERY OF THE ISLAND OF HISPANIOLA

selection was a difficult task, for everyone wanted to be among the first to dig into the treasure hoard of gold. But they were destined to suffer a very different fate from what they hoped. To this day the place of this first European settlement has remained nameless.

Columbus and Guacanagari parted on the best of terms on January 2, 1493. The Admiral now had a definite success to report and eagerly set out for home. He had a second very strong reason for haste: a few weeks earlier Captain Alonso Pinzón, with his caravel, the *Pinta*, had lost touch with Columbus during a storm and had seized this favorable opportunity of sailing into the blue with his speedier ship. Suppose he had also found gold and was perhaps on his way back to Spain to be hailed as the great discoverer? But on January 6 the two ships met again and, after Pinzón had apologized abjectly, were able, to the relief of both parties, to continue their daring voyage in company. Columbus sailed a few more days along the coast of Haiti, which he had christened Española (Latin version: Hispaniola). At the mouth of the Río Yaque del Norte, named Rio del Oro by Columbus, he found to his delight that the river was rich in gold; its waters harbored not only small grains but pieces the size of lentils. Even today gold is still found there.

Columbus experienced another excitement during this time: he saw three mermaids, who emerged from the deep sea. These creatures stirred the imagination of the sailors of those days violently, but Columbus was a sufficiently sober observer to describe them as "not so beautiful as depicted in paintings." Of course Columbus knew that these were not young women, rejecting all the sailors' yarns and comparing them with creatures he had already seen off the coast of Guinea—West African sea cows. These were in fact sea cows—but the manatees of the Caribbean with their well-formed heads and front limbs shaped like arms were much more like human beings than their African counterparts.

On January 16 Columbus at last set his course on Spain, strongly influenced in this decision by the growing lack of discipline among his crew.

The return voyage began with heavy gales, downpours, and raging seas; it was to be the Admiral's strongest claim to skill as a seaman. For of what earthly use was his great discovery if his two small ships—both leaking badly and in dire need of an overhaul —were swallowed up by the Atlantic's winter gales and nobody ever heard the news?

His luck held on the homeward voyage; while he thought he was on a true course for Spain, he was really steering too far north and ought to have finished up somewhere in the North Sea. Nonetheless, he found he was on the right course, and just because of his error; for it became known later that the quickest route for sailing-ships from Haiti to Spain was to sail north to the latitude of Bermuda and then pick up the prevailing winds that drove them thence to Spain.

Until the beginning of February the two ships made little progress. A bare diet of bread, wine, and Indian sweet potatoes was improved by catches of fish and birds. Columbus, by his daily changes of direction and continual new reckonings, gradually came onto the right course in a wide sweep. Comparison between his reckonings and those of his navigators and pilots shows that he was far ahead of them in fixing a position.

From the 4th to the 7th of February a wintry northwest gale drove them homeward at great speed. A few days later a trick of the weather, which might at any moment have proved fatal, struck them when two neighboring storms closing from different directions whipped up such tremendous cross-seas that the *Niña* several times nearly foundered. All day long the ships, with not a sail set, were tossed on the great combers; at night fearful thunderstorms raged overhead. On the 13th the wind abated a little, only to rage with renewed fury in the evening. The little convoy was hurled hither and thither; the great breakers poured over it and the ships could hardly keep any way on. The *Niña* was in special danger because she no longer had sufficient ballast aboard her. Every roller had to be carefully watched and the ship brought round to the right angle to meet it. Meanwhile, the gale drove the *Pinta* along more quickly; she disappeared over the horizon and was running for her home port, with the news and all the fame of the discovery in her keeping.

After two days the *Niña's* crew gave themselves up for lost. As all prayers remained unanswered, there was only one other possible appeal to the heavenly powers. In accordance with the usages of the day, Columbus organized a strange kind of lottery: the one who drew out of a sailor's cap a pea on which a cross had been marked undertook to make a pilgrimage to a certain church in Estremadura, in the event of their surviving the present ordeal. Chance decreed that Columbus himself drew the lot and with it the duty to perform the pilgrimage. But the furious seas took no heed of such vows and the despairing sailors instituted a second lottery. This time it was an ordinary sailor who bound himself to be the pilgrim; Columbus promised to give him the necessary money for the journey. During the day they tried once more, and this time it was again Columbus who had to take an oath: he would stay awake a whole night through and have a Mass read in the Church of Santa Clara de Moguer at Palos. But the heavens were not yet placated, and in the end the whole crew bound itself to walk in procession, clad only in shirts, and to offer prayers at the first shrine of the Virgin Mary they might meet with. On top of this, each undertook a personal penance.

SKETCH BY COLUMBUS OF HISPANIOLA

During the night of February 14 the storm at last abated, and on the following evening they sighted land. But contrary, veering winds prevented them from coming to anchor for a further three and a half days. It was not till Monday, February 18, that they were at last able to drop anchor and breathe again.

Columbus learned from the inhabitants that he was in the Island of Santa Maria in the Azores, a place he had wished to avoid because it was a Portuguese possession.

The inhabitants told him they had never experienced such a storm as had raged for the last few weeks, and they marveled that the caravels had survived its fury. The governor of the island, a young man named João de Castanheira, sent messengers to Columbus to say that he could not come himself that day because of the darkness, but that he would follow at daybreak. The messengers told of a little chapel dedicated to the Mother of God, and the sailors therefore decided to go ashore the very next day to fulfill their penances.

This first day back on the soil of the Old World provided a drastic lesson in the differences between that strange new world which still lay unrevealed and the old continent with clear-drawn boundaries whose violation involved swift retribution.

For the governer of the island imagined that the ships were coming from the coast of New Guinea, like so many others before them. But this, being a Portuguese possession, was forbidden territory to Spanish ships. Stray wanderers who paid no heed to laws, rights, and agreements must answer for their neglect before a Portuguese court. This is the explanation of what occurred in the following days.

Half the *Niña*'s crew immediately rowed ashore, awakened the priest, and began their promised procession to the Virgin Mary, clad in penitents' garb; the grumpy sailors took off all their clothes down to their shirts and reverently approached the little chapel, where they knelt in grateful prayer before the altar. Suddenly almost the whole male population of the place rushed up, on foot and mounted, and, falling upon them, took them prisoner. Naturally the sailors, trouserless and unarmed, could offer no energetic resistance.

Columbus waited many hours in vain for the return of his men. In the end he weighed anchor and sailed along the coast. Presently he noticed a great horde of horsemen, who dismounted and climbed fully armed into a boat, which immediately made for his caravel. Obviously they wanted to capture Columbus himself, an undertaking not so easy to fulfill on the moving waters as in a small chapel. The denouement took the form of a battle of words during which Columbus in his pitiful caravel tried to substantiate his claim to be Admiral of the Ocean and discoverer of the sea road to India. He even held his letter of credentials over the rail, though for obvious reasons he did not let the Portuguese boat get near enough for its occupants to be able to decipher the writing. After an exchange of loud but empty threats Columbus was compelled by wind and weather to sail on and look for a safe anchorage. But even there the mounting gale carried away his anchor tackle; so he had to seek safety on the open sea, where he cruised around for a whole day—a very difficult task, as there were only three trained sailors among the crew remaining at his disposal. So he turned back again to Santa Maria to see what diplomatic measures could achieve. The governor had already released the sailors, as he was interested only in capturing the Admiral himself; he now sent envoys, who looked over Columbus's credentials and then left the caravels and their crews in peace.

On February 23 Columbus departed from this inhospitable haven and sailed for Spain. Another heavy storm struck the two ships and made it impossible for them to hold their course. Once again the sailors gave up all hope and again consulted the pea oracle. Once again it was Columbus who drew the one with a cross on it—is it possible that even in the shadow of death that particularly hardbitten seafaring man saw to it?—and had to take upon himself yet another pilgrimage. But, for all their self-imposed penances—they were even willing to forgo a celebration on the first Saturday night ashore, in order to eat bread and water instead—the elements increased their fury. The tempest seemed to lift the ship into the air, and great columns of water poured over her from both sides at once.

On the evening of March 3 they sighted land, but that meant increased danger rather than safety, for they were being driven with great speed onto an unidentified coast. By strenuous exertions they managed to keep the caravels out at sea and preserve them from being smashed to pieces.

At daybreak they recognized the rock of Sintra, behind which the Tagus enters the sea. Having no choice, Columbus steered into the river mouth. Villagers, seeing the small, battered, and storm-tossed vessel, grew fearsome for its safety and spent the whole morning in prayer.

As the *Niña* entered the harbor at about 9:00 a.m. and at last came safely to anchor, numerous ships were lying in Lisbon's haven, held there by the contrary winds; many of the ships, indeed, had been there for the last four months.

The fury of the storm had, of course, driven Columbus into an enemy harbor; every addition to the strength of the rulers of Spain must have been an irritation to the King of Portugal. The first welcome for the returning discoverer was another attempt to arrest him. None other than Bartholomeu Dias, who had discovered the Cape of Good Hope, came with a boatload of heavily armed men and tried to bring him before the judiciary to account for his voyage. But Columbus fell back on his status as Admiral. After weeks of futile strife, of doubts and sleepless nights, with only his small band of exhausted sailors on a storm-battered caravel, he insisted on being accorded the courtesies of his rank and won his own way. Soon afterward Captain Alvaro Damão paid him a courtesy visit in full ceremonial, with pipes, trumpets, and drums.

A few days later Columbus was received with every honor by King João, who promised him his support and expressed his pleasure in the navigator's discoveries, though this cost him some effort, as his joy was simulated. Columbus, on the other hand, having come to João with his plans only to be sent away unsatisfied each time, was now, in the full tide of his success, by no means shy. His report naturally sounded somewhat galling to the ears of the King, who recognized fairly clearly what an opportunity he had missed for swelling his power. He therefore merely pointed out that the discoveries had been made within his Realms of Guinea and later pursued his claims to America by diplomatic means. Columbus's frontier-disrupting voyage meant that within a very short time much drawing of new boundaries would be required.

Hardly had Columbus taken leave of the King when the latter's courtiers surrounded him and made the bland suggestion that he should have the boastful and courageous Admiral murdered; in this simple way the whole enterprise of the Spanish rulers would come to an end. But João was well aware of the political repercussions that must follow such a drastic solution, and at least outwardly he maintained his friendly attitude.

On March 13 a favorable wind allowed Columbus to leave the harbor of Lisbon: he was in a hurry to get to Spain, for he was still afraid that his questionable comrade Martín Alonso Pinzón would try to arrive first with the century's most important news.

The *Pinta* had, in fact, been the first to reach a European harbor, though far from its intended destination. It was from Bayona, near Vigo and close to the Portuguese frontier, that Pinzón sent the sensational news right across Spain to his King and Queen, seeking at the same time an audience. The answer was a sharp rebuff: they would prefer to hear about it from the Admiral himself. So Pinzón set out in high dudgeon to sail home. There was still the possibility that the *Niña* had foundered in the storm and the unsympathetic upstart from Genoa with her, and that he might still walk the stage as the Great Discoverer; or he might at least reach home before Columbus. He lost the race by only a few hours: when his caravel entered the Río Tinto to make their home port of Palos, the *Niña* was already lying there, a close winner. This was too much for Martín Alonso Pinzón; he retired to his country house, took to his bed, and died. Columbus had arrived at noon on March 15—thirty-two weeks after setting out, seventeen long years after the waves had cast him ashore on the Iberian Peninsula. This was the zenith of his career, and he enjoyed a triumph that made all the toil and tribulation of the past worth while, though it was not to outweigh the bitterness of future events.

He spent a fortnight in fulfilling his penances and taking a little rest. Then he entered Seville, enjoying his due triumph to the full, and, as soon as the necessary invitation reached him, made his way to the royal court at Barcelona. The journey through several provinces was in the nature of a pageant; people thronged from far and wide to see this unique procession, consisting of the mariner who had suddenly won fame, several of his trusted followers, and six Indians in strange raiment bearing gold ornaments and cages full of brightly colored parrots. He reached Barcelona in the middle of April. The whole court retinue met him outside the gates, and the colorful reception took place next day at the Alcazar. When Columbus knelt to kiss the hands of Ferdinand and Isabella, they both rose from their throne and invited him to take his place next to them and the Infante Don Juan.

While Columbus was spending several weeks in banquets and celebrations, ennobled and honored in every possible manner, tremendous activity was going on in high political circles. Now that Columbus had crossed the frontier running somewhere across the Atlantic Ocean, order had to be restored in this part of the world. And before anyone even knew what he had discovered, strife had flared up as to whose property these new regions beyond the horizon should be.

The Pope was the main arbiter. As Head of Christendom, he had the right to partition new lands—lands outside the realm of any Christian king—among faithful rulers, to ensure their being brought into the Christian fold. Several Papal bulls had already awarded to the King of Portugal not only the African coast "as far as the country where the Indians serve Christ"—meaning the realm of Prester John—but also the rights over "any and every Island which might be found and possessed beyond [south of] the Canary Islands and on the hither side [west] of Guinea or in its neighborhood" (Bull "Æterni Regis" of 1481). So João of Portugal, with some justification for his plea that Columbus had invaded his sphere of interest, began to fit out a fleet to go forth and explore the newly discovered territories.

Spain hastily tried to establish legitimate rights over these regions, and the Pope quickly recognized that it was incumbent on him to parcel the world out anew. King Ferdinand had enough high cards in the political game to back his demands, for he had in the past made it possible for Rodrigo Borgia, who was a Spaniard, to be elected Pope, under the style of Alexander VI. He had also performed services for the Pope, providing three Episcopal sees in Aragon, a dukedom for Pedro, one of the Pope's sons, and two bishoprics for Cesare Borgia, the other son.

Now, in April 1493, Ferdinand asked in return that Columbus's discoveries be officially recognized as Spanish possessions. The Pope immediately issued four bulls, in which—in spite of Portugal's long-established rights—the Spanish claim was granted.

The first of these bulls (dated May 3, 1493) awarded to Spain all the islands and mainlands he had discovered, so long as they were not already in the posession of a Christian prince. But that did not satisfy Ferdinand. Two Spanish cardinals traveled to Italy and importuned the Pope; whereupon Alexander VI issued two further bulls, of which the first defined his previous awards to Spain, and the second drew a boundary line dividing the world between Spain and Portugal. This line ran from the North to the South Pole, "100 *leguas* [Roman miles] west and south of the islands commonly known as the Azores and the Cape Verde Islands." All land lying west of this boundary, including any yet to be discovered, was to belong to Spain.

Even this ruling seemed insufficient to Ferdinand and Isabella, and they contrived to persuade Alexander VI to adopt an even wider line in his fourth bull of September 26, 1493. "Since it is possible," it ran, "that your envoys, captains, or lieges may during their westward or southerly voyages come upon lands in eastern regions and there discover islands and mainlands which belong to India, we fulfill and enlarge our earlier enfeoffment to all islands and mainlands of any kind which are or may yet be discovered, when you permit sea voyages to be made westward or to the south, equally whether those lands be situated in regions to the west, south, or east of India." Earlier rights over the disputed regions were repealed and declared null and void, whether conceded to "Kings, Princes, Infantes, or to Religious or Military Orders."

It is not surprising that this was too much for Portugal, which was still the greatest sea power. João immediately began negotiations—not, indeed, with the Pope, but directly with Ferdinand and Isabella. The Spanish rulers had to take into account Portu-

gal's strength and ensure that their trading-ships, when they
sailed the new realms, incurred no danger. They consequently did
not obstinately stand upon their rights, but on the 7th of June,
1494, reached an agreement with Portugal, laying down the line

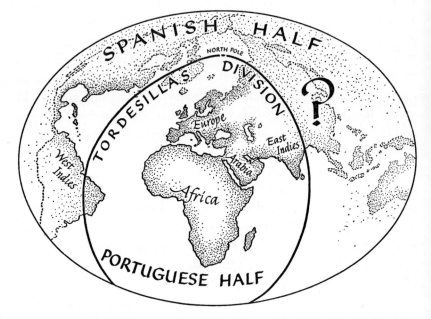

ONE HALF TO PORTUGAL, ONE HALF TO SPAIN: THE TREATY OF TOR-
DESILLAS DIVIDES THE WORLD

of demarcation 370 *leguas* west of the Cape Verde Islands. All
discoveries east of this line, even if made by Spanish ships, would
belong to Portugal; those to the west, even if made by Portuguese
ships, would all belong to Spain. Thus the world was partitioned
in the most peaceable way, and, thanks to this arrangement, Brazil
later became a Portuguese possession.

The dawn of a new era in which secular political power would
reign supreme was thus made noticeable immediately after
Columbus's discovery, because the two great Catholic powers ef-

fected the partition of the world by their own initiative, without allowing the Pope to interfere any further in their affairs. Another frontier had been crossed—this time one of spiritual authority, which had hitherto restricted the free play of the powers in developing power politics.

All this happened before anyone knew exactly where on the earth's surface the new regions lay. At first no one doubted that they were, as Columbus himself believed, a part of India. Pamphlets spreading the sensational news were printed one after another in Spain and Italy and were distributed all over Europe. The most exciting part was the report about the naked women: on a continent where women were wrapped up in masses of clothing, it seemed almost unbelievable that a female being could go about dressed in nothing more than a green leaf. Had Columbus discovered the Garden of Eden? Almost as exciting was the report that "almost all the rivers" in Hispaniola "ran with gold," for there was in Europe a dire scarcity of metal for minting purposes. In fact, the rapid increase of the treasuries of Europe, which soon resulted from the arrival of a stream of precious metal from America, was responsible for altering the entire economic life of the old continent so completely that it is from this point that the beginning of a new age has rightly been dated—the Age of Capital.

Columbus, who could have no idea of the tremendous changes his discovery was to bring in its train and who believed to his dying day that he had found the sea route to India, never even gave the new continent a name—a good example of how in this world almost more depends on publicity than on the actual facts.

A Florentine, by name Amerigo Vespucci, who went along on several early voyages and who, thanks to an outstanding and cultured gift of writing books about his experiences and discoveries, was able to give them widespread advertisement, declared ten years after Columbus's first voyage that the South American coasts could "rightly be described as a new world, since our forefathers had no knowledge of it; and so for all who hear thereof it is something quite new." Vespucci was lucky enough to have as his follower the German savant Martin Waldseemüller, at that time

Head of the Academy of Saint-Dié, famous for its geographical studies, who in 1508 confirmed that Vespucci had discovered a fourth continent. Waldseemüller, who had produced a large-scale map of the world and a globe in 1507, seized his opportunity to christen the new land mass. Encouraged by the German humanist

FACSIMILE OF A LETTER FROM VESPUCCI TO HIS FATHER

Ringmann, he gave it the name of "Amerigo's Land," or in Latin, which sounded more important (for instance, he styled himself "Hylacomilus"), "Terra America." He had no idea that he had hit the mark in one respect: Amerigo is the German name "Emmerich," which, being *Emmer-reich,* means "rich in wheat."

Posterity, adopting this name without question, wronged not only Columbus, but also a man who had discovered "America" before Vespucci.

No great mariner has had such a raw deal at the hands of the historians as John Cabot, though he had much more right than Vespucci to give his name to America. His ill-luck was to have discovered a region that at first sight offered less attractive prospects than Central and South America.

Neither the date of Cabot's birth nor that of his death is precisely known, but it is supposed that he was born about 1450 in Genoa, lived in Venice, was really Giovanni Gaboto by name, and was a superb navigator. In 1490 his business journeys brought him to England, where he settled at Bristol and took the name of John Cabot. He, too, pursued a plan to reach India or Cathay by a westerly route, though on a more northerly course than his compatriot Columbus. Bartholomew Columbus, who had been associated with his brother in preparing his plans for crossing the Atlantic and, like Christopher, was looking for a king to finance the operation, had already been to England and had dealings with

Lettera di Amerigo vespucci delle isole nuouamente trouate in quattro suoi viaggi.

WOODCUT FROM THE FIRST EDITION OF VESPUCCI'S *Letters*

Henry VII before Cabot's arrival. Bartholomew had interested the King in this great enterprise, but for various reasons had failed to clinch the matter. Moreover, the Columbus family had no vested interest in the idea itself, which had been in the air since Toscanelli's time; for instance, the German astronomer Hierony-

mus Müntzer laid the same plan as Columbus's before King João
of Portugal in a letter written in 1493, without having the slightest
idea that the Genoese had already come back from discovering
"India."

The news of Columbus's successful crossing of the ocean was
the greatest sensation of the day, and Henry VII at once recalled
the negotiations he had carried on with the explorer's brother. So
when Cabot discussed his intentions with the King, he carried his
suit without difficulty and, on March 5, 1496, received a patent
and widely monopolistic rights.

In 1497 the good ship *Mathew* sailed out from Bristol; John
Cabot, who was the leader of the expedition, had with him his
son Sebastian (Sebastiano Gaboto, born 1472), who later tried
to usurp his father's fame. Cabot's crossing took longer than Columbus's because on his more northerly course his flotilla had to
contend with fiercer winds and waves than Columbus had met.
But he made the first crossing of the North Atlantic since the
Vikings, land being sighted on June 24, 1497, after a voyage lasting eight weeks. It was the coast of North America, and Cabot
landed at a spot that scientists, after a keen controversy, agreed
to have been, in all probability, somewhere near Cape Breton.
Unfortunately, Cabot found nothing of any value—no gold, no
precious stones, no spices. The country, which he too believed to
be Asia, was cold and inhospitable. All the same, he was able to
report that its waters housed great wealth; and later the inexhaustible reserves of fish in the seas around Nova Scotia, Labrador, and Newfoundland drew fishing-fleets from the most diverse
European countries.

Cabot sailed northward up the American coast till floating ice
compelled him to turn back. His report was received in England
with the greatest interest, and for his discovery of America—or,
rather, of the sea route to India—he was awarded a "princely"
sum, equal to about £ 20.

Even if the harbors of "Asia" were cold and unfertile, Henry's
interest was by now so excited that he gave Cabot a second patent
and a fleet of six ships. It set out in the spring of 1498, cruised all
that summer in the waters of the North American coast, this time

in a southerly direction, and reached Cape Hatteras. After the successful conclusion of this journey he set out on yet another voyage of discovery. This great explorer's life ended tragically, for his ceaseless urge to explore the world sealed his fate. Somewhere off Iceland he lies buried at the bottom of the sea; no one will ever know when or where his third American journey ended or how he perished.

It was the discovery of North America which awakened the British colonial spirit. In the years just after the turn of the century a number of daring Englishmen made preparations for colonizing the new regions beyond the seas; overcoming many difficulties, they launched a small emigrant fleet, but at sea an organized mutiny of unknown origin broke out, forcing them to return. It is not improbable that the Admiralty had a hand in this, for they feared the outbreak of hostilities with Spain and did not want ships and crews to be far away when they might be urgently needed in the Channel. This event set back the start of North America's history by a century.

The Admiralty's worries were indeed not groundless, for Spain regarded Cabot's voyage with strong misgivings and had issued a violent protest against it, on the plea that the English were invading a part of the world where, according to the line of demarcation fixed by the Pope, they had no business to be. The artificial frontier was stronger than the natural barrier provided by the wide, stormy ocean; England had to give way and abandon any further voyages to America.

England was the more inclined to this concession because, after the death of Henry VII, who was interested in sea voyages of this kind, Henry VIII had ascended the throne and concentrated his political dealings on the mainland of Europe, so that he had no wish to fritter away his resources on distant corners of the earth. So when Cabot, Jr., arrived home from his most recent voyage of discovery shortly after the change on the throne, he found his news received with little enthusiasm, though he brought back momentous tidings: he had really discovered the long-sought passage to Asia. For sailing along the American coast Cabot had passed through the Hudson Strait (so named after a much later discoverer) and, entering Hudson Bay, had taken its apparently limitless expanse of water for the Pacific Ocean. He therefore had every reason to expect anything but such a cool reception. Seeing no more prospects in England, he entered the service of Spain, where as chief pilot of a fleet he was enabled to sail on further voyages of exploration; and in 1516 he sailed into the estuary of the Plata and on up the Paraná and Paraguay rivers to about the point where Asunción now stands. But even in Spain he did not, on his return, receive the recognition he expected. His fortune did not take the desired turn till in 1548 he found favor with Edward VI of England. Thus, Sebastian Cabot did not reach the peak of his career till he was over seventy, when he became one of the founders of England's sea power.

Although in his youth the success he craved most had eluded him—the discovery and exploitation of the northwest passage to Asia—now, as a graybeard of many years, he employed his unquenchable energies in another direction. The treasures of India and China still beckoned him from afar. The eastern and western routes through the southern hemisphere belonged to Spain and Portugal; in the northern hemisphere the search for the westward passage had failed, largely through the influence of Spain. There still remained a fourth possibility. Cabot laid on British mariners the task of finding a sea route to India which Columbus had never thought of: up in the north, around Scandinavia, in a northeasterly direction. And in 1553 the expedition set out under Sir Hugh Willoughby, Richard Chancellor, and Stephen Borough.

The little fleet was torn in two near the North Cape. Willoughby found himself compelled to spend the winter, without any suitable provisions, on the Kola Peninsula. This first "wintering" of the history of exploration ended in tragedy. The polar night struck panic into the sailors' hearts; they were racked by hunger, cold, and scurvy, until all the sixty-two members of the party perished. Chancellor and his ships fared better; he reached the mouth of the Dvina and journeyed thence to Moscow, where he negotiated a trade agreement, on terms favorable to England, with Ivan the Terrible. But he had not found the passage to India;

and after two more expeditions had failed to bring back favorable reports, the English decided to abandon these attempts.

Sebastian Cabot died in London about the year 1557, a man who had had his successes, but whose great aim had been denied him. As a young man he had lived through the dawn of a new era and been seized with a burning desire to rival the deeds of Columbus; he had even stood upon the soil of the American mainland before Columbus, though only when accompanying his father. His would have been the renown of a great discoverer, had he been able to achieve what Columbus had set out to do: to find the sea route to India. Vasco da Gama and Magellan had meanwhile found the right routes in the southern hemisphere— the one around Africa, the other around South America. Cabot attempted to do so in the northern hemisphere, by way of the American and Asian land masses alike. In both attempts he failed.

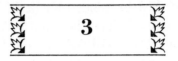

3

THE REAL DISCOVERY OF AMERICA

In 1492 not a soul doubted that Columbus had discovered what he believed he had: a group of islands off the east coast of Asia. People thought they lay about where the Moluccas are to be found on our maps. It did not become known till 1522, when the survivors of Magellan's crews came back from their voyage round the world, that Ptolemæus in ancient days had measured the world's girth better than Columbus and how far it really was to Asia. But Columbus held obstinately to his own views to the end of his days—nothing could have pained him more than to have been told he had discovered America, not Asia.

The age was not yet ready to sense the utter novelty of Columbus's discovery. Men swallowed the news about it greedily, but their interest was fixed just on those facts that linked up with the most distant past. Above all, on the natives, the unclothed women; they had never heard of such things, for the Portuguese, when they came across naked women in Africa, had kept quiet about it. The primitive innocence of the natives, their lack of a religion, their hospitality and peaceable demeanor led an educated European to believe that the "Golden Age" of classical belief had survived in a far corner of the earth. And when Columbus reported that "most of the rivers" in Hispaniola ran with gold, they recalled the story of King Midas and the Pactolus, a river for which the Portuguese had searched in vain on the west coast of Africa. The feeling of the age was directed much more toward the rediscovery of once-known and long-forgotten regions than toward the finding of an altogether new and unknown world, especially as it was thought that the earth's surface was already too well known for that to happen.

The gold that Columbus brought with him was a better argument than all his theories before the voyage began. By March 30, 1493, he had already in his pocket a decree from the royal pair for the outfitting of a new expedition, and on September 25 a fleet such as the history of exploration had never seen put out to sea: seventeen ships, mostly caravels and light-draft vessels, barks specially suited to the shallow harbors of the West Indies, and an impressive retinue of sailors, colonists, noble adventurers, officials, and reverend gentlemen.

The voyage of this magnificent fleet passed without serious difficulties, for Columbus sailed from the Canaries on October 13, when—though of course he knew nothing of it—the hurricane season is over.

On this second voyage Columbus instinctively found the shortest course from Europe to the West Indies; for four hundred years after him ships under sail steered the same course. After crossing the ocean the fleet reached a group of unknown islands: Dominica, Marie Galante (so named by Columbus after his ship), Guadeloupe, Désirade, and Les Saintes. Dominica with its lovely hills and rich foliage is one of the prettiest islands in the New World; Columbus looked for a harbor there, but the east coast was too steep and unapproachable. So he allowed the other ships to sail on while he cruised around the island, finding a bay, but deciding not to land after all. This was very lucky for him, because in later years it was established that the most savage of all the Caribs lived there. They killed and devoured everyone who landed on their shores—save monks alone, because after their first meal of monk they were overtaken by a heavy sickness. The Spaniards learned to make use of this idiosyncrasy, enveloping themselves in cowls when they went ashore to fetch water.

The islands and landscapes Columbus saw as he sailed by—Guadeloupe, where they tasted the marvelous fruit of the pineapple for the first time, Montserrat, Redonda, Virgin Gorda, and the countless other small islands of the Caribbean—offered to his eyes scenes of unforgettable, fairylike beauty: the sea, a shining mirror, bright with incomparable colors from sapphire blue to emerald green; volcanoes and high, cloud-capped mountains on islands whose lush blue-green forests, thronged with parrots, glimmered a shade less dark than the sea; above all, the night sky of the tropics, peopled with glittering stars.

But their inhabitants, unlike the peaceful tribes Columbus had learned to know till then, were terribly savage. These were the Caribs, whom Daniel Defoe described in the conversations of the sailor Alexander Selkirk in *Robinson Crusoe* (for the Robinson Island is not, as is so often claimed, to be found among the Juan Fernández Islands, but in the neighborhood of the Orinoco's mouths). Columbus's sailors soon found ghastly proofs of the cannibalistic habits of these Caribs: great chunks of human flesh, truncated limbs, shinbones to be used as material for darts. Later they found castrated boys from other tribes who had been specially fattened, and captive girls whose job was to bear children because babies ranked high on the list of edible delicacies.

These savages adopted an extremely hostile attitude toward the Spaniards and exhibited amazing courage. Peter Martyr, the first historian of the New World, gives his eyewitness's report: "They were dark-skinned and of a wild and terrible aspect, whose effect was heightened by the red and highly colored paint with which they daubed themselves; their heads were on the one side shaven, from the other there hung long black hair."

On a chance encounter four natives and two women attacked twenty-five Spaniards, in spite of the fact that the big ship lying off the island must have been to them something of a portent. They were overpowered after a terrific defense, but even on board ship "they laid not aside their savagery nor their terrible fury and comported themselves like Libyan lions in chains. No man was able to tame them, the beholder's bowels were turned with horror at the terrible, menacing, grisly aspect with which Nature had endowed them," wrote Peter Martyr.

The last island of outstanding importance to be discovered was Puerto Rico. Then the fleet reached Haiti (Hispaniola) and sailed along the coast in search of a haven. A party that went ashore at Montecristi made a gruesome discovery: two corpses tied with cords. On the next day two more corpses in an advanced stage of

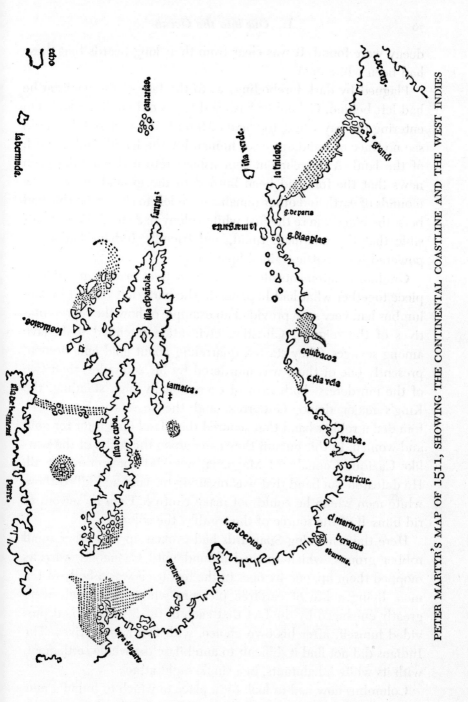

PETER MARTYR'S MAP OF 1511, SHOWING THE CONTINENTAL COASTLINE AND THE WEST INDIES

decay were found. It was clear from their long beards that these had been white men.

Plagued by dark forebodings as to the fate of the garrison he had left behind, Columbus hastened to his old landing-place. On entering the bay where the *Santa María* had foundered, he could see no trace of buildings or of human life the length and breadth of the land. A detachment sent ashore returned with the grim news that the fort had been burned to the ground; only a few mounds of earth and other remains were left to show that this had been the place where the first white colony had stood. Was it possible that the unarmed, timid, and friendly Indians had overpowered forty battle-trained Spaniards?

Gradually statements offered by the natives made it possible to piece together what had happened. The party left behind by Columbus had very soon provided an example of how the representatives of the reigning Christian civilization intended to behave among savages. They started quarreling about gold and women; presently one of them was murdered by his comrades, then two of the murderers—both men of exceptionally high standing, the King's major domo, Gutierrez, and the secretary Escobedo—founded a robber band that scoured the island on a hunt for gold and women. In this pursuit they came upon the realm of the warlike Cazique Caonabo of Maguana, who did not approve at all. He defeated the band that was ravaging his land and killed those white men whom he could not make captive. Then he set out to rid himself of the source of the trouble, the colony.

Here the remaining Spaniards had broken up into other small robber groups, which roamed around until Caonabo's warriors mopped them up, one by one. In the fort itself was a body of ten men, living a life of carefree pleasure whose attractions were greatly enhanced by the fact that each of the Spaniards had provided himself, after his own choice, with five native wives. The Indians did not find it difficult to annihilate the whole settlement, with its white inhabitants, in a single night attack.

Columbus now had to look for a place in which to found a new colony, but he had far too little time, because the domestic animals aboard the ships were threatening to die and most of his crews were either sick or exhausted by the continual sea routine. That was why he founded the first relatively permanent colony in the New World on a most inhospitable spot. He gave the place the name of Isabela, in honor of the Queen.

The loss of the first colony destroyed many hopes, more particularly the hope of collecting a few nice little kegs of garnered gold. The expenses of the first voyage had not yet been covered, the large fleet that was making the second had entailed a very considerable outlay; where now were the treasures of India which Their Highnesses in Spain were awaiting with such impatience? Columbus felt heavily pressed, with his name and fame at stake, so four days before the landing he sent out two search parties in quest of gold. The name "Cibao," which the natives used to indicate a ridge some way inland, raised his hopes to great heights: might not this be a corruption of "Cipangu"?

When the scouting-parties came back with samples of gold from the hills and from Cazique Caonabo's regions, Columbus was extremely relieved and began to entertain entirely unsupported hopes of starting a gold mine in Cibao. But first he had to solve the other, more pressing problem of how to keep his crews alive.

During the first few weeks ashore, half of the Spaniards were sick. Human nature could not stand such hard work so soon after weeks of exhausting sea-voyaging; moreover, the men were exposed to an unaccustomed climate, to deluges of rain, to swarms of fever-bearing mosquitoes, and, instead of their normal diet, were forced to live on strange fish, maize, yams, and cassava. True, they sowed wheat, barley, and other grain, planted sugar cane and the indispensable vine, but there was a long time to wait for the harvest. Realizing that the colonists must have their normal food as soon as possible, Columbus sent several ships back to Spain to fetch provender: salted meat, wheat, wine, oil, vinegar, sugar and molasses, medicine for the sick, and rice, almonds, raisins, and honey for those who were fit.

But in the meantime it was essential to prospect for gold. This was done in a manner soon to become the pattern for discoverers in the New World: on March 12, 1494, the trumpets sounded, the

Spanish flag fluttered, and the first march of the conquistadors set out in military formation, under the personal leadership of the Admiral—complete with archers, swords, and arquebuses, and, above all, the weapon that was soon to conquer a continent: armed men on horseback. Although Columbus was in the field only two and a half weeks on this first march, he set the pattern for the mighty enterprises of Balboa, Cortés, Pizarro, Almagro, de Soto, and the rest of the men who drenched American soil in blood and sweat and eventually reached every accessible spot in the enormous area stretching from 40° north to 50° south.

Hungry for gold, Columbus's column traversed scrub-covered steppes and crossed high, deeply riven mountain ranges and several rivers, marching through forests of tall palms, cotton, mahogany, and ebony trees, passing along lovely, fertile valleys whose coloring was of a heavenly beauty.

To his great disappointment, Columbus had to admit that his "Cibao," where he set up a base, had no connection with the long-sought Cipangu. He consoled himself with the gold, which was obtainable not only from the rock and rubble of the hillsides, but also from the hands of the natives, who in the friendliest fashion pressed gifts of food and gold nuggets upon the white visitors. These happy relations were soon besmirched: the whites habitually entered the Indians' huts and took anything they fancied. The owners in their unsuspecting innocence offered no objections, but when it occurred to them to appropriate a few trifles belonging to their guests, they were advised that such conduct would not be tolerated. The sight of the gold they had so burningly desired made the Spaniards lose all control, and Columbus found it necessary to impose ruthless punishments: anyone found black-marketing the costly metal was in danger of being thrashed or having his ears or nose cut off.

After their return to the settlement at Isabela, difficulties began to accumulate which Columbus was, in the long run, unable to dispel. The seven hundred sailors, adventurers, *caballeros,* and pickpockets under his command wanted to get rich quick, but after half a year's buffeting by land and sea they still saw no chance of so doing. Intrigues and treacheries were hatching; the hideous punishments that Columbus inflicted for indiscipline made him an object of hate, and finally even the peaceable Indians, provoked beyond bearing by brutal ill-treatment, became rebellious.

Columbus had the good idea of keeping the unruliest of his men busy with campaigns and the manning of garrisons on the island. For Hispaniola was an island, there could no longer be any doubt about it: and where was the mainland, the enormous mainland mass of Asia, which ought at least to be somewhere in sight? When the provision ships arrived from Spain, they were supposed to turn around and take back to the royal pair some definite news of sensational import. Columbus set up a council to guide the colony's affairs and on April 24 put to sea again with three caravels, the stout little *Niña* sailing as flagship, with the purpose of "reconnoitering the Indian mainland" and establishing relations with the Great Khan himself.

First he made for the extreme eastern end of Cuba. There was a cape to which he had on his first voyage given the lovely name of "Alpha and Omega" because he believed he was looking at the nearest and uttermost corner of the Euro-Asian continent. Columbus and contemporary geographers thought that it was possible to go dry-shod from there to the opposite end—namely, Cape Saint Vincent in Portugal—without having to cross any part of the ocean. It followed that the whole of the earth's population dwelt between these two headlands. Columbus, however, had no proofs of his theory; he prayed earnestly at night that he might succeed in proving that Cuba was an Asian peninsula.

On Cape Maisí, Columbus—following his practice in many places on his first journey to the island of Cuba, his supposed coast of Asia—set up a pillar surmounted by a cross, and proclaimed the annexation of the land to Spain. The little flotilla then bore southward—according to contemporary thought, there was less of value to be found in the north than in the south—and sailed along the coast.

Thus began a new phase of discoveries and observations, along the coast of Cuba, then Jamaica, then again the Cuban coast. On these voyages Columbus displayed an incomparable talent for navigation, piloting his ships in safety, in spite of unfavorable conditions, through the difficult waters off these coasts, full of uncharted sandy shoals. Less satisfactory was his failure to find a single proof of the presence of gold anywhere.

The inhabitants' behavior proved as variable as that of nature herself: whereas one tribe of Indians hurled their spears in fury at the high hulls of the caravels, another greeted the white men with gifts, sang songs of joy, and believed that the strange men and their ships came straight from heaven. True, many a riddle still remained unsolved. Where did the people who had tails like animals live? Whose was the light-skinned figure in a white cassock who met some archers on shore and then was never seen again in spite of the most diligent search? Was it, as Columbus believed, Prester John?

The riddle of Cuba's shape was solved by Columbus after his own peculiar fashion. As the condition of the ships and the morale of the crews demanded a return to Isabela without having sailed completely round Cuba (a bitter disappointment to Columbus), the Admiral persuaded some of his companions to sign a statement that it was useless to follow the coast any farther, seeing that it was a peninsula. Averse to any more exertions, the sailors—among them the cartographer Juan de la Cosa, who was to delineate Cuba correctly as an island—signed unanimously. Columbus did one more thing to bolster up his peninsula theory: he warned his people never to dare to support the opposite contention, threatening as penalty a fine of ten thousand maravedis and the cutting-out of the slanderer's tongue. Although many geographers of the day already recognized that Cuba was an island, Columbus's claim caused a great deal of confusion among cartographers of the Caribbean for years to come.

Back at Isabela, Columbus had to be carried ashore. Overwork, lack of sleep, and bad food had brought on a complete nervous breakdown, and at the same time there appeared the first symptoms of the gout that was to afflict him so heavily on his later voyages.

The news awaiting him was bad. The only pleasure he drew from it was that its bearer was his brother Bartholomew, who had

worked with Columbus so many years before on plans and preparations for the voyage to India and had also tried so hard later on
to get France and England interested in the idea; now Columbus
had asked him to join him in Hispaniola. Bartholomew's energetic
support was all the more valuable to Christopher because a
mutiny had meanwhile broken out. A column detailed to patrol

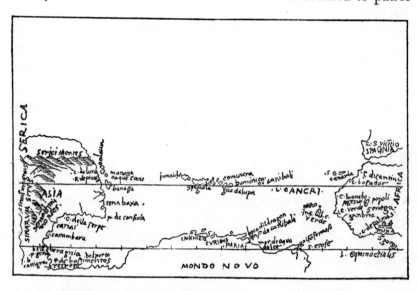

SKETCH MAP BY BARTHOLOMEW COLUMBUS, 1503

the country had seized gold by force from the inhabitants, as-
saulted their women, and stripped the natives of the barest neces-
sities; Las Casas reported that one Spaniard was "putting down
more in one day than a whole native family in a month." The
Indians were in a state of great unrest; when the leader of the
Spanish rabble received orders from Isabela to mend his behavior, he flew into a rage, stole three caravels, and sailed home
to Spain, taking with him his friend Brother Buil, who should
have been converting the heathen instead of making common
cause with a lot of ne'er-do-wells. On his return home, he went to
the court and joined a faction that was busy fanning the flames
against Columbus.

In spite of his ill-health, Columbus made efforts, from his sickbed, to restore the order that had been everywhere disrupted.

Unhappily, his activities as viceroy ushered in the blackest chapter in colonial history.

Small, unbridled bands of soldiers and disaffected colonists roamed about the island, stealing everything they could find. It was little wonder that the harassed savages eventually lost some of their good nature and did away with a few of these highwaymen.

But Columbus understood nothing of indulgence in such matters. His attitude was that a true Christian can never do wrong; so the heathens must be punished. He had the natives rounded up by horsemen and dogs, and made captives of fifteen hundred. This happened at an opportune moment, for the latest convoy of provision ships had just come in, and these were supposed to take back some of the treasures of India, which were at last to pay the high costs of the Columbus expeditions. But what was he to send? He still had not discovered the vaunted gold in Cibao, let alone started mining it; there were no pearls, no tropical hardwoods, no treasures of any kind.

So Columbus decided to ship the only thing of value the country had to offer: slaves. He selected the five hundred "best quality" of both sexes from the prisoners and put them aboard the caravels; of the remainder, each Christian was allowed to pick and keep what he wished. The remnants, four hundred in all, were chased away. Among them were many women who, in panic, left their nurslings anywhere by the way in order to be able to run quicker.

The Indians, herded like cattle in the caravels, were exposed to ghastly sufferings during the voyage. Two hundred of them died on the last stage between Madeira and Cádiz; the bodies were thrown overboard without further ado. In Seville the survivors were auctioned, naked and shivering with cold. A contemporary reports: "They were an unprofitable purchase, for the climate did not agree with them."

As soon as Columbus had recovered from his illness, he placed himself at the head of his military strength and advanced on an army of rebellious Indians, who were quickly mastered in battle; for the cavalry commanded by the daredevil Ojeda struck deadly panic into the simple children of nature, who took horse and rider to be a single living entity. Columbus returned to Isabela with a horde of new slaves and was able to leave the rest of the campaign to smaller detachments. Later his son Ferdinand was able to write: "By 1496 Hispaniola had been so completely subdued that a solitary Spaniard could go anywhere he pleased and obtain food, women, and pickaback rides absolutely free of payment."

Columbus, the man of perfect faith, who observed to the last detail of matins, vespers, and complin his daily duties of prayer and devotion, who believed he had a personal mission from God and planned to free the Holy Sepulcher, had no scruples about enslaving and exterminating the Indian tribes. Every inhabitant of over fourteen had to deliver a prescribed amount of gold each quarter—an amount far beyond his capabilities, even if the person concerned stood day and night in the river to retrieve the precious metal by washing the sand and shingle.

Life became unbearable for the natives. Many fled to the hills, but they were hounded out by dogs and had to suffer starvation and disease; thousands of these unhappy creatures took cassava poison in desperation. Others sought revenge and murdered their most persistent persecutors; this again led to reprisals on the part of the whites, who tortured and put to death not only the murderers but a number of those who lived near their abodes.

The Christians made a thorough job of it. Before Columbus's arrival Hispaniola could boast 300,000 inhabitants. Between 1494 and 1496 a third of them were slain; in 1508 there were only 60,-000 alive; four years later a further third of these had been murdered; in 1548 there were not more than 500 of the island's original inhabitants to be found.

The development of the Spanish colony fared badly. It remained an uneconomic venture not only during its first two years but ever after, because its inhabitants had no intention of settling there, but were interested only in hunting for gold and slaves before returning to Spain at the first opportunity as men of substance. Isabela had to be given up because of its unsatisfactory situation—nothing of it remains to be seen but a patch of grassland and a few relics of stone—and Santo Domingo was founded as the local capital instead. Columbus issued the orders for the move, but sailed to Spain in March 1496 shortly before the work started. Intrigues against him at court had flourished; Juan Aguado, an ex-official sent to Hispaniola to inquire into Columbus's administration, had adopted a very superior and authoritative attitude.

At the court Columbus was received respectfully, though with none of the ceremonial enthusiasm of his first return, and was able to make his own report. But at the same time he had to deliver a sealed dispatch from the great Juan Aguado, which was certainly not full of encomiums over Columbus's activities. All the same, the King and Queen showed goodwill and authorized the means for their Admiral's further plans to seek out, with a number of ships, the great continent that must stretch away somewhere to the south or southeast of the island of his discovery.

There was no apparent urgency to appoint Columbus viceroy of India, for fully two years were to elapse before his next sailing. It required unspeakable efforts to get his six caravels with their crews, equipment, and stores ready for the voyage, largely because there were more important matters afoot. The heir to the Spanish throne was to marry the Archduchess of Austria, while her brother, the Archduke Philip of Habsburg, son of the German Emperor Maximilian I, was to wed Doña Juana, the daughter of Their Catholic Majesties of Spain; and, for full measure, the eldest princess of Spain, Doña Isabel, was to become the King of Portugal's bride. Thus, in the eyes of certain European states left out of these arrangements, the world was being brought into the control of a single family, whose leadership the Habsburgs were destined, thanks to the demise of other lineages and their clever provision of male heirs, to assume.

These royal espousals absorbed vast sums of materials and money. In order to carry Doña Juana to her nuptials in Flanders, a fleet of 130 lavishly equipped vessels had to be fitted out; and these were to bring the bride of the heir to the Spanish throne back on their return journey. Columbus succeeded in foretelling the precise date of their arrival, and this trivial service won him so much new credit at the court that he at last found readier support for his comparatively unimportant business—the discovery of a continent—and was able to put to sea on May 30, 1498. Before doing so, he settled the succession and the distribution of his property among his own family and directed in his will that a church and a hospital be built in Hispaniola, as well as a training-college for divines, whose duty it would be to convert the Indians to the true faith. He left enough money for his wishes to be carried out after his death, but by then, unfortunately, there were no Indians left on whom the graduates could exercise their talents.

Columbus felt himself more fiercely driven than ever before on this, his third voyage. He still had to complete the great task he had set as his life's aim—the discovery of the western passage to the continent of Asia. The other essential was to counter the growing intrigues against himself and the loss of confidence of his King and Queen; somehow he must find something of the highest value and importance if interest in the Indian islands far across the sea were not to be blunted one day soon and the whole enterprise wound up on account of its insufficient dividends. Where, oh, where was the mainland, where the Great Khan himself, where the storied treasures of India?

This time he sailed on a more southerly course, at first on the very course another great navigator had held within the previous year—Vasco da Gama, who had later turned aside from it and, sailing round the southern tip of Africa, discovered the true route to India in precisely the opposite direction.

After a week of quiet sailing Columbus and his fleet were suddenly faced with a crisis. The gentle breeze ceased completely; the ships lay motionless on the calm waters. The great heat tortured the sailors, who never thought of casting off their heavy clothes; boredom and sickness racked their nerves. Luckily, after another week the sky clouded over and a breeze got up to carry them on their way. A trade wind had arisen which does not usually occur in that region at that time of year. Columbus threw himself on his knees in his cabin and earnestly gave thanks to the Holy Trinity for sending him this succor, promising to give the name Trinidad to the first land he might come upon.

A fair wind now bore the flotilla steadily onward. It was a

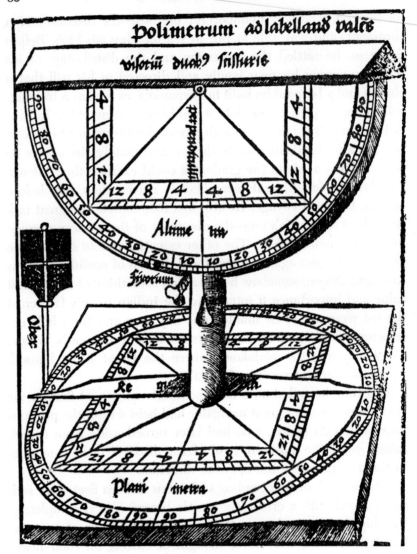

WALDSEEMÜLLER'S POLIMETRUM

lovely voyage over some of the loveliest waters in the world. But the farther they got from home, the more dubious grew the sailors as to their whereabouts, and in the end the old trouble of fear, doubt, and insubordination asserted itself once more. Water grew scarce, not a strip of land was sighted, and their hopes of a safe return to their homes began to recede.

The fleet would soon have run into difficult, reef-studded waters had not the sailor Alonzo Perez climbed up into the crow's nest at noon on July 31 and seen in the distance, beyond any doubt, the tops of three hills. The fact that the land he had promised to call Trinidad was first seen in the guise of three hilltops Columbus interpreted as a special miracle personally vouchsafed him by the Three in One. Nobody will ever know how the countless natives who perished as the outcome of this discovery interpreted it.

The first thing the sailors did was to go "very gaily" ashore, collect fresh water, and indulge in some carefree bathing frolics in the clear water of the river at whose mouth the flotilla had arrived. Then onward again, restored and refreshed.

While Columbus was sailing along the coast of Trinidad toward Erin Point, he caught sight of a distant coastline. It has so often happened in the world's history that those taking part in some great historical moment have failed to realize it; so now Columbus missed the vital significance of that pregnant minute. For he was looking at what he had come to see: the mainland. All unconscious that this was the actual discovery of America, he thought it was but another island that lay before him, and to it he gave the name Ysla Sancta—"Holy Island."

It was August 1, 1498. This is the date that should properly stand in the history books as the day on which Columbus discovered America, even though he was never to know in his lifetime that history would ultimately record him as the discoverer of the continent. It is, however, not the historically correct date for the discovery of America, for John Cabot had sighted the northern part of the continent and trodden the soil of the New World more than a year before.

Far from experiencing the elation of having discovered a new continent, Columbus now suffered the bitterness of a new disappointment. For the natives of Trinidad were no more the lieges of the Great Khan than any of the others, but again just savages of the Caribbean race he already knew too well. They were very suspicious and could not be lured on board, even by hanging brass chamberpots and other bright and shining objects over the rail. It took much negotiation before he could arrange a meeting with one of the caziques, at which the Indian exchanged his headgear for the red cap the Admiral was wearing.

After passing through the Gulf of Paria, Columbus dropped anchor in a small bay on the Paria Peninsula. This is where the Spaniards set foot for the first time on American soil.

Columbus sailed a whole week along the Venezuelan coast and still thought South America was an island, though he was somewhat surprised to find his ships cutting through fresh water, which could come only from very large rivers. The natives he found here were well advanced in the manufacture of cotton and metals. They owned countless objects, which they were glad enough to trade for copper. These were made of gold and of a metal that looked on the surface exactly like gold: this was an alloy of gold, silver, and copper.

Here Columbus missed one or two great opportunities. He refused to exchange his tinkling bells for neck ornaments as big as horseshoes, made of pure gold, wrongly taking them to be made of the alloy; worse, he neglected to look for the beds from which came the precious pearls that, to the great astonishment of the Spaniards, were worn by all the Indian women. In a hurry to get back to Hispaniola because his provisions were running out, he sailed, at no great distance, past the great banks of pearls, which were discovered not long afterward by Ojeda and which afforded Spain a sizable fortune for well over a hundred years. It was not Columbus's destiny to stand before his master with such a hoard in his hands.

Instead, he had much more sensational news to bring back with him. On August 14 he changed his mind. It had at last entered his head that he was sailing along a main land mass; he had never seen the estuary of so mighty a river as the Orinoco, where the flooded lowlands, as seen from the deck of a ship, seem to sink below the horizon. Now at last he believed that he was dealing with a huge unknown continent, and he backed his belief with the sixth chapter of the fourth book of Ezra, which says that six parts of the world are dry land and one part water. But what was the position of this continent? Columbus, who was still convinced that he was in the East Indies, placed it as south or southeast of the Chinese province of Mangi, which he identified with the "mainland," Cuba. This confusion of localities gave him the idea that he really had discovered something quite out of the ordinary—nothing less than Paradise itself!

Was it not generally agreed that the Garden of Eden lay at the far end of the Orient? And where else could he and his ships now be? The longer he thought about it, the more proofs he found: the moderate climate, the loveliest plants, the most luscious fruits, the precious gold—everything conformed to the description of Paradise. And the four rivers that poured into the Gulf of Paria could only be the four rivers of Paradise: the Nile, Tigris, Euphrates, and Ganges.

At the same time, Columbus developed a new theory of the earth's shape: it was not a globe after all, but a pear, a sphere with an excrescence shaped like a woman's breast. This breast pointed nearer to heaven than any other part of the world (a conclusion he reached by an incorrect observation of the Pole Star), and at the point of the breast lay Paradise.

They reached Hispaniola safely. But when on August 31 he cast anchor in the harbor of the new capital, Santo Domingo, after an absence of nearly two and a half years, he was met by bad news and the saddest events of his life.

After he had settled his brother Bartholomew as governor and himself left Hispaniola, things at first went well enough. The development of the new capital went ahead smoothly, and so did the slave trade; ships arrived from Spain with supplies. Bartholomew marched right across Hispaniola, but not on a warlike errand: this time he was paying a state visit to Behechio, a cazique in the southwest, in order to levy tribute. The Cazique, who possessed no gold, knew just how to deal with his white masters, so he got away with offering a skimpy gift of hemp, cotton, and cassava

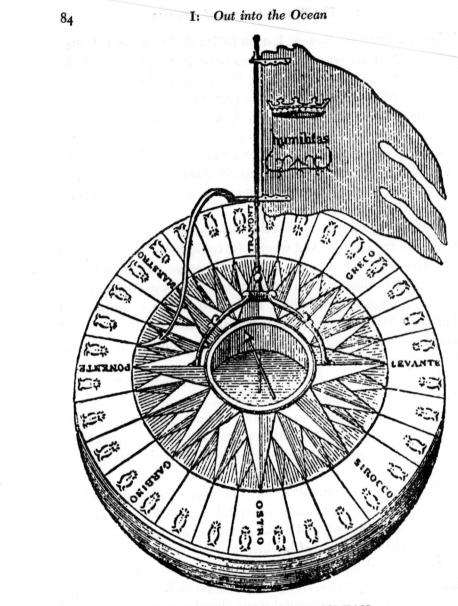

EARLY SIXTEENTH-CENTURY COMPASS

bread; he prepared a fine reception for the Spaniards and arranged a life of Arcadian pleasure for them. The celebrations lasted three days without a break: they feasted on delicious roast iguanas and other dainties, and delighted the eye with exhibition fights between the young men and dances by naked maidens. The peak was reached when Anacaona, whose loveliness was renowned (she was the sister of the Cazique, and widow of the savage Caonabo, who had laid the first colony in ruins), was carried in on a bed of flowers, in all her native beauty unadorned.

But every trace of the festal mood vanished when Bartholomew returned to the settlement. A rebellion had broken out there, and the struggle with the rebels lasted till Christopher arrived to find himself faced with a plethora of troubles. The natives were now filled with hatred for the white plunderers; the Spaniards were full of mistrust for the "alien" Columbus and his brother; one third of the white men were victims of syphilis; the latest supply ships from Spain had fallen into rebel hands. The rebels now commanded the farther side of the island, and Columbus had only an inferior force with which to face them. Finally, the ever present question stood in the forefront: how was he to defray the cost of his colonial venture, seeing that there was still no sizable amount of gold to be shipped back to Spain?

Columbus's correspondence reveals that he had by now lost all the nervous energy that had marked his earlier years. He came to a shameful agreement with the troublemakers which did great harm to his reputation and standing; the only solution he could find to the financial problem was to ship home more slaves, a practice he always considered justifiable. Indeed, this expedient was not new or of his own invention; he was only extending to men of different pigmentation the practice of the Christian lands of Spain and Portugal, where the habit of enslaving the natives of the Canary Islands and Africa was already established.

Dissatisfaction with Columbus's administration and the sorry state of affairs in Hispaniola eventually moved the royal pair to equip the sturdy old Francisco de Bobadilla with a very strong force and send him out to the colony to investigate. When in July 1500 he arrived at Santo Domingo, Columbus had just summoned up his energy to overthrow a fresh rising; the first thing Bobadilla saw from the harbor was a number of gallows, from which hung the bodies of seven rebellious Spaniards. This moved him to equal energy, and he had Columbus and his two brothers arrested. In October 1500 Columbus embarked on his return to Spain as a prisoner in chains. While Bobadilla took up residence in the land whose discovery and exploration had cost Columbus the seven best years of his life, the Admiral of the Ocean led a pitiful and disgraceful existence on charitable gifts from his fellow men, still a captive in prison. Six weeks passed before the royal pair allowed his release and had a small *solatium* of two thousand ducats allotted to him. On December 17 he was received at court; this is an eyewitness's report:

"The Admiral kissed the hands of his King and Queen and asked their pardon, with tears in his eyes, and as best he could; and when they had heard his plea they cheered him with much sympathy and spoke words that heartened him a little. And since his services were not to be gainsaid, though in some respects irregular, the gratitude of Their Princely Majesties could not permit the Admiral to be ill used; they therefore ordained that all revenues and rights which had been his and which on his arrest had been taken from him, should be immediately restored in full. Yet they gave him no promise to confirm him in his Command."

Columbus was never again invested with any powers of command whatsoever, though it had so often been confirmed in writing and under seal that he was to be viceroy of all the regions he might discover. It must have been an equally bitter blow that at the same time his fame as a discoverer languished and became overshadowed by that of his more fortunate successors.

When, in the autumn of 1498, the report of the voyage to the Gulf of Paria reached Spain, Alonso de Ojeda contrived to gain possession of Columbus's map and to obtain permission for a voyage of exploration in that area—over the head of the Admiral, who would of course have been available for such a voyage. Ojeda was an out-and-out go-getter, always the first on the spot where there was a chance of brawling and bloodshed. He had managed to attract attention as a young man at a popular fiesta in Seville, where the Queen happened to be holding court, by performing hair-raising tricks: he walked out onto a beam that projected at a giddy height from the cathedral tower, and pirouetted on one foot at the end of it; once on the ground again, he threw an orange so far into the air that the spectators thought it had gone as high as the top of the tower. He obtained command of a caravel, but distinguished himself on land as well as at sea. Columbus, in view of his prowess among the primeval forests of Guadeloupe, had delegated to him the command of the first expedition into the heart of Hispaniola, in search of Cibao's gold. On a later foray under his leadership Ojeda perpetrated his first crimes and horrors against the natives. When the mounting tension at last led to a rebellion of the inhabitants and to the battle with the Indians on Hispaniola, Ojeda hurled himself, at the head of his cavalry, on the native army and was responsible for their defeat; it was he, too, who later overcame the dangerous Cazique Caonabo by guile and treachery and finally "liberated" the island.

Now, driven by greed for gold and pearls, he was setting out on an expedition of his own. He was not to enjoy, however, the great reputation he was thus filching from Columbus: another—a Florentine named Amerigo Vespucci, then resident in Seville—was to inherit it. Vespucci took part in this voyage of discovery, as did Bartolomeo Roldan, who had been a pilot on Columbus's first voyage, and Juan de la Cosa, the cartographer who had been master of the *Santa María* on that journey.

Amerigo Vespucci knew well how to place himself in the right light—or, more correctly, in such a false one that the whole continent now bears his name (thanks to the two Waldseemüllers, as we have already seen); on this important voyage, however, he only played the part of fellow traveler. But Vespucci spun so fine a yarn about it that everyone fell for it and accorded him a wildly inflated stature. He was only too pleased to assist in the process: he simply suppressed the name of Ojeda, though it was not an easy matter to overlook the commander of the enterprise; and in order to consolidate his falsely acquired fame as an explorer, this braggart chronicler of travels merely antedated his report by two years so that on paper he appeared to have been in America before Columbus. Vespucci on his voyages did certainly make acquaintance with the greater part of the South American coastline; his greatest service, beyond any dispute attributable to him, is that he coined the idea of the "New World" and so laid open the way to a proper comprehension of these new discoveries.

Ojeda sailed to the Gulf of Paria and followed to its farthest point the coast Columbus had visited. There, with the keen instinct of a man greedy for gain, he located the invaluable beds

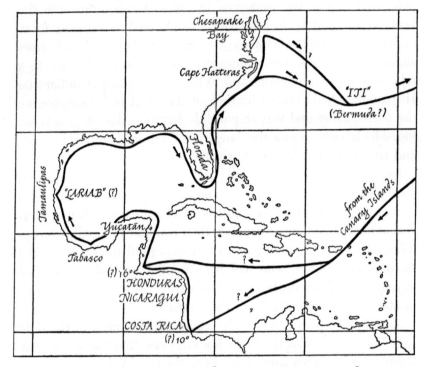

THE ROUTE OF VESPUCCI'S FIRST VOYAGE, 1497–8

of the pearl-fishers; no wonder that he, in contrast to Columbus, was able to win for himself an unassailable position in the eyes of the Spanish Crown. He discovered one or two islands—Aruba, Bonaire, Curaçao—and the Gulf of Maracaibo; to the mainland, because its inhabitants lived in dwellings built on piles amid the surrounding shallows, he gave the name of Venezuela—"Little Venice."

As soon as Ojeda had plundered the natives as far as the haste of a voyage of discovery permitted, he made for Hispaniola, where he attempted to usurp the leadership of the mutiny against Columbus, but without any conclusive results; then he sailed on to the Bahamas, loaded his ships to the full with slaves, and returned to Spain, successful and honored.

Ojeda was not the only one who was at that time cruising about the seas of Viceroy Columbus without his knowledge but with the blessing of the Spanish court. Pedro Alonso Niño, who had been one of Columbus's pilots, came back from these same waters in 1500 with an extraordinary load of pearls; Vicente Yáñez Pinzón, onetime captain of the *Niña* and brother of Columbus's rival who commanded the *Pinta*, undertook a noteworthy voyage during which he discovered the mouth of the Amazon and explored part of the Brazilian coast.

Every year the discoveries mounted in number. In 1500 the Portuguese mariner Pedro Alvares Cabral tried to repeat the voyage of his famous compatriot Vasco da Gama around the Cape of Good Hope with a fine fleet of thirteen ships. In trying to pick up the favorable trade winds he steered too far westward and was driven from his course and literally blown across the Atlantic; in this manner he arrived at the Indies—but the wrong ones. On April 22, 1500, Cabral reached a land that indisputably lay in the Portuguese zone of the world, so he annexed it as a Portuguese possession. Later, because of its wealth of red brazil wood it was given the name Brazil and long remained a Portuguese possession: even today its language is not Spanish, but Portuguese. After his discovery Cabral returned to his original objective. Off the Cape of Good Hope his fleet was overtaken by a storm, several ships sank, and it was here that Bartholomeu Dias, who had originally discovered the Cape, met his death by drowning. Cabral reached India safely, came back with a rich cargo, and so opened up trade between Portugal and the East Indies.

Diego Lepe twice rounded Cape Saint Augustine and explored the American coast to the southwest. In 1501 Rodrigo de Bastidas, accompanied by the indefatigable cartographer Juan de la Cosa, sailed round the Cabo de la Vela, which Ojeda had only recently discovered, opened up more than two hundred and fifty miles of

the Venezuelan coast, and reached the Gulf of Darien. Gaspar
Corte-Real and his brother Miguel discovered Newfoundland and
Labrador in Portugal's name. Both these brave navigators perished in 1502, and this was the end of Portuguese attempts to find
the northern passage to India. With all their zeal, the discoverers
had not the faintest notion how much more there was to be explored: in 1500 only a quarter of the earth's land surfaces and a
fifth of its oceans were known.

More and more people cruised about in Columbus's West Indian waters. Several of them, including the "best beloved" Amerigo Vespucci, sailed along South America as far down as the Río
de la Plata. Juan de Escalante, one of the officers on Columbus's
third journey, managed personally to lead an expedition; the
greedy, harebrained Ojeda got hold of four caravels at once and
went in pursuit of booty. The only one whose affairs were doomed
to stagnation was Columbus. True, he could have retired and enjoyed the rest of his life quietly, but he preferred to write letters
and treatises, to lobby and jockey for another chance.

And still, in spite of all these discoveries, the westward passage
to India remained undisclosed. In fact, the maps of those days
give a clear indication of the uncertainty as to whether there
really was a way through to India.

Juan de la Cosa's map, the first attempt by a cartographer to
delineate America, gives no indication as to the possibilities; its
author contents himself with putting in a figure of Saint Christopher at the doubtful spot, eschewing more detailed information.
The later Waldseemüller world map, on the other hand, shows
America as two disconnected islands (of which the southern, os-
tensibly discovered by Vespucci, receives the more serious treatment), so that apparently anybody could just sail through between them—if only he could find the right place! [1]

Columbus, doggedly maintaining that Cuba was the Chinese
province of Mangi, at whose western end must lie the Golden
Chersonese or the Malayan Peninsula, was of the opinion that the
passage lay somewhere in the great undiscovered gulf between

[1] See Plate XIII.

the Isla de Pinos and the eastern side of the Gulf of Darien. If only he could find it, he could sail right round the world and put Vasco da Gama in the shade.

On March 14, 1502, after sustained efforts, Columbus at last obtained the royal permission to set out once again for India. His brief was to discover new lands, find gold, silver, pearls, precious stones, and spices, but not to take any slaves; he was to bring back only natives who willingly accompanied him and would later be restored to their homes. Further instructions forbade him to touch Hispaniola on the outward voyage and only if absolutely essential on the way back.

On May 11 his small flotilla of four caravels put out from Cádiz. In the eyes of his contemporaries Columbus, at fifty-one, was an old man; his bodily strength had been sapped by his exertions and he was painfully racked by gout. It was destined to be a grim voyage, during which a quarter of his crews perished and the bitter fight against the elements and disasters was to be rewarded by no success of note.

On this journey Columbus recorded his fastest ocean-crossing, in twenty-one days. From Martinique he sailed past Puerto Rico to Hispaniola in order to sell one of his ships which had proved unsuitable, but he avoided entering the harbor of Santo Domingo. Instead, he sailed past the district some way out before landing and then sent an envoy asking permission for the discoverer to visit his own island and at the same time sending warning of an approaching hurricane.

A strong fleet of thirty ships was lying in the harbor, brought to Hispaniola by Don Nicolás de Ovando, a master of a knightly order and the governor of Hispaniola by royal appointment, but now due to return to Spain. On board was the disciplinarian Bobadilla, whose zeal for order was so keen that he had persecuted not only Columbus but the specially dangerous inhabitants as well—among them the lovely Anacaona and her daughter, who were tortured and hanged for "treasonable intentions." Bobadilla was indeed a pretty good man and could rightly count on his sovereign's acclaim, for in three years of activity he had squeezed considerable treasure out of the country and was now stowing some four million dollars' worth of gold, silver, and jewels aboard his flagship, the *Golden Hind.*

Columbus's messenger was received with contumely and contempt. Ovando read the Admiral's message aloud to his people, who greeted it with shouts of laughter. The "Prophet and Soothsayer" was told to clear out: they were not to be taken in by such tricks as his pretense of wanting to shelter in their harbor from an approaching hurricane.

Columbus put to sea again; Ovando's splendid fleet set sail for home, heedless of his warning. It had scarcely cleared the Mona strait when disaster fell. A furious gale tore down on it from the northeast. Some of the ships were immediately overwhelmed by the fury of the waves; others that were quick enough to turn and run were driven ashore and smashed to pieces; a tiny remnant fought its way back to Santo Domingo in a sinking condition. Nineteen ships foundered with all hands; more than five hundred perished, among them the captain of the flagship, Antonio de Torres, who had served as Columbus's second-in-command and was one of his best friends, and Bobadilla himself. Only a single ship escaped to reach Spain in safety; as ill-luck would have it, there was on board a sum of money destined for Columbus. This resulted in a further lowering of the Admiral's repute, for his enemies successfully spread the story that he had conjured up the fatal hurricane by black magic.

Columbus and his ships had sought the shelter of the coast in time, so far as he could do so without the provision of a haven. When the hurricane screamed down on them, the anchor cables snapped like twine; only Columbus's flagship, *La Capitana,* could be held at anchor. The other three caravels were driven out onto the raging sea. Through the darkness of the night they were hurled up and down on the mountainous rollers, their crews fighting desperately for life. The *Santiago,* whose captain, Porras, was thoroughly incompetent, had the worst time. Columbus had been forced to take him along on the orders of the head of the Castilian treasury: the latter bore the fine name of Morales, but he had a mistress who happened to be Porras's sister—and, as everyone knows, in the whole history of the world no one has ever been able to cope with a lady who has influence over a financier who himself has the decisive influence. Luckily, there was also on board the best sailor in the whole fleet, Bartholomew Columbus. He took command and saved the ship. Later Columbus in his bitterness wrote: "What son born of woman, save Job alone, would not have died of despair, seeing as I did how, while I was seeking refuge in such fearful weather for my son, my brother, my ship-mates, and myself, those harbors were denied me which I, with God's help and the sacrifice of my own blood, had won for Spain?"

A few days later the ships were reunited at a prearranged harbor in Ocoa Bay and found themselves fit to continue the voyage; but winds and storms hindered them to an exceptional extent, and it is doubtful whether any man but Columbus would have overcome such obstacles.

After discovering the lovely island of Bonacca on July 27, Columbus spent the first days of August sailing along the coast of Honduras in search of a strait and a passage somewhere thereabouts. It was a nerve-racking voyage, lasting almost a month, into continual cross-winds; day after day, at the expense of murderous exertions, a few short miles had to be wrung from the wind, under conditions Columbus described thus:

We suffered endless rain, storms of thunder and of lightning, and the ships were exposed to wind and weather, so that the sails were torn and anchors, tackle, and ropes, together with much cargo, lost; everyone on board was so exhausted and stricken that, in order to keep their courage up, they undertook to perform pilgrimages and, even more extraordinary to behold, confessed their sins to one another. I have lived through other storms, but none of such length and severity. Many of my old sea-"bears," on whose endurance so much depended, lost heart. My greatest trouble was to see my son, a boy of only thirteen years, suffering so and having to share in such heavy toil. But the Lord strengthened him with courage so that he himself gave courage to the others and comported himself throughout as though he had spent a whole lifetime at sea. That gave me new heart. I was sick and

*oft at the threshold of death, but I gave out my orders from a dog
kennel they had set up for me on the poop. My brother was in
the worst ship and I felt it keenly on my conscience that I had
persuaded him into sailing with me against his will.*

After four weeks of drenching by rain and sea, they rounded a
cape to which Columbus gratefully gave the name Gracias a Dios.
The coast bent southward, the winds and currents became more
helpful, and presently they were sailing smoothly along the coast
of what is today Nicaragua and the picturesque mountains of
Costa Rica.

On October 5 there was at last an opening in the coastline, but
this was not the entrance to the hoped-for passage; it was only
the Boca del Dragón, a great bay studded with islands. Soon afterward Columbus came upon a second opening, which he entered.
After winding their way through a narrow channel the ships eventually sighted a wide expanse of water, but again not an ocean,
for this was the peacock-colored surface of a great inland lake,
the Lagoon of Chiriquí.

Against this new disappointment Columbus could set the fact
that the natives possessed large quantities of solid gold. Trade in
the metal and the search for its source now began to preoccupy
the Admiral increasingly. In the following months, as he sailed
along Veragua and the Isthmus of Panama, rich in gold, he learned
from the Indians' reports that there was a great sea on the other
side of the land, but no waterway leading to it. So he gradually
abandoned his main plan and occupied himself more urgently
with the search for gold mines, though he had actually reached
the narrowest point of the American continent. And so he spent
Christmas and the New Year in harbor at the spot where the
Panama Canal now begins, without even trying to obtain a
glimpse of the enormous expanse of the Pacific Ocean and without giving any further thought to the search for a way through.

Columbus sailed up and down the broken coast; among the
harbors he visited was one that on account of its excellent situation and the beauty of its landscape he named Porto Bello—later

to be the gateway to the treasure house of the Spanish colonial empire.

In December the fleet renewed its acquaintance with the fury of the elements. For a whole month the caravels were tossed back and forth between Porto Bello and the Río Chagres without being able to progress against the winter gales. Columbus described vividly the dangers to which he was exposed:

The storm arose and harassed me so sorely that I knew not whither to turn. My old wound opened anew and for nine days I held myself for lost and had no hope of clinging to life. The sea was more terrible than any I had ever seen, furiously churned up and covered in foam. The wind not only forbade the least progress but prevented our seeking shelter behind any projecting land. So we were constrained to remain on that ghastly sea which boiled like a pot on a red hot fire. Nor had the sky ever looked more dreadful: for a whole day and night it sparked like the forge in a smithy, the lightning flashes crackled with such force that every time I thought them bound to carry away spars and sails alike, and so terribly did they bear down on us that we all feared the ships would be destroyed. The whole time water never ceased to pour down from the sky; nor could it be called rain but a cataclysm. So worn out in spirit were the men that they longed for death to put an end to their miseries.

When the storm was over they lay motionless in an unnatural calm, surrounded by shoals of sharks. The fish provided a welcome change in diet, for the ships' biscuits had grown so maggoty owing to heat and moisture that many of the sailors would partake of their porridge only after dark, so as not to see the seething mass of maggots in their food.

The year 1503 began with a favorable astronomical portent: the opposition of Saturn and Mars passed without incident. That was a good sign. Unfortunately, the Admiral's luck did not obey the behests of the stars; on the contrary, it confronted him with the most fateful trial of his life.

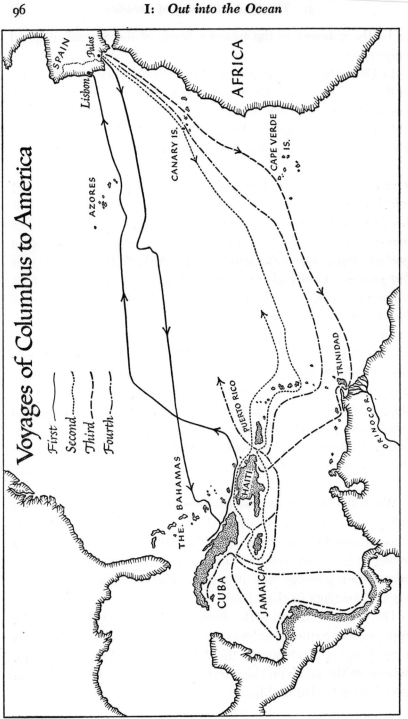

THE ROUTES OF COLUMBUS'S FOUR VOYAGES

At the beginning of January the fleet entered a river that Columbus named Río Belen (Bethlehem). Here he wished to wait till the rains were over; but while they lay at anchor there, it rained for three months without a break. However, they soon found another good reason for remaining: the Spaniards discovered gold-bearing soil out of which they could wring precious metal working with nothing but an ordinary knife. Here at last was a valuable find—Columbus would be able to stand before his King in full confidence with such a result to show for his voyage.

A settlement was founded in which Bartholomew Columbus was to take up residence till his brother could send out a new fleet from Spain. But before the ships could sail for home, the rains ceased and the water level in the river fell so suddenly that the caravels were caught fast behind a sandbank over which they had sailed safely on their entry. The attitude of the natives turned from friendship to hostility: they were obviously planning mischief, so Diego Mendez, a knight who had volunteered to join the expedition, offered to reconnoiter the position.

The Spanish conquistadors, those ruthless oppressors and greedy rascals, were anything but "nice characters." But their daredevilry was sometimes impressive, and Diego Mendez, one of the first of them, offered an unforgettable example that explains how a handful of these daring fellows came in a short time to subdue a whole continent. Casting off in a boat, he discovered a thousand savages gathered in an ambush behind a spit of land; so with all the pride of the superior Spaniard he went ashore singlehanded and interrogated the bewildered Indians! A few days later he walked straight into the lions' den, the Cazique's own hut in the middle of his military camp, and before the savages could make up their minds what to do with him, he excited their curiosity by sitting down calmly, producing unheard-of conjuror's tools—mirror, comb, and scissors—and allowing a companion to cut his hair. The Cazique was so impressed by the performance that he begged for his own hair to be cut. The imperturbable Mendez may have lost some of his locks, but nothing else, and was able to return with the important news that the Indians were preparing in every way to annihilate the white men.

From that moment things started in grim earnest. The garrison of the settlement was able to repulse the first attack by four hundred natives. In the meantime, three of the caravels had been hauled to the river mouth and were ready to sail, for a fall of rain had raised the river level. But further skirmishes, in one of which the Indians defeated a small group of Spaniards on their way to draw water, gave timely indications that the colony could not be permanently held, and Columbus was thus forced to change his plan. In face of the greatest difficulties, the colonists were brought on board ship again—the fourth caravel had to be abandoned—and Columbus set his course for Hispaniola.

By now it was the middle of April. The ships had for some time been in a lamentable state and should have been overhauled months ago. On the Belen River they had been attacked by a species of wood worm which made it very hard to keep them afloat at all—the pumps had to be manned day and night, and the water still gained, so that it had to be baled with kettles and kegs.

At Porto Bello, Columbus had to abandon a second ship, and he made his painful way along the coast with the two survivors. In doing so, he explored yet another unknown sector, then stood out to sea, discovered the Cayman Islands, and at last reached what he still held to be the mainland of Asia—Cuba; it was a miracle that neither of his ships foundered on the way. Then on to Hispaniola. When one of the hard-worked pumps broke down, they mended it and the crew meanwhile got the water away in kettles. In the end, however, one of the ships sank so dangerously low in the water that they had to steer hastily for the nearest shore. On June 25 the two battered caravels made land somewhere on the Jamaican coast—where at least they could not sink. With this inglorious safety measure ended one of the most wonderful navigator's careers in history.

Luckily, Diego Mendez found natives inland who had not yet seen glass beads, string, or falcon bells, and so was able to solve a critical position for a short time by trading for food, which had become all the scarcer since not a Spaniard had been able to catch fish or to add in any way to their slender provisions. The main question was how to get away from the island. The ships could not be made seaworthy; somehow or other help had to be sought. Diego Mendez, reliable as ever, volunteered to make a daring journey in a canoe (in itself a completely new thing for a Spaniard); he had to cover nearly a hundred miles across the sea to Hispaniola against winds and currents. From there he was to send back help, and himself sail on to Spain to deliver a dispatch from Columbus at the royal court.

This document contained a report of the whole voyage and finished with a few sentences that reveal the whole tragedy of Columbus's failure. For the man to whom the world owes the dawn of a new era and Spain the power of a world-wide empire had not succeeded in completing a single one of the tasks he had laid upon himself. He had not found the treasures of India, nor the Great Khan, nor the passage that led to them. The man who had sailed boldly out across the Atlantic as none other had dared to do had not the courage to stand up to his royal master; instead, he was as submissive and humble as toward God Himself. His dispatch is a terrible revelation:

When I was twenty-eight years old, I pledged my services to Your Highnesses; now is my hair white and my body worn and weak. Everything my brother and I still possessed had been taken from us and sold over our heads, even my cloak, a sore blow to mine honor. I cannot believe that this was done at Your Majesties' behest. The restitution of my honor and the compensation of my losses, as also the punishment of those responsible for all these wrongs, who despoiled me of my pearls and encroached on my rights as Admiral, will be to Your Worthy Majesties' advantage. A high degree of virtue and unparalleled fame as grateful and upright Princes will be the reward of Your Highnesses, if you do so, and your glorious memory will endure in Spain for it. My honorable efforts in Your Highnesses' service, rewarded by such unmerited ill-treatment, can never allow my spirit to suffer in silence, did I even wish it so. I beg Your Highnesses for pardon. As I have said, I am brought low indeed. Till now my tears have been for

*others; now, Heaven above and Earth below have pity on me
if my tears are for myself! In my empty treasuries lies not a single
blanca; in mental state am I indeed no longer able to maintain the
bare formalities here in the Indies. Alone in my pain, broken and
daily awaiting death, surrounded by a million savages who mean
us ill and are foully hostile to us, and sundered from the blessed
sacraments of Holy Church—ah, how lost must be my soul when
it parts from my body! Weep for me, ye who feel pity, truth, and
justice due to it! I entered not upon this journey for profit, for the
sake of wealth or fame; that is certain, for the hope of such things
was then already dead. I came to Your Highnesses with honorable purposes and righteous zeal, and this is no lie. Humbly do
I beg Your Highnesses to help me that if God should release me
from this place I may go to Rome and undertake other pilgrimages. May the Holy Trinity guard and sustain your health and
wealth!*

Written in India on the Island of Jamaica, July the 7th 1503.

Diego Mendez's first attempt miscarried, for on the Cuban
coast he had great difficulty in escaping the Indians, who were
determined to kill him. On the second occasion he reached the
open sea unmolested, but failed to reach his objective in the time
he had given himself. The occupants of the canoe suffered unbearably from thirst; one of the Indian paddlers died. After seventy-two hours on the high seas the friendly coast of Hispaniola
was at last sighted: some of the Indians drank so greedily of fresh
water at a spring that they died of it.

After a long coastwise journey and a march through the interior, Mendez, who was stricken with fever, at last reached the
governor, Ovando. That dignitary was not in the least put out by
the misfortunes of Columbus, now in ill-favor, and was in no haste
to aid him in any way. He was at the time on the point of "liberat-
ing" the Province of Xaragua, where an Indian revolt had broken
out. Eighty caziques were hanged or burned alive in the process;
so he had no time for other business. Mendez was kept under constraint for seven months, until Ovando gave him leave to make
his way to Santo Domingo on foot. But when he arrived there, he

learned that Ovando had given orders to deny him the small caravels that belonged to the government, so he had to wait once
again till fresh ships came out from Spain.

This long wait was much worse for Columbus, who had no
means of knowing whether Mendez had ever reached Hispaniola.
As always, inactivity led to failure of discipline among the crew,
and in the end, while Columbus lay dangerously ill, a serious
mutiny broke out. The mutineers carried out plundering forays
all over the island, while only a handful of loyal followers remained aboard the ships with Columbus. Provisions ran low, for
when the Indians had bedecked themselves with the cheap trash,
they lost all interest in trade.

The Admiral countered this setback in an original way. He had
with him the *Ephemerides,* a book by Regiomontanus, printed in
Nuremberg: in it the dates of the eclipses of the moon were calculated ahead for the next thirty years. A total eclipse was fore-
cast for the night of February 29, 1504. So Columbus prophesied
to the natives that the God of the Christians would in this manner
announce his displeasure at the meager provision they were making of the means of life and would doubtless impose worse punishments if the Indians did not show a great improvement. They at
first laughed at such warning, but began to beg and beseech
when the moon was in fact obscured. Then they promised Columbus all he asked, and the Christian God immediately pardoned them and allowed the moon to shine again. But besides
employing the eclipse for his stratagem, Columbus also used it
for a calculation of his latitude, which proved to be one of the
best reckonings of his time.

At the end of June a small caravel at last arrived, as Mendez
had arranged, and removed all the Spaniards, including the rebels, who had been in a pitched battle, to Hispaniola. Columbus arrived in Spain in November; no festive reception awaited him
there, nor was he summoned to court to report, as was the custom
with people of far less note.

The last years of his life, even if his privileges brought him in a
considerable revenue, were bitter indeed; they held for him only
an endless unsuccessful fight for vindication, for the punishment

of those who had wronged him, for the restoration of his rights as admiral and viceroy. For an unloved, obstinate old troublemaker like him who would not even accept the King's proposals for a compromise but insisted on all or nothing, there could not be even a hope of success. His sick and enfeebled body by now had little hold on life. On May 19, 1506, he made his will and in it even remembered the great object of his being, expressing the vain hope that his successors would accomplish it—the Crusade to liberate the Holy Sepulcher in Jerusalem.

On May 20 died Christopher Columbus, the man who had thrown open the door to a new era, without himself being able to cross the threshold. His death passed unnoticed by the historians, his funeral without recognition by those at court. Only his closest associates—his brother Bartholomew, his sons, Diego Mendez, and a few of his old salts—accompanied him to his grave.

Meanwhile, in America the hunt for wealth and power continued. Men who had learned everything in the school of the old navigator carried the banner of Spain ever farther, meeting new adventures on their way. Once the ocean had been crossed, they pushed on deeper into the lands they found. Juan Ponce de León obtained complete dominion over Puerto Rico, the island that Columbus had discovered on his second voyage; Juan Diaz de Solís and Vicente Pinzón explored all Yucatán. The old daredevil Ojeda undertook an expedition to the mainland in 1509 and settled the first colonies on it; in his retinue were Juan de la Cosa— how could he have failed to be there?—and two other men whose names were soon to be famous: Vasco Núñez de Balboa and Francisco Pizarro.

King Ferdinand generously granted rights over territories which he had once promised to his viceroy, Columbus—before he had discovered them. Ojeda became governor of the whole area between the Cabo de la Vela and the Gulf of Darien; Diego Nicuesa, who had founded his fortunes in Hispaniola, was given the governorship of the tract betwen Darien and Cape Gracias a Dios.

In 1510 Diego Velásquez conquered the island of Cuba, which Columbus had held to be the Asiatic mainland; in his company there was a very promising young man named Hernán Cortés. Ponce de León used Puerto Rico as the springboard for his expedition to explore Florida, while Pineda opened up almost the whole of the Gulf of Mexico and Vásquez de Ayllón sailed up the North American coast as far as Charleston. Thus it was that the continent beyond the ocean began to take on a firm shape in its coastal and outlying island areas as early as the first decade of the new century.

4

THE DISCOVERY OF THE OCEANS

O N T H E I R way to new coasts the navigators willy-nilly kept on making new discoveries; not, however, new lands, but water and ever more water—great expanses of sea nobody had ever dreamed of, for the extent of the oceans had been hopelessly underrated. Columbus himself had proceeded on the belief reigning in his time, that only a seventh part of the earth's surface was covered by water; did not the second part of the Apocryphal Book of Ezra, at the sixth chapter, verse 42, state clearly: "Six parts hast thou made dry"? A few dry figures plainly illustrate this:

Till the fourteenth century A.D. the West knew only 7 per cent (10,200,000 square miles) of the oceans, though at least 21 per cent of the land surfaces (12,000,000 square miles) was already known. This comparison alters fundamentally, once the peoples of the West were awakened from their idle sleep.

		SQUARE MILES	
A.D. 1500	*Known lands*	14,500,000	(25%)
	Known oceans	29,450,000	(20.9%)
1550	*Known lands*	18,700,000	(32.2%)
	Known oceans	46,800,000	(33.2%)
1600	*Known lands*	23,300,000	(40.0%)
	Known oceans	74,000,000	(52.5%)

These astonishing performances were produced under equally astonishing conditions. The crews of the ships that broke the horizons hemming Europe had to live in narrow cages and endure an existence that nobody would expect of a convict. Columbus's caravels were small ships indeed: their size was measured in tons which were really *tuns:* the number of wine tuns that the ship could stow below deck. This was normally fifty to sixty.

Everyone knows that these were wooden ships, but it must be realized how the wooden planks were held together; while there were iron bolts at points that had to take specially severe strain, elsewhere the planks were fastened to the frame only by long wooden pegs. The result was that the ships broke up very easily if they ran aground. On long voyages a thick crust of barnacles and seaweed fastened itself to the hull; wood worms settled greedily into its cracks and seams. Every month or two the ship had to be hauled ashore, scraped, and calked with a mixture of tallow and pitch: when, as on Columbus's fourth voyage, this was not done, the consequences could prove disastrous.

Draft, too, was a particularly important problem; when laden, the ship rode the water well enough, but without a cargo it became dangerous, for only comparatively recently have shipbuilders learned to add ballast to the keel. In those days the ship had to be weighted with sand and stones; there was sometimes so little margin that when the crew's provisions had been consumed, the empty keel had to be filled with sea water in order to provide any kind of ballast at all.

In addition to the fight against wind and wave, the sailors had to endure another hard and wearisome battle within their ships: a battle with the water seeping in, for the wooden hulls were never strong enough to keep it out. The wooden pumps were not merely called into use when a ship sprang a leak, but had to be manned day in, day out, in order to expel the water that collected in the bilge. Even so, the bottom of the ship could never be kept quite dry; there was always some leakage water, which, owing to the ship's motion, soaked the cargo and the provisions through and offered an ideal breeding-ground for those creatures whose nips never gave the sailors a moment's rest—the cockroaches. After a time the number of these permanent followers grew unbearable; worst still, the fearsome stench that arose from the bilges plagued even the sailors' hard-schooled noses beyond endurance. Then it became necessary for the ship to find shallow water; the cargo and provender were brought up on deck and the ship's inside was cleaned out. At the same time, as much new ballast as possible was taken aboard, the walls were thoroughly scraped, and all the woodwork was washed down with vinegar.

The tackle and rigging, on the contrary, were so excellent that in the matter of speed no substantial improvement has ever been made in later sailing-craft. But voyaging in such ships was seldom pleasurable, as was clearly proved when in 1893 the Spanish navy repeated Columbus's voyage in a modern replica of his *Santa María*. Owing to the short keel and the excessive roundness of the old ships, the crews were exposed to the fierce pitching and rolling of their vessel: in the modern replica even objects that had been fastened down were torn loose and hurled around, and hull and masts alike groaned and strained so much that the crew could not sleep. One sailor could only describe the ship's motion in the words: "She hopped backwards and forwards like a Bowery whore." Even this modern reproduction of the *Santa María* rolled so much that another likened it to a "washtub on the waves."

Shipbuilders of that early age had obviously given no thought at all to the crew. For the ordinary seaman there was neither cabin, berth, nor even sleeping-quarters. They simply had to lie down somewhere fore or aft in the stinking hold swarming with rats and cockroaches; or, in better weather conditions, on the deck, where they favored the cargo hatch, which, owing to the steep camber of the deck planking, was the only flat place. Columbus's voyage resulted in vast improvements and so made the lot of later explorers more bearable; in 1492 they made acquaintance with the Indian hammock and straightway took this comfortable object into use. So the primitive savages made this contribution to the white man's conquest of the world.

There was no galley aboard the old ships, nor was there that indispensable character in later seafaring romances, the sea cook. The only cooking-equipment was an open firebox, whose floor was sanded and whose rear wall was supposed to keep the wind out. Usually there was only one hot meal a day, served in wooden bowls and consumed with the help of fingers. While the provisions lasted, meals consisted of badly cooked, tough, salted meat, ship's biscuits or stale bread, peas or lentils, other vegetables or fish; the Spaniards never did without wine. Drinking-water was kept in open kegs on deck and soon began to be brackish.

The arrangements for dealing with nature's needs were equally uncomfortable. Seats were hung outboard over the rails, and the exposed user became an object of derisive and not too gentle seafaring ribaldry when he was unexpectedly subjected to a sousing from below.

The crews made up for the lack of radio programs by singing themselves. On long spells of work, such as the hoisting of a sail or the raising of an anchor, it was customary to sing a song—with pious words, like all official songs. One man intoned the first half of a line solo, then the sailors hauled with might and main on an "o," after which everyone sang the second half in chorus while they altered their grip. For example, the text of such a song that could be extended ad lib was:

> *Bu iza—o—dio*
> *Ayuta noy—o—que somo*
> *Servi soi—o—voleamo*
> *Ben servir—o—la fede*
> *De cristiano—o—malmeta*

and so on.

A particularly solemn occasion for the pious Spaniards was the daily Evensong, at which the Paternoster, Ave Maria, and Credo were offered, with the addition of the hymn "Salve Regina" sung in chorus. The singing may not always have been acceptable to trained ears. A humorist of the day wrote: "And now begins the 'Salve' and having each of us a throat we all join in . . . and since sailor men love multiplicity, seeing that they divide the four winds into thirty-two, so they also divide the eight notes of music into two-and-thirty other notes, so opposed, discordant and illsounding, that one could well believe our singing of the 'Salve' and the litanies were a hurricane of notes, so that we could certainly not be likely to beg successfully for forgiveness, if God and his all-glorious Mother and all the company of Saints were to look down onto our voices and notes and not into our hearts and spirits!"

The world was explored by a handful of intrepid, weather-beaten sailors in craft that, by comparison with a modern liner, were mere washtubs; and so were brought back fabulous treasures that revolutionized all previous living-conditions, so were empires built and systems of culture, power, and science in strange continents overthrown.

Columbus provided not only the direct impetus for the development of a new era, but indirect ones as well. It was a bitter pill for the King of Portugal that the uncouth Genoese, once written off as a wearisome importuner and plan-spinner, actually found land and that Spain thenceforward pressed with all her energy along the westward sea route to India. Since Bartholomeu Dias had discovered the bottom of Africa and at the same time the possibility of an easterly sea route to India, there had been no further attempts in this direction. Now, suddenly, time was of the essence: Portugal must establish herself in India before the Spaniards somehow or other arrived there by the other way round and spread themselves all over the land of immeasurable treasure.

The motives now at work were far more materialistic than the old search for Prester John, who had, moreover, been located in the meantime. For in 1487 João II had sent Pedro de Covilhão to the Levant with a mission to push on overland to India and carry a dispatch to the Christian King of Habesh (Abyssinia). After a long journey along the east coast of Africa, Covilhão actually reached the court of the Abyssinian ruler and delivered his dispatch, but was held a prisoner there for decades; it was not till 1520 that his compatriots found him again, some time after they had begun to sail the Red Sea.

In the meantime, Portugal's might had grown in an unexpected manner: all that Columbus had once promised as the outcome of the discovery of the sea route to India had come into that country's possession. King João died in 1495; his successor, Emanuel, knew of no greater example than Henry the Navigator and was filled with a burning zeal for great deeds.

This young king dreamed not only by day, but at night as well, of his triumphs to be: certainly the Portuguese poet Camões tells in his poem *The Lusiad* how Emanuel in a dream saw two reverend ancient men from whose hair and woolly beards ran water—the Ganges and the Indus, prophesying for him great conquests in India. Hardly had he awakened when he called his council to him, decided on the preparation of a fleet, and placed at its head a young nobleman called Vasco da Gama (born in 1469).

Da Gama left Lisbon on July 8, 1497, with three ships of 100 to 120 tons, as well as a store ship. The *Gabriel*, under Vasco's command, and the *Raphael*, captained by his brother Paolo, were brand-new three-masters; the *Berriot*, under Coelho, was a fast reconnaissance vessel. After three months of almost unbroken gales they reached the southern tip of Africa, which they rounded after four days of battle with a head wind. In Mossel Bay, da Gama found the heraldic pillars that Dias had erected ten years before. Here they burned the supply ship, whose provisions had been consumed, and from that point the fleet moved north along the African coast into regions where no European had ever been. On Christmas Day, after continual contests with currents and winds, they reached a region that da Gama named Natal (*Dies Natalis Domini*—the Lord's birthday) in honor of the occasion.

At the end of January 1498 the fleet made the mouth of the Zambezi in the realms of the Arabs, who carried on a lively trade with India. In preparation for the last part of the voyage using the sea routes followed by the Arabs, the ships were brought ashore and a month's labor was spent on refitting them. In the marshy, tropical flats of the Zambezi most of the sailors were afflicted by fever and scurvy, and many of them died of their sickness.

On March 1 the fleet came to Mozambique and encountered for the first time Arab dhows with their triangular sails. Vasco da Gama succeeded in nullifying Arab plots and the trickeries of the pilots, sailed on before a light breeze, and reached the haven of Mombasa, at that time established as an active Arab market. The light-colored houses and flat roofs reminded the Portuguese of home, but everything else was new and very different; for here the wealth of India had already made itself felt and all the trad-

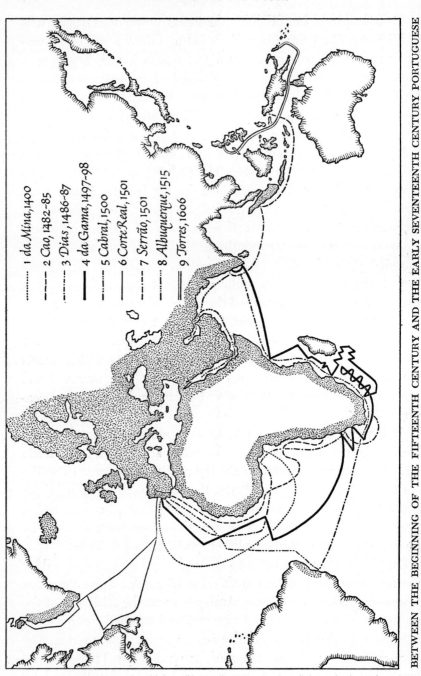

1 da Mina, 1400
2 Cão, 1482–85
3 Dias, 1486–87
4 da Gama, 1497–98
5 Cabral, 1500
6 Corte Real, 1501
7 Serrão, 1501
8 Albuquerque, 1515
9 Torres, 1606

BETWEEN THE BEGINNING OF THE FIFTEENTH CENTURY AND THE EARLY SEVENTEENTH CENTURY PORTUGUESE

Pedro Cabral,
Who Discovered Brazil in 1500
When Driven Off His Course
En Route to India

Vasco da Gama.
From A. F. G. Bell,
Portuguese Portraits

DOM · VASCO · DAGAMA

Gerhardus Mercator (*né* Kremer) and Jodocus Hondius, Sixteenth-Century Geographers

Ferdinand Magellan,
Whose Great Voyage Proved
the Roundness of the Earth

A Sixteenth-Century Spanish Galleon Bound for the New World

The Struggle for Control of the Seas—a Naval Battle in the 1580's

Queen Elizabeth I. From a Contemporary Portrait

Philip II of Spain. From a Painting by Rubens

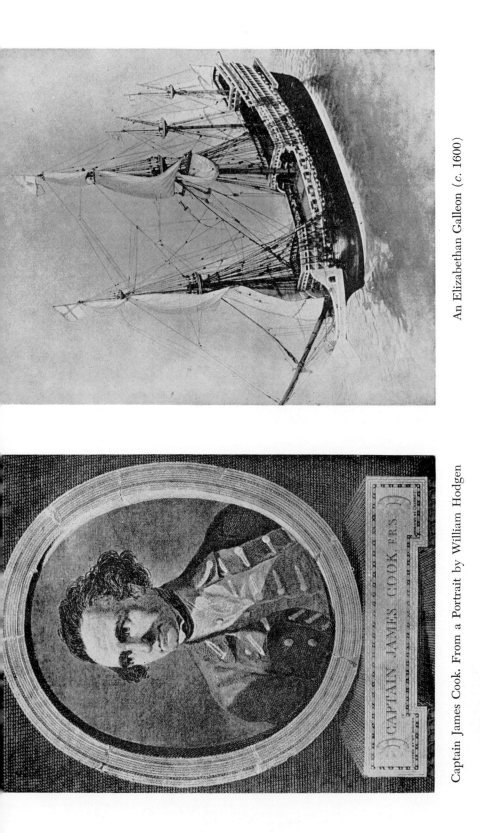

An Elizabethan Galleon (*c.* 1600)

Captain James Cook. From a Portrait by William Hodgen

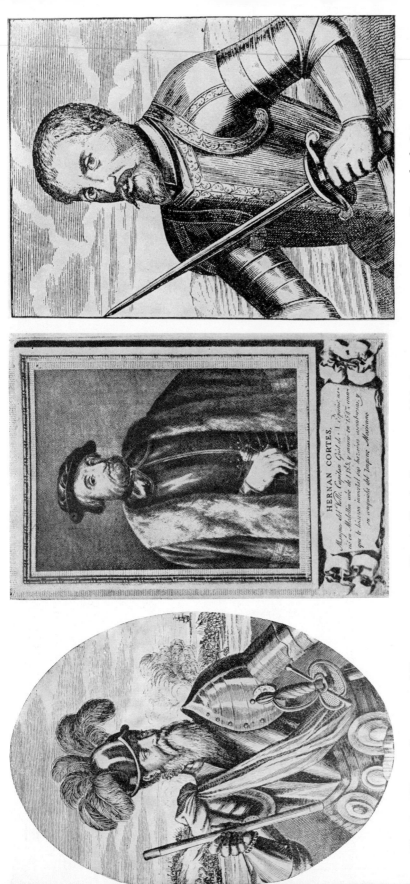

Hernando de Soto

Hernán Cortés, Conqueror of Mexico

Francisco Pizarro, Conqueror of Peru

The Forbidding Mountains of Peru over Which the Conquistadors Had to Pass.
Photograph by George R. Johnson, Courtesy of the American Geographical Society

Paramonga Fortress at the Southern Limit of the Inca Empire.
Photograph by Aerial Explorations, Inc., Courtesy of the American Geographical Society

Pizarro's Surprise Attack on Atahualpa. From Theodorus de Bry,
Collectiones Peregrinationum in Indiam Orientalem et Indiam Occidentalem

The Spaniards Advancing against the City of Cuzco. From de Bry

ing-posts were full of pepper, ginger, cloves, nutmegs, wax, and ivory. But here, too, after a friendly reception they were menaced by treachery and sudden assaults, so they did not stay long.

In Malindi (Kenya today) the Portuguese found a truly hospitable reception, however. Good nourishment enabled them to recuperate their sadly depleted numbers and when on April 24 they weighed anchor again, the King of Malindi gave them a reliable pilot, who steered the flotilla straight across the Indian Ocean on a favorable monsoon wind in twenty-three days to the Malabar Coast. On May 20 they ran into Calicut. The object of the voyage had been fulfilled.

And what an existence they found there at the junction point of the Arabian-Indian sea trade, one of the five great harbors of the world! A colorful mixture of tribes, every shade of pigmentation, a noisy mixture of languages. The astonished Portuguese heard Arabs crying in a familiar tongue: "Welcome, all! Praise Allah who has led you to the richest land in the world!"

Yet the Arab traders had every reason to regard with misgivings the appearance of the Portuguese on the scene. The first envoys to go ashore were greeted with curses in fluent Spanish by two Moors who laughed at the idea of finding Christians or Prester John out there.

Calicut was the capital of a sizable realm with highly developed cultural, legal, and political systems. Most of the inhabitants were Brahmins; the large community of Arab traders had been allowed to erect mosques and enjoyed religious freedom. The Emperor (Perumal), who carried the title of Tamutiri Rajah or "Lord of the Hills and Waves," was ready to give the newcomers audience.

Vasco da Gama, with a following of thirty, repaired to the Perumal's palace; he was borne there in a litter, accompanied by two hundred priests in ceremonial robes. At points on the route the procession halted at temples, where the white men said prayers. They believed the Indians to be Christians of long standing, and they knelt before a small picture in which they thought they recognized the Mother of God. They were all the more astonished at the outlandish images with their many arms and prominent teeth.

The Perumal, when he received the Portuguese, was reclining on a satin sofa richly decorated with gold fringe and embroideries. He wore a kind of tiara of pearls and dazzling jewels; his dress was of white muslin worked with flower patterns; his arms and legs were bare but adorned with bangles and precious jewels.

Vasco presented his petition to be allowed to make purchases in the bazaars and to carry on trade in the country. His words were translated by an interpreter into Arabic, then a second interpreter of the Perumal's retinue translated them into Indian, and finally a Brahmin addressed them to his master, for none but a member of the highest caste might have direct speech with the Perumal. The answer given to Vasco da Gama was short and to the point: the Perumal's land possessed cinnamon, cloves, ginger, pepper, pearls, and precious stones; gold, silver, coral, and scarlet were required in exchange.

This was not a very convenient answer for men who had come not with the intention of bringing anything, but of fetching what they could as cheaply as they could. The conventional presents that Vasco wanted to make to the Perumal showed how pitifully the West lagged behind India in resources: twelve pieces of striped cotton, twelve cloaks with red hoods, twelve washbowls, a case of sugar, and a barrel of oil—this was what the Portuguese had to back their diplomatic mission! The courtiers laughed outright when shown these costly gifts and omitted even to show their ruler such rubbish. In this part of the world the representatives of the medieval West found themselves the subjects, not the masters. But Vasco da Gama soon showed in what manner the Europeans could gain mastery.

While he was engaged in buying a valuable cargo of spices for his ships, the Arabs approached the court officials with complaints against the unwanted strangers. The Portuguese buyers were taken into custody on the ground that they had not paid the necessary export duties. So da Gama took six prominent inhabitants of Calicut aboard ship as hostages. But when the Portuguese were set free as a result, he did not reciprocate; instead, he fired with his cannon upon the boats sent to fetch the hostages and so gave notice to the Arabs that the white men were pirates and intended to disrupt the friendly trade that existed between Alexandria and India.

On August 29 he sailed away from Calicut, after trading his hostages for valuable goods and precious stones. The ruler of Goa —till so recently a Portuguese colony—established relations and entered into friendly dealings with the Portuguese. Then the flotilla sailed northward up the coast. The ships were refitted on a small island, and by the beginning of October it was possible to steer for East Africa once more.

The voyage back across the Indian Ocean was the worst the Portuguese had to contend with on the whole journey. Even more than by frequent head winds they were hampered by innumerable periods of complete calm, and these delayed them so much that it took three months to complete the crossing. During this time thirty men died of scurvy and in each ship only seven or eight men remained fit for duty; the rest lay sick or exhausted. The crews refused to sail on and mutinied, demanding an immediate return to India. Da Gama threw the instigators into chains, himself took over the navigation of his ship, and ordered the other captains, who were almost too weak to stand, to do likewise. A turn of the wind rescued the fleet in its moment of dire distress, and it was wafted in six days to the shelter of the coast. The friendly ruler of Malindi provided the worn-out sailors with good food, rest, and recuperation.

By the middle of January 1499 they were fit to sail on again, but they had to burn the *Raphael* for want of a crew to man her. They rounded the Cape of Good Hope and continued safely northward on their homeward way. At the Azores, Vasco had to bury his brother Paolo, who had captained his ship so stoutly for two years. Early in September, da Gama entered Lisbon at last, just two months after the *Berriot,* under Coelho, which had made the home port after being separated from the commander during a storm. Only a third of the original participants in the voyage reached home alive—fifty-five in all.

The sea route to India, sought by Portugal for a hundred years, had been discovered. Vasco da Gama's voyage confirmed clearly that the land discovered by Columbus was not India, but another

continent altogether. The Portuguese thenceforth had access to
the treasures of the real India. Within a short space the balance
of power in the Mediterranean shifted completely. The trading-
port of Venice, which had hitherto been the channel for the spice
trade into Europe, lost its glory and its wealth; the earlier trade
routes to India wasted away. The worst sufferer was Alexandria,
which, after the Turkish occupation of Constantinople, had held
a monopoly of the trade between Europe and the East. The dislo-
cation of commercial power was followed by that of political influence; Lisbon became the center of an impressive world power.

PORTUGUESE TRADERS IN INDIA

But first the sea road to India had to be made safe for use and
the Arab shipping-trade eliminated.

To achieve this, King Emanuel sent out his navies. The first was
under the command of Cabral, who on this cruise discovered
Brazil quite fortuitously and later founded one or two ephemeral
settlements in India. His successor was Juan Coelho, who returned
with a fabulously rich cargo from India and awoke the astonishment of the Old World. This whetted Portugal's appetite to gain
India's wealth in its entirety for herself. The most suitable man,
Vasco da Gama himself, was sent out to India with a fleet of three
squadrons of warships.

Da Gama carried out his mission with diabolic thoroughness.
Once in the Red Sea, he began chasing Arab trading-vessels,

whose activity it was his aim to suppress. The hunt went on in the Indian Ocean; in the course of it he captured a big Arab vessel carrying many important Indians back to their country from the pilgrimage to Mecca. The Portuguese Admiral demonstrated the superiority of the Christian way of life by stripping them of all their weapons and belongings, and then ordering the ship to be set on fire. The Arabs fought desperately for their lives, 260 men and more than 50 women; the women held out their children toward the Europeans and entreated for mercy—in vain. Da Gama spared only 20 boys to be brought up as Christian monks.

The Admiral performed his next act of heroism at Calicut, where he demanded that all Arabs living there be expelled. When the Perumal hesitated, da Gama had all the Arabs he held on board hanged from the yards, and their heads, hands, and feet cut off; then he sent the mutilated bodies to the ruler with a threatening letter. When da Gama received no reply to such bestiality, he fired on the city for two whole days with every gun aboard and then sailed on to Cochin, where he founded a trading-station. After setting up several bases he eventually returned to Lisbon with a cargo worth a million ducats;[1] and if the lion's share went to the Crown, he still had a tidy little sum of forty thousand ducats left for himself.

During the years that followed, the Portuguese made themselves masters of the whole of India's trade after bloody battles on sea and land. They first gained a firm footing in Cochin, where the Perumal lost eighteen thousand of his troops through fighting and a pestilence. In 1505 that ruthless man of iron, Affonso de Albuquerque, became viceroy of India. True, he met with a severe reverse before Calicut, but he captured Goa and was thus enabled to make the Perumal sue for peace; later he won the great naval battle of Diu (1509) and crowned his successes with the conquest of the rich port of Malacca, defended though it was by thirty thousand men with hundreds of cannon and a herd of war elephants. So the most important trading-city of southeast Asia, the approach road to the whole spice trade, which came from the Molucca Islands, fell into Portuguese hands; the way to Cathay

[1] A ducat is conventionally valued at about $2.25.

and Cipangu lay wide open. Finally Albuquerque also captured
Ormuz, the gateway to the Persian Sea. When he died in 1515
Portugal was supreme on the west coast of Africa, at the Cape,
along Africa's east coast and the whole of Asia's southern coastline
to the borders of China and Japan. The farther the Europeans
pressed on, the wider their hold on distant lands became, the
weaker grew what had once been the real aim of their longings
and the object of their voyages of discovery. The Portuguese
ships touched at the land of Prester John, Abyssinia—but what
use was this poverty-stricken, uncivilized region to them? Islam's
sea power, summoned to India's aid, was destroyed; wealth was
flowing in plenty to Spain and Portugal. No one gave a thought
any more to the recapture of the Holy Sepulcher.

In the fairyland of India, prosperity had risen to immense
heights. It was almost beyond the Crown officials to count the
treasuries of gold piling up, while the military commanders ravaged and plundered the land from end to end; fortune-hunters
possessed themselves of huge fortunes overnight, racketeering
was on the increase; rapacity and bribery, greed, gold-intoxication
and depravity, all these made it necessary to subdue the Indian
coast a second time. Once again a great fleet put to sea, once again
it was commanded by Vasco da Gama, suddenly recalled to the
royal memory after two years of cold storage. This time he sailed
against his compatriots as viceroy of India; he deposed the governors, mercilessly cleaning up and expunging the rackets wherever
he could. But not for long; a few months later, on Christmas Day,
1524, he succumbed to the ravages of a tropical life, aged only
fifty-five.

The sea route to India lay open, but open to none but the Portuguese. Jealously they ensured that no other nation's ships sailed
round the Cape to India and the islands of spice. Meanwhile, a
second partition of the world had taken place—this time "final"
and irrevocable. As Spain and Portugal could not agree about the
precise geographical line of demarcation, Portugal fell back on an
earlier bull of Pope Nicholas V dated 1454, which gave her the
monopoly rights over trade with India. So in 1506 Pope Julius II

drew a line from the North to the South Pole which sliced the world in two as clean as an apple 370 *leguas* west of the Cape Verde Islands. This side Spain's, that side Portugal's, and the threat of excommunication for anyone who did not observe it.

So Portugal had to sail eastward, Spain westward; but as the world is round and nobody knew much about its Asiatic side, there were a good many obscurities. For instance, did the Moluccas, those highly desirable spice islands, lie in the extreme confines of the East and so still in the Portuguese half, or were they in the Spanish?

While the Portuguese were comfortably shipping home the treasures of India by the eastern route around Africa, the Spaniards were still seeking the western passage that Columbus had failed to find. As a fly trying to get out into the light beats against a windowpane over and over again, so the Spanish ships in their attempts to reach India constantly came up against the mainland of America.

That is what happened to Juan Diaz de Solís. After the death of Vespucci in 1511, he had been made Chief Pilot of Spain as "the best man of the day in his calling." In 1508 and 1509 he had already sought in vain, in Pinzón's company, for a westerly passage. In 1514 he was given the task of sailing down the South American coast until somewhere or other he came to its end. Then he was to sail north along the west coast till he came to the Isthmus of Panama, over the waters of the "South Sea" that the conquistador Balboa had already sighted from that narrow neck of land.

In October 1515 three small ships set out, with a crew of sixty and provisions for thirty months aboard. As early as February 1516 Solís thought he had succeeded when he reached the broad delta of the River Plata and on its smooth, broad surface—he gave it the name El Mare Dulce, "The Gentle Sea"—tried to sail through to the "South Sea."

The shores of this huge river basin were sparsely inhabited, rolling pampas whose occupants lived by hunting and fishing. When the ships sighted a group of Indians, who waved in friendly fashion, Solís had himself rowed ashore. Hardly had he set foot on shore when the bloodthirsty savages fell upon him and his small company, killed them, and devoured the bodies of the slain before the horrified eyes of those on board. The undertaking was immediately abandoned and the fleet returned home without achieving anything.

What no Spaniard succeeded in doing was finally done by a Portuguese; yet, through extraordinary circumstances, his achievement was turned to good account by Spain.

Fernando de Magalhães (born *c.* 1480), better known as Magellan, was brought up as a page at the court of Lisbon. The lively traffic in this world seaport, the tradition of Henry the Navigator, the great voyages of Vasco da Gama and Cabral, and probably also the return of the storm-battered caravels of Columbus were among the inextinguishable impressions of his boyhood and youth. When he was twenty-five he attached himself to the Portuguese conquerors who followed Francisco de Almeida's fleet to India, and earned mention by his courage and circumspection in the wars against the Indians and Malays. In 1509 he served as an officer in the squadron commanded by Diogo Lopez de Siqueira at Malacca; at this time there was among his comrades in arms one Francisco Serrão, who was to provide the decisive impulse for the great achievements later performed by Magellan. During the conquest of Malacca by Affonso de Albuquerque in 1511 these two struck up a close friendship. In the following year Magellan returned to Portugal, while Serrão commanded one of three ships that sailed on to Amboina and Banda and so established the first direct link between Europe and the Moluccas.

On this errand Serrão's ship went down. After perilous hazards he succeeded in gaining the goodwill of the Rajah of the Island of Ternate, which by European standards possessed a measureless wealth of spices. He became commander-in-chief of the native army and spent the rest of his life in the Moluccas. In a letter to Magellan he wrote: "I have discovered yet another New World, greater and richer than Vasco da Gama's." He also described in detail the voyage thither; but in a very human attempt to exaggerate his deeds, he exaggerated the length of the seas he had traversed. This gave Magellan the idea that it must be quicker to reach the Moluccas the other way round the globe than by the Portuguese route around Africa and past India.

Magellan was less lucky than Serrão. When serving as an officer in Azemur, a Portuguese colony in Africa, he was wounded in the kneecap by a lance thrust during a skirmish with Berber tribesmen, and ever afterward he walked with a limp. On his return to court he asked the King for a modest rise in his modest pay: instead of the two and a half ducats a month which his services in India earned him, he requested three ducats, which was a remuneration more in keeping with his standing at court. Emanuel boggled at this modest half-ducat, refused it, and so lost the invaluable services of one of the greatest navigators of all time. Magellan in a rage abandoned his Portuguese allegiance and repaired—using the Spanish form of his name, Magellanes—to the land that for the most part owed its might to exploits of foreign mariners, such as Columbus, Vespucci, and Cabot.

At the end of February 1518 Magellan appeared before the young King Charles, later the Emperor Charles V. He carefully took with him a neatly painted globe to help him explain his plans exactly. These were to reach the Moluccas (where his friend Serrão was) by sailing the Spanish route westward to America and using the passage that existed far to the south. The American continent with its sharply contracting coasts could not stretch all the way to the South Pole, and if there really was no through passage, then one would if necessary have to sail round its farthest point, as had been done round Africa's Cape of Good Hope. This plan appealed very much to the King, because on Magellan's globe the rich spice islands were at last shown to lie in the right— that is, the Spanish—half of the world. The place where Magellan intended sail through was left unmarked on his globe. Did the navigator have more precise information and was he hiding what he knew from spying eyes?

After a little hesitation, on March 22 the King signed a contract according to which Magellan was "to discover the spice islands in the Indian Ocean, lying in the Spanish half of the World." Such things as the partition of resulting gains, the rights of Crown and discoverer were regulated; but the important thing for Magellan was that he obtained five well-armed sailing-ships—two of 130, two of 90, and one of 60 tons—with provisions for two years and a crew of 234.

Before these ships, which were fairly old and not too seaworthy, could float down the Guadalquivir in August 1519, Magellan had to overcome many obstacles. Portugal tried everything to upset the preparations: the Bishop of Lamego gave the advice, abounding in "Christian neighborliness," that Magellan should be done away with. The Spaniards, on the other hand, mistrusted him because he was Portuguese. They compelled him to sack a number of Portuguese sailors he had hired; and when he hoisted banners with his own device on his ships before the Spanish flags were out of the designer's hands, officials of the Spanish Admiralty with drawn swords compelled him to haul them down. Luckily, this foolishness of the flags had less serious consequences than on certain other famous historic occasions.

On September 20, 1519, the little fleet left the harbor of Sanlúcar and made for the open sea under the joint flags of Spain and Magellan. The command of the flotilla and of the *Trinidad* lay with Magellan himself, Juan de Cartagena commanded the *San Antonio,* and Gaspar de Queseda the *Concepción.* The captain of the fourth, the *Santiago,* was the trustworthy Portuguese Juan Roderiquez de Serrano. The last ship, the only one destined to return successful, symbolically bore the name *Vittoria* and was commanded by Louis de Mendoza.

Magellan ordered that the fleet should set course during the day by the mast of his ship, during the night by a torch burning on his deck; if at night the *Trinidad* in addition showed a burning rope made of rushes, the other ships must show a light to reveal their position. This caused the first conflict over the measure of Magellan's powers of command; the small, lame man with the unquenchable energy had to battle not only with the sea and winds, but also with distrust and envy in his own squadron. When at a conference Captain Juan de Cartagena demanded a division of the supreme command, Magellan seized him bodily, declared him a prisoner, and gave him into the care of Louis de Mendoza. And so he straightway suppressed any doubt as to the level of his rank.

The voyage proceeded slowly, with unfavorable winds and heavy rain showers, furious storms and flat calms alternating. Huge sharks swam in shoals about the caravels; flying fish and

ASTROLABES OF THE SIXTEENTH AND SEVENTEENTH CENTURIES

wonderful birds that appeared to have no backs to their bodies were observed. After sixty-nine days the ships approached the Brazilian coast on November 29.

The sailors were at last able to go ashore and recover from their exertions in the lovely bay where Rio de Janeiro now stands. Fresh water, precious pineapples, dainty chicken (six pullets could be bought for a playing-card) soon restored them. A month later the voyage was resumed into the unknown regions south of the River Plata.

The farther they pressed southward along strange coasts, the colder it grew and the more vicious the force of the short, danger-ous squalls. The mainland proved rugged and bare—partly snow-covered, too, for it was wintertime in that region. At the end of March, Magellan decided to winter ashore on the 49th parallel. This was too much for the Spaniards, accustomed to the warmth of sunny Spain—rain, snow, storms, bitter cold, and all on short rations! But Magellan insisted on the building of living-quarters ashore and punished one or two of the sailors who were squealing too vociferously for a return home.

When on Palm Sunday, April 1, he invited several officers to dine with him, the only one to appear was Alvaro de la Mesquita, whom he had promoted to the captaincy of the *San Antonio* to replace Cartagena when he arrested him. During the night Gaspar de Quesada with Juan de Cartagena, whom Mendoza had set free, attacked the *San Antonio* at the head of thirty armed men, threw Mesquita into chains, and struck down his first lieutenant, who tried to rescue his captain, with dagger thrusts. The crew were given arms and treated to wine and a feast.

Only Captain de Serrano remained loyal to Magellan; the three other ships—Cartagena's *San Antonio*, Queseda's *Concepción*, and Mendoza's *Vittoria*—were in a state of open mutiny. Magellan sent a boat with a few sailors under Gonzala Gomez de Espinosa to Mendoza to arrange a parley, and when with a superior smile he rejected the proposal Espinosa thrust his dagger through Mendoza's throat and one of the sailors finished him off with a blow on the head. Espinosa's companions then took charge of the ship without further resistance. During the next night the *San Antonio* cast her anchor and bore down on the Admiral's ship, which promptly fired a salvo; in a short time this ship, too, was brought to subjection, and not long afterward the remaining ship in the mutineers' hands capitulated. Magellan insisted on making an example. Mendoza's body was quartered (a burial practice then in force in cases where it was desired to ensure that the delinquent should not be able to arise on the Day of Judgment). Captain de Quesada was beheaded, Juan de Cartagena and a chaplain who had stirred up the crews to mutiny were abandoned in the desert. The forty sailors who had taken part he pardoned after the death sentence had been pronounced over them.

The winter sojourn in this inhospitable place lasted five months.

At the beginning of May, Magellan sent the *Santiago*, under Serrano, to reconnoiter southward. Caught in a severe storm, the ship was driven on the rocky coast ten miles south of the Río de Santa Cruz. The shipwrecked crew had to endure two months in the desert; they were supplied with the utmost difficulty from the base camp and somehow fought their way back to Magellan through deep snow.

Nobody knew whether there were any people in this inhospitable land till one day a giant turned up. Of course it wasn't really a giant, but the inhabitants the Spaniards saw seemed unusually tall to them; so in the later versions of the story they grew just a little more. Be that as it may, this giant approached, as described by the Italian knight Antonio Pigafetta, the chronicler accompanying the expedition, "continually throwing dust all over himself" and "executing in the sand the oddest leaps, singing and dancing the while." The sailors made friends with him; he kept on pointing to heaven, thereby indicating his conviction that the white men came from thence. Magellan presented him with a few small objects, including a mirror. When the poor giant looked into it and saw his image, he fell over backward in his fright with such force that he knocked over four sailors who happened to be standing behind him.

The Spaniards found it very striking that these big natives, who lived in the grand style, wore footgear of hide. These were called "*patagons*," and after these the Spaniards named the land and its inhabitants (who were, incidentally, lucky enough not to excite any further interest in the Europeans because they had no gold; to that circumstance they owe their survival as a tribe to the present day).

After months of waiting the weather improved by degrees; on August 24 the ships were at last able to resume their southerly course. Near the River Santa Cruz they ran into a fierce storm that would almost certainly have destroyed the whole fleet had not the frequent St. Elmo's fires about the mastheads made it possible to keep their positions. They anchored in the river mouth, filled up with fish, water, and wood, and on October 18 continued on their way.

Shortly afterward, on the 24th, they sighted a cape to which Magellan, in honor of the day, gave the name "Cape of the Eleven Thousand Virgins," commemorating the legendary virgins who went on a sea voyage with Saint Ursula for three years and came to a fearful end in Cologne because the city happened to be overrun by the Huns on the day of their arrival. Behind this cape a deep inlet into the coastline was revealed. Magellan sent two ships into the channel.

This was a very daring move, for steep mountains rose to over six thousand feet straight from the shore. Glaciers and sharp rocks enclosed the narrow channel, and that very night a fierce storm broke out.

Two days passed and the detachment had not returned. The sailors began to plague Magellan with tears and plaints to turn back. But he would not let himself be turned from his purpose.

Suddenly they heard cannon shots—the ships they had thought lost were coming back, bringing with them the tremendous news: "We have found the passage!" After sailing through a narrow channel and a bay they had observed that the flood tide was plainly overtaking the ebb. So the channels must connect with a great ocean!

Despair was turned in an instant into jubilation. Even the dour Magellan lost control, burst into tears, embraced and kissed men who clung to each other for joy.

They then pressed on into the passage that the world's best navigators had sought so long. But first one of the most experienced pilots, Esteban Gomez, warned Magellan: "Commander, we must turn back! We have only three months' supplies. Nobody knows how vast the South Sea may prove to be." Magellan, however, remained immovable. "We promised the King to find the Spice Islands," he declared. "Our oath is binding. Death henceforth to any man who speaks of our returning."

On November 1, 1520, the fleet ventured into the narrow, twisting labyrinth of channels; rain drove down on them continuously, their view was barred ever and anew by deeply riven, rocky cliffs. On shore the natives burned open fires on account of the rawness of the climate; these provided the only gleam of light to be seen in the whole monstrous dark surroundings. And so the country got its name of "Fireland"—Tierra del Fuego.

When the *San Antonio*, the most seaworthy of the ships and the one carrying most of the provisions, was sent out to reconnoiter a confluent arm of the strait, her pilot, Gomez, finally lost heart. He put his captain under constraint and altered course—for home. Gomez had suggested to the King of Spain even before Magellan that a search for the Moluccas by the westward route was worth while, but his plea had been rejected. It must have been with bitter feelings that he saw his successor truly launched on the right course. Gomez could now return home with the report of Magellan's successful discovery of the westward passage, even if he did not reach his original objective, the Spice Islands.

Magellan spent a few days in searching for the missing ship, but was finally compelled to continue the voyage with the three ships remaining to him; he never learned that the *San Antonio* had deserted him, but believed to the end that she had gone down. The laborious journey through narrow channels, past reefs and rocky cliffs, always in the teeth of dangerous westerly gales, took five weeks. Since then innumerable shipwrecks have made the Magellan Strait so hated by navigators that they finally preferred the route around the storm-lashed Cape Horn to the hazards of its menacing rocks.

On November 28, Cabo Deseado—"Cape of Yearnings"—was sighted, and the ships sailed out into a vast, unexplored ocean that Magellan named El Mare Pacifico because he first saw it in fair weather and calm conditions.

They were now sailing a sea so immense that it was "almost beyond man's wit to conceive"; Magellan had no idea how close he sailed to groups of islands—he sighted no land except two barren little coral atolls, which gave his crews an opportunity to rest a little and obtain fresh water supplies. On top of their exertions in the difficult passage between cloud-capped mountains, they were immediately exposed to the agonies of the scorching South Sea sun. Pigafetta described their sufferings:

The voyage across this calm ocean lasted three months and twenty days. During this time we had no fresh food; it was a dreadful time. The biscuits we had to eat were no longer bread but only dust with which worms were mixed, having eaten through the biscuit, and all smelling unbearably because of the urine of mice. The water we had to drink was yellow, foul, and stank to heaven. So as not to starve to death we were forced to eat neat's leather, with which the main yard was covered to prevent the ropes from tearing. These bits of leather, which had been exposed for years to the sun and the winds, were so hard that we had to let them hang in the sea for five days to soften them a little. Then we roasted them on coals and ate them. In our dire distress we frequently consumed sawdust. Even rats, so abhorrent to mankind, were a much-sought delicacy. We paid a ducat apiece for them, but alas there were not enough. As a result of this bad nourishment a strange disease fell upon us. The upper and lower gums swelled so greatly as to cover the teeth, so that the sick man could take no food. Nineteen men died from this evil. To add to this, about 30 men lay sick with pains and even open sores in their arms, chests, and legs, or other parts of the body. But these recovered.

On March 6, 1521, they at last reached an island, the sight of which did much to raise the low spirits of the crews. Little boats full of naked olive-brown natives surrounded the caravels; the islanders climbed nimbly aboard them and began with great skill to steal everything they could lay hands on. Even a small boat made fast to the prow of the ship was taken, and Magellan had to undertake a punitive expedition into the island to get the boat back; he also brought back coconuts, yam roots, and sugar cane for the nourishment of his enfeebled crews. Because some of the natives had been killed during the fight ashore, it became necessary to leave these islands, which the sailors had christened Ladrones—"Thieves' Islands." Even as the ships sailed away, the natives' boats flitted adroitly in and out among them; a cat-and-mouse chase resulted, with the Spaniards bearing down on the boats under full sail while the natives hurled stones and managed most skillfully to avoid being rammed.

Six days later the flotilla came upon a large, hilly island, but dared not land on it; a smaller uninhabited islet was safe enough for Magellan, however. It was the island of Samar, one of the Philippines. The sick were brought ashore. Magellan had a pig slaughtered, and fresh water assuaged the men's parched throats and tasted better than vintage wine.

Those suffering from scurvy recovered with amazing speed; soon it was possible to resume the voyage with strength refreshed and renewed. At the beginning of April, Magellan reached Cebu, the capital of the Philippines; he was now in the area of the Malayan-Chinese culture, so the Moluccas could not be far away. Yet it was not Magellan's destiny to see the promised land, near though it was.

In spite of an attempt on the part of an Arab trader to stir up the ruler of Cebu against the white men on the ground that they were "of the same warlike race that had conquered Calicut, Malacca, and other large islands," Magellan was able to come to friendly terms with this chief. A grand banquet was held to seal the friendship; there were turtle eggs and palm wine, which was served in kegs and imbibed through small reed pipes. Four pretty young girls almost as white as the Europeans provided a musical accompaniment on drums, tuned kettledrums, and triangles.

After this prelude Magellan was able to get down to more serious matters: trade and conversion to Christianity. A lively barter trade set in during the first days. The islanders brought scales, and prices were quickly agreed on: fourteen pounds of iron brought the seafarers ten pieces of gold, each worth about fifteen ducats; for beads and other trifles the islanders paid in pigs, rice, and other foodstuffs. Conversion proceeded at a breath-taking pace. The King was the first to be baptized, on Magellan's promise that he would thus become the most important ruler in all the islands; then five hundred of his vassals, and in the afternoon his wife, with forty of her retinue, joined the queue. A number of idols were destroyed; the ships' chaplains baptized another two thousand islanders within the next few days, while Magellan's sailors stormed and burned to the ground every village that resisted this conversion drive and killed the inhabitants. Wherever such a village had stood, they erected a consecrated cross.

In order to prove the power of the Christian God, Magellan undertook to help the King of Cebu in the conquest of the Island of Mactan, lying to the eastward. In vain did his companions entreat him to eschew this venture and sail on to the Moluccas. Magellan set out at midnight with three sloops, carrying three cannon and sixty heavily armed Spaniards. Twenty-five barges with a thousand warriors from Cebu went with him.

They sighted the enemy island at dawn. Lightheartedly refusing any assistance from his native allies, so confident did he feel, Magellan waded ashore with his men, not even troubling to load the cannon. A village near the shore had been abandoned by the islanders, and this the white men burned down. At this moment the men of Mactan bore down on them, with three detachments of about five hundred men coming from different directions; in their left hands they bore great shields of wood, in their right bamboo spears. Magellan gave orders to fire on all three fronts, but the muskets failed to have the desired effect; the natives skillfully covered themselves with their shields and were only more angered by the shooting; and though the balls tore through the tough wood of the shields, the wounds they inflicted were not serious. The small company of Spaniards was overwhelmed by a hail of stones, lances, and darts. When Magellan gave the command for an orderly retreat, most of his men fled before the menacing weight of numbers and only a few remained with their commander to cover the withdrawal.

Magellan was struck high upon the thigh by a poisoned dart, a stone knocked his helmet of steel from his head. He had nearly reached the safety of the boats and was already knee-deep in the water when an enemy lance struck his forehead. With grim determination he turned the lance on an attacker and drove it deep into his back. He tried to draw his sword, but as he did so a savage blow paralyzed his right arm. A Malay sprang at him and dealt him a deep wound in the left thigh with his cutlass. The commander sank down in the water, and the natives threw themselves on him and hacked his body to pieces with spears and cutlasses. With him died Cristobal Rabels, captain of the *Vittoria,* and six of his sailors. Then at last the Spaniards contrived to open fire from the sloops with their cannon and drove off the islanders.

"So slew they our mirror, our light, our support, our steadfast leader. While they were dealing him his death wounds, he turned several times to see whether we were all safe in the boats," wrote Pigafetta. The inhabitants of the Philippines honored the name of the great navigator for centuries; the descendants of the men of Mactan inherited the slur that their forefathers had slain this outstanding man.

Magellan achieved what Columbus attempted in vain—he found the western sea route to India. He also discovered the passage that Columbus had failed to find. It may be that the fixing of his name on this difficult and little-loved passage has to some extent detracted from his tremendous achievement; for he threw open to the Western world a sector of the earth's surface of whose vast extent the geographers of the day had no conception. By sailing across the Pacific for the first time in history, Magellan provided the true knowledge of the world's size; and by facilitating the first circumnavigation of the globe (for from the Moluccas onward the ships had only to sail a known route) he confirmed its proper shape by turning a more or less credible theory into an irrefutable fact.

The leader's death was followed by a further disaster for the fleet. The unexpected defeat had robbed the Spaniards of their aura of invincibility, and now the King of Cebu wanted to undo his act of submission. So he treacherously invited the Spanish officers to a great farewell festivity.

Only one of them foresaw the foul deed: Juan de Serrano, the last of the original leaders, the only sea captain who had remained loyal to Magellan during the mutiny, and the best seaman in the fleet. He warned them not to accept the invitation. But Durate Barbosa, whom the Spaniards had elected joint commander with Serrano, objected that one could not so insult a king who had become a Christian.

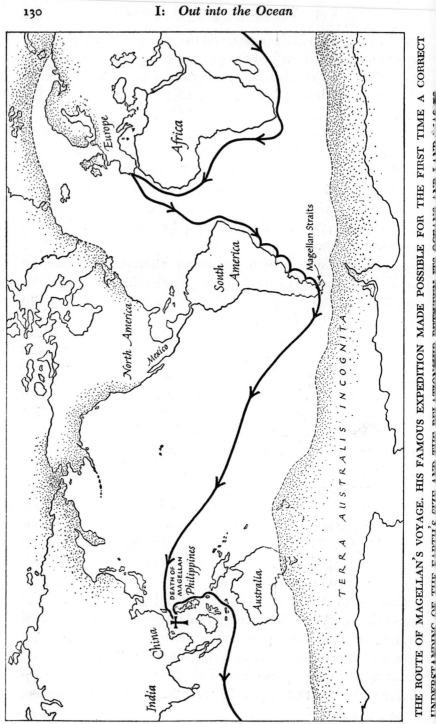

THE ROUTE OF MAGELLAN'S VOYAGE. HIS FAMOUS EXPEDITION MADE POSSIBLE FOR THE FIRST TIME A CORRECT

In order to clear himself of the taunt of cowardice Serrano was the first to jump into the boat that was to take him and Barbosa, with twenty-four of the most important Spaniards, ashore. The native ruler received them with honors, and a festive banquet was served under palm trees. While the Spaniards were enjoying the costly fruits and the palm wine, a horde of armed warriors fell upon them and butchered them like cattle. Only Serrano, who was loved by the islanders for his gentle and just character, was spared.

The horrified Spaniards on board the ships watched aghast as the bodies of their murdered officers were dragged to the shore and flung into the water. Then a howling mob appeared with Serrano in their midst, in chains and almost naked. Serrano shouted to his comrades: "Fire two cannon on them! Then they will let me go and I shall be freed. Help me, for the love of the Holy Mother of God!"

They were just rushing to the cannon when Serrano's brother-in-law, Juan Carvalho, shouted to them to stop so as not to incur any further danger. The crews, who had lost not only their leaders but their heads, hauled in the anchors and hoisted sail. Deserted, Serrano stood on the shore wringing his hands, and in the end the inhabitants dragged him back from the shore. As his comrades sailed away they could hear hideous war cries as Serrano, the noblest captain of the Age of Discovery, fell a victim to the lances of the blood-crazed mob.

Of 265 sailors only 108 now survived, too few to handle all three sailing-ships in gales and heavy seas. So everything usable was taken off the *Concepcion* and she was then burned. The sailors elected Juan Carvalho as commander and captain of the *Trinidad*, Gonzala Gomez de Espinosa captain of the *Vittoria*.

After further hardships and sufferings they arrived at the island of Palawan and were glad to replenish their stores and lead a pleasant life again.

Then on to Borneo, where they entered the harbor of Brunei. A barge embellished with gilded serpents and decorated with blue and white banners brought on board, to the accompaniment of drums and bagpipes, eight high dignitaries, who presented as gifts betel and areca, jasmine and orange blossom, chickens, goats, some bundles of sugar cane, and three kegs of arrack.

The Spaniards went ashore with their reciprocal gifts and first of all visited the palace of the King, to whom they had to do reverence by bowing thrice with their hands folded on their heads and simultaneously raising alternate feet. In addition to these acrobatic exercises they handed over their presents and after a solemn audience were led to the home of his prime minister by the betel-chewing monarch, surrounded by his richly bedecked wives. Here there was a tremendous feast: roast veal, capons, chicken and peacocks, turtles and fish—thirty separate courses, of which the rice and the sweetmeats were eaten from golden spoons. And with each course, according to local custom, a small porcelain cup, the size of an egg, had to be emptied.

In spite of this banquet, the friendship did not last long. When, next day, five Spaniards were sent ashore to buy pitch and tar, they did not return to the ships. Instead, three junks and a hundred and fifty boats appeared and began to swarm about the caravels until the Spaniards fired a few shots and boarded one of the junks. The Spaniards released their prisoners in exchange for a good sum of gold and a promise to free the white men who were held on shore. As a result, four of them were set free, but not the fifth, Carvalho's son.

A little later the Spaniards noticed thousands of warriors gathering on the shore. Carvalho did not venture to attack them, but instead hastily ordered the anchor ropes to be cut and sail to be set. It was not only the anchors he left in the lurch: after his brother-in-law Serrano, now it was the turn of his own son. The Spanish crews were anything but satisfied with their leader, who displayed neither the courage and energy of Magellan nor the prudence of Serrano. A further occurrence robbed him of their remaining respect. Carvalho had caused the powder barrel to be placed in his cabin and was checking its contents when he flew into a rage and started shouting at a sailor for not having cleaned the candle properly. Angrily the sailor cut the burning snuff off and threw it aside—and unluckily the glowing wick fell straight into the open barrel. While Carvalho stood pale and trembling awaiting the annihilating explosion, the sailor with great presence of mind plucked the smoldering fragment out of the powder and threw it scornfully at his commander's feet in mockery of his cowardice. Carvalho had him clapped into chains, but that was the end of his authority. Next time they rested on an uninhabited island the crew deposed their captain unceremoniously. They chose instead Espinosa as commander-in-chief and captain of the *Trinidad* and Juan Sebastián del Cano as captain of the *Vittoria*.

Then they refitted the ships. This heavy task took forty-two days with every man lending a hand. Besides the usual work of unloading, scraping, and so on, there were now new beams and planks to be made. Shoeless—they had choked those down at the time of their starvation diet—they hacked a way through the thorny jungle undergrowth teeming with scorpions and poisonous snakes, then dragged heavy tree trunks to the coast and there fashioned them.

They put to sea again and at last reached the Moluccas on November 6, 1521, thus attaining their objective at the end of twenty-seven months of voyaging. Some happy weeks followed while they reveled in the enjoyment of rare, good fruits and spices, abandoning themselves to well-earned idleness. But at last the ships were fully laden with spices, and on December 18 began the voyage to a very exciting destination—home! The *Trinidad*, however, did not reach the open sea; she was leaky and the water poured into her heavily. So while the *Vittoria* departed under full sail, Magellan's flagship had to return for repairs.

Even after patching, this vessel had no luck. She sailed back again in an easterly direction toward Panama, with fifty-three well-tried sailors aboard under the energetic leadership of Espinosa. They fought the wind and the weather for seven months, three fifths of the crew died of starvation and sickness, and finally the ship was forced to return to the Moluccas. Here they found that the Portuguese had installed themselves in the meantime and were determined to prevent any other nationality penetrating the area. The hard-tried crew of the *Trinidad* were imprisoned; for years Magellan's companions languished away. Only Espinosa and three of his men ever saw their homes again.

Magellan's original intention had not been to sail around the world, but to reach the Moluccas by the westerly route and then sail back again. But when the *Vittoria* left the islands, del Cano preferred the risk of sailing the Portuguese sea route to the murderous perils of the Pacific. In the *Vittoria*—seventy feet long and with a beam of twenty-five feet—he succeeded in crossing the Indian Ocean and reaching Africa unnoticed by the Portuguese. Then the gallant ship had to fight for weeks with gale after gale before rounding the Cape.

There followed two months of northward voyaging up the African coast. Thirty-two of the worn-out sailors died. Near the Cape Verde Islands they barely escaped from Portuguese pursuers; the pumps had to be manned day and night to keep the rotten vessel afloat.

But on Monday, September 8, the *Vittoria* ran safely into Seville harbor and fired all her cannon. Of 265 who had set out three years before, 13 sailors tottered ashore. Next day, barefoot and carrying candles, they made a pilgrimage to Santa María de Antigua, as they had vowed to do when in deadly peril in the Timor Sea. And they had to crave forgiveness for a serious sin indeed: they had celebrated all the Sundays and saints' days on the wrong day—for, though Pigafetta had kept his journal most accurately, Europe was a day ahead of them with its date. How angry God must be with them that he saw fit to cancel a whole day out of their lives! However, the Venetian ambassador, Contarini, who was at the court of Charles V, advised them that on a voyage eastward round the world—counterclockwise—you gain a day, and vice versa; and so they were comforted.

Captain del Cano's fame soon outstripped by far that of Columbus or Vasco da Gama. It was as if the man who had sailed round the world had brought to the marveling human race a new relationship to their own planet. The royal house, too, had grounds for gratitude. The *Vittoria*'s cargo, seventy-seven thousand pounds of cloves, cinnamon, nutmegs, and other spices, was sufficient to defray the various expenses of the undertaking—the cost of five ships, their equipment and trading-cargoes, as well as the crews' pay. Over and above, the Crown kept many thousands of ducats as clear profit. Small wonder that the mariners received princely rewards. Del Cano was awarded, besides a life pension, a coat of arms embodying clove branches, nutmegs, cinnamon, and a globe with the legend: *"Primus circumdedisti me!"* ("First didst thou sail around me!")

Unfortunately, this haul of spices had to remain an exception for Spain, because as long as the two Catholic powers continued to rule, the earth remained tidily halved; the Spaniards plundered America, the Portuguese exploited Asia. The chief differences between the two colonial empires lay in the much shorter distance the Spaniards had to sail to reach their oversea possessions, and in the fact that they could maintain their sea supremacy more easily, even though they had to deal with vicious attacks from French and British pirates or from privateers, which managed to capture many a heavily laden galleon. The Spaniards pressed deep into the jungles and mountains of their continent, destroyed the native kingdoms, and made certain of their hold on the new possessions by the extermination of a few million Indians.

It was quite the opposite with the Portuguese, who, in spite of all their power and wealth, were not strong enough to maintain their mastery. For in Asia they had only bases on the coast; their strength was concentrated on the safeguarding of the long sea route. This required three hundred warships, and the succeeding centuries proved that this was too heavy a task for Portugal's small population. And soon new sea powers appeared on the scene: England and Holland.

Portugal was defeated in 1580 by Philip II, but as early as 1588 Spain suffered a portentous reverse when her proud Armada was destroyed in the English Channel between Dover and Calais. In 1600 the English, pressing energetically abroad, founded the British East India Company, and in 1602 Holland followed with a Dutch East Indian one. By 1615 the power of the Dutch was already sufficient to enable them to defeat decisively the combined Spanish and Portuguese fleets at the Battle of Malacca.

The first circumnavigation of the world had solved old riddles and set new ones. It proved once for all that America was a separate continent and not a part of Asia. The old theory of three

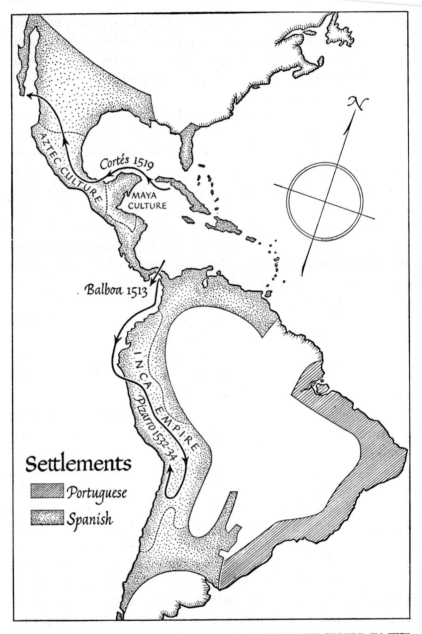

THE SPANISH AND PORTUGUESE EMPIRES IN THE NEW WORLD IN THE
SIXTEENTH CENTURY

continents was exploded; were there only four—or five perhaps? Since it was known how large was the northern land mass of the globe, it was thought that the earth must be balanced by the presence in the southern half of a large, unknown continent: the maps contained an entry *"Terra australis nondum cognita"*—"the southern continent yet to be discovered." But nothing more was to be found out from them.

Indeed, during the second half of the sixteenth century the maps exposed a baffling confusion of ideas. Some held to the scholastic science, some used Ptolemæus' projection, others reproduced isolated new discoveries, still others combined them with old and false representations. Magellan's voyage had left a strong impression of the vast extent of the Pacific Ocean. It had also made clear the dangers of sailing this tremendous desert of water. Why had he not sighted the southern continent, which was supposed to stretch up to the equator?

The huge Pacific did not seem a particularly inviting field to the explorers of the time and, because it lies inconveniently on the borderline between the Pacific and Indian oceans and far from all the main trading-routes, Australia was later identified as the northern edge of New Guinea or part of the islands of Oceania. Moreover, the power-political rivalry of the sea powers brought it about that the few pieces of information which were obtained disappeared either in the Portuguese state archives at home or in the Dutch records in Batavia.

So we do not know whether Portuguese sailors from the Moluccas reached the north coast of Australia that lay so near at hand, though it would be surprising if they failed to do so. One thing is certain, however: in 1601 the Portuguese Godinho de Eredia reached it from Melville Island.

But the first news about that area reached Europe through the Dutch, who contributed most to the opening up of that unknown area of the ocean. Even if there was nothing to trade in or to conquer on the coasts of its numerous islands, the voyages of exploration did at least produce new geographical data: Dutch scientists were able to delineate on their maps Tasmania, New Zealand, Fiji, and the Friendly Islands among other island groups.

In 1605 the Dutch East India Company entrusted Captain Willem Janszoon with the task of accurately charting the immense island of New Guinea, first sighted as long ago as 1526; on this mission he ran up against the Australian coast in the Gulf of Carpentaria. The following year brought one of the most important discoveries of the time, but nobody outside the body of competent experts employed by His Catholic Highness of Spain heard anything about it. Luis Vaez de Torres began an important voyage in 1605 with a view to rediscovering the Solomon Islands, first seen in 1567. Taking a more southerly course than his predecessors, he discovered Tahiti, the Manihiki Islands, and the Torres Islands, which form part of the New Hebrides. Sailing farther west, he discovered the Louisiades and traversed the strait, which was afterward to bear his name, between New Guinea and Australia—thus proving that the former really was an island and not part of the southern continent everyone was looking for.

All these sensational results were kept secret; a hundred and fifty-six years later when they captured Manila the English found among the secret archives a map in which the Torres Strait was shown and so helped the discoverer to win posthumously the fame he earned so long before. It was not till 1770 that Cook repeated the passage of the strait.

During the following years Dutch discoveries along the Australian coast—they called it New Holland—increased in number. Dutch captains en route to Java, the first and almost exclusively Dutch trading-post, learned that they reached it more quickly if, after sailing round the Cape, they allowed the favorable west winds of the southern hemisphere to fill their sails as long as possible. In this way any ship that did not turn north soon enough came upon the coast of the Australian mainland. The first to land on it was Dirk Hartog, whose ship, the *Eendragt*, cast anchor in Shark Bay in 1616. Hartog put up a post with an inscription and left the spot hastily, as it looked most inhospitable. In 1624 Captain Vlaming came to the same place with the *Geelvink*: as there was nothing to remove, he left his mark—another post. Gradually the west coast became quite well known, and in 1627 Pieter Nuyts reconnoitered part of the south; but still nobody knew whether this was the "south continent" or just another large island. So in 1642 Anton Van Diemen, governor general of Java, sent out Captain Abel Janszoon Tasman, who had sailed to Japan three years earlier, to look for the southern continent. Thus began the first great expedition into the waters of Australia and Oceania; its completion marked Tasman out as one of the century's greatest navigators.

Tasman ventured farther south than any previous commander and so reached the southern point of Tasmania, which, however, was not named after him till much later; he himself called it Van Diemen's Land, but without knowing that it was an island. Continuing his voyage, he discovered New Zealand, to which he also gave a name—Statenland—that did not endure. He gave it that name because he thought he was looking at a part of those Staten Islands, lying off South America, that those energetic sailors Le Maire and Schouten had discovered; he also believed it formed part of the southern continent. Then he followed its west coast northward and discovered the southern Tonga Islands, the Fiji group, New Ireland (New Mecklenburg), and New Britain (New Pomerania). On the other hand, when he returned in June 1643 he had never sighted an inch of the east coast of Australia, though he had circled the whole continent. As a result of his voyage, the great tract in which men expected to find the southern continent was appreciably reduced in size; what is more, the idea that Australia stretched away to the South Pole was no longer tenable.

By this and a further voyage in 1644 Tasman proved that Australia could not be the great "southern continent." It was smaller than expected, but appeared bigger than it really is because on his second voyage Tasman missed the strait that Torres had discovered and consequently declared that Australia and New Guinea were one solid land mass. Near Australia's northwest coast he found several tracts of unknown land, among them that now known after him as Tasman's Land.

From the economic point of view his reports were disappointing. According to the ideas of the time, only the east and south coasts of Australia would have been worth possessing and neither of them was as yet known. So the Dutch put an end to their exploratory voyages and thereby missed a great opportunity to obtain possession of a promising and valuable continent.

The fifth continent was left unmolested—only the English pirate and adventurer William Dampier carried out a voyage of discovery in Australian waters toward the end of the century—until 1770, when interest in Australia reawakened. It was the British Admiralty that took the decisive step after Bougainville in sailing round the world had failed to reach the east coast of Australia in 1768. They ordered James Cook to "sail southwards, to discover the Continent [still meaning the undiscovered 'south continent'] to latitude 40° S., if you do not come upon it sooner. If you see no signs of land whatever, look for the Continent in a westward direction between 40 and 35 degrees until you discover it or meet the east coast of New Zealand. If you do not discover the Continent, fix New Zealand's geographical position as exactly as possible." Never has there been a clearer brief for the discovery of a new continent, and if all the geographers had not been wrong Cook would surely have found the legendary land mass that was supposed to maintain the earth's balance. As it was, he failed, but the results of his voyages were more important than their original aims; for they put an end for all time to the possibility of great geographical errors and brought the age of the great voyages of exploration to a close.

James Cook (born in 1728) was of humble origin and worked his way up in the merchant service. He made such a mark by good scientific work at the survey of the Saint Lawrence in Canada and also in Newfoundland that the Royal Geographical Society nominated him for the command of a ship in an expedition planned to observe an occurrence of the first importance to the world of science: the transit of Venus across the sun's face on June 3, 1769, which was certain to have an important bearing on the measurement of the distance between the earth and the sun. This was the first instance of a new mental attitude among the peoples of Europe as the motive for voyages of exploration and discovery. Since the discovery of America there had awakened a general drive to obtain exact knowledge of the world, of nature, of facts, to spread knowledge of these things, and to test them in the light of scientific criticism. Now it was no longer a wild urge for adventure or a bigoted zeal for conversion, no longer the hunger for gold, spice, or riches, no longer the desire for power or fame, but mainly a spirit of inquiry into facts and a longing for exact scientific knowledge that drove men out to seek distant horizons.

In the course of the seventeenth and eighteenth centuries the spirit of the scientists had come to the support of the keen sense of adventure which had moved the great navigators to press on into the unknown. The captains of the sailing-ships no longer relied on their luck, their knowledge of seamanship, and a kind of sixth sense, like Columbus, in order to find their way about the oceans; on the contrary, they were continually in a better position to make use of new improvements.

Thanks to the progress of cartography, nothing that came to men's knowledge was lost any more; everything could now be entered on maps and charts and handed on to the sailors of the future. In 1589 Gerhard Kremer (1512–1594), who in the prevailing fashion had adopted the excellent name of Mercator, soon to become famous throughout the world, published for the use of seafarers an epoch-making map of eighteen sheets which showed the whole of the earth as then known. For it he used a projection that he did not actually invent, but whose general adoption and use throughout the world he certainly ensured. On a remarkable new principle—the distance between the parallels being measured by lines at increasing distances apart—it was possible to join two given geographical points in such a way that the line joining them cut all the meridians at the same angle. This enabled sailors to plot their course with obvious ease.

It was not only the increasing number of maps or the improvements in their presentation which made deep-sea navigation so much easier, but also the provision of all sorts of new instruments in this period of blossoming scientific activity. In 1604 Zacharias Janssen constructed his telescope; this invention helped sailors not only by its direct use but also in a very roundabout and complicated manner, by enabling Galileo to observe the moons of Jupiter. Because these looked like small points of light which now and then went out as they circled the planet, they provided a cosmic signal that could be observed from widely separated points on the earth's surface at the same time and so made it possible to establish geographical longitude if one knew the right time. After 1729, when the chronometer was constructed, this of course no longer presented any difficulty. In 1731 the reflecting sextant arrived as a simple method of taking reckonings. Since 1755, when the first reliable moon tables were produced, the fixing of longitude and latitude has gradually reached a perfection that was at the disposal of all mapmakers as well as all map-users.

James Cook was given command of the warship *Endeavour* for his voyage of astronomic observation and geographic exploration, and first sailed round Cape Horn to Tahiti. The transit of Venus was observed there in good weather conditions, and Cook then turned to the second part of his mission: the search for the southern continent. He reached latitude 40° without meeting any land, so he turned toward New Zealand, which was supposed to be part of the continent.

Cook was the first since Tasman's day to approach that country. He was able to establish that this was certainly no great land mass, but rather two islands separated by a narrow passage—the Cook Strait, which he discovered and which bears his name. The inhabitants were warlike cannibals, on whose closer acquaintance Cook set no great store.

After reconnoitering (and charting) the coasts in these unknown waters, where for three weeks fierce tempests raged and the ship was continually threatened with shipwreck on steep cliffs, he sailed to Australia at the beginning of the antarctic winter and on April 19 reached the east coast, which no European had yet seen. He cruised along six hundred sea miles of unknown coast through waters thick with perilous reefs and shoals and, in spite of the continual danger of shipwreck, charted the position of these atolls, shoals, and reefs. He even collected new botanical knowledge; nearly four hundred unknown plants were brought to light. Finally, the British government profited handsomely from this voyage, for Cook annexed the whole of the east coast.

Although ships and navigation had improved considerably since the early voyages of discovery, the dangers had not dimin-

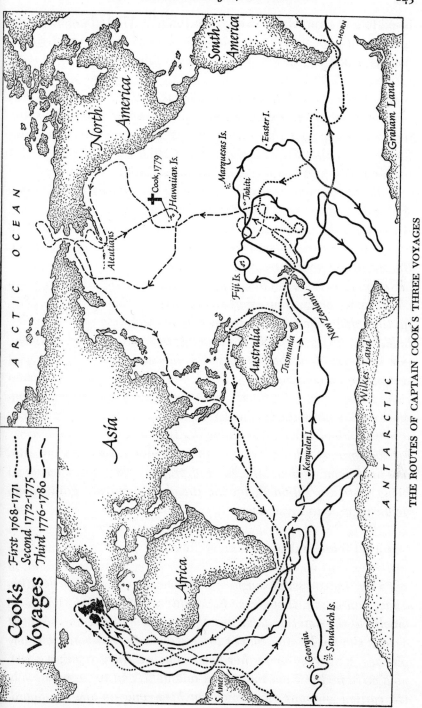

Cook's Voyages

First 1768-1771 ·········
Second 1772-1775 ————
Third 1776-1780 — — —

THE ROUTES OF CAPTAIN COOK'S THREE VOYAGES

ished to any appreciable extent. On June 10, 1770, the fate of the
Endeavour appeared to be sealed; she lay on a hidden reef. Cook
has described this desperate situation as follows:

*In this situation all the sails were immediately taken in, and the
boats hoisted out to examine the depth of water round the ship;
we soon discovered that our fears had not aggravated our misfortune, and that the vessel had been lifted over a ledge of the
rock, and lay in a hollow within it. . . . To our great misfortune
and disappointment we could not move her: during all this time
she continued to beat with great violence against the rock, so that
it was with the utmost difficulty that we kept on our legs; and to
complete the scene of distress, we saw by the light of the moon
the sheathing boards from the bottom of the vessel floating away
all around her. . . . This however was no time to indulge in
conjecture, nor was any effort remitted in despair of success: that
no time might be lost, the water was immediately started in the
hold, and pumped up; six of our guns, being all we had on deck,
our iron and stone ballast, casks, hoop-staves, oil jars, decayed
stores, and many other things that lay in the way of heavier materials, were thrown overboard with the utmost expedition, every
one exerting himself with an alacrity almost approaching to cheer-
fulness, without the least repining or discontent; yet the men were
far too imprest with a sense of their situation, that not an oath
was heard among them, the habit of profaneness, however strong,
being instantly subdued, by the dread of incurring guilt when
death seemed to be so near.*

But all these endeavors seemed in vain:

*To our inexpressible surprise and concern she did not float by
a foot and a half, though we had lightened her near fifty ton, so
much did the day tide fall short of that in the night. . . . At two
o'clock she lay heeling two or three streaks to starboard, and the
pinnace, which lay under her bows, touched the ground; we had
now no hope but from the tide at midnight, and to prepare for it
we carried out our two bower-anchors, one on the starboard*

quarter and the other right a-stern . . . that the next effort might operate on the ship, and . . . draw her off from the ledge upon which she rested, towards the deep water. . . . We observed at the same time that the leak increased to a most alarming degree, so that two more pumps were manned, but unhappily only one of them would work; three of the pumps however were kept going, and at nine o'clock the ship righted, but the leak gained upon us so considerably, that it was imagined she must go to the bottom as soon as she ceased to be supported by the rock. . . . We well knew that our boats were not capable of carrying all of us on shore, and that when the dreadful crisis should arrive, as all command and subordination would be at an end, a contest for preference would probably ensue, that would increase even the horrors of shipwreck, and terminate in the destruction of us all by the hands of each other. . . .

To those only who have waited in a state of such suspense, death has approached in all his terrors; and as the dreadful moment that was to determine our fate came on, everyone saw his own sensations pictured in the countenances of his companions: however the capstan and windlass were manned with as many hands as could be spared from the pumps, and the ship floating about twenty minutes after ten o'clock, the effort was made, and she heaved into deep water. It was some comfort to find that she did not admit more water than she had done upon the rock . . . but having now endured the excessive fatigue of body and agitation of mind for more than four and twenty hours, and having but little hope of succeeding at last, they began to flag; none of them could work at the pump more than five or six minutes together, and then, being totally exhausted they threw themselves down upon the deck. . . .

In this situation, Mr. Monkhouse, one of my midshipmen, came to me and proposed an expedient he had once seen used on board a merchant ship, which sprung a leak that admitted above four feet water an hour, and which by this expedient was brought safely from Virginia to London. . . . To this man, therefore, the care of the expedient, which is called fothering the ship, was immediately committed . . . and he performed it in this manner:

he took a lower studding sail, and having mixed together a large quantity of oakham and wool, chopped pretty small, he stitched it down in handfulls upon the sail, as lightly as possible, and over this he spread the dung of our sheep and other filth. . . . When the sail was thus prepared, it was hauled under the ship's bottom by ropes, which kept it extended, and when it came under the leak, the suction which carried in the water, carried in with it the oakham and wool from the surface of the sail. . . . By the success of this expedient our leak was so far reduced, that instead of gaining upon three pumps, it was easily kept under by one. This was a new source of confidence and comfort; the people could hardly have expressed more joy if they had been already in port; and their views were so far from being limited to running the ship ashore in some harbour, either of an island or the main, and building a vessel out of her materials to carry us to the East Indies, which had so lately been the utmost object of our hope, that nothing was now thought of but ranging along the shore in search of a convenient place to repair the damage she had suffered, and then prosecuting the voyage upon the same plan as if nothing had happened.

Cook now set out on his homeward voyage, traversing for the first time since its discoverer the Torres Strait and thus at last bringing it to notice; then around the Cape and back to England, where he was accorded an enthusiastic welcome. His reports about New Zealand's good harbors, its well-watered plains and lovely forests, and its temperate climate led to the later colonization by Europeans. Australia, too, the forgotten fifth continent, began to attract more attention, now that it seemed to have more to offer than its arid western regions had promised. Incidentally, the continent was still known by the name "New Holland," which the Dutch had given it; it was Matthew Flinders who, after completing the exploration of the Australian coastal regions, proposed in 1814 that the new continent should be given the name of Australia, in memory of the southern continent for which men had searched for so long.

James Cook's second voyage, which he carried out in the ships

Resolution and *Enterprise* between July 1772 and July 1775 and which took him through the whole unknown South Seas from latitude 60° to 70° south, proved that the search for a southern continent was a work of supererogation. He twice crossed the Antarctic Circle, meeting huge ice fields and bergs, without finding a trace of it anywhere. All the same, he surmised correctly that there must be behind that enormous wall of ice a considerable mass of land lying around the South Pole, and even thought he had caught a glimpse of it. The voyage certainly put South Georgia, the Sandwich Islands, and New Caledonia on the map.

The West Prussian naturalist Johann Reinhold Forster and his seventeen-year-old son Georg took part in this voyage; the father, one of the first German explorers, earned a great reputation for his geographic and naturalistic observations and measurements and was the first to recognize Australia as a separate continent. The son later published his father's scientific facts and notes in books that established him as one of the masters of travel description in the German language; but owing to a wrong-headed enthusiasm for the French Revolution whose professed aim was the cession of Mainz to France, his world-wide fame did him no good. He was thrown out of Germany and died lonely and in pitiful circumstances. Nonetheless, as Alexander von Humboldt's teacher he contributed an indispensable chapter in Germany's spiritual development and was for that reason re-Germanized later by those who demean intellectual achievements by sticking a nationalistic label on them.

James Cook went on a third voyage, this time as captain rather than as a mere lieutenant. In 1776 he set out with the ships *Resolution* and *Discovery* to try to find the northwest passage at the top of America which had been so eagerly sought since Cabot's time. Parliament had offered a prize of £20,000, in 1745, to anyone who discovered a passage through Hudson Bay and later one of £5,000 to whoever might approach to within a degree of the North Pole.

Apparently Cook preferred to sail round the world one time too many rather than too few, for he did not cross the Atlantic to the northern tip of America, but betook himself to the opposite hemisphere and looked for the passage from back to front. The course he took was round the Cape to Tasmania and thence into the Pacific.

In December 1777 Cook came to a group of islands about which nothing useful had come to light for a long time; he charted their western half and called them the Sandwich Islands (naming them not after the snack, but in honor of the First Lord of the Admiralty, to whom he owed his commissions). Today they are known as Hawaii. Then he pushed on as far north as possible.

The reverse side of North America was all too scantily known. Since the days of Drake, who was very inaccurate, nobody had bothered about improving geographical knowledge in these parts. Cook established that the coast went farther west than was believed, and charted the whole completely unknown northwest coast of America as far as Alaska. He then cleared up a question about which only the vaguest ideas had hitherto reigned: the relation of the northern corners of the two great continents of Asia and America. Cook charted with exactitude both Bristol Bay and Kuskokwim Bay, sailed through Nelson Strait into Norton Sound, and on August 9, at a point 65 degrees 46 minutes north, reached the extreme western point of the American land mass, the eastern boundary of the narrow strait between the Old and the New worlds.

This strait Cook named the Bering Strait, after its discoverer. Fifty years earlier the Dane Vitus Bering (born 1680), serving as a Russian officer, had accepted a mission from Peter the Great to establish whether Asia and America were one land mass or two separate ones, and had sailed along the Siberian coast. This voyage made it clear that the two great continents were sundered by a sea: in the fogs through which Bering had to sail he failed to realize that the strait which later came to bear his name was only a narrow passage and not a broad sea.

After passing through the Bering Strait, Cook succeeded in forcing a way northward into the Arctic Ocean. He pressed on to latitude 71 near Icy Cape in northern Alaska, then, halfway to success, an impassable ice field barred his way. Nobody had ever been so far north, and he had probably not expected to have to go so far into the polar circle to look for his northwest passage. He established that the long-sought passage could bring no economic or transportational benefit, but decided all the same to complete his voyage to the Atlantic. Till then he only interrupted his mission.

Cook sailed back, in his farsighted way, straight from the polar night to the tropical sunshine of Hawaii; the months during which winter reigns in the arctic he would use to the best advantage in exploring those fertile islands.

For two months the inhabitants of Hawaii were well disposed; then one day the *Discovery's* sloop was stolen—it was February 14, 1779—and Cook went ashore to take the local chief aboard as a hostage until it was brought back. But when the women got excited, he decided against this plan and wanted to return to his ship. Just at this critical moment the news arrived that English boats had fired on fleeing natives and had killed a princeling. This roused the natives to extreme fury; the men wrapped themselves in war mats, armed themselves with lances and stones, and attacked Cook and his companions.

Lieutenant King, who continued Cook's diary, described the events as follows:

One of the natives, having in his hands a stone, and a long iron spike, came up to the Captain, flourishing his weapon, by way of defiance, and threatening to throw the stone. The Captain desired him to desist; but the man persisting in his insolence, he was at length provoked to fire a load of small shot. The man having his mat on, which the shot were not able to penetrate, this had no other effect than to irritate and encourage them. Several stones were thrown at the mariner; and one of the Erces attempted to stab Mr. Phillipo with his pahooa, but failed in the attempt and received from him a blow with the butt end of his musket. Captain Cook now fired his second barrel, loaded with ball, and killed one of the foremost of the natives. A general attack with stones immediately followed, and was answered by a discharge of musketry from the mariner and the people in the boats. The islanders contrary to the expectations of everyone, stood the fire with great firmness; and before the mariner had time to reload, they broke in upon them with dreadful shouts and yells, what followed was a scene of the utmost horror and confusion.

Four of the marines were cut off amongst the rocks in their retreat and fell a sacrifice to the fury of the enemy; three more were dangerously wounded; and the Lieutenant, who had re-
ceived a stab between the shoulders with a pahooa, *having fortunately reserved his fire, shot the man who had wounded him just as he was going to repeat his blow. Our unfortunate Commander, the last time he was seen distinctly, was standing at the water's edge, and calling out to the boats to cease firing, and to pull in. If it be true, as some of those who were present have imagined, that the marines and the boat-men had fired without his orders and that he was desirous of preventing any further bloodshed, it is not improbable, that his humanity, on this occasion, proved fatal to him. For it was remarked, that whilst he faced the natives, none of them had offered any violence, but that having turned about, to give his orders to the boats, he was stabbed in the back and fell with his face into the water. On seeing him fall, the islanders setting up a great shout, and his body was immediately dragged on shore, and surrounded by the enemy, who snatching the dagger out of each other's hands, showed a savage eagerness to have a share in his destruction.*

Next day the natives sued for peace and the English succeeded in retrieving part of Cook's body, which the superstitious natives had cut to pieces, and committed it to the sea.

Clerke took over the command and, in spite of his sufferings from a lung ailment, tried to complete the mission that Cook had taken upon himself to discover the northwest passage, but the weather proved even more severe than the year before. Shortly before reaching the 70th latitude, huge icebergs compelled a retreat; before the ships reached Kamchatka, Clerke died.

Lieutenant Gore led the return to the coast of China and thence round the Cape back to England, which they reached on August 22, 1780, after an absence of more than four years.

While in the great age of exploration the voyages only opened up trade routes, Cook on his voyages explored remote regions and established a correct picture of the oceans and of the relation of the land and sea areas to the earth's surface. He put an end to the legend of a "southern continent" and provided the first knowledge of Australia; after him there remained no expanse of sea and no land mass to discover, with the exception of Antarctica—and he had shown the way to that. This is the judgment of his companion Georg Forster:

Taking Cook's three great voyages together, they constitute a great whole, which included all the unknown geographic regions accessible to ships, and replaced them with reliable knowledge of areas spread north and south beyond latitude 70. From now on, a few isolated islets may be discovered in the Pacific, the position of a few which have already been sighted may be properly fixed, and charts prepared of certain harbours in New Zealand, New Holland and New England which Cook either did not visit or whose entrances he contented himself with indicating. But there can be no further discoveries of any great significance, and the globe is at last known from end to end.

Part II

*Into the Heart of
the Continent*

5

THE CONQUISTADORS

THE NAVIGATORS who first set foot on the strange coast of the American continent came too soon. The Western world was quite unready to occupy, colonize, and rule a continent that suddenly and unexpectedly rose up out of the waves of a dark ocean. The only recipe they knew was unbounded enrichment by plundering the new regions.

The painful history of Spain's conquest of America is not, as is so often claimed, the story of the acts of a few exceptionally criminal individuals. It was the work of medieval man, with his virtues, vices, usages, and ideas at the point they had just then reached, but in a distorted order of importance, resulting from the entirely strange conditions and the astronomic wealth of the new continent.

Long before a new spirit slowly began to develop in Europe which gradually aimed at greater humanity among men, the daring of seagoing men sent the most adventurous and ruthless types far afield across the ocean. Had not this spirit of adventure been so violent and had it set in a hundred years later, the technical as well as the spiritual conditions for the discovery of America would have been much more favorable; better ships, better navigational equipment would have reduced the perils of the seas, and if Dutch navigators rather than Spaniards had discovered and colonized America, their more humane outlook might have spared mankind one of its blackest epochs.

Columbus's voyages to America were not synonymous with the foundation of the Spanish colonial empire. Haiti was, after all, only one more island being added to the Spanish realm. The point where Columbus first set foot on the American mainland was as unsuitable a starting-point for colonization as the islands of the Caribbean, including Trinidad. It was not till some decades later that the first settlements were attempted on the Atlantic coast of South America, and these came to grief. The natives of the continent, like those of the islands, were dangerous cannibals who seemed to be beyond taming. Consequently, settlement in these parts began only when it was already the usage to obtain Negro slaves from Africa to look after the sustenance and support of their work-shy white masters. The rise of the great Spanish colonial empire could never have happened on the side of America which was first discovered, its Atlantic shores. Its development was to unfold along the other side, up the Pacific coast and north toward Mexico. The history of the Spanish Empire really begins on the day when Balboa waded breast-deep into the water of the Pacific with drawn sword, waving on high the banner of Castile, and declared this ocean and all its adjacent lands to be Spanish possessions.

Two men became prominent at the same time on the American continent. Ojeda, the old daredevil who had accompanied Columbus, and the *nouveau-riche* cavalier Diego Nicuesa approached King Ferdinand almost simultaneously and sought the right to settle colonies in America. They were both granted permission, and a broad strip of Central America was apportioned to each.

Ojeda borrowed money to fit out four ships; his rival prepared five ships and two brigantines out of his own resources. Ojeda's fleet was the first to leave Santo Domingo, and after a passage of only four or five days it reached the coast of Caramairi, as the Caribs called it, where now stands the port of Cartagena. The inhabitants were accounted to be bloodthirsty cannibals, and consequently the Spanish Crown had given leave to enslave them. Ojeda was determined to improve the state of his finances by instituting a little man-hunt, though his commander on the spot advised him strongly not to. This was Columbus's old companion and cartographer Juan de la Cosa, who well knew these tribes to be by nature keen traders who flew into a warlike rage if attacked. They had, too, a most dangerous weapon: their darts were poisoned with the juice of the manchineel tree and this poison ensured that the slightest wound produced an incurable delirium in the victim, who died in great agony. Ojeda, however, took no notice of any warnings and attacked the Carib village of Calamar at dawn; all its inhabitants who did not flee were either slain or placed in chains. Eight Indians who were resisting in a hut were burned to death with it. On the next day Ojeda continued his man-hunt in the hamlet of Yurbaco, a few miles away, but found no victims there; all its inhabitants had betaken themselves to places of safety. While the Spaniards were amusing themselves in their carefree way, plundering the huts and swinging in the hammocks they found there, the natives bore down on them like lightning and butchered them one after another. Ojeda, Cosa, and one or two sailors escaped into a hut and fought desperately. Ojeda, being small, was able to cover himself entirely with his shield and avoid all the Indians' darts, but one by one his comrades sank to the ground at his side. Cosa, who had once deserted the sinking *Santa María* and left Columbus in the lurch, now saw Ojeda, trusting to his swiftness of movement, run away. Soon the poison began to rage in Cosa's wounds; he and his companions perished in agony.

In vain did the ships wait for the eighty Spaniards who had gone ashore. When a search was made of the shore, they found no one but Ojeda, who lay utterly exhausted, hidden in a mango thicket, clutching his sword. On his shield they counted three hundred arrow hits.

When next day Nicuesa appeared with his fleet, the Spaniards joined forces in a fearful punitive expedition. The native women were so terrified at the sight of the unfamiliar double shapes of horse and rider that to escape they threw themselves with their babies in their arms into the flames of their burning village.

After a gruesome day of slaughter the Spaniards found Cosa's horribly swollen body. This sight robbed them of any desire to spend the night on land, and they withdrew to the ships with the gold they had pillaged.

All the same, a short time later Ojeda went on another round-up of human beings and captured a considerable haul of slaves. At the beginning of 1510 he founded a settlement on the Gulf of Urabá, which he named San Sebastián. But the numbers of the Spaniards were woefully reduced by the arrows of the Indians, by starvation, and also by the death sentences Ojeda enforced on mutineers. He himself never changed a jot. One day, when chasing Indians, he fell into an ambush and a poisoned arrow pierced his thigh. He immediately had an iron made red-hot and ordered his surgeon to cauterize the wound with it. When the doctor showed some reluctance, Ojeda threatened him with hanging, so he carried out the emergency treatment and the incorrigible hothead was actually cured.

Next, Ojeda sailed to Cuba and marched through the marshy tropical wilderness on foot. Within a month half of his seventy men had perished. They lived on roots, their thirst was assuaged only by brackish, salty water from the lagoons. When after these wild ventures Ojeda was finally rescued by ship and brought to Santo Domingo, he arrived penniless as a beggar and in no state to obtain help for his colony. Soon afterward he died, an unsuccessful adventurer, and was buried, as he had desired, under the threshold of a church.

Those who had remained behind under Pizarro's command were rescued, after all, for the advocate Martín Fernández de Enciso, Ojeda's partner in finance, had set out from Spain with supplies and reinforcements before Ojeda's return. He had a stowaway on board, one who was running away from his creditors; once at sea, he came crawling out of a barrel in which he had been hiding. He was a strong, intelligent man thirty-five years old, by name Vasco Núñez de Balboa.

To Enciso's great discomfiture, this Balboa soon found out how to make himself indispensable and win a position of command, for he was better than anyone else at disciplining a rabble of reckless, fighting, starving adventurers. When San Sebastián was abandoned, he found a more suitable site on the Gulf of Darien and founded the colony of that name. Here he soon got himself elected alcalde and then found a reason for getting Enciso arrested and shipped back to Spain—but later Enciso found a lawyer's way to revenge himself cruelly through his reports at court.

Enciso had been imprudent enough to ban the gold trade between the colonists and the natives. The settlers had immediately
discovered that the Advocate's word went for nothing in these
regions, which lay in the sphere allotted to Nicuesa. Two ships
bringing supplies destined for Nicuesa were greeted with enthusiasm, unloaded, and then sent in search of the Governor.

He had meanwhile suffered every setback and hardship attach-
ing to this kind of enterprise—faction, mutiny, starvation, exhaustion, pestilence, and shipwreck. Of his considerable force of seven
hundred hardened fighters there remained only forty emaciated
bodies by the time he was found and brought to Darien. "Desic-
cated by extreme hunger, filthy and horrible to behold" was a
comtemporary's description of his condition.

Nicuesa started off with a bad mistake: laying claim to all the
gold that had been gathered without his authorization. It is not
surprising that he immediately incurred violent hostility in Darien. Balboa pretended to be very friendly, but let things take their
course. Eventually Nicuesa was made a prisoner and, with sixteen
of his cronies, placed on board a rickety brigantine without any
provisions whatever. He begged his opponents to keep him in
durance, but nobody listened to his plea; without further ado the
wrecked vessel was pushed off shore and never seen again.

Balboa now had nobody above him, but, at the same time, no
authority to play the master on the American continent. So it
seemed to him prudent to ingratiate himself with the Crown by
some outstanding and notable achievement. He developed from
a rude usurper into a level-headed leader who on campaigns and
forays was the best friend of his subordinates, who organized a
respectable army and laid in stores of provisions and sowed fields
of maize. When he married the daughter of one of the local chiefs,
he gained many powerful allies among the Indians.

One day when they were weighing gold, one of his Indian
friends suddenly struck the scales a resounding blow and, pointing to the south, cried aloud that in that direction lay an ocean
and a land richer in gold than Spain in iron, a land that could be
conquered by a thousand men.

That was the beckoning prize which had lured all Spanish ad-

venturers into American waters and which had already destroyed
so many of them. Balboa set out with 190 of his best men and 600
native carriers on the first conquistadorial march into the continent; he sailed west from Darien under the guidance of Indian
pilots to the narrowest point on the Isthmus of Panama and, again
guided by Indian pathfinders, began a march of sixty miles. This
"march" led through sixty miles of a jungle so impassable that not
till 1854 did anyone dare to repeat Balboa's venture at this point;
then an American expedition attempted it and came to grief with
heavy losses.

The Spaniards had to fight their way through a jungle whose
mighty trailing undergrowth and tremendous tree trunks barred
all progress and rarely allowed a sunbeam to penetrate its darkness. The fetid air was heavy with poisonous vapors from mo-
rasses and swamps, while mosquitoes and sandflies swarmed everywhere. The men had to cross mountain ridges and rivers. The
climate and sickness sapped their energy, spiny thorns lacerated
their clothing, snakes and wild animals lurked in the undergrowth
to make prey of them. Balboa had to reach an understanding with
the savage natives, for he could not afford to have enemies in his
rear. His diplomatic measures succeeded in establishing friendly
relations, for he was not so ruthless a murderer of Indians as the
rest of the conquistadors. But he could be tough. When the Cazique of Quarequa tried to forbid the use of a mountain pass, the
Spaniards slew him and five hundred of his warriors in a night
attack; moreover, Balboa passed a savage sentence next day on
all the natives who (unusually for Indians) wore women's clothes
and indulged in the "Oriental vice." He had them torn to pieces
by bloodhounds. To the terror of the Indians, all the conquistadors were accompanied by these hounds, which dismembered
countless numbers. The dogs, like the soldiers, received a share of
the booty (which their owners naturally put to their own account): some of them even had their names and deeds entered
in history books.

This manner of liquidating Indians and other methods used
were not the result of sheer brutality. It must be remembered that
the conquistadors brought with them from Europe to America the

customary methods of liquidation and torture and applied them
with a frequency merely heightened by the grim conditions of
existence. In medieval Europe men were quite accustomed to
carrying out such punishments as mutilation, burning by fire or
boiling oil, quartering, and flogging to death.

From Quarequa, Balboa marched on with the sixty-six who had
managed to cheat sickness or death. On September 25, 1513, toward ten o'clock, the Indian guides indicated that the sea would
be visible from the ridge in front of them. Balboa called a halt
and went ahead alone to be the first to set eyes on the new ocean;
and there on the crest of the hill he enjoyed the unforgettable
thrill of being the first European to gaze upon the Pacific. Balboa
fell on his knees and, with arms upheld, shouted in greeting to the
waters of the "Southern Sea," as he named it. He gave thanks to
God for His grace in allowing "a man so poorly gifted as himself
and one of humble origin" to bring so great an undertaking to
fruition. And, indeed, his discovery stands historically second
only to that of Columbus, achieved twenty-one years earlier, for
it unveiled the greatest secret held by the New World and allowed mankind its first comprehensive view, beyond all previous
frontiers and horizons, over all the continents and oceans of the
world in their proper relationship to one another.

When Balboa and his small body of men went down to the
shore, the army of the Cazique of Chiape was awaiting them,
drawn up in battle order. But the firearms of the white men soon
decided the issue, for the natives into whose eyes the wind drove
the smoke from their muskets were stricken with terror, believing
that the strangers were belching thunderbolts and destruction
from their mouths. Here Balboa followed his earlier tactics of
coming to terms with the defeated foe, once they had felt the
might of his weapons.

Soon afterward Balboa undertook a daring journey out into the
stormy ocean in a frail Indian canoe and discovered rich pearling-
beds. After an absence of five months he returned to his base
harbor of Darien, bringing with him a treasure of gold and priceless pearls, a part of which he sent to the Spanish court.

But this tangible proof of his ability arrived too late. Enciso's testimony against him had resulted in the appointment of a new governor of Darien, who soon arrived with a strong force. He was astonished to find Balboa not arrayed in pomp and circumstance but, clad in working-clothes, helping his Indians thatch a roof.

The new governor, Pedrarias, set in motion a train of shocking cruelties against the inhabitants; his lieutenant, Juan de Ayora, fell into the habit of attacking the Indians in their sleep and either roasting his prisoners alive or having them torn to pieces by hounds if they failed to deliver enough gold. Balboa, who had been appointed commandant of the "Southern Sea" and two provinces adjoining it, sent a complaint to the Spanish court because the whole of his great work was being undone by the annihilation of his native allies. When Pedrarias summoned him to appear before him, Balboa set out on a journey. On the way he was intercepted by his old friend Pizarro and, to his amazement, made a prisoner. Balboa was put on trial in the very Darien he had founded, accused of uttering treasonable plans in a speech. The alcalde, Gaspar de Espinosa, whose inhuman methods of hunting slaves had horrified even the hard-bitten colonists, sentenced Balboa to death. So, with four of his comrades, the discoverer of the Pacific, second only to Columbus in importance in founding the Spanish colonial empire and revealing the true picture of the world to science, was beheaded at the age of forty in the prime of his life, while his insignificant enemy, Pedrarias, watched the executioner between the boards of a near-by building. Pedrarias lived a long time in Darien and later succeeded in obtaining the governorship of Nicaragua. When in 1530 the tyrannical old man was laid in earth after sixteen years of rule on American soil, he was, according to the computation of the contemporary historian Oviedo, responsible for the enslavement or slaughter of two million Indians.

A new and important chapter in the history of Spanish discoveries was opened when a group of disgruntled adventurers became bored with Darien and sailed to Cuba, which one of Columbus's earliest shipmates, Diego Velásquez, had conquered and colonized. He provided the fortune-hunters, who had chosen a capable leader in Francisco Fernández de Córdoba, with three ships and sent them out to look for new lands. Sailing from the west coast of Cuba in February 1517, they came upon the coast of Yucatán, which, oddly enough, had escaped discovery, and there lit upon a strange civilization of a type undreamed of here by any European. The presence of people in colored cotton clothes cultivating maize fields, the masonry of a city's tower rising skyward, and finely carved idols, raised a number of questions. But these inhabitants were warlike—not even the all-conquering Aztecs had been able to conquer this Maya civilization—and the Spaniards were driven off, returning to Cuba with less than half their force. Ten days later Córdoba died of his many wounds.

A second expedition, three times as strong, sent out by Velásquez, likewise failed. So for the third he appointed an exceptionally capable commander, the Alcalde of Santiago. This man, who had spent a wild youth at the University of Salamanca and had nearly been stabbed to death in an amatory escapade, had decided in 1504 to seek his fortune in the New World and had distinguished himself at the "peaceful occupation" of Hispaniola. Velásquez had brought him to Cuba as his secretary, where the promising young adventurer soon made himself highly popular as a gay companion and daring leader. Involving himself in madly wild gallantries and love affairs, he was compelled to marry; he was also forced on one occasion to swim for his life, and on yet another landed himself in prison; but he soon regained the Governor's goodwill and now at last got his chance to show his outstanding qualities as a leader. His name was Hernán Cortés (born in 1485).

After collecting his force of devoted followers—whose loyalty he won by such actions as cutting the gold buttons off his coat so that one of his officers might buy a horse—he sailed in February 1519 with his fleet of five ships, carrying a hundred sailors, five hundred volunteers, and eleven small cannon.

The Spaniards had to face their first decisive encounter against an enormous army of natives on landing at Tabasco. The chronicler Bernal Díaz, an eyewitness, described how the enemy's host covered the entire plain:

They dashed around like mad dogs, encircled us on every hand, and flung upon us so many arrows, spears, and stones that at the very first assault above seventy of us were wounded. Our cannoneers, musketeers, and archers strove hard. Mesa, our master-of-arms, slew many of them, who piled up in thick heaps before him. But in spite of all losses they let themselves not be driven off. The whole of this time we waited for Cortés and the cavalry, fearing by now lest some misfortune have befallen him. When we shot, the Indians cried aloud and whistled, throwing grass and dust in the air, that we might not assess their losses. Their drums and bugles noised incessantly and thereto they did roar "Ala Lala!" At length our horsemen appeared. The dense hordes of Indians, intent only on attacking us, heeded them not and were taken by them in the rear. And as the ground was level and our men were good horsemen, having among their mounts many tractable swift steeds, they cut the enemy down to heart's content and dealt with them so sorely that the Indians, hard pressed by us also, soon turned tail and sought safety in the neighboring woods—for they, who had never before seen horse, imagined steed and rider to be one Being. We buried our dead comrades, tended the wounds of man and horse with the fat of a slain Indian, and set up a watch. Then did we take our evening meal and lay down to rest.

Cortés made peace with the Mayas and then sailed farther along the coast, taking with him a concubine, who, being an Aztec woman of noble lineage, proved of great service to him. Doña Marina was a brave, intelligent woman who clung faithfully to her lord and eventually bore him a son.

On Good Friday, 1519, Cortés encamped at the harbor of San Juan de Ulúa, founded a settlement there, and within four months had taken under feudal control, without a fight, two large provinces. He contrived to have himself promoted from his burgomastership of Villa Rica de la Vera Cruz to governor and commander-in-chief of New Spain and so to cut himself free from his chief, Velásquez; he wanted to serve the Crown of Spain directly, without any intervention.

Montezuma, the ruler of the great Aztec Empire, kept himself fully informed from the first about every movement of the white man, and sent a mission to Vera Cruz bearing costly gifts, among them a slab of gold "great as a cartwheel and with many pictures thereon" representing the sun, and a still larger one of silver depicting the moon. At the same time, Montezuma begged earnestly

MAYAS BRINGING GIFTS TO CORTÉS; DOÑA MARINA STANDS NEXT TO CORTÉS'S HORSE. FROM A CONTEMPORARY INDIAN DRAWING

that the foreigners should stay away from Mexico; but his priceless gifts naturally excited in them the keenest desire to conquer the land that had produced these objects.

Montezuma had good reason to fear the presence of the strangers. In the religious beliefs of the Aztecs there was a protective deity, Quetzalcoatl, who had taught their forebears many useful arts and then sailed away in a magic ship, promising to return. This god was white-skinned and bearded—exactly like the strangers on the coast. To make matters worse, the priests had foretold that the time for the god's return was now at hand—very awkward notions for a king who was at the same time high priest. There are several possible explanations of how this mythology of the Aztecs came to exist, especially when it is taken into account that the Aztec religion had several similarities to the Christian. It embodied the stories of Eve and the serpent, the Flood, and the Tower of Babel; its ritual included baptism, confession, and communion in a slightly different form; its holy symbol was a cross, and there were other likenesses. So it seems likely that the prototype of this god was a Nordic visitor who had long ago put in here. This myth of course favored the progress of the Spaniards.

Another factor that furthered the conquest of the mighty Aztec

CORTÉS ON THE MARCH TO MEXICO.
FROM A DRAWING BY A SIXTEENTH-CENTURY INDIAN CHRONICLER

Empire by a handful of Spaniards was the tyrannical regime, which exacted heavy tribute from the neighboring tribes under its yoke and demanded of them youths and maidens as sacrifices to the Aztec gods; so the Spaniards found powerful assistance from them, as well as from the free race inhabiting Tlaxcala, who were offering a bitter resistance to the Aztecs.

When the Spanish force—fifteen horsemen, four hundred foot soldiers, two hundred Indians to haul the small cannon, and forty native nobles with their retinue—set out from Vera Cruz in mid-August 1519, it immediately had to face a hard march over narrow mountain passes to Mexico, two hundred miles distant. It took three months to reach the land of Tlaxcala, whose brave warriors put up a fierce resistance, but who served Cortés as terror-inspiring allies after their defeat.

Montezuma again sent presents and a message: "Do not come to Mexico!" Still Cortés marched on, reinforced by a body of Tlaxcalans thirsting for a fight. He had a friendly reception in Cholula, the first place on Aztec territory, but soon his mistress, Doña Marina, learned from one of the inhabitants that an attack was being treacherously planned. Cortés made short shrift of the Cholulans: his men fell upon them and slew three thousand in an hour.

Thence the way led over the mountains to Mexico. The cities near which the Spaniards passed sent presents—gold, cotton, feather coats, and women—and complained to Cortés of the Aztec oppression. His army had meanwhile been strengthened by another four thousand Indians, but was still far too small to risk, as it marched down into the Mexican plain, a pitched battle with Montezuma's hordes.

A nephew of Montezuma, borne in a marvelous litter by eight noblemen, greeted the invaders and accompanied them to the city of Ixtapalapa. Marching over a broad dam, the Spaniards could hardly believe their eyes and felt as if they had been transported into fairyland. Díaz records:

When we beheld so many cities built in the water and again so many on dry land and saw this dam which leads straight and continually through water to Mexico, we were astonished and oft-times said that it was like to the magic things which stand written in the book of Amadis, for these towers and temples and buildings were all of massive masonry. Some of our soldiers even asked if this which they beheld be not a mirage. I know not how to describe all these unheard-of, nay, undreamed-of sights. . . . And how marvelous were the palaces of Ixtapalapa, in which we were quartered; its gardens and its many kinds of trees, its paths full of roses and other flowers. . . .

All this glory was to last only a short time; the result of the Spanish invasion was that all these wonderful buildings were razed to the ground.

Cortés marched on to Tenochtitlán (Mexico) along a dam broad enough for eight riders abreast. This was the capital city of the Aztec Empire, surrounded entirely by water. The Spaniards noted with qualms that the dams had many gaps spanned by re-

Chalco.

CORTÉS CROSSING THE MOUNTAINS.
FROM A CONTEMPORARY DRAWING BY A TLAXCALAN

movable wooden bridges. They were marching straight into a trap.

Montezuma received them in a royal litter, accompanied by eleven hundred nobles. A huge crowd watched from the streets of the city, from roofs, and from boats as the Spaniards were guided to a princely abode close to the royal palace, where Montezuma dwelt in unimaginable splendor. There was no limit to the Spaniards' astonishment.

From their palace they looked out on the dams leading to solid land, the aqueduct bringing in fresh water, the countless canoes laden with goods, the marketplace thronged with people, and streets so clean that, as one Spaniard said, a man passing along them soiled his feet as little as his hands. In this city built on piles were a colossal temple pyramid, obelisks, hospitals, menageries, botanical gardens, barbers' shops, Turkish baths, fountains, carpets and paintings in lovely feather-mosaic, goldsmiths' ornaments, tortoise-shell ware, carved ceilings of sweet-scented woods, perfume sprays, hot-water systems, gorgeously colored cotton coats, marvelous leatherwork. There was a highly developed police force and civil service; the postal system delivered the latest news along cunningly built ways and flights of steps with uncanny speed. Meals consisted of the most *recherché* food and drink: game, fish, waffles, preserves, soups, spicy dishes, and such unusual items as the delicate turkey, *pulque*—an alcoholic beverage made from aloes—and a tasty cream confection called *chocolatl.*

Montezuma's state ceremonial was also fabulous. At every meal countless courses were served on hot copper dishes, but none of the plate was used twice. Dancers, acrobats, and clowns supplied diversion. Everything spoke of immeasurable wealth—his armories and enormous granaries, his aviary and his zoo full of wild animals, his gardens stocked with lovely flowers and sweet-smelling trees. But the Spaniards were, from the first, not granted a sight of his well-filled treasuries.

Another source of wonder was the honesty of the Aztecs: no citizen ever locked the door of his house; on leaving it, he laid a small cane rod in front of the doormat as a sign of his absence and never gave a thought to anything untoward. Yet in this highly civilized city the Spaniards were horrified when they were allowed to enter the holy place at the top of the great pyramid. For here human sacrifice was practiced. Five priests forced the victim down on a convex stone; a sixth slit his chest open with a knife of stone, tore out the heart, still beating, and burned it before the image of the god. The body was hurled down the steps to be devoured by caged beasts of prey. The Spaniards were used in their homeland to burnings of heretics and such horrors, accompanied by orgies of hate, while the grim Mexican ceremonies were part of a rigid religious ritual so well established that from time to time believers voluntarily submitted to it. Nevertheless, the Spaniards were revolted by these cruelties.

After a week of entertainment Cortés decided to take the friendly Montezuma prisoner in his own land. The Spaniards

MONTEZUMA PAYING TRIBUTE TO CORTÉS.
FROM A CONTEMPORARY INDIAN DRAWING

spent a whole night in prayer while preparing for this desperate coup. On the next day Cortés and six armed men of his entourage succeeded without much difficulty in surprising the King and constraining him to accompany them to the palace where they lodged. In tears, his nobles bore him away to captivity on their shoulders.

From now on, Cortés had the whip hand. The Aztec King accepted his fate and, when feeling well disposed, made his jailers presents of golden finery, costly raiment, and lovely women.

Meanwhile, the Spaniards were collecting unheard-of treasures in his kingdom. "It seems incredible," said Cortés, "that any worldly ruler should possess such riches." The King of the Aztecs studiously carried out the Spaniards' commands. He not only gave up his own treasure, but saw to it that gold was collected in all his provinces for the account of the Spanish Crown; moreover, the section of the Spanish force detailed to supervise the plundering of the gold mines was, at his instruction, left in peace. Nonetheless, the Spaniards soon succeeded in arousing ill-feeling among the population by their rapacity and excesses.

After five months Cortés was suddenly compelled to hurry back to the coast because his actual chief, Governor Velásquez, had sent an army to take charge of the country. Cortés managed to take the detachment by surprise and win them to his side. But in the meantime his chief lieutenant, Pedro de Alvarado, whom he had left in Mexico, perpetrated a great mischief; he had some Aztec nobles, who were celebrating a summer festival with his full permission, murdered during a ritual dance, and so touched off an uprising.

Cortés gathered thirteen hundred infantry, ninety-six cavalry, and four thousand Tlaxcalans and hastened by forced marches to the relief of the garrison besieged in Mexico. As soon as he got there, he was attacked from all sides. He sent Montezuma in full imperial array up onto the palace roof. For a moment the strife was stilled; but when Montezuma called for peace and asserted his friendship for the white men, this provoked obstinate murmurs of opposition, and then the full fury of the mob broke loose. The King was struck on the head by a flying stone and, refusing the attentions of all his doctors, died three days later. Guatemotzin, the leader of the attack against the Spaniards, who lost half of their men, was immediately elected king in his place.

The situation of the surrounded Spaniards grew more and more desperate; their casualties continued to increase, their supplies to shrink. In this dire crisis Cortés was forced into a decision to abandon everything and risk an attempt to break out. The main treasure hoard was left behind, but each man was allowed to take along what he wanted to. When darkness fell, the Spaniards attempted to force their way out and crossed the first breach in the broad dam on a portable bridge they had built. But when the head of their column reached the next gap, it proved impossible to move the bridge, which had stuck, weighted down by the load of the whole army's passage over it. Then began a ghastly night, long remembered by the Spaniards as *"Noche triste."*

While the column was in confusion, innumerable canoes suddenly swarmed to the attack across the darkness of the water. The Aztecs hurled lances at the horses and dragged every man they could lay hands on into the lagoon. Many of those who tried to swim to safety were pulled under by the weight of the gold they were lugging along. A third of the Spaniards, some thousands of the Tlaxcalans, the cannon, the powder, and most of the horses were lost.

The rest succeeded, by swimming or by using the bodies of horses and men as bridges, in fighting a continual rear-guard action until they reached the city of Tacuba and took shelter in a kind of fortified temple on high ground. From there the exhausted and continually shrinking force, constantly under harassing pursuit, marched on for six days more, till, near Otumba, they were attacked by an Aztec army.

This was the decisive battle for Mexico. The starving, stricken band of Spaniards saw themselves, deprived as they were of their superior weapons, exposed to the onslaught of an army so superior that it could crush them by sheer weight of numbers. But Cortés with only a few horsemen charged the attacking enemy at the very point where the commander-in-chief was in position, clad in golden armor. The standard-bearer was laid low with a lance thrust, and as their banner fell to the ground, the Aztecs lost their stomach for the fight. Suddenly glimpsing the hope of victory, the Spaniards butchered a fearsome number of the enemy, who were mostly wedged together in a helpless mass.

The victorious Spaniards had just about enough strength to drag themselves to friendly Tlaxcala, where at last they found food and rest.

Reinforcements had, in the meantime, reached Vera Cruz. The expeditions sent out to support the various governors went over to Cortés, for nothing else seemed so attractive as serving under the great conquistador. On December 26, 1520, just six months after the *"Noche triste,"* Cortés received a new army, with which he intended to reconquer Mexico: five hundred infantry, forty horsemen, eight cannon, and the supporting army of Tlaxcalans. A most determined enemy had entrenched himself in the city of Mexico itself. Cortés advanced very cautiously and spent three months in "mopping up" all enemies in the neighborhood. He had thirteen ships built so that he could attack from the lagoon. In May 1521, after cutting off the city's fresh-water supply, he invested Mexico; and so began one of the saddest chapters in the New World's story.

The Aztecs several times repulsed the Spaniards when they had almost broken through. Hideous forms of murder were used by both sides. While the men of Tlaxcala literally hewed their prisoners into small pieces, the Spaniards, when seventy of their comrades were taken prisoner, had on one occasion to watch from a distance for ten days while the Aztecs drove them up the steps of the great pyramid with blows, forced them to dance, and then did away with them on the sacrificial stone.

Finally Cortés decided to raze the city to the level of the ground. "I knew not," he wrote, "how we were to help ourselves without the destruction of this, the most beautiful city in the world, for they showed themselves as undaunted as ever. . . . So I formed the plan of tearing down each house in turn as we broke into the city and to go no step forward till all was laid waste." The daily battles, together with starvation and pestilence, cost the besieged a hundred thousand victims by the time the survivors, who had been living for weeks on roots and bark, capitulated three months later in the ruins. Cortés ordered the clearance of the debris, and a column of homeless refugees moved slowly past the Spanish victors for three days—"so thin, so filthy, so yellow and stinking, that it was pity to behold them."

Even so, the riches the Spaniards had hoped for did not fall into their hands. In spite of every torture imaginable, the last king of the Aztecs did not reveal the secret of where the great treasure lay hidden—perhaps on the slimy bed of the lagoon. Montezuma's gold remained hidden, the disease-ridden ruins of the city held nothing for the pillaging soldiery, and Cortés was forced to send his disappointed veterans out into the country.

The former Aztec Empire was explored and brought effortlessly under subjection in a number of campaigns. The bounds of the region over which Cortés held sway in October 1522, when the Crown accorded him official recognition as governor of New Spain, were still further extended by the successful campaigns of the impressive but touchy Alvarado, who in the course of two years brought Guatemala and northern Honduras under the yoke.

Meanwhile, Cortés devoted himself earnestly to the organization of his empire and the rebuilding of Mexico, a task during which countless Indians perished. He built a harbor, founded another city, Pánuco (now Tampico), laid in powder, bronze cannon, and ships, and thus laid a firm foundation for the Spanish overlordship, which was in the end to include a large slice of what is now the United States. Alexander von Humboldt later pointed out that Spanish was spoken in an area whose length equaled that of Africa.

In 1524 serious difficulties arose, quite different from those inherent in the discovery, exploration, and conquest of a continent; they sprang from the rapacity of the Spaniards themselves and were to result in some bloody decades throughout the newly discovered land. Cortés now learned that the unification of his remunerative territories in the south was encountering the opposition of plunder-hungry Spanish columns pressing forward from Panama through Costa Rica as far as Nicaragua, pocketing a large booty of gold and pearls on the way, and then proceeding to invade even Honduras. In order to restore order, and also because he was beguiled by the will-o'-the-wisp idea that in Nicaraguan waters he would find the long-sought passage from the Atlantic to the Pacific, Cortés undertook a conquistadorial march of five hundred miles through unexplored country where even today there is no railway line and only narrow mule tracks provide a difficult means of progress through tropical jungle and broad swamps, while steep mountains and deep rivers bar progress.

Cortés set out in true Montezuma style, with gold and silver plate, musicians, jugglers, and acrobats to provide distractions, and two native kings in his train, one of whom he did away with on a trumped-up pretext on the way. Hardship, starvation, and disease were not long absent, but, faced with the rigors of this jungle hell, the conqueror of Mexico recaptured all his old energy and skill in leadership and saved the expedition from disaster.

AN AZTEC PYRAMID TEMPLE

Seven months elapsed before Cortés, hollow-cheeked as a ghost, arrived in Honduras. Thanks to his great authority, he succeeded in occupying that land without internecine strife among the Spaniards.

It was high time for him to hurry back to Mexico, for rivalry and faction had broken out among his officials there. But the jealousies and feuds continued even after his return. So a few years later, in 1529, he sailed in high dudgeon for Spain to report at court.

He was received with acclamation and loaded with honors. But in spite of the titles, liens, and rights showered upon him, he had to admit on his return to the New World that the rule over New Spain was no longer conducted by him, but by a council of officials. He sent out four more exploratory expeditions during the following years, to sail along the coasts in the ships built at his shipyard in Zacatula. These sought in vain for the passage to the Pacific, but they did carry Cortés to California before anyone else had seen it—though he was unable to establish definitely whether it was mainland or an island. Above all, they piled up enormous costs.

The continual bickering about his rights upset Cortés so much that in 1539 he again set sail for Spain. This time his reception was very cool. He was accorded no place of political significance in either the New World or the Old. He had done his duty, and though Spain filled its coffers out of his conquests and enjoyed the fruits of his labors, he had henceforth to live the life of an unimportant private citizen till he died at his home in 1547.

But at the time of his first enthusiastic reception at the Spanish court there appeared on the scene a poor colleague of his who had somehow scraped together the money for a passage from Panama to Spain. He had plans for the conquest of an empire similar to that of the Aztecs. It was Pizarro, and the fabulous land of gold he promised to discover was called Peru.

The moment was favorable. Cortés's support may have been of some assistance. Pizarro won his first decisive round. Charles was about to be crowned Emperor of Germany; his greatest enemy, Francis I of France, had been captured with the aid of German mercenaries at the Battle of Pavia; Cortés's reports and gifts gave a most favorable impression of the rich, newly won land of New Spain. So the King generously endowed Pizarro with the rank of governor, admiral, and chief justice of all the lands he might conquer.

Cortés was thirty-five when he conquered Mexico; Pizarro (born in 1475), who had once been a swineherd and who never in his life learned to write his name, had to wait till he was over fifty (an age that in those days wrote a man off as scrap) before he got the great chance that completely altered his life. His past was a story of fruitless endeavors carried out with obstinate toughness.

After marching with Ojeda, accompanying Balboa's push to the Pacific coast, and witnessing the imprisonment of his former commander, Pizarro had settled in Panama as a cattle-breeder. His business associate was Diego de Almagro, a wandering adventurer who had also shouldered the burden of five decades; he was a cheerful, sociable character, but he had just murdered someone in a brawl and fled to Darien in consequence. These two joined forces with a priest, Hernando de Luque, who had two splendid recom-

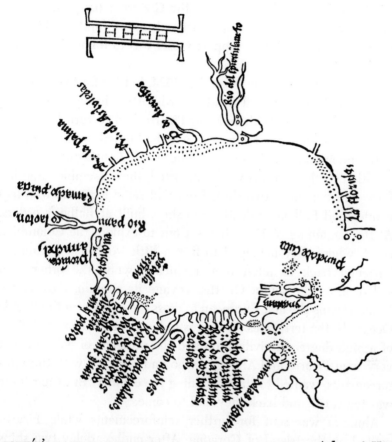

CORTÉS'S MAP OF THE GULF OF MEXICO, 1520. FROM *Atlas of Historical Geography*, CARNEGIE INSTITUTE OF WASHINGTON

mendations: money and good relations with Governor Pedrarias. This trio brought a rather considerable business into being, which embraced mining, agriculture, and also a slave trade in both Indians and Negroes (the destruction of the natives was soon counterbalanced by the import of slaves from Africa). But now they began a project on a very different scale.

Ever since Balboa's discovery of the "Southern Sea" there had been rumors of the powerful empire of the Incas, which the natives called "Biru." In 1522 Captain Pascual de Andagoya undertook a voyage to the Peruvian coast and there learned a few things about the land and its treasures. This was the incentive for the three business friends to ask the Governor for permission to embark on an expedition and to use Luque's funds to fit out a ship for Pizarro, while a support vessel was to follow later under Almagro.

The venture began in December 1524, but for four years it was to reap only failure and deadly perils. After heavy losses from hunger and battles with Indians, Pizarro had to turn back from his first venture. So did Almagro, who had failed to make contact with him and had had an eye shot out while fighting on land.

Although their means were exhausted, they assembled another force and borrowed two ships from that same Espinosa who had condemned Balboa to death—two ships built at Balboa's orders. At the beginning of 1528 they set out to explore the Colombian coast, where they managed to find a little gold. Then Almagro hastened back to fetch reinforcements, while the other ship sailed on to the south. On this voyage its captain, Bartolomeo Ruiz, became the first European to cross the equator in the Pacific Ocean. In the territories of what is today Ecuador he found signs of a high degree of civilization and the presence of gold, so that very soon Pizarro and Almagro, who had returned with the reinforcements, wanted to start subduing the country. But their force was too small, and back they had to come.

Almagro was sent for further reinforcements while Pizarro waited on the Island of Gorgona. After endless delay two ships did arrive, but only to fetch him away. A new governor in Darien wanted to put an end to this useless venture that had already cost so many lives. But the ships also brought a secret message from Almagro and Luque, counseling Pizarro to see it through.

In a very few minutes a handful of greedy clods came to a decision affecting the fate of a vast empire. Pizarro drew a line in the sand with his sword, pointed to the south, and shouted: "Shipmates and friends! There lies the hard way, leading to Peru and wealth." Then, pointing north: "That way lies Panama and peace and rest, but also poverty. Take your choice!"

Then he crossed the line. Thirteen men, whose names are known, followed him.

These fourteen resolute men had to wait seven miserable months before Almagro arrived with a ship, bringing provisions and ammunition but not a single volunteer over and above the crew.

With this dozen or so adventurers the trustworthy pilot Ruiz sailed to the Gulf of Guayaquil and then down to 9° south, whence they returned to Panama. During this voyage Pizarro collected valuable information about the Inca Empire, and when he returned to the royal court in Spain he was able to give all sorts of exciting reports and show proofs of them: one or two llamas, the "sheep-camel," which had never before been seen; fine vicuña wool fabrics; vessels and trinkets of gold and silver. Undoubtedly these objects contributed to the success of his visit and to a display of his authority.

The empire that Pizarro wanted to conquer ranged from north to south for more than two thousand miles and embraced today's republics of Ecuador, Bolivia, Peru, and northern Chile (except the tropical forests east of the Andes). The inhabitants had reached standards of civilization higher, if possible, than those of the Aztecs. The land was full of engineering marvels, with countless canals, aqueducts, irrigation terraces and marvelously constructed roads that crossed difficult terrain by scientifically constructed suspension bridges, on long staircases hewn in the living rock, or through lengthy tunnels. In agriculture the Incas used guano fertilization, a method unknown in Europe and adopted there only much later. The art of weaving had reached a high level of development, and the style of this civilization was exemplified by its huge buildings, especially the Sun Temple in Cuzco, whose massive blocks of stone were covered by golden slabs encrusted with jewels and whose dome was a huge sheet of gold representing the sun.

The land was ruled by an aristocratic order at whose head stood a monarch, to whom were accorded godlike honors. The conduct of his court was unimaginably splendid: everything in use was artistically wrought in gold or silver, and in the lovely gardens surrounding the palace you could even see all sorts of flowers imitated in precious metals.

The conquest of this domain was rendered all the more difficult by nature's obstacles, for the home of the Incas lay on the far side of the Andean plateau, flanked on either side by the gigantic walls of the eastern and western Cordilleras. To reach it from the Pacific the invaders had to make their way over huge mountains; in this they were at least aided by the good roads and ample stores of food provided by the Incas themselves. Another development favorable to Pizarro's invasion was that disputes about the succession to the throne, though settled by Atahualpa's victory, brought about a critical weakening of the internal structure just at the moment of the Spanish attack.

On his return from Spain, Pizarro had at first to combat the anger of his partner Almagro, who rightly complained that Pizarro had cashed in on the lion's share of the royal concessions, leaving him only a very secondary position. He had also to counter the reluctance of the colonists; the long casualty lists of the first voyages to Peru had damped their ardor, and the first volunteers for the new venture came forward halfheartedly. Not till 1530 was Pizarro in a position to set out with 180 men and 27 horses, while Almagro once again was searching for new sources from which to keep them supplied.

For two years Pizarro organized the necessary support points along the coast. His men had to march and fight under the scorching sun in coats of mail and padded doublets. Epidemics and casualties thinned their ranks, but pillage and golden booty kept their interest in the venture alive and even attracted new adherents. An exceptionally valuable addition to Pizarro's strength was the arrival from Nicaragua of two ships under the brave cavalier Hernando de Soto.

At last Pizarro felt strong enough to march with a tiny army of 106 infantry, including twenty bowmen and three musketeers, 62 horsemen, and a few small cannon into the high Andes, over icy heights and through narrow gorges where the Incas could have disposed of the strangers at one blow. Instead, Atahualpa sent messengers bearing gifts to meet them, having no idea of the kind of brood which wished to make its nest in his kingdom. When the Spaniards, at the end of an exhausting series of marches, descended into the valley of Cajamarca they found themselves confronted by the camp of an army thirty thousand strong; but there was no sign on its part of any hostile intent.

On November 15, 1532, Pizarro led his band into the town of Cajamarca, which was apparently deserted, took up his quarters there, and sent his brother Hernando and Captain de Soto with a few horsemen into Atahualpa's camp. Hernando carried an invitation to the Inca to come and visit Pizarro. De Soto rode right up to the Inca as he sat in state and reined in so late that his horse's head was right above Atahualpa's; but, in spite of his never having seen a horse, the Inca did not move. He had some of his dignitaries beheaded for showing too plainly their terror of the unfamiliar snorting beast. Atahualpa's stoical immobility recalls the ancient Roman general who remained perfectly calm when at a conference his adversary tried to scare him with the sudden appearance of an elephant.

Next day the Inca sent Pizarro a message that he would come and his men would be armed, since Pizarro had sent armed warriors to him. The Spaniards, resorting to methods that would shame many a bandit, answered the herald: "Tell thy master that he may come when and how he wills, but that in whatever state he may come, I shall receive him as a friend and a brother." Thereupon the unsuspecting Inca answered that he and his men would come unarmed.

Pizarro now prepared a reception such as has—happily—not often been seen in the world's history. He concealed his armed detachments in various places, had the cannon loaded and laid, and gave strict orders to the twenty men whom he picked to overpower the Inca that he must be captured alive. As the signal for this treacherous capture of a true king by a real swineherd, he chose the holy war cry "Santiago!"

Atahualpa drew near with pomp and heraldry. He was borne in a litter "like to a golden castle": a host of servants swept the way before him, cleansing it of every speck of dirt; behind them came a troop of singers and dancers, followed by the main retinue of nobles with crowns of gold and silver, who took turns to bear the royal litter. In addition there was a long train of dignitaries in litters, with a host of retainers.

Pizarro sent the Dominican friar Vicente de Valverde with an interpreter to meet Atahualpa. The monk spoke a short address and handed the Inca a Bible, which he tried to open, though he had of course never seen a book before. Valverde stretched out his arm to help him, but the Inca, unaccustomed to being so closely approached, struck his arm away, opened the book unaided, looked at it—unlike the other natives—without a sign of astonishment, then threw it away. Then he said: "I know full well how ye Christians have comported yourselves on the way here, how ye have misused my princelings and stolen raiment from my storehouses. I will not quit this place till all is restored."

Valverde then returned to Pizarro. What happened next is described by an eyewitness, Don Alonso Henriquez, a lieutenant: "The rascally friar, who was certainly the one responsible for breaking the peace, forthwith spoke in a loud voice: 'I call upon ye, my brethren in Christ, to avenge the slight here done to our holy creed!' "

Thereupon Pizarro fell upon Atahualpa with four other Spaniards, seized him by the arm, and cried "Santiago!"

Immediately all hell broke loose. Trumpet signals blared, cannon boomed, mounted men dashed forth from their hiding-places, foot soldiers swarmed to the attack. Panic flared up among the Indians; none of them defended themselves, while all their leaders were being banded close about the Inca and cut down piecemeal. Within half an hour some thousands of the natives lay dead, the rest had fled, Atahualpa was a prisoner—and Pizarro was master of the Inca Empire.

He treated his captive well. The prisoner learned to understand the mentality of his captors so accurately that he made them a proposal that would probably have saved him, had they been ordinary robbers. He offered to fill the room in which he stood—sixteen feet by ten—with gold up to the level of his outstretched arms, in exchange for his freedom.

This deal suited the Spaniards perfectly. In spite of the huge booty they had already taken, their eyes filled with tears as they watched the room being filled. Next, they did not know how to divide among themselves all the beautifully wrought plates, dishes, pots, pieces of jewelry, and art treasures. So for five weeks Indian goldsmiths had to labor at melting down these proofs of their artistic talent into exactly similar bars of even weight!

Atahualpa had fulfilled his side of the bargain; now it was Pizarro's turn. He acted in full accordance with his villainous nature. Instead of releasing the Inca, he trumped up a charge against him and had him condemned to death. Then he sent de Soto, who had rebelled against such a travesty of justice, out on a reconnaissance and, while he was away, had Atahualpa—who suffered his fate with great dignity—publicly strangled in the marketplace.

The next town to suffer at the Spaniards' hands was Cuzco. The inhabitants resisted de Soto's advance guard, so Pizarro had Atahualpa's former commander-in-chief arrested and, in spite of all his protestations of innocence, burned alive. It was proposed that the victim should first allow himself to be baptized, but he rejected the offer with the words: "I do not understand the white men's religion."

In Cuzco, the capital of the Inca Empire, the Spaniards were able to wallow in plunder, pillaging the natives right and left and enriching themselves even further, though each soldier was already possessed of a considerable fortune. And still they were not satisfied.

While Almagro and his active captain, Belalcázar, marched into the kingdom of Quito and subdued it, Pizarro set to work organizing the administration of the Inca Empire. As its new capital, he founded close to the spacious harbor of Callao the city of Lima, to remain the chief city of an enormous empire under Spanish administration for two hundred years. But unfortunately the overthrow of the Inca Empire was not the end of the bloody story

of South America's early history. The conquerors oppressed their
new subjects till they rebelled and became embroiled with one
another, so that many bloody decades ensued, during which the
conquistadors made off with each other's booty, continually penetrated and subdued new regions, and almost all paid for their in-
sensate gold lust with their lives. In this inferno of unbridled
greed it was the inhabitants who had to pay the heaviest price.
Their crops were destroyed, their women violated, their villages
laid waste, and they themselves brutally forced into either war
service or slavery.

The bloody discord in the ranks of the conquistadors began
when Almagro found out that Chile, which he had taken two
painful years to subdue, held no hidden treasures. During a march
across the icy heights of the barren province of Las Charcas he
had failed to notice the silver deposits that were soon to become
world-famous for their richness. Almagro, feeling himself neglected in the division of posts and lands, wanted at least to get
hold of Cuzco; the loose manner in which Pizarro's realm and his
own had been outlined left it debatable to whom the city belonged. After a long march through a waterless district—the desert
of Atacama alone is a hundred miles long—he arrived just in time
to rescue the city from rebel Indians, who had been besieging it
for a long time. At the same time he captured Francisco Pizarro's
brothers, Hernando and Gonzalo, but released them on Francisco's definite promise that the city should be his. But open war
soon broke out between the two former partners, and Almagro
was defeated, captured, and sentenced to death. His son Diego
later avenged his father by having Francisco Pizarro murdered,
which was the signal for the outbreak of another civil war of terrifying savagery during which Diego suffered defeat and subse-
quent decapitation. Of Pizarro's brothers, Hernando, who had
reached Spain with an enormous treasure, spent twenty-two years
in prison for Almagro's death, while Gonzalo instigated a revolt
against the new viceroy sent out from home, made himself king,
and obtained a height of power not seen again in South America
till the days of Simón Bolívar.

But Gonzalo's dictatorship was based on feet of clay. The Spanish Crown sent the priest Pedro de la Gasca to America. He arrived with only his cassock and breviary, but with incredible skill brought about the disaffection of Pizarro's officers and soldiery till with a mounting army at his disposal he was able to march into Cuzco unopposed and have Gonzalo beheaded.

The hair-raising history of the endless conquistadorial wars is a long romance of banditry in which countless figures appear, marching through jungles, swamps, and mountain ranges and so achieving their exploration and discovery. Cortés's commander Pedro de Alvarado, who first marched through Guatemala; his successor, Belalcázar; Pedro de Candia, the first to venture through the rain-sodden primeval forests to the eastern fringe of the Peruvian Andes; Pizarro's captain Alonso de Alvarado, who reached the River Huallaga; Pedro de Valdivia, whose exertions over a period of fourteen years resulted in the reduction and colonization of Chile, which Almagro had both misprised and despised, till he himself fell in a fight against rebel Indians; Diego de Ordaz and Alonso de Herrera, who navigated the Orinoco. For the mighty streams of South America were sailed upon two hundred years before the comparable rivers of Africa, though these lay so much nearer at hand.

In 1541 Gonzalo Pizarro, at his brother's orders, undertook an expedition to discover the country where the cinnamon trees grow and the golden land of El Dorado (the object of almost every voyage of exploration). Gonzalo took with him 200 Spaniards, 4,000 Indians, 5,000 pigs, more than 1,000 hounds, and a herd of llamas; with them he marched right through the Andes from Quito to their extreme eastern foot. He found neither of his objectives. When after eighteen months of almost unimaginable hardship he returned to Quito, barely half of his white following had survived. They brought back nothing but their swords. A vast number of the Indians had succumbed to their sufferings.

In the depths of the unhealthy tropical forest, on the banks of the River Coca, where they had nothing left to live on but "grass, nuts, and poisonous worms," Pizarro ordered his lieutenant, Francisco de Orellana, to build a boat. Shortly after Christmas 1541

Orellana with seventy men embarked on a voyage downstream to look for food. The Coca flowed into the Napo, and that river into the Amazon. After eight days of navigating the rapids of the turbulent stream they came upon an Indian village and actually obtained provisions, but they decided it was impossible to paddle upstream against such currents and so get back to Gonzalo Pizarro.

Thus began one of the most fantastic voyages of the whole history of discovery, which took them right across the immense continent, downstream and ever downstream, for three thousand miles of the unknown, perilous waters of the world's mightiest river, hedged in on either bank by impenetrable forests.[1]

Orellana was so impressed by the many wonders he was the first to see and the adventures he lived through during his seven-month voyage that he gave the river his own name. During a fight with the natives, the white men noticed that their opponents were led and urged forward by women, who distinguished themselves by their unusual courage. Scientific research later confirmed that the Spaniards were not victims of their overheated imaginations or of the effects of some tropical fever, but that a warlike tribe consisting only of women really existed somewhere here in the green wilderness. Nobody knew where the village of these creatures, so strangely similar to the Amazons of Greek mythology, was situated. Many Indians who found their way to it remained absent a year or two from their tribe; they were treated extremely well by the Amazons and led a life as pleasant as it was exhausting. The Amazons kept only their girl children, the boys being given away after a year to their progenitors. The men, who were very reticent about their experiences on returning to their tribes, wore as a decoration a rare green stone presented by their hostesses in recognition of their services.

Oddly enough, when he returned to Spain his contemporaries gave no credit to this story of Orellana's, as if they did not regularly accept plenty of other cock-and-bull stories altogether too

---

[1] To give some idea of the Amazon's size: its length is 3,500 miles (the third-longest river in the world); its basin covers 2,722,000 square miles (the second-largest is the Congo with 1,428,600). Its mean flow is 157,000 cubic yards per second (the next-greatest is the Congo with 39,500; that of the Elbe is 930).

fabulous to be believed—which really applies as much today as it did then! At all events, Orellana was held to be nothing but a braggart till later explorers like La Condamine and Humboldt justified him. He lost his life while trying to make his way upstream against the Amazon's mighty current in 1546 when he returned to South America in search of the legendary El Dorado.

The huge Río de la Plata, too, South America's second-greatest river, the natural gateway to the richest, most fertile, and healthiest regions of the continent, came to be known quite early. Ten years passed after Juan Diaz de Solís perished there so tragically: then a Spanish fleet sailed up the Río de la Plata. It was under Sebastian Cabot's command. He was at that time Chief Pilot of Spain, and his brief was to sail with four ships along Magellan's newly discovered route to the Moluccas and look for the fabulous lands of Tarsis and Ophir, but in any case to trade gold, silver, jewels, medicaments, spices, brocades, and other valuables.

Apparently this program was too comprehensive for Cabot: the state of his ships, too, may have seemed too doubtful for a crossing of the Pacific. Whatever the reason, he rejected the voyage through Magellan's Strait and chose to enter the Río de la Plata, sailing up it and undertaking a difficult voyage along one arm of the Paraná delta. He believed he would make important discoveries in the heart of the continent and was encouraged in his mistake by the silver objects offered him along the riverbanks by the Indians; these he carried back in triumph to Spain and named the river the "Silver River" (Río de la Plata) after them. Unfortunately, however, the silver came from very far away—in fact, from Atahualpa's treasure house. It was by this roundabout route that the first articles of Pizarro's booty reached Spain and created an unfounded fame for the area of the Plata.

Cabot, whose crews had shrunk to half their original numbers, frittered away four years before he next returned to Spain with such optimistic reports that—a true sign of the rage for discovery— the largest expedition yet to leave a Spanish harbor was sent out under Pedro Mendoza. A hundred German subjects of the Emperor Charles V took part in it. One of them, the mercenary Schmiedel, later wrote an outstanding report of its experiences.

Mendoza's expedition by no means lived up to the high hopes placed upon it. He reached the mouth of the Plata at the end of 1535 and founded a town where Buenos Aires now stands. But everything went wrong—wars with the Indians, starvation and pestilence eventually forcing him to abandon the town, and Mendoza himself dying aboard his ship from the universal cavalier-sickness of the conquistadors.

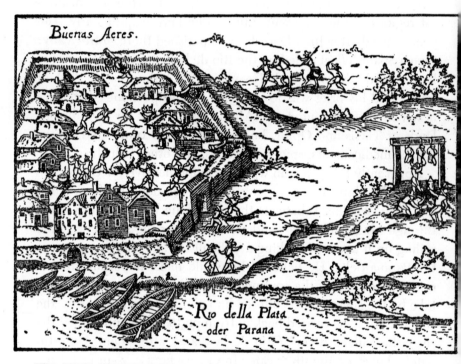

THE FIRST SETTLEMENT OF BUENOS AIRES. FROM A DRAWING BY A GERMAN MERCENARY ON MENDOZA'S EXPEDITIONS

His successor, Juan de Ayolas, who founded the settlement of Santa María de Asunción farther to the north, was rather more successful. The town remained the most important Spanish post in the area for eighty years. From it were dispatched later expeditions that made contact with the Spaniards coming across from Peru. Strangely enough, however, the opening up of the great tract of the Pampas was achieved not from the Atlantic but from the Pacific side. The strong impetus of the conquistadors Pizarro and Almagro drove their tireless successors on to reach even these districts. The decisive protection and extension of the area of Spanish suzerainty from the mouth of the river was not achieved until in 1580 Juan de Garay sailed south from Asunción and founded a second Buenos Aires.

In the Spanish-occupied area there was, besides the Aztec and Inca civilizations, a third culture, that of the Chibchas, whose highly developed skill in goldcraft had given rise to the El Dorado legend; but they lived in such isolation—huge mountain walls and boundless plains, on which lived poor and primitive tribes, some of them still cannibalistic, cut them off from the world outside— that the Spaniards had no knowledge of this rich country and its inhabitants, skilled as they were in agriculture, pottery, and weaving. And so "New Granada," today the Colombian Republic, was the last part of South America to be discovered and explored. Besides finding the gold and precious stones, the Spaniards made a find there which was to prove more valuable to the common folk of Europe than any dream treasure house of riches, a find that was to put an end to the ever present danger of famine continually menacing hundreds of thousands of lives. This was a strange plant with "scattered dull-purple flowers and mealy roots of a pleasant savor," a choice delicacy for Indians and Spaniards alike: in short, the potato. Yet it was not this vegetable but gold that lured the foreign invader on into this land, which proved so peace-loving that its conquerors did not incur a single casualty. All the same, the occupation of the Chibcha Empire was an achievement of great difficulty, for the way to it had first to be found. And the first people to be anywhere near it, the Germans, failed to find it.

Charles, the Habsburg King of Spain, and Francis, the Chevalier King of France, were at a daggers-drawn rivalry with each other; so gripping was this enmity in all its hypotheses and forms of expression that world history might almost seem to have created these two figures intentionally, at the outset of the new era, in order to stage a dramatic melodrama. The first open clash between these two mighty opponents was over the Imperial Crown of the Holy Roman Empire of the German Realm.

Maximilian, its ruler, had founded a new royal power by uniting the thrones of Germany, Burgundy, Spain, Bohemia, and Hungary in his own family by a skillful policy of intermarriage. The choice of his cousin, Charles of Spain, as second German emperor would have created the mighty empire of his dreams, but, in spite of every effort of the Reichstag of 1518, Maximilian found it impossible to achieve his aim. He died, the German throne fell vacant, and three claimants appeared: Henry VIII of England; Francis I of France, who reigned over the most flourishing country in Christendom, where he was heralded as a young Cæsar and had already been asked in 1517 by German envoys if he would accept the crown of Germany; and finally Charles of Spain, aged only nineteen.

The last-named pair entered upon a fiery private battle for influence among the seven princely electors who had to choose the emperor. It was a decisive moment in the fate of Europe. How the hotly contested issue resolved itself in Charles's favor is now history. The results that might have followed had Francis won the vote—a choice that might perhaps have united Europe—will ever remain conjecture.

The decision lay in the hands of the seven electors. They (with the exception of the one honest man among them, Frederick the Wise of Saxony) chose, in a mood of cold calculation, the candidate who offered them most. Francis emptied his coffers and mortgaged great slices of his royal estate, but his poor hundred thousand livres could not match Charles, who promptly obtained a loan of 143,333 gulden from the banking-house of Welser.[2] Even that was not nearly enough for the demands of these businesslike princes, especially for him of Brandenburg; but when the house of Fugger, closely related (as creditors) to the Habsburgs, came to the rescue with 543,580 gulden and an Italian bank added another 65,000, Charles's election was assured.

Of course Charles could never repay these vast debts in capital, so in the end he mortgaged to the Fuggers income drawn from the Tirol and Spain, whence the knightly orders of Santiago, Alcantara, and Calatrava furnished dues. The Welsers had to con-

---

[2] In interpreting this, one must not belittle it, for gold had a very different value at the time. A gulden could then buy four to five bushels of wheat.

tent themselves with more dubious security: Charles allotted to them a region in the New World—Venezuela—giving them the right in perpetuity to appoint governors there.

The banking-house energetically undertook the expensive business of prospecting for unknown treasure in an unknown land. In 1528 they sent three hundred men to America to found two towns and three fortresses, to start mining-operations, and to look for El Dorado. The expedition was placed under the Welsers' agent in Santo Domingo, Ambrosius Ehinger (born in 1500), whom the Spaniards called Ambrosio Alfinger. Leaving his merchant's desk, he went out as governor and military commander into the wildernesses of the New World.

This, of course, could not produce results, in spite of all expectations of success. Thousands of Indians were herded together to provide transport, gold-washers and miners from Joachimstal came along from Europe to send back the masses of gold without delay; but nothing whatever materialized. From Coro, Alfinger made the first German conquistadorial march to Lake Maracaibo, founded a settlement there, and after a year's absence returned to Coro to collect supplies. Amassing the necessary funds by slave-trading, he started out on his second march into the valley of the Magdalena in 1531.

The inevitable hardships soon began to take toll of this expedition, too. Slaves who fell by the wayside were ruthlessly beheaded by the Spaniards, for to release one of them it would otherwise be necessary to undo the chains of all those in front and behind. In the end, Alfinger sent back to Coro a party with six hundred pounds of gold (which he had got by barter and pocketed) to fetch further provisions: but this detachment came to grief on the way, and the main body's distress grew even greater.

Alfinger attempted to save the situation by pressing farther ahead. Scouts reported that beyond the Cordilleras to the east lay fertile, healthy valleys. Many Spaniards and Indians died on the icy passes they had to cross. Alfinger pressed on as far as he could, but at last, only ten miles from his objective, he turned back. On the return march he was killed in a fight with natives. The pitiful remnants of his expedition struggled back to the place they had started from, reaching Coro two years and two months after leaving it.

His successor, George Hohermut, whom the Spaniards called Jorge Espira (Georg von Speyer), pushed forward in a three-year march toward the rich land that was supposed to lie near the sources of the Meta, beyond the hills. He reached the river, but his scouts reported that the mountains were impassable, so, like his predecessor, he turned aside and changed direction only a little way short of his objective. It is possible that on these marches Hohermut actually penetrated the Amazon basin before Orellana. He covered more than two thousand miles through the tropical forests of the Orinoco, and if he had not been slightly lacking in common sense, in energy, or in luck, which prevented his reaching the plateau of Bogotá, he might well have become one of the greatest figures in German history.

Among his companions was Philipp von Hutten (born about 1510), the brother of the famous knight Ulrich von Hutten. Philipp, who described his experiences in the New World most graphically (his letters were published in 1880 in the annual report of the Munich Geographical Society), became Hohermut's successor when the latter died during preparations for another expedition. In 1541 began another march during which Philipp pushed farther south than his predecessor, thence to the eastern plains in the region between the rivers Inírida and Guaviare, where he found a fairly advanced culture among the inhabitants of the land of the Omegans. The emaciated Germans managed somehow to withstand the attack of fifteen thousand Indians, but a further advance was unthinkable. Philipp von Hutten returned to Venezuela, having traversed in five years more of the interior of Venezuela and Colombia than any man before him: nor were the districts explored by him revisited for another three hundred years.

Hutten never got back to Coro—he met a typically conquistadorial end on the way. During his long absence the Spaniards in Venezuela had, contrary to the agreement with the Welsers, appointed a Spanish governor. Hutten was not equal to his guile. When in Easter week of 1546 he unsuspectingly accepted an invitation at El Tocuyo, he and his companion, Bartholomäus Welser, the son of the great banking house, were attacked while asleep, taken prisoner, and murdered. This set the limit to the German colonial attempt in Venezuela, which was finally abandoned in 1555.

But even before Hutten's great march, fate had played the house of Welser a particularly sorry trick. Among the German conquistadors there was one, Nikolaus Federmann (born *c.* 1500), who in his gift for leadership and ambition closely resembled the Spanish conquerors. In 1550 he had already come to Venezuela in the service of the Welsers, and in that year he made his first march, which took him to the Río Cojede and into the Llanos near the Río Portuguesa. In 1532 he returned to Europe and then went back to Coro in 1535, serving there under Hohermut, though he would have preferred to be in command himself. Hohermut began his march of discovery in the same year, while Federmann set out in February 1536 to look for El Dorado—some say on his own initiative, others at Hohermut's behest—after wasting much valuable time in preparation. In the upshot he marched through the same plains as Hohermut at the same time, apparently avoiding all contact with him. Federmann crossed the Arauca and the Río Meta; he was not daunted by the mountain walls, but scaled them by breakneck tracks. After three dreadful years and with only a third of his original force, he reached the plateau of Bogotá from the southeast. He succeeded in doing what every other German had failed to do: he stood at the heart of the Chibcha Empire, that land so rich in gold. But he was too late.

The discovery of this unapproachable country, whose conquest was finally achieved with 160 men whose firearms were useless because their powder had been spoiled, was the reward of a long, patient fight against every possible hardship a tropical wilderness could inflict. The man who had already achieved it before Federmann got there was originally by profession a lawyer, by name Gonzalo Jiménez de Quesada (born *c.* 1500).

In April 1536—two months after Federmann's departure—a force of nine hundred men set out under his command on the long march to conquer the legendary land of gold about which one had heard only the vaguest rumors. Marching across arid wastes, through forests and swamps, they reached the River Magdalena, whose course they then followed. The column fought its way forward along the flooded shore in the rainy season. A chronicler writing a hundred years later wrote: "God preserve me if I can grasp how men of flesh and blood could break a way with their hands through 200 miles of impenetrable forest, a jungle so dense that in spite of the uttermost exertion it was possible to go forward at the most a mile or two a day! How many there were that perished of feverish diseases while still their hands worked to the very last . . . how many devoured by wild beasts and crocodiles, how many laid low by hunger and thirst, how many accounted for by the poisoned arrows of the natives!"

Jiménez, whose force was ever shrinking before his eyes, left the Magdalena and followed the Opon upstream, farther and farther into the dense forest, till, about eleven months from the outset, he reached the plateau where dwelt the Chibchas. Of his force of 900, he mustered only 166. Thanks to extraordinary pains, he still had sixty-two horses at his disposal. Now they began life anew; the starved scarecrows of Spaniards soon filled out on a good diet, and then they set out to occupy the country. In so doing, they met with all sorts of strange experiences: Sucklings were offered to them as sustenance because they were taken for cannibals. At the doors of the houses hung narrow rows of gold plates, whose tinkling announced the country's great wealth. The Spaniards received presents of golden hearts, weighing two pounds each, and saw with astonished eyes how the inhabitants prospected for emeralds. In the palace of one princeling they took so much booty that the pile of gold and jewels was tall as a man.

In this pleasant land there was not a single fight with the peaceable inhabitants, who were in many places so fearful that they threw themselves flat on the floor to avoid the sight of the horses. Jiménez had no difficulty in founding the city of Bogotá, which became in the course of time the capital of a well-organized province.

In February 1539 Jiménez experienced a most unexpected

double surprise. First there descended upon him from the hills to the east a rabble of exhausted, half-naked, fur-clad white men: Federmann and his troupe. Then, soon afterward, there appeared a second army, this one well equipped and well provided with three hundred sows in farrow. This was a Spanish expedition under Pizarro's onetime captain, Belalcázar, who came by way of Popayán and Cali. So it came about that three armies of conquistadors suddenly encamped at one and the same time on the savannas of Bogotá. The avoidance of a battle with the two explorers who had arrived too late was due not to a miracle but to Jiménez's skillful diplomacy in feeding Federmann's soldiers and presenting him with forty pounds of gold.

After pillaging the realm of the Chibchas from end to end, the three leaders followed the Magdalena back to the coast in company and then journeyed together to the royal court in Spain. In spite of active lobbying, Federmann got nothing. Indeed, the Welsers instituted a tedious suit against him, but it came to nothing with his early death in 1542. It is interesting to note that the German conquistadors, unlike the Spaniards (particularly the illiterate Pizarro), had literary tendencies, and Federmann has described his journeys of discovery in a book entitled *Indianische Historia*.

Belalcázar pursued his services and claims so pressingly before Charles V that he obtained the mayoralty of Popayán, but Jiménez did not know how to gain influence and was passed over. A ne'er-do-well, who had soon to be relieved, was appointed governor of "New Granada," the region known today as Colombia, which Jiménez had discovered. But Jiménez received only a lifelong post as councilor in Bogotá, to which place he soon returned. There he lived as a valued and honored citizen till he died at the age of eighty—a man of parts to whom neither his own time nor posterity accorded his rightful due.

The wealth of South America continued to attract new ventures, but after the conquest of Mexico the progress of the explorers in the North American continent faltered. Failure followed failure. Juan Ponce de León (born *c.* 1460) had conquered the island of Puerto Rico and set out in search of a land that the

Indians told him was called Bimini and that harbored a Fountain of Youth. The elderly conquistador found, instead, the Bahama Islands and Florida, where he tried to found a settlement; but he was wounded in a fight with the Indians and died in 1521 on his return to Cuba. Another attempt, by Vásquez de Ayllón, to found various colonies in North Carolina between 1520 and 1526 also came to grief.

Especially bad luck came to Pánfilo de Narváez (born *c.* 1470), who had taken part in the conquest of Cuba under Diego Velásquez and had been sent out by him in 1520 to bring Cortés to reason after he had declared his independence. But Cortés had won Narváez's soldiers over and for a time even imprisoned their leader. Velásquez, the only one of Columbus's companions who still counted in the New World, would gladly have discovered a land flowing with gold, and he sent Narváez out again in 1528 to follow in Ponce de León's footsteps and land in Florida with four hundred settlers. Almost as soon as they got there they lost several ships. Half the expedition died on fruitless marches into the interior; the rest struggled back to the coast, built themselves some rickety boats, and sailed along the coast as far as the Mississippi. Here a storm annihilated the little fleet. Of those who managed to reach the shore, all but a handful were killed by Indians. The rest finally died of starvation. Only two saved themselves by joining a nomad Indian tribe and pretending to be medicine men endowed with magic powers.

These two, Álvar Núñez Cabeza de Vaca and the Negro slave Esteban, were unwilling wanderers on the North American continent for six and a half years, during which they traversed two thirds of its breadth on foot. In 1536 they at last encountered white men again on the northern frontier of "New Spain." These were Spanish slave-hunters who could not believe their eyes when a fellow countryman suddenly appeared out of the unknown regions to the north.

Cabeza de Vaca's tales of his plight and the poverty he had met among the North American tribes did not stimulate anyone to further incursions into that country, which was henceforth written off as useless. When Cabeza de Vaca returned to Spain, however, he altered the gist of his stories and gave an impression that he knew important secrets he dared not reveal. Just at this time Hernando de Soto was staying at court. After playing his part in the conquest of Peru as an underling of Pizarro's, he wanted to lead his own expedition to discover a land like Mexico or Peru and had already obtained leave from Charles V. His plan was to go to North America and there seek the treasures no one else had succeeded in finding, and as a result of Cabeza de Vaca's wicked pretense that there was really something to be found there, de Soto began his luckless venture.

His march with 660 men, 213 horses, and plentiful bloodhounds began on May 28, 1539, from Tampa Bay (Florida) and lasted four years. Suffering frightful hardships, the Spaniards marched the length and breadth of an unexplored area 350,000 square miles in extent. They wandered from latitude 28 to 36 and longitude 82 to 100, without finding anything to repay all their trouble.

In May 1541 they reached the Mississippi at the point where Memphis stands today; then they wintered at the confluence of the Arkansas and Canadian rivers, where for the first time in their lives they experienced a snowfall lasting a whole month. Next spring they dragged their weary footsteps back to the Mississippi in sorry plight, and there de Soto died. His successor, Luís Moscoso de Alvarado, marched in burning summer heat across the prairies to the upper waters of the Brazos, and, as this effort too brought nothing but disappointment, the remnants of the expedition fought their way back to the mouth of the Arkansas, built frail boats, and sailed down the Mississippi for two months to reach its estuary. Even on the final stage of this fruitless expedition many a Spaniard lost his life, but the survivors were sufficiently hardened to be able to laugh at one another's faces swollen with mosquito bites and to deride the poverty of the inhabitants of the first Spanish settlement they came upon.

Equally fruitless was another Spanish incursion into the north which the viceroy of Mexico, Antonio de Mendoza, had carefully prepared. His men, under Francisco Vásquez Coronado, pushed

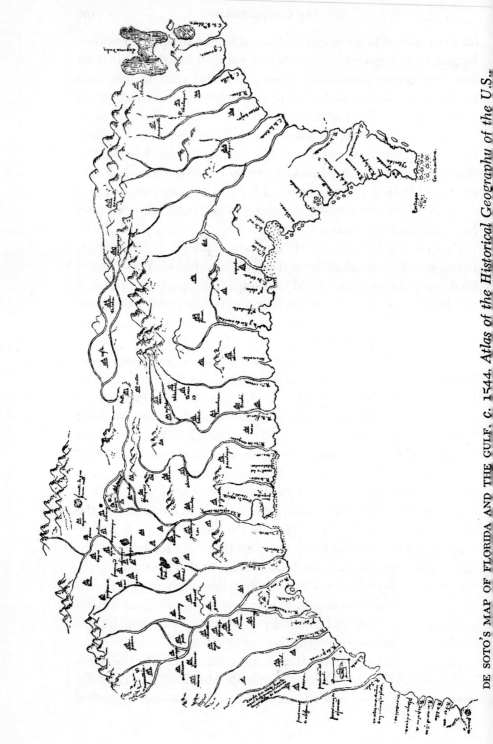

DE SOTO'S MAP OF FLORIDA AND THE GULF, c. 1544. *Atlas of the Historical Geography of the U.S.*

forward to the Grand Canyon of Arizona and on to Quira (between the Arkansas and lower Kansas rivers), but found no more gold or big towns than those before them—only pueblos, prairies, herds of buffalo, and the fact that the farther north they went, the colder and less hospitable the country became.

With that the attempts to extend the Spanish colonial empire into the North American continent came to an end. The great age of discoveries came to a close about 1550. Now Spaniards and Portuguese concentrated mainly on cashing in on what they had discovered. Half a century after the first landing in America the broad outline of its coasts, its mountains, and its main river basins was known and the New World was an open secret. The great impetus of the conquistadors had died out, and many of the regions they had penetrated were left untrodden for centuries and fell into oblivion—regions they had traversed clad in iron armor and leather jerkins, in spite of scorching heat, the pangs of hunger, and the pains of tropical diseases, in spite of steep mountains, treacherous swamps, raging rivers, and the dense undergrowth of vast jungles. At other points, maps were improved by assiduous detailed work, at which the Jesuits particularly were masters. The Spaniards' chief interest still lay in great sources of wealth where gold and silver were to be won. The New World was open—but only to its possessors. In truth it lay closed. Where earlier the ocean and nature's savage forces had barred the way, now political frontiers not to be crossed prevented all access. No other land but Spain—with the sole exception of Portugal, which owned Brazil—could approach it, no ship dared run into American waters, no trader might hawk his wares there.

For the outside world it was as though America had never been discovered. No news was spread abroad; the reports, observations, and descriptions of Spanish explorers disappeared in the archives; nobody learned any of South America's geography, botany, or zoology, its rich ores or its sources of mineral wealth. As ever, harsh political boundaries meant harsh spiritual limitations. Every book about South America had to undergo a rigorous censorship, first by the King, then by the "Holy" Inquisition, then by the

Council for India, and finally by the Casa de Contratación (the governing board for American trade). And so things remained till a generation other than that of the conquistadors set out on new ventures of discovery—a generation of men imbued with the same old daring, but with the new and different urge for exploration which had in the meantime developed in Europe.

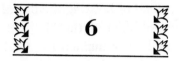

THE DAWN OF AMERICAN HISTORY

As LONG as Spain had the power to do so, she made the New World part of the Old; the fate of the continent beyond the ocean was decided entirely in Europe. The only new things about it were its nature and the wealth that flowed from its mines; for the rest, it had to adapt itself completely to the Old World.

Meanwhile, the power that Spain enjoyed in the Old World did not remain unchallenged. The enmity between Charles V and Francis I smoldered unceasingly and five times between 1525 and 1544 burst into the flames of war. And alongside the official conduct of recognized warfare, the century following the discovery of America brought an entirely new form of warlike acts which flourished in waters that, before Columbus, had lain equally far from politics and shipping-routes.

Hernán Cortés, who in 1522 had every reason to ingratiate himself with his royal master in Spain, decided to send a specially selected treasure of gold and silver ware and ornaments to Madrid from his Aztec Empire. But this precious offering never got there; off Cape Saint Vincent it was intercepted by a French privateer and carried off to France. This was the beginning of the favorite activity of French, English, and Dutch sailors, an activity that was to be long practiced with indescribable ardor. With their swift, handy ships, they fell upon the cumbersome galleons bearing the Spanish treasures to Europe and plundered as much as they could lay hands on of what the Spanish themselves had won by plunder.

These piratical acts were mostly sanctioned by official "letters of mark" issued by the privateers' governments, but the captains were so thorough and so clever in carrying out their orders that occasionally they far exceeded their authority. A later development of this highway robbery at sea was the activity of unbridled adventurers who, instead of hoisting the flag of a state, ran up the skull-and-crossbones emblem of the "Jolly Roger." The favorite field for booty throughout remained the Caribbean Sea with its islands and hidden coves where the buccaneers[1] found ideal hiding-places and springboards for their attacks on Spanish treasure galleons and coastal towns.

In 1523 Francis I sent the Florentine Giovanni da Verrazano on a reconnaissance into the far north of the American continent to discover the passage to Asia, but he did not succeed where the Cabots and Corte-Reals had failed. However, he probably mistook Chesapeake Bay, of which he caught a glimpse across the flat, sandy land spit from Delaware Bay, for the Pacific and thereby gave an impetus to the later search for the passage to that ocean. Then he sailed on northward and reconnoitered the coasts of New Jersey and Maine, finding as he went the harbor on which New York now stands.

But none of the early voyages produced any results that encouraged further attempts. Here were only fog, ice, and bitter cold, a confusion of islands and sand dunes, poverty-stricken Indians or Eskimos; here was certainly no place for a new Mexico or Peru. And yet Jacques Cartier (born in 1491), whom Francis sent out in 1534 with two ships to look for the passage, believed in its prospects for a short time. When he saw Labrador he wrote in horror: "I tend to the belief that this is the land God gave to Cain." But the island group of the Magdalens, with their wild-grain crops and their fruit, seemed very attractive to him, and on journeying farther to Chaleur Bay he recorded how rich the waters were in fish, seals, and walruses, how densely wooded their shores. Indian tales of three mighty lands—Saguenay, Hochelaga, and Canada—moved Cartier to sail to America again in the following year and to follow the course of the Saint Lawrence.

---

[1] The name adopted by the free brotherhood of the independent pirates. The name is derived from the Spanish and is related to the salting of the veal that these sea robbers used as provender.

Still looking for the Pacific Ocean, he pressed on into Canada and found there a fertile country: grapes, nuts, maize, melons, beans, pumpkins, and tobacco grew there in profusion, there were shoals of fish beyond number, walruses and seals in its waters, and a charming variety of bird life.

The rock fortress of Stadacona, in which lived the Montagnais Indians, was of course very different from Montezuma's palace. The hospitable inhabitants were greedy for the white men's iron, brass, and steel articles and tried to deter their visitors from continuing their journey to Hochelaga, at first in the friendliest way, by presenting them with a thirteen-year-old girl and two little boys, then by trying to frighten them. "Three Indians, covered in black and white dogskins, with horns as long as an arm on their heads and their faces dyed pitch-black, came in the guise of devils, and prophesied in the name of the God Cudouaghy that there would be so much snow and ice in Hochelaga that they were all bound to perish."

The French, however, were presumptuous enough not to heed this warning by the Devil and to sail on up the river until they reached the considerable village of Hochelaga, fortified by palisades. The Hurons, too, received them kindly, but had to admit that here there were no treasures to be found nor any possibility of driving on to the Pacific. Cartier named the high hill at whose foot the village lay "Mont Royal," and so the city that now stands there is called Montreal.

The Frenchmen had to cover about a thousand miles to get back to the coast. There they wintered and did not even suffer from scurvy, because Cartier had contrived by guile to get possession of an Indian remedy—a brew of conifer buds and bark. But Francis I was naturally not satisfied with the results of this expensive expedition when they got back to France. Once again the King stood facing a war with Charles V and, instead of bringing the gold he so badly needed, here was Cartier asking for more. But a Huron chief whom the explorer had brought along on a visit awoke fresh hope by regaling them with all the fairytales that were current around the Indian campfires; according to him, there were, deep in his homeland, many cities, great reserves of gold, copper, and rubies, besides other valuables, also dwarfs, winged men who flew, one-legged men, and even people who neither ate nor digested.

France could of course spare no funds for freaks and oddities, but the hope of wealth from the unexplored New World moved Francis to fit out a splendid expedition of eight ships, four hundred sailors, three hundred soldiers, and a host of laborers and builders, complete with ladies of extremely doubtful repute and provisions for two years, to found a colony.

This infuriated the Spaniards, who could not bear to see anyone sharing American soil with them. When they referred him to the Pope's division of the world between Spain and Portugal, Francis replied scornfully: "I should much like to see Adam's will and learn how he divided the earth."

At least one Spanish grandee saw little danger to Spain from this French colonial essay and solaced Charles with words that hit the nail on the head: "Because of idle chatter the French believe this region to be rich in gold and silver and so hope to achieve what we have achieved. But they are enmeshed in error, for the whole of that coast down to Florida has nowhere anything at all to offer. Therefore they will come to grief or, at the best, stay only a short while, losing a few of their people and the better part of their cargo."

The colony that Cartier founded near Quebec in 1541 was, in fact, unable to maintain its footing in the bitter Canadian winters, and he was compelled to withdraw his people in 1544. But before this he had made a sensational find: prospecting-operations revealed a glittering type of stone in which the Frenchmen thought they recognized gold, silver, and diamonds. The triumph was short-lived, however, for it was later established that they had brought back a heap of worthless treasure; the stones consisted of pyrites, mica slates, and crystalline quartz.

After such disappointments Francis lost his zeal for similar ventures. France's resources were too heavily strained by the war with Spain and later by civil war to allow her to develop an official colonial policy. Instead, religious refugees from France twice tried to found places of safety for themselves in America.

Fort Coligny was founded by the Calvinists in 1555 and its site on the Bay of Río formed the central point of an "Antarctic France," but the fort perished of its internal factions and Portuguese attacks. Then in 1562 and 1564 Huguenots fled to North America under the leadership of a sailor called Ribault; this time they went not to Canada in the far north, but to Florida, where they set up a fortress called "Charlesfort" after their king. But the Spaniards gave them short shrift, capturing the settlement and butchering the inhabitants to the last man. This showed plainly enough that no one but the Spaniards had anything to hope for in America. After the blood bath of Florida (1565) several decades passed without any further attempts at colonization.

France was too exhausted. The appearance of some new power was needed before she could fly at the throat of Spain—a Spain that now enjoyed unheard-of heights of power. Philip II had succeeded his father, Charles V, who, since his abdication in 1556, was occupying himself with horticulture and watch-mending in a monastery. Philip increased the span of his empire by the old Habsburg recipe of intermarriage; his spouse was Bloody Mary, Queen of England, and as the fruits of a previous Habsburg marriage Philip also inherited the throne of Portugal, so that he ruled over both halves of the world at once.

But his marriage to the Catholic Mary, who forbade her sea-loving subjects to sail to America, was to provide one of the germs of later trouble. Philip's wedding present to Mary consisted of ninety-seven cases in which fifty thousand pounds of silver was brought to the Tower of London. This drew the attention of men in England more sharply than was good for Spain to the fabulous riches of America. Bloody Mary died in 1558, and in the same year Henry VIII's daughter Elizabeth became Queen of England.

The Habsburg strategy misfired completely where she was concerned. She rejected Philip II's offer of marriage and later was strong enough to oppose his hostile intentions with great success. She was enabled to do so by a generation of tough mariners who from now on showed the flag of England on the seven seas and showed small respect in attacking the Spanish might.

The Spaniards, however, brooked no competitors at sea any more than ashore. Sailors caught in American waters had to suffer fearsome tortures in the cells of the Inquisition and hardly ever survived their sufferings. But the catching of them grew more and more difficult.

The last great success against the British sailors was in 1569 off Vera Cruz, where the Spaniards inflicted heavy losses. The ships engaged were under the command of John Hawkins, who had recently started a very profitable business; in his ship *Jesus of Lübeck* he fetched slaves from Africa, sailed into the forbidden American waters, and sold them there at top prices. But both Hawkins and his captain, Francis Drake (born 1540), escaped at Vera Cruz, and as a consequence the Spaniards soon had to suffer much more serious trouble than black-market trading in Negroes.

Very soon afterward Drake began a series of piratical exploits under the very noses of the all-powerful Spaniards. He helped himself to as much gold as his ships could hold at Nombre de Dios, "the golden storehouse of the West Indies"; he towed a galleon away from the middle of Cartagena's harbor; he burned Porto Bello to the ground, pillaged Vera Cruz, scattered three Spanish convoys, and returned to England, after breathtaking adventures, with a considerable fortune. Elizabeth now commissioned him to destroy Spanish trade in the Pacific, and he immediately sailed through the Magellan Strait, ravaged the west coast, and was the first ever to reach Vancouver Island. To avoid the Spanish fleet lurking off the southern point of the continent to cut off his return, he imitated Magellan and sailed onward—the second to do so—right round the world. His skill in navigation was of the greatest service to the development of British seamanship, and under his guidance there grew up a generation of devil-may-care sailors—Walter Raleigh, Frobisher, Howard, Cumberland, Essex, and other masters of the sea. Skillfully using improvements in ship design, rigging, and armament, the English also developed a new type of vessel which was soon to make its mark on world history—the freebooter.

Elizabeth, that great Queen, had already been on the throne a quarter of a century, Catholicism had at last been forced to give way to the Anglican Church, the might of England had increased sensibly, Shakespeare's plays were entrancing London audiences, Francis Bacon was diverting thought into a new channel that aimed at modern scientific investigation when Walter Raleigh, pirate, admiral, and statesman, sought to destroy the power of Spain by entirely new means. England must gain a footing in

SIR WALTER RALEIGH

America. His idea eventually cost him his life and altered the course of the world's history considerably, for its final result was the appearance of the U.S.A.

Walter Raleigh (born *c.* 1552) began as an ordinary seaman, fought in the Huguenot cause for some years, and after an adventurous career at sea came to Elizabeth's court, where he helped to plan and organize the intensification of the British attack on Spanish colonial possessions by piracy, voyages of exploration, and pillaging raids. But this was not all: Raleigh had realized that Spain's great colonial empire must be undermined from the mainland, and it was in North America that he made his first attempts. Later he staged a direct invasion into the heart of Spain's empire by sailing up the Orinoco in 1595; in 1617 he once again set foot on the South American continent, but high politics compelled James I, Elizabeth's successor, to heed Spanish complaints to the extent of withdrawing his support and having Raleigh sentenced to death. Raleigh walked calmly to his execution with a pipe in his mouth: he was not only an energetic fighter and explorer, but also a man of considerable parts who left behind him a fine account of his South American voyage of discovery, a mass of political and economic writings, and even books of poetry.

In 1585—the same year that John Davis (born *c.* 1550), following in Frobisher's wake, made the second discovery of Greenland and sailed through the strait between Greenland and North America later named after him—Raleigh had sent out 108 men to found a settlement on North American soil. According to a reconnaissance by Captain Arthur Barlowe and Philip Amandas, the island of Roanoke lying close to the mainland was an ideal spot for the venture. Raleigh would dearly have liked to lead the expedition himself, but the growing threat of a Spanish attack on England anchored him at home and he therefore commissioned John Lane to command it. Lane, who incidentally provided England with a rich source of profit by bringing tobacco back with him, founded a settlement, the core of which was a fort named after Sir Walter Raleigh. The part of the continent selected for this first colonial essay was given the name Virginia, in honor of Elizabeth the Virgin Queen; though many historians have questioned this aspect of the Queen's life, there is no doubt that the name was bestowed at the time in all respect and had behind it a definite feeling of admiration.

At all events, the name was admirably suited to the unspoiled tract of country it covered—a land that plagued the British settlers with problems very different from those which Central and South America had set the Spaniards. The terrible wilderness, peopled with hostile Indians, imposed on them a bitter struggle for existence, so unexpected that they had not even brought the necessary materials and provisions with them. So after an agonizing year they were compelled to sail home again in ships commanded by Francis Drake; fifteen courageous men remained behind to man the fort and were rewarded by the arrival, shortly afterward, of the plentiful shipment of supplies intended for the whole colony.

Although Elizabeth could ill spare a ship or a crew from the war with Spain which was obviously imminent, Raleigh refused to abandon his plan and in 1587 sent another party of intrepid settlers to Roanoke. The three ships, with 121 people and their colonial gear on board, took eight weeks to cross the Atlantic. On arriving at Roanoke, they were greeted by an evil omen; the fifteen defenders of the fort had been murdered by the natives. Nothing daunted, they began the war against the primeval forest under the skillful leadership of the governor, John White, and his son-in-law, Ananias Dare. During the first month of this grim existence, weatherproof blockhouses were built, ground was plowed for crops, and Mrs. Dare bore a daughter. This girl, who was christened Virginia, was the first North American of true European extraction, and even if her fate remains a mystery, the name Virginia Dare has for centuries remained a symbol of the endurance and confidence of American pioneers.

The little colony flourished in spite of all hardships and difficulties, but supplies ran dangerously low. In the late summer Governor White returned to England to report and obtain stores, equipment, and clothing.

But world history nullified his intentions. The settlers in Roanoke must have searched the sea day after day in vain, longing for the ships that never came; however pluckily they fought for life, there was to be no rescue. Slowly and surely the colony perished, and when, later, Raleigh five times sent ships out at his own expense to look for the settlers, no trace of them could be found.

For in the meantime the fate of the world—both New and Old —had been decided in Europe.

When Governor White arrived in England, he learned to his amazement that not a ship or a man might leave the island stronghold. The decisive battle with Spanish world power was plainly at hand; Elizabeth had to reckon from day to day with an invasion of England. So all the pleas of White, Raleigh, and the relatives of the deserted settlers proved vain; in face of the country's deadly peril, the Queen remained obdurate.

Philip II of Spain prepared with loving care the stroke that was to annihilate the English heretics who had gone over from the true Church, who plundered Spanish galleons with their pirate vessels, who with their fire raids in South America were at one and the same time constituting a growing danger to his colonial empire and refusing to recognize the famous Line of Demarcation. He fitted out the greatest fleet the world had ever seen: 130 great vessels from Portugal, Andalusia, Vizcaya, Guipúzcoa, and Italy, with a veritable army on board them. The "Armada" was a symbol not only of Spain's military but her economic power; it represented in round figures a treasure of two hundred million ducats.

In July 1588 this incomparable, invincible fleet of the ruling world power sailed into the English Channel in order to wipe out the bothersome English spoilers of the peace, who could not muster even half the number of ships that bore down upon their waters. Under Admiral Lord Howard and Francis Drake, the host of small but handy privateers, whose crews had braved the storms of every ocean, flung themselves on the Spaniards. Had the battle been fought on the classical lines of naval tactics and strategy, the British would have had no hope of survival.

Instead of the customary battle at close quarters, in which ships lay alongside and their crews tried to board one another, the British contented themselves with gunfire from a distance. The Spaniards, of course, had a far greater weight of cannon, but the very weakness of the British fleet—the fact that it consisted only of small vessels—turned out to be a vital advantage; the shots from their low decks bored irresistibly into the towering hulls of the Spanish men-of-war, whose salvos were mainly wasted on the masts and rigging of the English ships.

For three whole days the mobile English sailors, taking their lives in their hands, attacked the Armada, firing their guns, turning away, and running in again to fire. The losses and confusion of the Spaniards mounted apace, their cumbersome fleet was maneuvered into unfavorable waters close inshore and began to scatter, battered galleons fell an easy prey to the British, and finally a heavy storm sealed the fate of that proud fleet. Most of its ships capsized or ran onto the rocks, where they broke up. Thousands died in the waves. The impossible had happened; Spain's sea power had suffered a blow from which it was never to recover.

The battle in the English Channel was more than the repulse of an attack on England; at one stroke it robbed Spain of the mastery of the seas and of the world. The sea lanes, especially those leading to America, were now open to England, which was soon to develop into a world power; the barriers that Spain had imposed on other countries by her might were down once for all. The fate of America, too, had been decided in the Channel: Spain could no longer prevent the colonization of North America, starting from its Atlantic coasts, by the English, the Dutch, and the French. Gone forever were the days when a Pope could divide the world between Spain and Portugal.

A nine-year-old boy with the very ordinary name of John Smith enjoyed the heartfelt celebration of England's great victory in his birthplace, Willoughby in the County of Lincoln, where the people danced around a Maypole and did rare justice to the fatted ox that Lord Willoughby had roasted to mark the occasion, and to the liquor that was plentifully laid on. This John Smith was more adventurous than other boys; the early death of his parents gave him the opportunity to go out into the world at a tender age and get to know foreign countries. When he was only fifteen he enthusiastically entered the French army, then joined the Dutch forces two years later; after which he took to the sea and eventually found a profitable occupation when he took part, in Hungary, in the war against the Turks. Here he distinguished himself by his exceptional courage, and was soon promoted from the ranks to be captain in command of two hundred and fifty men. After being wounded, he was made prisoner by the Turks and at first lived very agreeably in Constantinople as the slave of a young lady, later less agreeably as her brutish brother's in an obscure place. Finally one day Smith killed his master. After a desperate flight he managed to reach safety with friends; he traveled through Europe to Morocco, survived a few storms and naval actions on board a French ship, and in 1604, at the age of twenty-five, returned home with a tidy fortune and a thirst for adventure by no means quenched.

Captain Smith soon heard reports about the colonial efforts in America and talked to sailors who had been in Virginia. On ma-

ture reflection they thought it might be worth while to visit the
new continent, for there the Indians exchanged valuable skins
and furs—beaver, otter, seals, deer—for a trifle; they also had
copper that was not much use to them; one could sail home with
shiploads of furs, cedarwood, and other goods and do a very
nice trade. The beauty of the American countryside, the endless
expanses of its forests, the wealth of fish in its waters, the prospects of trade and adventure seized the imagination of young
Smith, so he joined a group of adventurous people who wanted
to make another attempt to found a colony.

They spent a whole year in vain planning, for the funds they
commanded were insufficient, but by patience and careful saving they slowly made progress. By a patent of April 10, 1606,
James I, Elizabeth's successor, gave them permission to settle
colonies and plantations in Virginia or any other part of America
on condition that a fifth of the yield from gold- and silver-mining
should fall to the Crown. (He could equally well have asked for
more or for less, for he was never to receive a grain of the much-
prized metal from Virginia.) The wealth found by the Spaniards
in America led not only the King, but also many later explorers,
into the error of believing that there must be precious metals in
North America too; here again the thirst for gold—though there
was none—quickened the pace of discovery and exploration.

A company formed to pursue the development of Virginia
eventually provided the necessary funds, and a flotilla set out on
December 19, 1606; there were one ship of a hundred tons and a
pinnace of twenty, with a hundred emigrants herded together on
board.

Unfortunately, they sailed at the worst and stormiest time of
year. They cruised for six weeks within sight of the British Isles;
many were helpless with seasickness; doubt and despair were
loudly voiced. At last it was possible to set course out into the
open sea, the ships following practically the same course as Columbus, past the Canaries and the West Indian islands, then
turning north. On April 26, after almost missing their objective,
they at last landed on the coast of Virginia.

John Smith came ashore under duress, for many of the emigrants had trumped up false charges against him. However, when the sealed orders were opened, he had to be set free, for the London Company, as organizers of the expedition, had established the rules for its conduct. It was laid down that a council of seven, including John Smith, should take over the administration and elect a president. The settlers, from whom the company expected a quick haul of riches, were not only to found a settlement, but to explore the country with the object of finding a passage to the "South Sea" and to the treasures of India.

These European colonists sailed for the first time up a river into the North American interior in a sloop constructed of parts they brought with them. After reconnoitering upstream for seventeen days, past broad plains of a rich green, through pleasant hills and valleys set in well-wooded landscape of oak and walnut trees, with a rich abundance of fruit, vines, and berries, they found a suitable spot about forty miles inland from the mouth of the river (which the natives called Powhatan), and there on May 13 founded their first settlement, which they called Jamestown in the King's honor.

Smith soon left the settlement to explore the country farther upstream. Near its source he erected a cross and named the river King's River as a further honor to the King, who, like most kings, had the least trouble but the greatest credit from the whole venture.

John Smith established friendly relations with the natives he met in their villages and in the capital, Powhatan. But he returned to Jamestown just in time to save it from destruction, for it was on the point of being overpowered by savages. Seventeen white men already lay wounded, one dead, and—thanks to the criminal stupidity of the President, a man called Wingfield, who neglected even the simplest means of defense—the fate of the colony would have been sealed then and there, had not the loud report of a cannon from the sloop scared the attackers away.

A few days later the ships in which the emigrants had come from England sailed for home, and Wingfield, one of Smith's bitterest enemies, conceived the splendid idea of having him sent home forcibly on the ground of the earlier accusations. As the future was to show, that would have been tantamount to the suicide of the whole colony, for Smith was the only one who knew how to look after provisions and come to terms with the Indians. However, he himself insisted on a trial and was acquitted on all counts. So he was permitted to stay, and Wingfield was heavily fined instead.

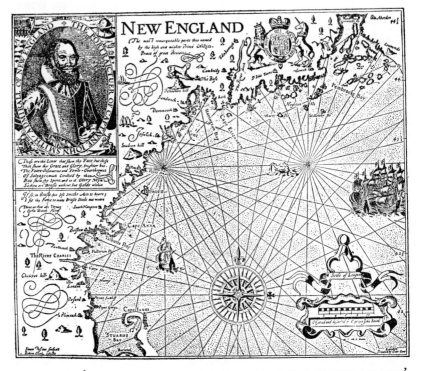

JOHN SMITH'S MAP OF NEW ENGLAND, FROM CAPTAIN JOHN SMITH'S *General History*

Intrigues and trials—these marked the start of colonization in North America. But worse was still to come. The food supplies had been cut far too fine, and ten days after the ships left for England to fetch new provender only a few of the settlers were fit and on their feet; the rest had been laid low by hunger, weakness, and sickness. The daily ration was a half-pint of wheat and the same amount of barley, and this tiny dole was actually more garbage than food, for twenty-six weeks of storage in the ship's hull had left the grain full of worms and cockroaches.

Between May and September fifty died: had the Indians launched a second attack during this time, the colony would have been wiped out. By September there were hardly any provisions left, but then a miracle happened: the Indians, anxious to trade, came of their own accord with fruit and great quantities of sustenance. Gradually the settlers regained their strength. John Smith worked with might and main to get houses built strong enough to withstand the approaching winter. When the Indians suddenly stopped bringing food, he went off on another journey in the sloop. He succeeded in making a deal with them and obtained considerable quantities of venison, turkeys, bread, and other foods. But when he returned to Jamestown, hell had broken loose again: the colonists were at loggerheads, and some of them had used force to get hold of the pinnace and were on the point of sailing for England. Smith trained the cannon of the newly built fort on them and brought the ringleader to trial, as a result of which he was sentenced to death and shot.

Although the Indians came several times to Jamestown with provisions to trade and barter, there were far too few supplies to last through a winter. Nobody cared, however, as they were all for the moment well fed; it is one of the peculiarities of the story of this attempt at colonization that its inhabitants did little to provide for their future and cheerfully traded with the Indians their most valuable possessions, even powder and shot, for small quantities of food. In the end, only one course lay open: Smith had to go out on another trip.

This time he penetrated even farther into the unknown than before. The upper reaches of the river presented serious difficulties because of innumerable tree trunks that had fallen across the channel and had to be sawed through. When the water became too shallow, Smith went on in a canoe with two Englishmen and two Indian guides. Twenty miles farther on he came to a great expanse of swamp. In his anxiety to obtain supplies for his people, he went ashore to shoot birds, and so began one of the most romantic chapters in the whole adventurous early history of America.

One of the crew of the sloop had gone ashore, in spite of orders to the contrary, and had there been attacked by Indians and killed. Two hundred Indians then followed Smith's trail and surrounded him. There was a sharp fight in which he killed three of them and wounded several more. He would have escaped had he not fallen into a marshy stream, into whose mud he sank; this left him the choice between capture and a lingering death. So the savages were able to bear him away in triumph.

Smith, who had learned their language, asked permission to speak to the chief, and was led to an Indian with the sonorous name of Opechankanough, whom he was able to dissuade from any intention to murder him by showing him a compass and delivering, as best he could, a lecture on the sky, the stars, and the earth. The Indian listened eagerly for an hour, but in the end they tied Smith to a tree and made a show of shooting him with their arrows. But at the last moment the Chief made a sign and he was untied and brought into an Indian village.

There a victory celebration took place which Smith described as follows:

They led me along bound by cords to two strong savages, whilst the others danced about me, looking like very devils. Their town, truly, was not much, for it consisted only of thirty or forty hunting lodges, built up of mats, which they remove as they please, as we do tents; and all the women and children came staring to look at the wonderful white man. Then did they exalt themselves greatly, and, setting me bound in their midst, they cast themselves into a ring, dancing in such several postures, and singing and yelling out hellish noises and screeches; being strangely painted, with every one of his quiver of arrows, and at his back a club. They were clad in fox or otter skins, or some such matter, their head and shoulders painted scarlet, which made an exceeding handsome show. Their bows they carried in their hands, and had the skin of a bird, with its wings spread out, dried, with a piece of copper, a white shell, a long feather, a small rattle from the tail of one of their snakes, or some such toy in their hair.

The ceremony ended with three wild dances, and after that Smith was well treated, magnificently fed (which made him think they were going to eat him later on), and exhibited as a phenomenon in all the villages along the Rappahannock and Patawomek rivers. At the end the Indians brought him to Merenocomoco, the home of their paramount chief, Wahunsona-cock or Powhatan.[2] Further celebrations and war dances took place before Smith was brought into a big house. Here the Chief was seated near a fire on a throne that reminded Smith of a bed-stead. The room was full of savage warriors who engaged in long consultations and in the end decided to do away with Smith. They seized the Englishman and laid him on two great blocks of stone; then two of the savages raised their clubs to smash his skull.

At this very moment an Indian girl flung herself on the prisoner, threw her arms around him, laid her head against his, and claimed possession of John Smith. It was impossible to refuse her request, for she was the Chief's favorite daughter, a child of ten years. Her tribal name was Matoaka, but in her relation to the white men she was called Pocahontas ("The Outcast").

Ten days later things took another turn for the better: Chief Powhatan declared that he and Smith were now friends and that he intended to present the land of Capahowosick to him and re-gard him as his son. Captain Smith was allowed to return to Jamestown, but had to leave two guns and a whetstone as pledges.

Once again it was high time for him to return to the colony, for once again a disaffected section had obtained possession of the pinnace and wanted to sail for England. Smith fired a few shots from his cannon to bring the rebels to their senses and later had the ringleaders sent home in chains.

The affairs of the little colony, which was on the verge of starva-tion, now improved greatly, for Pocahontas visited it every fourth or fifth day with her retinue and brought food. In spite of this, even Smith's best friends tried to persuade him to give up the whole enterprise and go back to England. But Smith faced his friends with peaceful persuasion, as he had the mutineers with warlike measures, and managed to counsel them to endure.

Their steadfastness was well rewarded. The trading-company

[2] The appearance of two different names is due to the fact that the Indians, fear-ing the white man's magic powers, adopted other names when dealing with him.

had not forgotten them, but had sent two ships with supplies. The first of these now arrived, bringing not only tools and materials but considerable quantities of food.

Hardly had they laid in new stores of provisions when fate struck the colony a fresh blow. A fire broke out and destroyed the whole settlement—even the stockade was burned down. Supplies, materials, arms—everything went up in flames in the midst of the hard frost of the winter of 1607. Smith incurred further hatred by the energy with which he urged on rebuilding measures. In the spring the second supply vessel, which had been blown from off Virginia to the West Indies by unfavorable winds, at last arrived, bringing a substantial cargo of food, and new settlers as well. How little idea the company had of existence in their colony was shown by their choice of newcomers, among whom there were hardly any laborers or craftsmen, but in their stead—besides a goodly company of adventurous good-for-nothings—jewelers, goldsmiths, and even a pipe-maker and a perfumer.

The regulations that the company had sent with them did nothing to add to the ease of life in the wilderness. It was absolutely forbidden to do any harm whatever to the natives, with the result that pilfering, encroachment, and even hostilities became much easier for the Indians. The company also insisted that gold and the passage to India must be discovered, so the crew wasted so much time in looking for gold and washing the sand of the riverbed that every man of them had his fill of it and the captain, taking John Smith's advice, sailed for home with a cargo of cedarwood.

Smith himself set out on a further expedition in a big open boat with a crew of fifteen, intending to explore Chesapeake Bay. On this voyage, which lasted seven weeks, he discovered the islands that bear his name, also some other islands. Then he traveled up some rivers into the mainland and established friendly relations with a number of Indian tribes.

Of course when he got back to Jamestown he found he had to settle new quarrels and to bolster up the morale of the newcomers, who had all fallen sick in the unaccustomed climate. Smith did his best to restore order, and three days later was off again on another seven-week journey because the Indians had told him tales that roused his hope that he would find the way through to the "South Sea," supposedly close at hand.

Once again Smith explored long stretches of the coast and the interior, and had friendly and unfriendly encounters with Indian tribes. Once again he had to restore order when he returned to the settlement. This, however, was an easier matter, for just about then a ship arrived from England bringing his appointment as president of Virginia—a fine promotion for a man who fifteen years earlier had been a poor, hungry orphan.

The London Company had issued instructions to the ship's captain which it was quite impossible for the poor man to carry out; he was forbidden to return without a heap of gold and must at all costs find the passage to India. With this end in view, he had been provided with a ship fabricated in five parts, to enable him to explore the country far upstream. Near the source of the river the boat was to be carried by hand across the mountains—an assignment that would have required five hundred men—and then sail down a river on the other side, thus certainly arriving at the "South Sea."

The only mission the Captain was actually able to carry out was the delivery to Powhatan of a crown, a scarlet robe, a bed, and some other gifts.

The Chief was not prepared to fetch these presents, but sent a message saying: "If your king sends me gifts, I too am a king and this is my country. I shall expect to receive them within eight days." So a small party left the settlement, delivered the gifts to the Chief, and explained their use to him. Everything went pretty well till the actual act of coronation. Powhatan refused to assume the robe; it needed a great deal of persuasion and many assurances that he would come to no harm before he would put the festal garment on.

Still more difficult was the placing of the crown on his head. He could not grasp the meaning of this strange object and could not be persuaded to kneel down. Every explanation and demonstration proved unavailing till the white men grew tired of their efforts, but they dared not take the crown back with them. In the end Smith and the Captain succeeded in leaning on Powhatan's shoulders in such a way that he had to bend forward a little, whereupon the sailors, who were standing in readiness, jammed the crown on his head, all awry.

When Smith got back to Jamestown he was faced by a fresh threat of starvation. The ship had brought seventy settlers from England, but no provisions for them; the Indians screwed up their barter prices all the time and were bringing food to the colony much less frequently. So there was nothing left but to sail up a river into the interior and trade a large amount of supplies.

In this they were successful, Smith returning with three boats full of grain, fish, and fowl. Needless to say, he returned to find the usual mutiny going on and had to deal with the rebel faction before he could get on with his work.

So life went on: shortage of food, fresh trading-trips, difficulties with the Indians, dissatisfaction and revolt in the colony. It grew steadily worse, for Powhatan wanted to exterminate the white men. He arranged for Smith to be murdered, but Pocahontas saved him again by warning him at the last moment. Was this a case of the love of a child or mere human kindness? The true nature of the relationship between the bearded swordsman and this young blossom of the wilderness cannot be learned from John Smith's extremely reticent reports. Women several times saved his life during his adventurous career, but nobody knows whether there was the slightest mutual feeling involved. Smith only once mentions the word "love": once when the Indians wanted to accord him a specially worthy reception, he found himself in a hut full of naked women and girls, whose wild dance was continually interrupted by their cries of "I love you!" According to Smith, that was as far as things went, even on that occasion.

This second rescue by Pocahontas was all the more remarkable because Smith observed that Dutch and German fortune-hunters had allied themselves with the Indians and were also anxious to annihilate the settlement. In spite of every kind of treachery, Smith succeeded, through sheer force of character, in browbeating the natives and concluding a lasting peace with them.

In 1609 the company realized that their great expectations of wealth from the colony were not going to materialize. The King's patent was returned to him, and presently a new commission was set up, with greater funds at its disposal. A flotilla of nine ships with five hundred men reached Virginia, and that proved sufficient support at long last to ensure the colony's permanent survival.

But the arrival of the newcomers meant that Smith had to suffer new difficulties and struggles for authority. Being totally ignorant of the country and its conditions, they made so many mistakes in the building of new places that Smith had to save them from disaster, and almost as soon as he had done so they threw his wise counsel to the winds.

John Smith was depressed and full of cares at the dissensions that were spreading through his colony. But the burden of responsibility was suddenly lifted from his shoulders. Some villain exploded Smith's powder bag while he was asleep; this was the second attempt to murder him. The Captain's wounds were so serious that he had to be sent back to England, for the colony's medical resources were totally insufficient.

Smith survived an agonizing voyage, took a long time to get well, and then had to take a lengthy period of leave; in this way he lost his close ties with Virginia and later, in 1614, became interested in other enterprises. He joined a trading-expedition to New England—which name, incidentally, was originated by John Smith, who first used it on the map he constructed there.

On his last sea voyage, in the following year, he once again met adventures sufficient to fill a long novel. He found himself aboard a French pirate ship and had to take part in its raids and fights against his will till he was at last able to escape and get ashore in a boat—and the pirate ship sank that very night.

In 1616 he returned to England and began the peaceful life of a retired citizen, out of which he was shaken when he learned that Lady Rebecca Rolfe had arrived in that country. Smith immediately wrote to Queen Anne, setting out at length that lady's services, with the result that the unknown stranger suddenly found herself treated with the respect due to a princess. And indeed Rebecca was the daughter of a king, even though his skin was red—for this was Pocahontas.

The captain of a trader, with peculiar ideas of decency, had enticed her on board and taken her prisoner, planning to extort a ransom from her father and force him to a peaceable understanding with the colony. Pocahontas never returned to her tribe, for during her time of ill-treatment and durance a young Englishman fell in love with her. This was John Rolfe, the man to whom Virginia owes its wealth. Rolfe grew a new type of tobacco plant far better than any known in England, whose particular aroma is still known all over the world as "Virginia."

After Pocahontas had learned English and been baptized, Rolfe married her and took her home with him. In England there was a moving reunion with John Smith, but it was to be short-lived, for a few months later Pocahontas died of smallpox, her last words being: "I am glad my child is alive."

Rolfe went back with his son Thomas to Virginia, where—thanks largely to his marriage to the Chief's daughter—all was at peace between native and white man. Even the Spaniards left the colony alone, though they regarded it with hostility. Fifty years earlier they had been able to keep the continent clear of bothersome competitors, but now an attack on Jamestown would have meant war with England, so the Spanish Ambassador at the court of King James confined himself to a protest. The King's reply was that he could do nothing, for the colony was a private enterprise.

The colony was thus safe from external attack, but when Powhatan died just a year after his daughter, war broke out again with the Indians. During the fighting John Rolfe was killed. The most famous Virginian families are now proud to trace their descent back to the union of one of the first settlers with the lovely princess of the wilderness.

The growth of the colony could not longer be put off. A ship with a strange cargo—marriageable women—brought the colonists all that had been missing to make the settlers feel at home in their new home.

By 1619 there were as many as eleven settlements in Virginia, and the colonists founded a council for their political representation. In 1624 Virginia became a royal British province, and henceforth the governor was appointed by the King himself, not by the privileged Virginia Company, and a parliament or "Assembly" was provided to assist him.

Farther north a number of similar attempts by the company to found settlements had failed because of the unfavorable ground. In 1620, however, the "Pilgrim Fathers," who had sailed in the *Mayflower* in search of religious freedom, landed on the New England coast. While great plantations and cultivated areas had come into being in Virginia, here the Puritans had to maintain life by grim hard work in a raw climate. And so the differences between the southern and northern states of the future U.S.A. showed themselves from the very outset.

John Smith lived to see these beginnings—not as an active participant, but in the seclusion of his native village, where he "drank" (as they called it) his pipe of good Virginian tobacco and told the village boys his breath-taking tales of adventure. He died, aged fifty-three, forgotten and neglected by those to whom his experience in opening up a new continent might have been invaluable.

In 1607, the same year Smith landed in America to look for the passage to the Pacific, another Englishman was given the same task and tried to carry it out farther north. This was Henry Hudson (born *c.* 1550), who, in the service of the Muscovy Company, was sent to find a sea route into the "Warm Sea" and so to China by way of the North Pole or some more easterly route. Between Spitsbergen and Greenland pack ice compelled him to turn back. His geographic facts lacked precision, but his reports about the rich animal life of the north led to the great sealing-voyages of the next two centuries. In 1609, during a later voyage on behalf of the Dutch East India Company also in search of the elusive passage, he discovered the mouth of the river that now bears his name, and as a result of his reports the Dutch founded New Amsterdam, later to become New York.

A newly formed English company obtained the services of the

now famous mariner and in April 1610 sent him out in quest of the fateful passage. Hudson was not of the same breed as the robust, energetic British captains of his day, for, though a splendid navigator, he was often timid and unsure of purpose and had already given way once or twice to the will of mutinous crews. On this voyage his lack of energy proved fatal.

CAPTAIN HENRY HUDSON

After he had run into the Hudson Strait at the end of June and been again and again compelled to alter course by fog, floes, and icebergs, the crew's attitude became dangerous. Everything contributed to a low, miserable state of mind—the pale, smooth walls of ice breaking sheer into the sea, the sharp rocks with their myriads of screeching birds, the shifting mists, the endless sounding and tacking.

Hudson explained what was at stake: only a little longer and they might reach the Pacific, then Cathay, India. On August 3 he enjoyed the great moment of his life when he at last saw open sea ahead and could set course for China. But soon afterward he suffered the bitter disappointment of finding his way barred by a swampy coast, where he sailed back and forth along hideous shores looking in vain for a way through.

Then the ice closed and there followed a fearful winter of bitter cold, hunger, and scurvy before Hudson was able to put out again in June 1611. Once again he was so vague, so uncertain in his plan, that the men feared they would die of starvation. Hudson's

THE *Half Moon* IN THE HUDSON RIVER

clumsy handling aided the outbreak of open mutiny. In order to have a free hand to search the ship for provisions he was supposed to have hidden aboard, the mutineers put him, his son, and five sailors in the shallop, which was being towed. The ringleader, a cynical young rogue called Greene—Hudson had once espoused his cause—ordered the tow rope to be severed. A seaman had already raised his ax when the ship's carpenter declared his allegiance to his captain. He took his tools, his musket, and his cook pot with him and joined the unfortunates in the shallop.

So this grim day in an unpeopled waste of loneliness saw both an act of treachery and a fine example of human greatness.

The little shallop moved slowly toward the bare, rocky shores of the bay. None of its occupants was ever heard of again. The mutineers fared scarcely better. Their leaders were killed in an attack on an Eskimo food store; others died of privation; a handful eventually reached England safely and escaped hanging only because Hudson's diaries and the new geographical facts they brought were useful to future trading and exploratory voyages.

But the greatest gains to North American exploration during the first century of its colonization were provided by the French.

True, Cartier's plans failed, but the wealth of fish life he dis-covered encouraged French fishermen to sail across the ocean. Their visits to the fishing-grounds, from which they returned with ships packed full, did not in themselves enrich men's knowledge of the distant continent; but other French ships were soon to follow the same course, and then wealth of a quite different kind was discovered in that part of the New World which had so cruelly disappointed all hopes of gold, spices, and the passage to India.

The impulse came from the hat-makers. A new material pro-duced an unexpected increase in their trade: the downy hairs of the beaver fur produced such an indestructible felt that the same piece occupied a hat-maker over and over again. A hat that had been worn could be worked over—and more than once—thanks to the lasting qualities of this material. About the middle of the seventeenth century the hat industry in La Rochelle was furiously busy: there they made new hats, worked up old ones, renewed still older ones (which were sent back to La Rochelle) for resale to Spain, repaired worn hats from Spain to sell in Brazil. And as the beaver felt was not worn out even then, these hats proved valuable objects for the Portuguese to barter along the African slave coasts on their last lap.

Now dealers, trappers, hunters, and backwoodsmen began to land in North America, where they started up a lively trade in valuable furs and skins, and in its pursuit pressed ever deeper into the wild interior. They had two objects in so doing: they were forced to extend their sphere of operation on account of the rapid extermination of the beavers; and their jealous competitors, the eastern Indian tribes, tried to prevent trade between the Indians in the heart of the country and the whites who possessed such valuables as steel and powder. The French were thus forced to press forward and make contact with distant Indian tribes.

It was probably in 1581 that French merchants in Saint-Malo first sent ships up the Saint Lawrence in order to trade in furs with the Indians. They gradually came to know the country by journeys close to the riverbanks, until Samuel de Champlain (born in 1567) arrived in Canada, learned to force a way through the wilderness like an Indian, pushed far into the interior in Indian canoes, and laid the foundations of a French colonial empire by placing a settlement there.

Champlain had come to know the New World early, for he had a relative who was one of the great Spanish pilots and who took him along in 1599 to the West Indies in the annual treasure fleet. The Frenchman remained in the Spanish colonies for two years. When he returned to France he published his experiences and reports, which attracted great attention and obtained royal support for his plan to make Canada "by means of its trade, another Venice, Genoa, or Marseille."

When he sailed up the Saint Lawrence in 1603 and, much to the disgust of the trading-company that backed him, put his geographical explorations before all other activity, he found no trace of the towns of Stadacona and Hochelaga, once visited by Cartier. In an area unvisited by any white man, where the bloodthirsty Iroquois were once again on the warpath, burning and slaying, he charted with the precision of a schoolmaster every single tributary of the Saint Lawrence and collected information about its upper reaches.

His personal contributions to the opening up of this unknown world were outstanding. He founded Quebec in 1608, a city soon to become the market for the fur trade. In the following years he explored the country on both sides of the Saint Lawrence, discovered the lake that bears his name, sailed up the Ottawa River, reconnoitered the lakes of Nipissing and Huron, blazing the main trail of the fur trade in so doing, visited Lake Ontario and Niagara and forced a way so deep into this trackless wilderness that the Indians themselves were amazed and believed he had dropped from heaven. Finally he became governor of Canada and ruler over all "New France" as his reward. Besides which he shaped the future pattern of exploration which alone could further the development of this inaccessible territory by acting as teacher and example to a host of fearless young people who conquered the wilderness by adapting themselves to it.

Champlain rejected white men's accomplishments and adopted the technique of the natives. He became a backwoodsman fight-

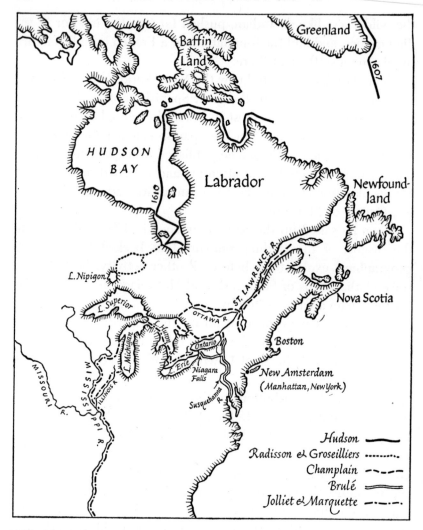

THE ROUTES OF THE FUR-TRADERS AND PATHFINDERS IN NORTH
AMERICA

ing his difficult way through undergrowth, thicket, and primeval forest, carrying his possessions on his back; he became also a canoeist who learned to master the difficult waters. The canoe—a light ribbed vessel of white cedarwood with closely knit birch-bark strips covering its frame, the whole made watertight with pine resin—was the only means of transport up the Canadian rivers. Having no keel, it needed an expert to steer it; but Champlain was soon as accomplished as an Indian and was thus able to force the swift course of the Ottawa, often barred by rapids. He described the labors of such travel as follows: "Sometimes we carried our canoes on our backs, at others we were able to tow them on ropes through the seething rapids. We were also 'humping' our clothes, provisions, and arms—a sore trial for one not accustomed to it." And the trials were redoubled when it was a question of overcoming sections of the river where he met with one rapid after another over a distance of thirty-five miles.

Under Champlain's leadership, the dour battle with the wilderness developed an extraordinary type of man, those *voyageurs* and *coureurs* who, utterly self-reliant and endowed with amazing courage and instinct, became completely familiar with the forests, lived among Indians, sometimes took red-skinned wives, helped their friends the Hurons against the terrible Iroquois, learned to know the country better and better until they gradually made it their own—all this without any great military operations or slaughter. Their prototype—forgotten by posterity—was a man like Étienne Brulé, who at the age of eighteen came to Champlain in 1610 and explained that "he would like to go to the Algonquins, to learn their language." Champlain was glad to support this plan, which would enable the young man to find out a great deal about the nature of the country and to explore it as far as the "Great Lake" (Lake Huron). The young man actually lived for some years among the savages, particularly the Hurons, learned the languages of several tribes, and explored far and wide on his own initiative.

When in 1615 Champlain was assisting the Hurons in a war against their permanent plaguers, the Iroquois, he sent Brulé to call the Andaste tribe out onto the warpath. The Hurons failed to capture the great Iroquois stockade deep in the forests and Brulé arrived after their withdrawal. He could only withdraw likewise with his Indian friends, and he sojourned at first in their villages near the source of the Susquehanna—the scene of Cooper's immortal *Deerslayer*. Clad in Indian garb, he traversed vast territories untrodden by the foot of a white man. Then he set out for the coast, following the Susquehanna and traversing the present states of Pennsylvania, Maryland, and Virginia till he reached the sea. He thus discovered a waterway from the region of the Great Lakes to the Atlantic which did not involve the difficulties of the Saint Lawrence.

Before he could get back to his Huron friends, Brulé was set upon by Iroquois, managed to escape, and wandered about in the wilderness until, half starved, he decided that his only hope of survival was to make straight for an Iroquois village. His enemies showed not the least sign of hospitality: "They fell upon me, tore my nails with their teeth, burned me with red-hot stakes, and pulled the hairs of my beard out one by one." When he no longer had a grain of hope left, a terrible thunderstorm suddenly broke out—apparently on his command—and frightened the savages so much that they hastily loosed his bonds, tended his wounds, and led him in safety to the territory of the Hurons.

While the French continued to explore new regions during the succeeding years, their position in Canada was rendered precarious by the political weakness of the mother country. Along the Hudson and the neighboring rivers, Dutch merchants established themselves firmly and wrested a large slice of the trade with the natives by undercutting the French prices. Canada was captured by British pirates in 1628, but was returned to France when a king of England happened to be short of money; for when his wife, the French king's sister, received her considerable dowry, which had been withheld, in cash, Canada returned to France. That was the first occasion on which the sovereign rights of a state were obtained by payment, but the New World later provided several examples of how considerable territorial changes can be brought about without shedding a drop of blood, as when Louisiana, Florida, and Alaska were acquired for money.

But leaving out high politics, the French Canadians pushed farther and farther into the unknown. Brulé reached Lake Superior (the greatest fresh-water lake in the world) and later discovered fertile country to the north of Lake Erie, which he described with enthusiasm. But he was killed in 1632 by the tomahawks of his onetime friends, the Hurons.

ENGLISH SHIPS OF THE EARLY SEVENTEENTH CENTURY

Champlain, the great pioneer, died in 1635; before his death he handed on important missions to the backwoodsman Jean Nicolet. The latter, hoping to reach the Pacific and perhaps even China, carried with him through the forests a ceremonial robe of Chinese damask embroidered with gay flowers and buds; it was not in China that he put it on, but when he reached Lake Michigan and visited the Winnebagos who lived on Green Bay. Wearing his finery and with his pistols spitting thunder and lightning, he found it easy to play the part of Wakontanka, the Spirit King, and bring the terrified savages to submission.

Nicolet pushed on westward to the Wisconsin and was told he was close to the "Great Water"; this was surely the Pacific, and he turned back so as not to fall into Spanish hands. At that point he was only three days' journey from the Water, which was, however, not an ocean but a mighty river, the "Mich Sipi": and so he failed by a touch to discover the Mississippi.

During the next few years the activities of the Canadian pathfinders were halted, for the great Iroquois war broke out. In the spring of 1642 they captured the Jesuit Father Jogues, who on his tireless missionary and exploratory journeys had traveled as far as the Sioux country. The Iroquois tortured him for a whole year by every practice of their devil's craft and made him perform the most menial services as their slave. They took him along on one of their journeys to the fishing-grounds of the Hudson, and some Dutchmen whom they met bought from them this wreck of a human being. As soon as he was restored to health, the courageous Father immediately took up his missionary work again—and right in the lions' den at that, among the Iroquois themselves. Here he was struck down from behind with a war club as he was entering a hut.

From then on it was impossible to maintain friendly relations with the Iroquois for a long time to come. Between 1643 and 1663 almost without a break they were on the warpath, barring the Ottawa—sometimes for years at a time—crossing the Saint Lawrence, overrunning all the tribes that were friendly to the whites, burning and plundering, tying Hurons and missionaries to the martyr's stake, scalping and murdering them. They exterminated the Indian tribes from Lake Michigan to the Tadoussac, drove the pitiful remnants of reds and whites before them till they sought safety in Quebec or Montreal, and would eventually have settled the fate of "New France" had not their bloody campaigns proved too costly; in the summer of 1653 they were so exhausted by their losses that the French colony was granted a breathing-space till the spring of 1658, which saved it from destruction.

During this interval the French, undeterred, started on new reconnaissances. Several thousands of Hurons and Ottawas had wandered to the Mississippi and thence on to Lake Superior in their flight before the dread Iroquois. In their company were Médart Chouart, who called himself the Sieur de Groseilliers, and his brother-in-law, Pierre Esprit Radisson. These two arrived in Montreal, by way of Lake Huron, French River, and Ottawa, with—to the great joy of their countrymen—a huge fleet of sixty canoes heavily laden with valuable furs, and three hundred warriors to boot.

RAFFEIX MAP OF THE GREAT LAKES. *Atlas of the Historical Geography of the U.S.*,
CARNEGIE INSTITUTE OF WASHINGTON

But, as the future was to show, the two backwoodsmen were worth far more than a cargo of furs. Radisson had turned himself from a European into a child of the wilderness; the Iroquois had captured him at the very outset of his career and adopted him. Later he ran away, but they got him back again; finally the Dutch on the Hudson bought him into freedom. He was very scornful of his white compatriots, whom he found better at boasting than at forcing a way through the primeval forests of Canada. Said Radisson: "Is there a better defense work than a good tongue, especially when a man can see the smoke of his own chimney or can kiss his wife or his neighbor's wife at leisure? It is a very different matter when the very means of subsistence are lacking, and when one has to labor hard for whole days and nights and has to lie on the hard ground. Sometimes one stands with one's backside in water, has fear in one's belly, an empty stomach, tired bones, and a great desire to sleep possessing one's whole body. And all of it in evil weather which must be borne, for it is an affliction against which there is no protection."

After many years of indefatigable hunting, tracking, and fighting, packed with adventures, perils, and trading coups, the two Sieurs found out how to avoid the unbearable efforts so many had till now rashly incurred. They discovered that there was a great sheet of water, Hudson Bay, which could be reached from the region of the Great Lakes, and that from it the fur cargoes could be carried to the ocean in big ships. The penetration to Hudson Bay from the interior and the recognition of its possibilities forged the link between the pioneering ventures of Hudson and Champlain and shaped the future of Canada once for all.

A pigheaded French governor, who did nothing but put administrative difficulties in the way of the two backwoodsmen and once even commandeered their fleet of canoes with its cargo of skins, angered them to such an extent that in 1668 they entered the service of the more farsighted English, who then sent two ships to Canada: one under the command of Radisson, whom head winds prevented from reaching his destination, the other under Groseilliers, who, when he anchored in James Bay at the end of August, was the first to steer a ship into those waters since Hudson's tragic death. In 1670 the Hudson's Bay Company [3] was established and, to the disgust of the French, soon began to control the fur trade, to remain in secret but powerful control of it for two hundred years.

The obstruction of a hidebound governor in the north was counterbalanced by French pluck in a southerly direction. The eternal lure of the passage to the Pacific was still present, and this caused a new and energetic governor, the Comte de Frontenac, to send out in his service an explorer named Louis Jolliet. With him went the fearless Jesuit priest Jacques Marquette, one of the many brothers of his Order whose contributions to the exploration of the continent were to add far greater luster to their names than their missionary successes among the Indians. After a severe winter on Lake Michigan the two set out together at the end of May 1673, sailed down the Wisconsin, and a few weeks later committed their fortunes to the impressive Mississippi, though the Indians had uttered insistent warnings of fearsome monsters that would undoubtedly swallow up their canoes and the men in them.

But while the daring explorers were on one occasion scared by a sudden piercing caterwaul, their experiences were at first quite pleasant; they were as charmed by the varied landscape, alternating between prairies and wildwoods, as they were astonished at the richness of fowl, fish, red deer, and fruit, and, above all, at the sight of huge herds of buffalo grazing on the lush grassland.

The swift stream bore them rapidly down the ever broadening river, while thick swarms of mosquitoes plagued them day and night. Jolliet was disappointed to find that the river flowed on and on to the south—his hopes of reaching the Chinese Ocean evaporated daily.

One day a huge stream coming from the west joined theirs and mingled its yellowish clayey waters and dangerous driftwood with the Mississippi's clear course. It was the Missouri joining the Mississippi in a seemingly endless waste of waters.

Jolliet had the notion that the new, mightily rolling tributary

[3] To this very day the company bears the romantic name of "The Governor and Company of Adventurers of England trading into Hudson's Bay."

could lead to the missing ocean—but the first job was to reconnoiter the double river, with its swarm of islands, its insect-ridden swamps and lagoons, its shimmering heat, and its lurking alligators.

Another great river came pouring into the Mississippi: the Arkansas. Here they finally came upon people, an Indian tribe, and learned that a day or two downstream lived unfriendly natives and unfriendly white men: the Spaniards. From their reports Jolliet at once realized where the river led—not the Pacific, but the Gulf of Mexico. These were the waters that the luckless conquistador de Soto had traveled and named Río del Spiritu Santo. So there was nothing left but to turn back and fight their way home by sheer paddling labor yard by yard against the current of the longest river in the world.

Bitter as was this disappointment, the knowledge that the Mississippi did not flow into the Pacific gave the immediate impetus to some intelligent and far-reaching plans taking shape in the mind of René Robert Cavelier, Sieur de La Salle—a man misprized by his contemporaries but honored by posterity. For his ideas were far ahead of the times and, indeed, brought nothing but heartbreak to their originator till his tragic death.

La Salle, who began his career in the New World as a fur-trader and got involved in an ever deepening imbroglio of business deals, was deep in debt. Possessed of the unhappy, melancholy temperament of his age, he often seemed to be hovering on the borderline of madness, dealt clumsily with the Jesuits, and made enemies everywhere; but he saw the only chance of making France mistress of all America. This was to lay down a chain of forts stretching from the Saint Lawrence to the Gulf of Mexico and taking in the rear the slowly developing English and Dutch settlements right through the continent. Such a lifeline in the interior could not fail to bind the whole of the trade with the Indians to France and make her position in America utterly unassailable. Unfortunately, Louis XIV, failing to see what a priceless colonial empire was there for the taking, preferred to waste his powder on the limelit battlefields of Europe. Nonetheless, he issued a patent giving La Salle the right "to explore the western part of New France, where a way can probably be found to Mexico," to build forts, and to carry on trade along the Mississippi with a five-year monopoly; but that was all, and there was no sign of the necessary funds for either the Sieur or Canada, under its Governor Frontenac, to establish a colonial empire.

La Salle tried to carry out his plans unsupported, and so began a tragedy. To start with, he improved on the old canoe method by building a solid freighter, the *Griffin*, which he loaded with valuable furs and sent to Canada by way of the Lakes in order to keep his creditors quiet. Then he began his preparations for the great voyage down the Mississippi, following in Jolliet's tracks and paddling and marching with his men down the Illinois right through the territory of the rebellious Miamis. On the banks of the Illinois he founded a fort to which he gave the defamatory name of Crève-Cœur—"Fort Heartbreak"—which was soon to prove a bad omen.

As there was no news of the *Griffin* (which had sunk somewhere on the way), La Salle, greatly concerned, eventually set out with six Frenchmen to look for his ship. And this was in March! Through ice, melting snow, and slush they footed it, through forests and marshes, carrying on their backs heavy leather packs, out of which new soles or entirely new moccasins had to be fashioned every evening. They were continually on the watch for the roving Iroquois, and their only food was maize—without which indestructible and easily carried grain the exploration of thinly populated North America would have had to be postponed many a long day. They traveled in a canoe of their own making to the site of the present-day Detroit, past Niagara, and without a halt on through the heaviest rains to Cataraqui at the mouth of the Saint Lawrence—a marvelous feat. But all in vain: of the *Griffin* they found no trace. La Salle had covered a thousand miles in sixty-five days, only to meet, at Fort Frontenac, with tidings to try a Job: the *Griffin* had foundered, an even more valuable supply ship from France had been lost at sea, his property had been impounded by his creditors.

La Salle did not allow the news to discourage him. Soon afterward he was in Montreal and there received further disastrous news: the garrison of "Heartbreak" had mutinied. He hurried to the place, only to meet another stunning blow. The fort had been burned to the ground and the whole valley laid waste by the Iroquois.

LA SALLE'S LANDING IN TEXAS. FROM HENNEPIN

Even this did not defeat La Salle. After two years of preparation, just nine years after the journey of Jolliet and Marquette, he started out with a fleet of canoes on the great venture down the Mississippi. On April 9, 1682, he reached its mouth.

They sang the hymn "Vexilla Regis" and a Te Deum; then La Salle erected a cross and a column bearing the arms of France, into whose keeping he now took all the territories from the river's source in the icy north to its delta in the sweltering south. To this area he gave the name Louisiana, in honor of the Sun King, Louis XIV, and the name has survived in the southern corner of that gigantic plain.

After a return journey involving heroic labors La Salle founded Fort Saint-Louis on the Illinois to protect his realm; but there had also to be a permanent base at the river mouth if his work was to endure.

Now at last La Salle managed to obtain support at the French court at Versailles; this enabled him to leave France on July 24, 1684, with four ships and two hundred men—soldiers and colonists —to found a settlement sixty miles above the Mississippi's mouth, between Florida and Mexico.

Unfortunately, the captain in command, one Beaujeu, was a difficult character. While La Salle lay seriously ill, Beaujeu, instead of sailing on a direct course, circumnavigated Cuba, with the result that La Salle lost his bearings and was unable to find the mouth of the Mississippi. After cruising about for some time they came in sight of a coast and later the mouth of a river. It was the Río Colorado, which debouches six hundred miles west of the Mississippi in the fever-ridden marshes of Texas. La Salle went ashore with his men, but hardly were they over the side when Beaujeu was up and away without even allowing time for the cannon, muskets, and powder to be unloaded.

Cut off from the whole world, La Salle's settlement on the spot eked out a miserable existence till it perished. Twice in the first two years he started out on important reconnaissances. His companions succumbed to starvation and hardships in the swampy, magnolia-starred thickets, died of fever and snakebite, fell victims to tomahawks and alligators. From both journeys La Salle returned alone.

In the hope of saving the remnant of forty-five suffering specimens of misery to which his company had now shriveled, he conceived the crazily courageous plan of a forced march to Montreal to fetch help—twenty-five hundred miles through unknown wilderness, endless prairies and llanos, untracked forests and poisonous swamps, without provisions, the necessary firearms, or so much as a map!

With a few companions La Salle set out on January 7, 1687, from the devilish Matagorda Bay, crossed the Brazos and San Jacinto at high water, and reached the Trinity River, where he met his fate. A group of his men, weary of his remorseless energy, murdered him from behind during a hunting-expedition, stole his clothes, and left his body lying in the undergrowth. The murderers joined a tribe of Indians, but his brother, Jean Cavelier, continued the march and was able to reach the safety of a blockhouse near the mouth of the Arkansas, where two French backwoodsmen were living.

As soon as Henry de Tonti, the commandant of Crève-Cœur, heard of La Salle's death, he started off in spite of the unfavorable time of year. He made his way from the post in Arkansas to the Red River, searched many months for the body of the unlucky Sieur, and made endless inquiries of the Indians. When at last his provisions ran out, he had to withdraw from that inaccessible region without having accomplished his purpose. His report closes with the words: "In short, in my life never have I suffered as on this journey." And so upon the dark end of La Salle, a man hunted by jealous deriders, debtors, and foes, there falls the solitary ray of a comrade's human dignity and fellowship.

Even after La Salle's death the French did incomparably more for the exploration of the continent than all the other nations put together. Their backwoodsmen pushed forward up the Ohio and the Tennessee and reached South Carolina in 1699. During the next century they pressed on westward to the Rocky Mountains; it was Varennes who discovered Lake Winnipeg in 1734, and his sons, following the course of the Assiniboine and the upper Missouri, also reached that range.

But there was a great difference between discovery and possession. In the Seven Years' War, Prussians, Austrians, Frenchmen, and Russians struggled with one another till Frederick II conquered and retained Silesia; and in the forests of the New World there were also a few skirmishes between frontiersmen and Indians. But the conclusion of peace brought a twist in world his-

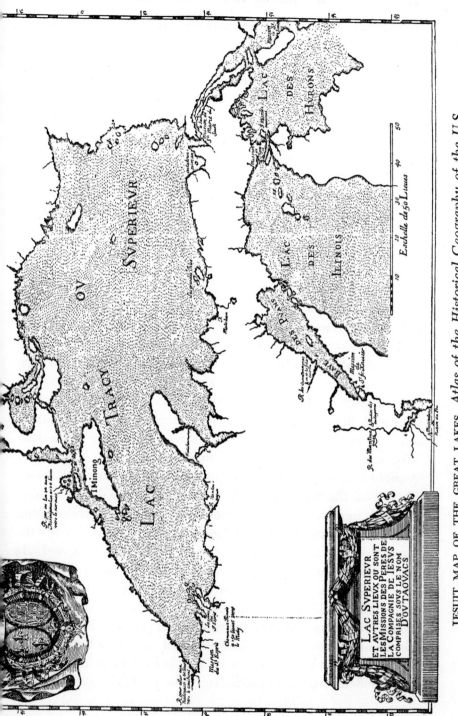

JESUIT MAP OF THE GREAT LAKES. *Atlas of the Historical Geography of the U.S.,*
CARNEGIE INSTITUTE OF WASHINGTON

tory, for the French were compelled to cede their American possessions to England.

The Anglo-Saxon colonists who were to be the possessors of North America undertook no great solitary journeys on the French pattern, but pressed slowly forward in numbers and on a broad front; settlers followed hard on the heels of the explorers. The dense forests and high hills of the Appalachians, populated by warlike Indian tribes, for a long time constituted an impassable barrier between the eastern coastal areas and the heart of the continent, but after the Seven Years' War the movement to the Missouri and Mississippi basins set in. Even after the American War of Independence, however, the greater part of the continent remained unexplored.

The opening up of America, when it came, was not due to isolated personalities of great fame, but to innumerable unknown adventurers, explorers, hunters, trappers, traders, slayers of Indians, and settlers; it was, in fact, the work of all those pioneers who, in the steps of Christopher Gist, crossed the fourfold heights of the Alleghenies and who, somewhere between the Monongahela, the Kanawha, and the Ohio, surrounded by spiteful Wyandots, Lenapes, and Shawnees, sought for cultivable settler's land —or who, in order to be free of such burdensome objects as taxes and supervision, moved south into the fertile valleys of the Holston and Clinch. Indeed, when in 1768 the British government wanted to fence in these restless souls and put a barrier between them and the wilderness, the outraged backwoodsmen crossed the hills in droves, made for the "dark, bloody" Kentucky lands, and followed the trail of that lonely explorer Daniel Boone (the prototype of "Leatherstocking") as he moved ever westward. He had known Kentucky in its unspoiled natural state: the green cane, high as a man's head, the groves and coppices of hickory, white elms, oaks, date plums, sugar acorns, and sycamores, the countless herds of elks and bison, the wolf packs and black bears, the teeming flocks of parrots, doves, quail, eagles, and turkeys, the lynxes and the pumas. Later he had helped to defend settlers' posts in fierce wars with the Indians, had lived as a prisoner of the

Shawnees in Chillicothe, had once again rescued the land from swarms of attacking Indians, had seen the population grow in five short years from 198 to nearly 20,000 who shot the wild creatures down without let or hindrance. Then, plagued by speculators, lawyers, and underlings, at the age of sixty, a legendary figure— exactly as in the "Leatherstocking" stories—he pressed on through the Indian hunting-grounds into the prairies beyond the Ohio and wandered ever farther west. Along the Green River, the Cumberland, the Tennessee, and the Mississippi he roved and, in the end, pursued by the madding crowd who left him no peace, moved on into the wide savannas of Louisiana, where Spanish subjects gave him a broad stretch of land. Even there he found no rest, for the settlers came hard on his heels, so he went on to the Osage River. Still living the life of a hunter and explorer, ever and again mixed up in wars with the Indians, he even managed a journey of some hundreds of miles through forests and across prairies at the age of eighty-two.

During Boone's century North America had altered fundamentally from an unknown wilderness where danger lurked at every step, to a much-prized area of colonial enterprise in which rush tactics, initiative, and a keen business sense reigned supreme. But there were still unexplored regions, and the link between ocean and ocean was yet to be forged.

Strangely enough, for centuries the exploration of America, once it had been discovered, was still governed by the same yearning that had sent Columbus out onto the wide ocean. His aim had been to find the way to Asia's treasures; once it became obvious that another continent barred the way, the search turned to the discovery of a passage through it. Columbus had failed, Solís, Ojeda, and many another had sought in vain. Magellan had found a useless route, Cook had been caught in the ice, Hudson had perished tragically, John Smith had been continually urged to find the way through, Champlain and the French woodsmen had gone well on the road to it—all to no purpose, for what does not exist (at least not in the desired shape) cannot be found. All these labors had resulted in so great an improvement of geographical knowledge that the days of chasing a mirage were over. But no one had yet succeeded in crossing the continent from sea to to sea anywhere outside the Spanish sphere of influence. Now a new and pressing reason had presented itself for doing so at the first possible moment. It was the unheard-of wealth of America's fur resources, not valuable spices or fabulous Indian treasures, that provided the final impulse.

It had remained uncertain for a long while after the discovery of America whether the New World was really a separate continent or whether it was joined somewhere at its northern tip to the Euro-Asiatic land mass. The Cossack Simon Ivanov Dezhnev tried to solve the riddle when in 1648 he sailed in boats from the mouth of the Kolyma through the Arctic Ocean, round the most easterly cape of Asia (which later received his name) to the Gulf of Anadyr in the Pacific. In this way he proved that Asia and America were separated, but his discovery was not published till, in the eighteenth century, Vitus Bering rediscovered Dezhnev's sea route first in the archives of Jakutsk and later by retracing it at sea.

Although Bering did not know how broad the strait was which bears his name, he had no doubt that the distance to America was trifling. After living down a period of displeasure at the Tsar's court, he obtained sufficient financial support to enable the *St. Peter*, under his own command, and the *St. Paul* under Tschirikov to sail in pursuit of his plans. Both ships reached the Pacific coast of America, though at widely different points. Bering died of scurvy on the voyage, but it resulted in an unexpected success, for the Russians found immense quantities of the two most beautiful furs in the world, Alaska seal and sea otter. Russia immediately set up supply posts on the Aleutians and Bering Island; they made the natives produce the valuable furs for them, and by the middle of the century the world was wide-eyed with astonishment at the vast quantities of furs which Russian traders were selling in China. The Russians had discovered a new treasure house in the northern Pacific and on the west coast of America, and there was an immediate rush of Spaniards, Dutch, and Frenchmen as well as of English merchants from China and India and American traders to the area. But on the continent itself the hostile powers in possession took every possible measure to prevent a Russian expansion into America.

Among the Spaniards in the south the spirit of the conquistadors flared up once more, if rather belatedly. To the north of them lay California, straight in front of their noses, a dry, mountainous country with a narrow span between its coasts, and in it there was supposed to be a mythical city called Quivira. In 1603 the navigator Sebastián Vizcaíno had been sent to find it, but had failed; instead, he discovered the sheltering Monterey Bay. At the end of the century German Jesuits (the Fathers Eusebius Kino, Jakob Sedlmayr, and Wenzeslaus Link) accomplished missionary journeys into the rocky valleys between Altar and Gila which laid the preparations for the great advance to northern California and the coast; this was eventually undertaken in 1796 by José de la Sonora Gálvez, inspector general of New Spain, in the course of two land and three sea expeditions intended to forestall the Russians in San Diego and Monterey.

The Spaniards, under Fernando de Rivera and Gaspar de Portolá, marched through sandy deserts, thorn bush, and bouldery wastes to San Diego and thence to Monterey, where they arrived after months of continuous scrambling up and down hills. But even then they were not where they wanted to be, for nowhere on the whole bay could they find the harbor they were looking for. So they decided to risk the hardships of marching still farther and reached a bay that they thought at first was Drake Bay. Actually it was a great unknown harbor, past whose entrance—the Golden Gate—ships had till now sailed unsuspecting of its existence. The city that the Spaniards afterward founded there was given the name San Francisco.

Up in the north, where Canada reverted to the English after the Seven Years' War, they were determined at last to reach the Pacific. In 1781 Alexander Henry set out in a memorandum (which contained some errors) the possibilities of so doing and also the advantages that must accrue to the fur trade. Ever since Cook's last voyage the desire to cross the continent had grown stronger; and when Peter Pond, the explorer, who had set up a station on Lake Athabaska and bagged an unexpected haul of valuable furs,

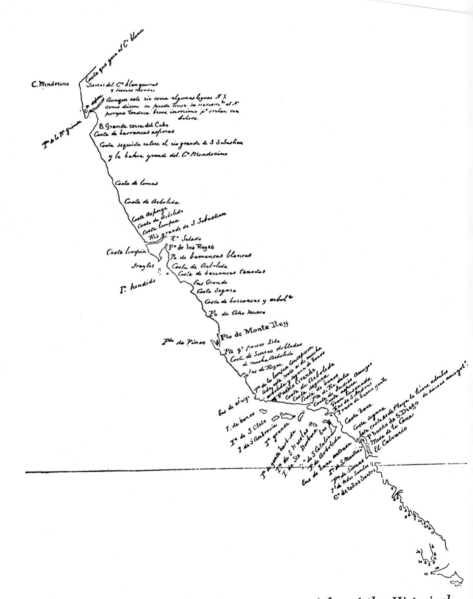

VIZCAÍNO'S MAP OF THE CALIFORNIA COAST. *Atlas of the Historical Geography of the U.S.,* CARNEGIE INSTITUTE OF WASHINGTON

reported that reliable Indians who had been to the Pacific coast said a Russian factory had already been built there, it seemed high time to do something decisive.

The Merchant Company of Montreal chose twenty-four-year-old Alexander Mackenzie, who much preferred the role of explorer to that of fur-trader, to carry out this mission. Mackenzie spent a whole winter with the aged Pond at his station on Lake Athabaska; then, in the summer of 1788 he built Fort Chippewyan as a base for his expedition and after the most detailed preparations set out on June 3, 1789, on the first of his two great journeys, which were to unmask the geographical secrets of northwestern America. With a few companions, whom his restless energy compelled into a number of tight corners, he paddled with great speed down the swift-flowing Slave River to the Great Slave Lake, which fortunately began to thaw the day after his arrival, June 10.

Threading their way from island to island through racing shoal water, the little bark canoes adventured across the lake's three-hundred-mile-long and fifty-mile-broad waters under the heavy spring storms. On its north bank, after six days of toilsome search, he discovered the river, later to bear his name, by which he hoped to reach the Pacific. Progress along it was easy, but on the morning of July 2 Mackenzie's hopes were dashed: the river, meeting a high, rocky range (the Mackenzie Mountains), turned away to the north.

The farther they went, the less prospect there was of reaching the ocean. The Indians on the bank stared amazed at the pale-faced apparitions and only by gifts could they be lured into approaching. They gave warnings of horrible monsters lurking downstream. One of the chiefs said: "It takes several years to reach the sea, and it is as old men that ye will return."

Where did the river really end? The country grew barer and barer, the Indians lived almost exclusively on fish and rabbits and went in great fear of Eskimos. But Mackenzie needed no years for his journey. He reached the sea on July 10, a matter of days—but it was the Arctic Ocean, by which, had not ice utterly forbidden any progress, he would in any case have been more likely to reach the North Pole than the Pacific.

So, in order to avoid being caught by the polar winter, he had to turn back. When, after a journey lasting 102 days, Mackenzie arrived at Chippewyan, he had covered about 2,750 miles by canoe, had measured and mapped Canada's second-longest river —but had failed to reach his objective. However, his second journey, which brought him fame, ended in success.

But first, dissatisfied with his scientific results, he returned to England to study surveying and geography, and to provide himself with the best scientific instruments. After deciding on his new route and siting a more satisfactory base at the junction of the Peace and Smoky rivers, 250 miles farther west than Chippewyan, he set out on his second great canoe journey on May 9, 1793. During the same month he almost came to grief in the eddies and cascades of the Peace River, but he and his woodsmen succeeded in defeating this dangerous sector by breakneck climbing among the rocky canyon walls, with their canoes on their backs. In June, after a toilsome journey up the Parsnip, Mackenzie learned that the Fraser did not, as he had hoped, flow down to the sea but became impassable farther down and then swung away from the ocean in a great bend. So that was that!

But Mackenzie did not give in. Although his expedition was in no way equipped for it and in spite of the refusal of the local Indians to act as guides—they were afraid of the coastal tribes, whose association with Russian fur-traders was doing them no good—he set out on a cross-country march that meant each man had to carry a load of from seventy to ninety pounds on his back. They climbed and marched for fifteen days. On the evening of July 19 they stood, at last, on the shore of the Pacific.

A few weeks earlier, another explorer had surveyed this coast from the sea, but Mackenzie failed to decipher the "Macubah" of the Indians' report as a jumbled version of George Vancouver's name. Vancouver had first entered North American waters as one of Cook's companions and had later explored the whole coastline from southern California to Alaska.

The Indians were openly hostile, but, in spite of the nervous tension, Mackenzie was not satisfied till he had taken precise observations of latitude and longitude by day and night over the course of a week. After exciting experiences, he got back to his base on August 24—the first European to have crossed America. Then, at the age of thirty, he abandoned his work as an explorer and settled in Montreal; it was only by gradual degrees that the world learned of his remarkable feat. Thanks to his journeys, the maps of North America were vastly enriched, and all over the world men began to read his account—*Voyages on the River St. Lawrence and through the Continent of North America,* a work as full of keen comments as of attractive descriptions of nature. His renown spread as fur-traders and geographers followed in his tracks. He died in 1820, famous as the man who had not only completed the work of the great navigators but had also proved that the passage they had sought lay not upon the waters but overland.

Taking into consideration the immense difficulty of traversing the rough and icy terrain of North America, it is easy to understand why the push forward to the Pacific coast was achieved at a comparatively late date. But for us today it remains an astonishing thought that as late as the start of the last century the huge tract beyond the Mississippi was a wilderness almost as unknown as in Columbus's day.

Since 1787 an American fur trade had developed on the Pacific coast alongside the Russian; its center lay at the mouth of the newly discovered Columbia River. In 1803 President Jefferson set preparations in motion for creating an overland link with the Pacific coast. Yet another development favored the exploration of the unknown region. Louisiana, the large tract of country at the Mississippi mouth which had been under the suzerainty of a declining Spain, had gone over to France. Jefferson managed, by buying Louisiana, to almost double the area of the United States. Napoleon, who needed money urgently for his campaigns and had not the slightest conception of the value of this possession far across the seas, sold it for sixty million francs—about four cents an acre. This was the last time that a decision taken in Europe effected a great territorial change in the New World, which henceforth struck out on its separate existence.

Jefferson had no real idea of what he had bought, and the expe-

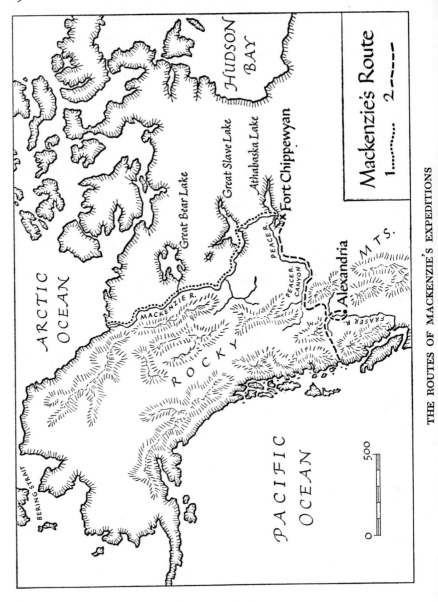

THE ROUTES OF MACKENZIE'S EXPEDITIONS

dition sent to explore the land to the mouth of the Columbia was therefore all-important to him. It was placed under the command of Jefferson's former private secretary, Meriwether Lewis, and William Clark, a young man who had distinguished himself in the wars against the Indians; they were instructed to follow the Missouri to its source, cross the mountain range beyond, and then find the best waterway to the Pacific. This venture in a wilderness untrodden by any white man was carried to a successful conclusion in spite of all its perils, thanks to meticulous preparations and extremely careful methods. Of the team Lewis and Clark had trained with great thoroughness for six months, only one man was lost.

The expedition left the mouth of the Missouri at the end of August 1804, moved slowly upstream, and wintered in the territory of the Mandans. Here Lewis had the luck to make the acquaintance of a person who later contributed materially to the party's success. This was Sacagawea, an Indian woman of the Shoshone tribe who had married a Canadian trapper.

On April 9, 1805, they proceeded on their way in hollowed tree trunks. Below the Missouri falls they met with serious difficulties, having to drag the boats through shallow water in long periods of chilling rain. "The men often laboured standing up to their shoulders in icy water and groped their way forward over spiky rocks."

Lewis, the ex-secretary, who had been sent out one day on reconnaissance, had the good fortune to become the discoverer of the Missouri falls and the first to enjoy "the sublime spectacle of this stupendous object, which since the Creation had been lavishing its magnificence on the desert, unknown to civilisation."

It took thirty days of great exertion to master the ten-mile stretch of rapids. The party was menaced day and night by grizzly bears and rattlesnakes reluctant "to yield their dominion over the neighbourhood."

On August 10 Lewis, sent ahead to reconnoiter with three woodsmen in Shoshone territory, reached the continental watershed. As they climbed a steep path "the stream gradually became smaller, till after going two miles it had so greatly diminished in width that one of the men in a fit of enthusiasm, with one foot on each side of the river, thanked God that he had lived to bestride the Missouri."

After resting among the Shoshones for a fortnight, the expedition resumed its exhausting march through trackless mountains riven by gorges. Once they lost their way in a blizzard, suffering severely from hunger and sickness, and only just in time reached a plateau where they could recuperate. This was on September 20. From here, in cedarwood canoes of their own fashioning (using for the first time the Indian method of burning out the tree trunk, not hollowing it), they were able to start their journey down the Salmon River to the Columbia. Thanks to the skill of the Canadians, they steered through the seething rapids without a serious accident and finally reached the sea on November 15, suffering from seasickness, hunger, thirst, and cold. Utterly worn out, they worked through a continuous period of rain, hail, and snow to build a blockhouse, in which they spent the winter on insufficient food without salt, but with plenty of fleas they had brought with them from the Indian villages.

On its return across the divide and down the Yellowstone and Missouri to Saint Louis, where they arrived in September 1806, the expedition delivered a mass of new knowledge which paved the way for the final geographical exploration of this new region of America. Lewis and Clark had found the link between the basins of the Mississippi and the Columbia; but it was not known till much later what efforts it had cost them both. Lewis died on his journey home from Saint Louis. Clark was overwhelmed by so many different kinds of work that it was 1814 before an edition of their reports was published by Nicholas Biddle. For a more detailed look into the diaries of Lewis and Clark, the general public had to wait till 1904, when these were at last published—and then not in their complete form. In 1935, in two abandoned writing-tables in an attic in Saint Paul, Minnesota, were discovered sixty-seven books containing entries from December 1803 to April 1805, together with numerous maps and sketches that might perhaps have lost their novelty value after one hundred and thirty years, but had certainly acquired greater historical worth.

7

THE REDISCOVERY OF SOUTH AMERICA

O NE of the problems that have occupied the attention of geographers since time immemorial is the size of our planet. This, of course, demands great precision of measurement. The discoverer of the law of refraction, Professor Willebrord Snell van Royen, of Leyden (1580–1626), who called himself Snellius, executed the first measurements with his new method of triangulation, which permitted very exact results. The method consists of dividing the area to be measured into large basic triangles, whose corners are marked by stone pyramids, then subdividing these areas into smaller triangles, measuring the angles (which gives more accurate results than measuring the length), and working out the results. In 1671 Jean Picard adopted this method in France and put it to very successful use.

Jean Baptiste Colbert, Louis XIV's finance minister, was a patron of the sciences and was particularly interested in geographical exploration and survey. It is not surprising that he gave his interest a practical application in the direction of enlarging the French realm; at the end of his lifetime France still possessed Canada, the whole Mississippi basin, many West Indian islands, Guiana, strips of Africa's northwest coast, and the Island of Madagascar. Colbert founded the Academy of Science; this body saw the provision of precise measurements as one of its chief duties.

They began by producing first-class maps of France; the savants Picard and La Hire undertook the measurements, and later the famous Italian astronomer Cassini was added to the team. The work was completed in 1682. Incidentally, as a result of the precision of their astronomic observations, the amendment of the existing maps resulted in a reduction of France by two degrees longitude and three quarters of a degree latitude. Louis XIV playfully remarked to his astronomers: "I am sorry to see that your journey has cost me a large slice of my realm."

Next a sharp assault was made on the exact measurement of the whole globe. After Picard had undertaken the measurement of a degree between Corbeil and Amiens, in France, in order to facilitate the fixing of the earth's shape and size, a lively scientific argument resulted in the Academy sending out two expeditions to measure the length of a degree at two widely separated points on the earth's surface and so to allow of a comparison.

This purely scientific enterprise was, oddly enough, the start of an entirely new era in the history of exploration. It was no longer the call of far-off lands or a longing for adventure, nor the search for new trade routes or the hunt for wealth from gold or spices, nor the zeal to win new souls for Christendom, but the desire for purely scientific knowledge which now drew learned men, whose natures were very different from those of the mariner or the conquistador, across the seas and on through unexplored jungles, deserts, and primeval forests. They navigated dangerous rivers and climbed towering mountains, risking their lives without a thought of personal gain, covering thousands of miles for the sake of a millimeter's precision. With them, a new generation of discoverers came on the scene—men who could not rest because mankind's fund of knowledge was so pitifully small.

At the start of the eighteenth century Europe was bleeding itself white with wars concerned with the power of Louis XIV, with the Spanish succession, and with all sorts of other things that interested the masters on the thrones and shed the blood of their subjects. During one of these campaigns a French army was besieging the Spanish frontier town of Rosas. While the cannon were firing on the city with noisy roar, an eighteen-year-old French nobleman, Charles Marie de La Condamine, who had distinguished himself by various deeds of gallantry, was sitting in camp and listening to the tales of a Spanish prisoner. This hostage of war had just come back from the colonies oversea and could tell stories of the huge mountain range, the Andes, that skirts the whole length of the Pacific coast, of raging rivers, and impassable forests, of the marvelous palaces of the Incas. The young Frenchman had no idea at the time that one day he would see for himself all these legendary things that were then unapproachable for him, but what he heard bent his thoughts in a direction that was to influence heavily the future course of his life.

La Condamine, who was born in 1701, now devoted his interest to science, particularly to mathematics and their practical application to land measurement, and worked with tireless enthusiasm in this sphere. At the age of twenty-nine this gifted young scientist was elected a member of the Academy of Science and got his first chance to accompany an expedition to a foreign country. He made the fullest possible use of his mathematical and astronomical capacities along the African coast of the Red Sea and also on the ocean, and returned to Paris, after two adventurous years, as a famous scientist and organizer.

Among his friends was one of the most shining spirits of all time —Voltaire. This friendship provided Voltaire with a nice sum of money, and La Condamine with the chance of a lifetime.

La Condamine had met the famous philosopher when as a young man he attended a dinner given for a controller of finances who was on the point of organizing a lottery to replenish the city purse. At the table La Condamine, working on a precise calculation, advised Voltaire that there were too few tickets in the lottery, and that anybody who bought them all would make a handsome profit. Voltaire made a protest against the lottery; but when the officials would not hear his complaint, he bought all the tickets and won five hundred thousand francs.

Later Voltaire used all his influence with the Academy to ensure that La Condamine might contribute his share toward the settlement of the contentious problem about which the whole scientific world was then at fever heat—the shape of the earth. Scientists knew that it was not an exact globe, but what did it really look like? In England the great Newton claimed that it was flattened at the poles and swollen at the equator. This contention was of course correct (the earth's bulge at the equator amounts to about thirteen miles), but between the discovery of a correct scientific theory and its general acceptance there lies, in most cases, a bitter period of differences of opinion. Newton's theories —his views about the atmosphere as well as about the earth's shape—met with a particularly cool reception in Paris. For at this stage the followers of Cassini, who ruled the roost in Paris, were especially obstinate, seeing that Cassini had produced a very different theory.

Both parties kept on deploying new arguments. The dispute was carried on with great acrimony. Voltaire, who had been to London, energetically supported Newton's views against those of his countrymen, thereby setting a shining example and showing that it is unworthy of a great mind, occupied with the battle for the truth, to allow its views to be influenced by considerations of nationality. To the credit of the French savants, in spite of all the excitement and bitterness of the conflict (including highly defamatory utterances on both sides), they finally settled the question of the earth's shape in the way that becomes pure scientists —not by a battle to be won by the strongest, but by strenuous exertions to find a factual proof strong enough to compel general acceptance.

Such an objective proof could be obtained only by the most precise measurements. A degree had been measured in France; now it was proposed to measure one in the far north and one on the equator, in order to obtain a comparison. So an expedition was sent to Lapland under the leadership of Pierre Moreau de Maupertuis (1698–1759), a famous physicist who was later to become president of the Prussian Academy of Science in Berlin.

There was only one place where the other expedition could carry out its measurements on the equator. Equatorial Africa was still unexplored, Borneo a sealed book, the lower basin of the Amazon a swampy wilderness. Only the Audiencia de Quito (today's Ecuador) offered a suitable site for the work. Surprisingly, the King of Spain, on political considerations, gave his royal permission; this was the first time in the course of two hundred and fifty years that the ban on entry by foreigners into Central and South America had been lifted.

La Condamine used every means at his disposal to further this

venture. His good relations with the court and with Voltaire
played an important part; he threw a hundred thousand livres of
his own fortune into the pool; he offered to take along the nephew
of the Academy's treasurer (the same old story: whether it was
La Condamine, Columbus, or Stanley, somebody had to be taken
as a passenger for financial reasons); and eventually he obtained
an offer of leadership in an expedition that was to take him to a
country he had for years longed to visit.

When on May 16, 1735, the little party of astronomers, bota-
nists, and mathematicians sailed on board the French warship *La
Rochelle*, the history of America's discovery began all over again.
The book of the New World, which Columbus had first opened,
had been closed and sealed again by the political rulers, so that
the world in general had learned nothing of it. Now it was to be
reopened—and from this day South America became part of the
known world.

At Cartagena de las Indias, one of the most important tranship-
ment ports in the Spanish Empire, the expedition made its first
acquaintance with the marvels of this unknown continent—with
the flaming beauty of its exotic flowers, the scent of vanilla, the
blossoming balsams and acacias, the juicy pineapples, the cocoa
trees (that expensive treasure, for in Paris only the richest people
could afford to taste chocolate).

The strangers from Paris found not only nature, but the system
of government unfamiliar. It had bogged down in the Middle
Ages; the French were amazed to find that freedom of expression
in written word and speech did not exist. Alongside the temporal
examples stood that of the Tribunal of the Inquisition, unrivaled
in power and authority, which censored most rigorously every
expression of spiritual thought.

The explorers were treated with the greatest kindness and co-
operation by the Spanish administrative officials, who went so far
as to put two scientists at their disposal: Don Jorge Juan y Santa-
cilla and Don Antonio de Ulloa. These two were occasionally useful because of their knowledge of the country and its people, but
were much better at their real task of keeping a watch on the
others.

Then began a journey of many months into the interior to reach their objective. The delicate instruments had to be handled most carefully; in order to avoid mule transport, the expedition traveled as much as possible by waterways.

The first stage was one of 230 miles overland to Porto Bello, that fever-ridden spot that had so often been attacked by pirates because it was the key to invading the Spanish colonial empire; Hawkins, Drake, whose bones rested on the bottom of the sea somewhere hereabout, and especially Henry Morgan had left their mark on it. Then they traveled for two days in boats up the Río Chagres through jungle and forest that hemmed in the river like green walls. Another cross-country march took them to Panama, whence they took ships along the coast across Pacific waters to the province of Quito—but not till formalities and the delay in the ship's departure had consumed many weary weeks of waiting.

La Condamine landed at Manta to start measurements and make his way to Quito. The only member of the expedition who cared to accompany him on this difficult venture was Pierre Bouguer; the rest sailed on in the frigate to Guayaquil and set out from there on the road to Quito. Bouguer was a headstrong crank who deeply mistrusted La Condamine; he was more inclined to lean toward Cassini's followers than toward Newton's, and would have liked to carry out the measurements and calculations quite on his own. So they cannot have spent a very companionable time together.

They worked for a week or two in the desert of Manabí; the flat plains assisted their measurements, but continual fogs hindered their astronomical observations. At last, on March 26, 1736, the weather improved and they were able to observe the eclipse of the moon. This enabled them to fix the exact position of this most westerly point on the South American coast, and all the eighteenth-century maps of South America were based on this result.

When they traveled seventy miles farther north through the jungle and savanna country to Cape Pasado to start their observations and measurements on the equator itself, they made their first close acquaintance with some of the local pests. There were blood-sucking flies the size of a pin's head, which settled by the dozen on every unprotected expanse of skin; stingless bees that hung in their hair to absorb the sweat; and, at night, swarms of mosquitoes and cockroaches the size of mice. One of the worst trials was the *niguas,* insects about the size of a flea, which bored unnoticed into the soles of their feet and their toes and lodged deep under the skin.

But here La Condamine—who, unlike Bouguer, wanted to extend their stay—met with one of his pleasantest experiences, for Pedro Vicente Maldonado appeared on the scene and asked leave to join him. Maldonado, three years La Condamine's junior, was one of the most outstanding personalities the colony had ever produced. Educated at the Jesuit school in Quito, he had for years taken upon himself the hardships of exploring the jungles and deserts of his native land. In this way he had surveyed and mapped a considerable area of the Spanish colonial territories. His services to La Condamine, as a first-class observer, mathematician, and cartographer, backed by his knowledge of the country, its inhabitants, and the language of the Indians, were invaluable. It was due to the friendly collaboration of these two explorers, urged on by a common thirst for scientific knowledge, that La Condamine was able to push on into the inaccessible wilderness and later return to Europe with such exact information about South America.

They sent Bouguer to Guayaquil with the heavier instruments and thence by the usual way to Quito, while Maldonado showed La Condamine a hitherto untrodden route along the Río Esmeraldas which enabled him to familiarize himself with the heart of the tropical forests in all their beauty. There were brightly colored birds with sweet songs, jaguars, monkeys, alligators—much to remind him of Africa and much that was quite new—especially that rare elastic webbing that the natives called *caoutchouc.* La Condamine was fascinated as he watched the "milk" flowing from the trees and turning into rubber. He had a bag, impermeable by water, made from the material to protect his instruments.

Before this, Cortés had watched the Aztecs playing with hard rubber balls, and travelers since his time were familiar with rubber; Peter Martyr and the Spanish chronicler Juan de Torquemada had also described it, but these stories had awakened no echoes. So La Condamine became the modern discoverer of rubber, and his reports attracted the attention of Europe to it. He was the first to make scientific experiments with it and to bring samples of the valuable material home with him. After La Condamine's revelation of the value of rubber, a British botanist in 1786 smuggled several sacks of seed out of South America to London, whence thousands of young hothouse plants were taken to India, where they were planted with outstandingly successful results.

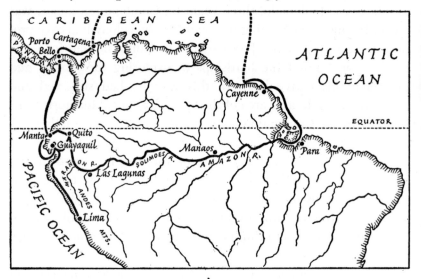

THE ROUTES OF LA CONDAMINE'S JOURNEYS IN SOUTH AMERICA

While La Condamine was establishing the course of the Esmeraldas, making preparatory observations for his equatorial triangulation, and collecting plants and mineral samples, he discovered another object of great value. This was a metal called *platina* by the natives; scientists in Europe, after exhaustive tests, recognized it as a precious element and christened it platinum.

The last part of the way to Quito demanded heavy exertion. From the Esmeraldas they had to scale the Andes, which rise many thousands of feet and inflict tremendous variations in temperature in a very short space of time. Rain poured down incessantly, soaking everything and turning the ground into slippery mud. The two explorers slipped, fell, got up again, stumbled onward, and sank deeper and deeper in the morass. The Indian porters who had come from the plains were allowed to go back from the three-thousand-foot level when the cold became too much for them.

Indian hillmen, not so happy and gay as the plainsmen, took the work on. Banana trees and palms gave way to Alpine trees, bushes, ferns, and mosses that covered the rainy, foggy landscape. At last they crossed the upper limit of vegetation. On June 4 La Condamine measured a height of thirteen thousand feet; he had singing sensations in his ears and could hardly keep pace with Maldonado.

After crossing the backbone of the range they came upon scattered hamlets and found it possible to hire horses. Near Quito the mists lifted, and La Condamine saw what he described as the most impressive and wonderfully beautiful sight in the world. Beyond the gray-green landscape fifteen snow-covered volcanoes leaped to the sky. He was gazing at the peaks of Imbabura, Cotacachi, Cayambe, and, beyond them, Altar, Corazón, Cotopaxi, and the greatest of them all, Chimborazo. Between the towers of Pichincha and Cotopaxi, down in the green valley of Anaquito lay a city—Quito. After nearly a year he had arrived at the point where he could set to work on his task.

The French scientists, reunited here, were amazed to find such fine and stately buildings in so remote a district; Quito was the largest and most impressive city they had seen since leaving home. Equally astonishing were the enthusiastic reception and the many celebrations in their honor; their arrival was the most sensational thing that had happened since 1546, when the first white woman came to Quito.

The difficulty now was to decide where to start operations. The huge cones of the volcanoes and the deep gorges were by no means an ideal terrain for survey work. They had to lay down a base line on which all the triangles would depend; this base line must be absolutely exact and had to be measured inch by inch with an iron measuring-rod. Where in such a district could they find a pitch of the necessary length with no inconvenient height differential in it?

It was Pedro Maldonado who solved the problem for them. On the plain of Yaquí, northeast of Quito, he found a suitable piece of ground, and there it was agreed to lay down the base line. Just before they got to work, the expedition suffered its first casualty; one of the team died of a serious attack of malaria in spite of the efforts of Dr. Jean Seniergues, the expedition's doctor.

The first job, which took several months, was the preparation of maps of the area in which it was proposed to measure the triangles. The base line itself was laid down by La Condamine, Maldonado, and the two Spaniards, Juan and Ulloa. On the bare, desert-like plateau the daytime heat was unbearable, but at night the temperature fell to freezing-point and cold winds swept over the plain. One after another, the explorers fell ill; one of the Indian attendants died, the others left the camp for a while. La Condamine had to summon up all his reserves of toughness to prevent the work from being interrupted.

New difficulties arose. A deputation from Quito visited the explorers to see close at hand what was going on, and they were amazed at what they saw. Measurements were being made with theodolites, octants, and measuring-rods; the foreigners were doing such incomprehensible and therefore suspicious things to the ground that there could be only one reasonable explanation—they must be looking for the buried treasure of the Incas.

The Governor of Quito immediately started to make difficulties; he had the explorers' servants questioned, sent inspectors to spy on the scientists, and interrupted the execution of the survey. In the end there was only one way out—to send La Condamine and Juan to the Viceroy in Lima and ask him to solve the dilemma. This gave La Condamine a chance to clear up some of the expedition's financial difficulties, and he therefore set out on a journey that took him on foot and on horseback and in a litter a thousand miles along the Andes and allowed him to see more of the continent than he had ever dared to hope.

In July 1737, after eight months' absence, he returned. The Viceroy had instructed the Governor not to interfere with the "Nature Philosophers," and so their important work was allowed to go on. In the meantime, the base line had been measured and all was ready for the triangulation—work that was to occupy years. They measured out a great number of triangles from the ends of the base line, northward to the town of Ibarra, southward toward Cuenca—a surface covering more than three degrees in a district demanding continual climbing over mountains.

With their theodolites, measuring-rods and chains, and other instruments, the explorers scrambled up high volcanoes, wandered over riven lava deposits, past craters, and across vast plains. They suffered from cold, driving storms of biting hail; they were hampered by mist and lack of provisions. Not a spot in the Ecuadorian Andes, a landscape that looked like the moon's surface, was left untouched. They surveyed, mapped, recorded temperatures, air pressures, magnetic deviation, the force of gravity, the speed of sound, and other data, suffered from sickness and internal dissensions that broke out in their seclusion from the world, and in June 1739 at last reached the town of Cuenca, about three degrees south of the equator.

They brought to Cuenca, four years after leaving Paris, a sensational result, quite beyond the comprehension of its inhabitants. Their tremendous efforts had solved the great controversy; their triangles had produced mathematical proof that Newton's theory was correct. Their fame would rest, in the history of the world's scientific progress, on having been the men who proved it.

And then they received a letter from the Academy in Paris. It explained politely that the expedition which had gone to Lapland under Maupertuis (which numbered the Swede Celsius among its scientists) had completed its task, had measured an arc of 57 minutes longitude, and had returned to the capital after eighteen months. Their contribution was the proof that Isaac Newton's theory was right: the earth is a spheroid flattened at the poles.

Gone with the wind was the fame of being the first in the field, in vain were all their afflictions and privations. The expedition wanted to break up; the disappointment was too bitter. What was there left for them to do?

In this critical situation La Condamine exhibited a greatness of human stature rarely equaled by the most famous heroic figures in history. True, it was too late to earn renown, but their scientific aims must be fulfilled without counting personal ambition or outward success. That was his contention, and he succeeded in keeping his colleagues together.

So they went on with the work. They were now engaged on the last triangle, and as one of its corners was the cathedral tower of Cuenca, they stayed in this town for some time.

Cuenca, with twenty thousand inhabitants, most of them Indians, was the second-largest city in the Audiencia de Quito. The explorers, after all their exertions, enjoyed the opportunity to rest in a house in this fairly poverty-stricken township, little suspecting what excitement awaited them.

For as time went by, a rumor had spread from tongue to tongue and with ever increasing force through the whole province that the strangers were looking for the treasure of the Incas and were preparing maps for the use of England, Spain's deadly enemy. The inhabitants of Cuenca showed particularly fierce hostility to the Frenchmen. Here, as elsewhere, ignorance bred enmity. Explanations of the true nature of the measurements were misunderstood, and at the best the explorers were thought to be crazy.

The situation was uncomfortable enough, but when Dr. Seniergues got mixed up in a local family quarrel it took a much worse turn. Among the patients whom he was in the habit of treating without payment was the old-established Queseda family, with a pretty twenty-year-old daughter, Manuela, who was engaged to a young man called Diego de León. As has so often happened before, with catastrophic results in little nests, the young man jilted his lady and married another. The Queseda family now enlisted the doctor's advice and assistance. As a polished man of the world, he was quite prepared to approach Diego and discuss compensation, for in so small a community Manuela now had no prospects of marriage. With such narrow issues at stake, it is not surprising that Diego regarded the proposal as an affront to his personal honor. He spread a rumor that Manuela was conducting an affair with the foreign doctor. This infuriated the doctor, and when he met Diego in the street he flew at him with his sword after an exchange of words. Bystanders disarmed both contestants, and from then on the doctor and his French colleagues incurred great hatred.

The quarrel between inhabitants and strangers grew more bitter and ended in tragedy when Dr. Seniergues attended a bullfight with Manuela and her father and was subjected to insults as soon as he had taken his seat in a box. Fierce recriminations roused the fury of the mob, which murdered the doctor before La Condamine and his companions could come to the rescue.

The explorers were compelled by the uproar to take refuge in a monastery, where a further tragedy occurred. The botanist Joseph de Jussieu lost his collection of plants, owing to the carelessness of his servants. He had spent five years of fiendish labor on his careful collection of the Andean flora and had gathered a treasure worth more than the gold of the Incas to the scientific world; and now it was all gone. This loss afflicted the unhappy scientist so severely that he went down with a nervous collapse and never really recovered his mental faculties.

When order had been restored, another unfavorable event hampered the expedition's progress: the two Spaniards, Juan and Ulloa, were summoned to Lima, war having broken out between Spain and England. Spain allowed only a single British ship to enter Porto Bello each year, so there was lively smuggling along the frontiers of the continent. If the Spaniards caught anyone at it, he did not find it amusing, and an example was Captain Robert Jenkins, in command of a merchant ship, who lost an ear while undergoing the usual torture. This resulted in a declaration of war.

Two British fleets were dispatched to attack South America. One, under Vice-Admiral Anson, captured Paita in Peru; then, avoiding further hostilities against the mainland, it rounded up a Spanish treasure fleet and sailed right round the world to return home with a booty of £500,000. The conquest of America had failed at the outset. The other fleet, under Admiral Vernon, which was intended to capture Cartagena, was repulsed. Greater than the famous Armada, it suffered heavy losses—half its ships and eighteen thousand men—and was forced to break off the encounter with Cartagena's weak garrison after fifty-six days. But the

balance of power had altered so fundamentally since the days of
the Armada that this defeat had no bearing on the world's history.
England's sea power remained unchallenged; she had only missed
the opportunity of conquering South America.

Naturally these events heightened the mistrust toward the
strangers from Europe who were still resident in the country.
There they had been for six years, measuring, mapping, experimenting with incomprehensible instruments; what was all this designed to conceal? A nobleman in Quito put the question this
way: "What could move men of decent standing to live so miserable, lonely, and laborious a life, traversing mountains and deserts
and observing the stars—unless there was some high payment at
stake?" And then a very alarming piece of news arrived: La Condamine and Maldonado were building pyramids bearing the emblem of the French lily and King Louis's arms, at the point between Baraburo and Ayambara where the base line was sited.
When Don Jorge Juan came back from Lima and heard these rumors he immediately went to establish their truth or falsity with
his own eyes.

Now, the Academy in Paris had ruled before the expedition's
departure that the basic measurement line should be marked by
such monuments of a permanent nature. La Condamine had attempted to carry out these instructions, ignoring the fact that the
moonlike cratered area was about as unsuitable as it could be for
the erection of such pyramids. He had to dig a canal to get water,
build a kiln to bake bricks, level the ground with planks, and
bring up wood from distant regions lower down to provide tablets
for the inscription.

The pyramids were completed after months of work. At that
moment the Spaniards arrived and were furious to discover that
the inscriptions did not include the names of the expedition's
Spanish members. His Catholic Majesty the King of Spain was not
even mentioned, and the French flag was flying from the top of
the monuments!

The differences between the two sides were at first the subject
of argument, but later of litigation. La Condamine defended himself skillfully against the Spaniards' charge; he was quite prepared

to alter the inscriptions, but, in defense of the disputable banner with its lilies, pleaded the close relationship between the French and Spanish royal houses.

The lawsuit dragged on for two years and the dissolution of the expedition could be delayed no longer, especially as another member had died when he fell from a scaffolding while helping with the building of a church. Now, after seven years of exhausting work, the party had to mourn three fatal casualties. Two more of the scientists were suffering from incurable nervous breakdowns, one had meanwhile accepted a post in the local administration, and two had married wives of the country.

But an astronomical observation to check the existing measurements was still lacking, and La Condamine decided to carry it out with the help of his old rival Bouguer.

In 1742 the court at last gave judgment. The names of the Spanish explorers must be added to the inscriptions and the fluttering lilies removed. The pyramids themselves were spared—but only for six years: then the Council for India, which considered the verdict too concessionary, ordered the pyramids destroyed. So the spirit of chauvinist narrow-mindedness celebrated one of its chief triumphs. Not till Ecuador was declared an independent republic was the replacement of the monuments sanctioned, and then the substitutes were not so solidly built as the originals.

With their work completed, Bouguer and La Condamine were at last free to return home. Their fortunes had aroused great interest—not only was there the excitement of La Condamine's early report, but a great deal of feeling had been aroused by the murder of the doctor and the row about the pyramids; moreover, public interest in the Spanish colonial empire in South America was growing.

Bouguer traveled to Cartagena and took the next ship home, but La Condamine undertook a very different journey. With two servants and a few mules, which had to carry a twenty-foot telescope, he left the Andes of Ecuador, made a detour to Cuenca, where, in spite of his depositions, the murderers of Dr. Seniergues were still at liberty, visited Loja, where he collected quinine plants and seeds to be planted in France, and reached the Amazon at Borjas. It was his intention to become acquainted with the whole thirty-five hundred miles of this mighty river's dangerous course.

Maldonado's elder brother was a Jesuit priest and, thanks to him, La Condamine had been able to establish contact with the brothers of his Order in Quito and obtain access to their secret archives. Among them he had seen a document of the highest scientific value, the first map of the Amazon. A priest, Samuel Fritz, had drawn it after spending twenty years in the Amazon basin, most of them on the river's lower reaches, where the Jesuits maintained numerous missions among the Indians. The holy father's map and diaries contained such a mass of important material that La Condamine was moved by them to want to produce a scientifically correct map of the river's course.

And now, after eight years of work in the Andes, he stood on the threshold of a new world full of wonders and riches that so far, like the rest of the continent, was hidden and unexplored.

A few hundred miles downstream he met Maldonado, who was to accompany him on his journey down the great river. For two whole months they worked together in uncovering a new scientific realm; they recorded the volume of the stream, its depth, its levels, and its speed. The map they eventually produced was so exact that it could still be used today.

Where the dark waters of the Río Negro join those of the Amazon, La Condamine met with a new problem: he learned from Indians that there was a connection between the Río Negro and the Orinoco, a thing no geographer had yet remarked. La Condamine was almost convinced of its existence, however much his contemporaries thought it a myth. His question: "Where is the confluence of these great rivers?" remained unanswered until an explorer of the next generation went out to South America especially to solve the riddle—Alexander von Humboldt.

La Condamine reached the mouth of the Amazon on September 19, 1744, with his collection of scientific material and observations greatly enriched. In the following spring he at last returned to Paris, ten years after setting out with the intention of measuring a single degree and no idea that he was going to rediscover a whole continent into the bargain.

From then on he devoted the whole of his life to the evaluation of the immense amount of material he had brought back with him. Almost at once he had to defend himself against the spiteful attacks of Bouguer, who had traduced him in the meantime. Then followed years of scientific controversy and proof, to which La Condamine gave all his drive and tough energy. This involved not only geographical and mathematical problems, but also the questions of quinine and rubber, the speed of sound, the legends of the Amazon, the poison used by the Indians on their arrows—curare— and vaccination against smallpox, which he was the first to effect successfully.

Charles Marie de La Condamine was the man, later to be revered and honored everywhere, who opened the gate to the South American continent and made it one of the known parts of the world. He had to pay a heavy price. In spite of all his mental resilience, his body succumbed to the exertions to which he had subjected it. He had set out on his mission a young man, admired by all the ladies; it was as an invalid that he returned, with one leg lamed and one ear so deaf that he had to use an ear trumpet.

His illness grew apace. In his later years he was nursed by a niece twenty years younger than himself, whom he married. While his spirit never wavered, his body continued to deteriorate; by 1763 he was a complete cripple. He now had to dictate his books and articles, but his bodily ills could not hinder the execution of his work, which became all the more famous as interest in South America continued to grow.

When in 1774 he died, crippled and deaf, he left behind him a harvest of scientific knowledge and also a task. The man who was to inherit it from him had already seen the light of day—he was still a little boy of five, living a dull and cheerless childhood in the city of Berlin and in the charming park of Tegel.

Alexander von Humboldt (born on September 14, 1769) came from a family of Prussian soldiers, but made his mark by gifts more intellectual than those of his forebears, who had fought in Prince Eugene's and Frederick II's campaigns. The old King of the Prussians must have been very astonished when one day on a visit to the little château of the Humboldts in Tegel he spoke to the two sons of their widowed mother. He asked the elder, Wilhelm, how old he was. When the boy said: "Ten, Your Majesty," Frederick suggested he was the right age to join a cadet organization. Wouldn't he like to be a soldier? Wilhelm immediately gave a negative answer and said he would prefer to follow a literary career.

So Frederick turned to his eight-year-old brother. "What is your name?"

"Alexander von Humboldt."

"Alexander—that's a fine name, reminiscent of one who conquered the world. Would you like to conquer the world, too?"

"Yes, Your Majesty—but with my head."

By the time he was thirty Alexander von Humboldt was within sight of the realization of his desires. He had worked with that single end in view. After studies in the natural sciences, he had published original works on geological, botanical, and physiological subjects, had visited Paris, the bright center of culture and the sciences, and would have taken part as natural historian in an expedition all over the world, including the South Pole, had not Napoleon's warlike enterprises, which contributed nothing useful to the human race, interfered with that scientifically valuable venture just before it was due to leave.

Nevertheless, Humboldt managed to reach distant parts of the world after strenuous efforts; the King of Spain gave him permission to travel to South America and gave him more freedom of movement than had ever before been accorded to any non-Spanish European. For that he had to thank an enlightened Spanish minister, Don Mariano Luis de Urquijo, who was interested in the sciences.

Humboldt could now sail up the Orinoco, climb the Andes, visit Bogotá, Lima, Quito, and Mexico, and spend five years in collecting plants, examining stones, and studying the climate and the tides. He managed to put together so much material about

Incas Resisting the Spanish Invaders. From de Bry

Pizarro Supervising the Collection of Booty. From de Bry

Montezuma Seated on His Throne. Also Shown Are the Special Palace Chambers Reserved for War Councilors,

Spinning. In the Second Panel a Boy and Girl of Eight Are Being Cautioned against Deceitfulness. The Next Two Pan-

The Virginia Massacre, 1622. From de Bry

Pocahontas, Daughter of Powhatan and Later Mrs. John Rolfe

Ætatis suæ 21. Aᵒ. 1616.

Matoaks als Rebecka daughter to the mighty Prince
Powhatan Emperour of Attanoughkomouck als Virginia
converted and baptized in the Christian faith, and
Wife to the worᵗᵗ Mᵗ Thoᵗ Rolff.

Sir Francis Drake's Fleet before Cartagena. From de Bry

Drake Attacking the Spaniards on the La Plata. From de Bry

A Sea Battle in the Age of Privateers

De Soto Discovering the Mississippi in 1590

Alexander von Humboldt.

Raleigh at the Mouth of the Orinoco in 1595

A Nilotic Sailing-Boat of the Eighteenth Dynasty

An Egyptian Bark of the Third Millennium, of the Type Employed for Coastal Navigation

Pigafetta's Map of Africa. Late Sixteenth Century

the country and its people, and to publish it in such a clear and scholarly form, that this hitherto dark continent lay revealed as an open book to anyone who wanted to read about it. Unlike earlier discoverers of the continent, Humboldt risked the dangers of the climate, the sickness, toil, and exertion of crossing so vast a territory with no thought of enriching himself; on the contrary, he paid expenses of about thirty-eight thousand thalers out of his own pocket, thereby reducing his modest fortune considerably.

Some words he wrote to a friend just before his departure show that Humboldt had dedicated not only his mind but his heart to the enterprise: "What good fortune has come my way! I am giddy with joy . . . for a man must pursue what is good and great."

He traveled to America by almost the same route as Columbus and at once began, in Paria and Caracas, to collect his natural-history data, with the help of a young French botanist, Aimé Bonpland, who proved a valuable assistant and a stanch companion—until a period when he was consumed by the flames of a violent love affair with a "Samba," an Indian girl with an infusion of white blood. The brown-skinned beauty, a servant in the house, had turned his head to such an extent that he not only pursued her but actually made an offer of marriage. She accepted it, but shortly before the wedding day she disappeared with a good-looking Indian boy, never to be seen again. The love-crazed Frenchman went after her, hoping to find her somewhere in the wilderness; he was fortunate enough to happen on a district whose rare butterflies and plants turned his attention to collecting again, and he soon came to his senses.

Unlike Bonpland, who contracted a serious tropical fever into the bargain, Humboldt remained unaffected and healthy; he was thus able to continue enthusiastically with his collecting, measurements, and observations in a country where, since his earliest childhood, he had longed to be. As an example of the extent of his work, he and Bonpland had already dried sixteen hundred plants and recorded six hundred unknown species in Paria alone.

When the rains ceased in the interior Humboldt was able to start on his journey up the Orinoco, to solve the riddle of its junction with the Río Negro. Long ago, in 1595, Walter Raleigh and his devil-may-care companions had fought their way up this great river, first when they rowed up against its fierce currents, then at the battle for the Spanish fort of Saint Thomas, where, incidentally, his son was killed. Raleigh raved effusively about the beauty of the country, the like of which was nowhere to be found. But since his day no foreigner had been in a position to visit the Orinoco and the interior of the country.

In 1745 a book about the Orinoco had been published by a priest, José Gumilla, in which it was firmly denied that the river joined the Río Negro. La Condamine was at the time voicing the opposite view, so the Spanish government sent out an expedition to clear the matter up once and for all. In 1754 a party 325 strong, under Captain Solano, moved forward into the forests, in whose wild depths it met with fearful disaster, only thirteen of its members returning safely from this unsuccessful venture.

Humboldt was to have a more than sufficient personal acquaintance with the difficulties the river opposed to all its invaders. The sufferings from mosquitoes, stinging flies, *piumes,* and other blood-sucking insects was almost unbearable for the Indians, let alone the explorers, who had to put up with a ceaseless downpour of rain and the pangs of hunger—their diet consisted of bananas, manioc, water, and occasionally some rice. On April 6, 1800, they nearly perished in a disaster. A storm struck their small craft in the middle of the immense stream; water rushed in and filled two thirds of the boat. It was risky to swim for the shore, for the waters swarmed with crocodiles; and even if they reached the unpeopled shore, they would certainly have come to grief, for the primeval forest, full of wild beasts, was so densely hung with lianas that it was impossible to find a way through. As Humboldt said: "The strongest man armed with an ax could hardly have covered a French mile in twenty days." At the critical moment a puff of wind came to the aid of the boat in its dire distress and filled out its sails; its occupants escaped by a hair's breadth, with the loss of only a few books and some provisions.

In spite of all these troubles, Humboldt was at last in a position to write: "I have pushed on to the source of the Orinoco. . . . I have fixed the latitude and longitude in more than fifty places, observed many occultations and emersions of planets, and will be able to issue an exact map of this immense land, inhabited by more than two hundred Indian tribes, most of whom have never seen a white man, and use different languages and cultures."

For many weeks Humboldt, penned in his narrow craft, mastered huge stretches of the river, forcing his way up the Orinoco, in a breakneck struggle through the raging eddies where the Río Meta pours into it, then farther upstream, and later southward up the Atabapo and the Tuamini, with a final four-day march overland, carrying the boat. Then down the Río Negro to the Brazilian border and back again to the mouth of the Casiquiare. This was the river Humboldt was seeking, which unites the Orinoco and the Amazon: he sailed down it back into the Orinoco, reached Esmeralda safely, and then turned for home. He arrived at Angostura on June 15, where he took a well-earned rest, then continued overland to Cumaná, the harbor on the Venezuelan coast, and so on to Havana.

While the conquistadors devoted all their thought and effort to the gathering of a hoard of gold and jeweled treasure, the scientists garnered a different type of riches, no less valuable to them. So Humboldt was truly depressed when he wrote: "What a wealth of plants is there in that marvelous country, thick with impenetrable forests, inhabited by so many new kinds of monkeys, between the Orinoco and the Amazon! Yet I have been able to collect hardly one tenth of what we have seen. . . . It is almost in tears that we open our plant-cases. The immeasurable dampness of the South American climate, the rankness of its vegetation, which makes it difficult to find fully grown foliage, have ruined more than a third of our collection. Every day we come upon new insects, which destroy papers and plants alike: using camphor, turpentine, tar, pitch-boards, or having out the cases in the fresh air, all these methods, so successful in Europe, are useless here, and we are beginning to lose patience. After an absence of three or four months, one's *herbarium* is scarcely recognizable. Five out of every eight samples had to be thrown away, especially in Guiana, el Dorado, and the Amazon country, where we were daily drenched by rain."

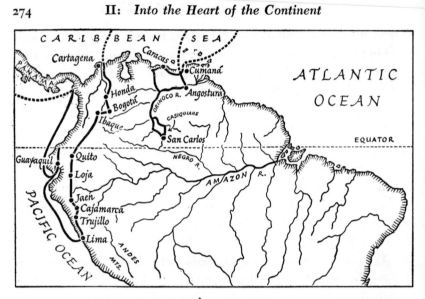

THE ROUTES OF HUMBOLDT'S JOURNEYS IN SOUTH AMERICA

Humboldt had spent sixteen months in the Orinoco area. "We crossed a tract from Mondavaca to the Volcano Duida, from the borders of Quito to Surinam, an area of eight thousand square miles in which there lives no Indian, indeed nothing but monkeys and snakes—and all the way with hands and faces swollen by mosquito bites." And now he felt impelled "to cross the tremendous Cordillera of the Andes, for thus alone can I draw from my own observations a properly founded map of all South America to the north of the Amazon." For this purpose he chose not the comfortable journey by ship along the coast, but the difficult route through the interior of Colombia, up the Río Magdalena to Honda, and then up over the Andes. His way to Quito led him through Santa Fe de Bogotá, where he visited the celebrated botanist Don José Celestino Mutis; but Quito when he got there was in a state quite different from when La Condamine visited it. A ghastly earthquake had struck there on February 4, 1797, sweeping the whole province and killing forty thousand at one blow—a monstrous tragedy when one remembers that by present standards the area was sparsely populated. So long-lasting were the effects of the earthquake that even the climate was affected;

Humboldt's measurements everywhere revealed lower temperatures than those recorded by La Condamine's expedition.

At that time the majestic Chimborazo was held to be the highest mountain in the world. Humboldt, following in La Condamine's footsteps, made an attempt on its snow-covered summit; after the Indian porters had deserted, he climbed through gales and hailstorms, in biting cold and suffering from the rarefied air, accompanied by Bonpland and two others, till finally a rocky face brought them to a halt. They had reached a point three thousand feet higher than La Condamine, but the purpose behind these exertions did not spring from any wish to achieve a sporting record, but was purely scientific. This ascent on Chimborazo and Humboldt's later journey to the Altai Mountains in 1829 served to underline the significance of conditions at high altitudes to geographical science generally.

When he made his way down from the Andes to the Amazon, Humboldt again followed La Condamine's route, with a view to improving the French explorer's maps, if this should prove possible. He also continued his predecessor's work in the study of special subjects such as the development of quinine.

Humboldt went to Lima in order to observe in detail the transit of Mercury across the sun on November 9, 1802. At Callao he stood for the first time on the Pacific shore. This is what he wrote: "The sight was a joyful one for him who has drawn part of his education and the direction of many of his desires to his contacts with one of Captain Cook's shipmates. . . . Forster's attractive description of Otaheiti awakened, especially in Northern Europe, a general—one might almost say a yearning—interest in the islands of the Pacific."

The stay of this inquiring scientist had unexpected results for Chile, for here Humboldt learned about guano and was instrumental later in introducing that valuable fertilizer into Europe. The states of Chile and Peru had really no hand in the fact that the sea birds nested there and deposited their droppings, which became so extremely valuable because they contained nitrogen and phosphorus; the two countries contributed equally little to the German scientist's journey or to the energetic propaganda he made for their product. But the important revenue fell into their laps and only ceased when in 1912 the Haber-Bosch process was developed and hydrogen could be extracted from the air. At the end of December, Humboldt took ship to Guayaquil, where he had a thorough look at the almost impenetrable forests of Babahoyo; in February he traveled on to Mexico and there spent almost a year, exploring the Cordilleras all the way across to Vera Cruz. His American journey ended with a visit to the United States and a meeting with President Jefferson.

Back in Paris, the greater part of Humboldt's labors began. This was the cataloguing of the sixty thousand plants he had collected with Bonpland during a journey of thirty-seven thousand miles, the fifteen hundred measurements he had taken, the innumerable notes he had made on geologic, astronomic, volcanic, archæological, and other topics, and the thirty enormous cases of material he had brought back. He paid his publisher 180,000 francs—almost all of what remained of his fortune—to issue his great volumes about America: twenty-nine magnificent books with 1,426 maps and illustrations. Among the many attracted to and inspired by him was a young South American who had come to ask the great explorer and liberal thinker for information about the high political outlook in the Spanish colonial empire. Humboldt insisted that South America was ripe for independence, but that she lacked anyone who knew how to achieve it. He was talking to the man who was to bring South America her independence—Simón Bolívar.

Humboldt not only concluded the immense task of editing his scientific publications and continuing to make other discoveries, but even embarked later on a second exploratory journey, through Russia and Siberia to the Yenisei; though this relatively small venture, in 1829, was in no way comparable to his South American expeditions.

When he was sixty-six Humboldt began the publication of a work that he alone among natural scientists could have contemplated. *Cosmos* was intended to offer a comprehensive exposition of the physical world. Humboldt worked on it till his death in 1859.

The exploration of South America proceeded rapidly, especially after her emancipation from Spanish rule. Brazil was explored by W. L. von Eschwege (1811), Prince Maximilian of Wied-Neuwied (1814), and Von Martius and Von Spix (1817); poor Bonpland stupidly got caught in the whirlpool of political faction and in 1816 was captured by the dictator of Paraguay, Dr. José Gaspar Rodriguez Francia, who kept him in prison for ten years. After his liberation he devoted himself entirely to his botanical work, remaining in correspondence with his old companion.

Humboldt did not die without seeing evidences of the great strides being made with the further exploration of the continent. Between 1831 and 1835 one of his most enthusiastic followers, Charles Darwin, traveled through Argentina, Patagonia, southern Chile, Peru, and the Galápagos Islands; between 1835 and 1859 the brothers Robert and Richard Schomburgk explored Guiana; in 1838 J. J. von Tschudi made journeys through Peru; and in 1848 Henry Bates and Alfred Wallace were busy in the green jungles of the Amazon. In the following year one of the greatest explorers of the Amazon basin began his work; his name was Richard Spruce. He achieved perhaps the most remarkable single performance of all, for he spent seventeen years deep in the heart of the Amazon and Río Negro country, where he disclosed one of the most inaccessible tracts, unconsciously paving the way for the modern world of industry and commerce which was to wring from nature not scientific secrets but a raw material, rubber. But Spruce himself remained a scientist; he started a collection of plants which far surpassed anything known before, and put the history of the botany of South America on a firm basis. To every branch of science which was affected—medicine, chemistry, and the like—he provided the premises for the evaluation of botanical facts, and ultimately it was he who gave the geographical discoverers a second chance; he collected with meticulous care a hundred thousand separate seeds of the cinchona tree, which were eventually planted with great success in India; the resulting quinine later facilitated the exploration of other tropical regions, particularly those of Africa, which white men had not yet penetrated. But though his achievements were little inferior to those of a La Condamine or a Humboldt or a Darwin, he gained no noteworthy honors from them, nor did he ever find time to publish a book about the results of his researches; and he died the same poor devil he had been all his life.

In discovering a new continent Alexander von Humboldt had at the same time heralded the high summer of all exploration. Once the explorers had discovered what a fantastic wealth of new knowledge lay hidden in South America, the continent became the happy hunting-ground of all explorers, and the study and observation of nature became the favorite pursuit of the age. And then—in the year in which Humboldt, the representative scientist of his time, died, with his *Cosmos* still unfinished—a new era dawned for the natural sciences. For it was then that Darwin published his *Origin of Species,* a work establishing biological laws which would have seemed strange and even revolutionary to Humboldt. But it was as a disciple of Humboldt's, and through the study of his South American researches and commentaries, that Darwin evolved the fundamentals of his evolutionary theory.

8

THE SECRETS OF THE DARK CONTINENT

THE DISTANT continent across the Atlantic was explored from end to end a few centuries after its discovery, but the one which lies nearest to Europe and whose existence had been known for thousands of years—Africa—kept unrevealed a myriad of secrets. While the coast had been charted so long ago that it had been forgotten and had to be re-surveyed, the interior of Africa presented far greater barriers to penetration than did the American interior. Its huge rivers, unlike those of North and South America, were not suitable for navigation, but faced the inquisitive invader with falls, rapids, and whirlpools. In the north, the Sahara opposed the approach of all traffic with its inhospitable sandy wastes; along the coasts lay a depressed belt full of swamps and mangrove thickets where noxious fevers spelled death to travelers. In the interior lay the menace of sleeping-sickness, dealing death to millions, and it was impossible to introduce horses, donkeys, or cattle because they contracted sores, for which the tsetse fly was mainly responsible. Beasts of burden, draft animals, and mounts could exist only in North Africa or in the non-tropical districts of the south; camels could endure only a dry climate, and the only means of transport was unreliable columns of porters.

The first people to know anything about Africa's shape were the inhabitants of Egypt, an ancient civilization, who certainly sailed in their ships to the incense land of Punt, south of the Somali coast, three thousand or perhaps even four thousand years before Christ. About 1500 B.C. they ventured even farther south in search of gold, silver, and copper. They may quite possibly have sailed down the Red Sea and right round Africa.

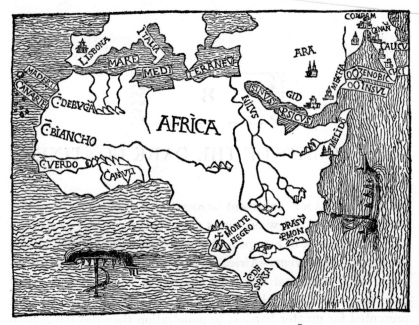

AFRICA AS UNDERSTOOD IN 1508

Of the seafaring Phœnicians we know that they discovered the
Canary Islands and, in spite of the denials of many historians,
sailed round the Cape of Good Hope in the service of the Egyptian King Necho in about 595 B.C. This journey—one of the greatest voyages of discovery in all history and the first reliably recorded circumnavigation of a continent—started out from the Red
Sea. It was twice interrupted at the appropriate times of the years;
the sailors went ashore, sowed corn, reaped the harvest, and so
provided themselves with food for the continuation of the journey.
The Phœnicians returned to Egypt by way of the Strait of
Gibraltar after an absence of three years. The report of the
Carthaginian admiral Hanno about his famous African voyage
(already mentioned in the first chapter of this book), recorded on
tablets in a temple at Carthage, has been preserved in a Greek
translation called *Periplous*. Apparently Hanno sailed with sixty
fifty-oared vessels, in about 530, 525, or 465 B.C., to visit existing
Carthaginian settlements on the west coast of Morocco and to
found new ones. He afterward followed the African coast to
Senegal, sailing along it a short way and then rowing on south-

ward to a point that it is impossible to identify. Many evidences point to his having got as far as the great Cameroon mountain in the Gulf of Guinea. It was nearly two thousand years before the next ships were seen in these waters, and then it took the Portuguese almost a generation to re-explore the northwest coast of Africa.

Other sea and land expeditions undertaken in ancient times were those of the Greek Euthymenes (*c.* 530 B.C.), the Greek historian Herodotus (*c.* 450 B.C.) and various Roman generals, who penetrated to the sources of the Nile, to where Merowe is today, to the Atlas Mountains, and into the area around Lake Chad. When, in the second century after Christ, Ptolemæus made a final collection of all the existing information about Africa in his *Geographica,* his data remained the most important source of African research until well into the nineteenth century. His work contained much correct information; naturally it also included many errors, the chief of which was the statement that the east coast curved eastward toward the south of Africa and so entirely enclosed the Indian Ocean, making it into an inland sea and entirely precluding any possibility of a sea route to India.

White men took no further interest in Africa until the time when Henry the Navigator and his Portuguese captains began their new explorations on the African coast. Later, when—drawn there by the prizes of trade in slaves, gold, and ivory—the Portuguese, English, Dutch, Danes, and Brandenburgers set up supply posts and settlements, they confined their attentions to the coastal strips, particularly those of Guinea, and let themselves be scared away from any attempt at further penetration by the rain-drenched tropical forests.

When, in the eighteenth century, the first voyages were made by explorers—the French in Senegambia, the Jesuits Paez and Lobo in Abyssinia, and Europeans of various nationalities in the region of the Cape—they were really not original. The interior of Africa had for the most part been opened up in the interval—not by Europeans, but by men from the Orient.

As early as A.D. 946, Abdul Hassan, called Massudi, came from Baghdad and traversed not only Egypt, but all northern and eastern Africa; the Moorish princeling al-Idrisi (1100–1166) wandered through the hinterland of Morocco into the rear of Africa and drew a map on which almost all geographers relied till the eighteenth century. A decisive contribution to the broadening of knowledge were the journeys of the Berber Mohammed ibn-'Abdullah ibn-Batuta of Tangier (1304–1377), who won fame as the greatest overland traveler of any time and any place. In thirty years of traveling he made himself familiar with Egypt, Persia, Asia Minor, southern Russia, Turan, India, the Maldives, the Sunda Isles, China, Spain, and finally Africa, where he reached Kilwa on the east coast, pushed up the Nile as far as the Cataracts of Dongola, crossed the Sahara into Senegal in the west, and made his way through the western Sudan to the Niger and to the great trading-center of Timbuktu. His books contain valuable reports and scientific data about natural phenomena as well as about the social and economic conditions in the countries he visited.

Another Arabian scientist, the Moorish princeling al-Hasan ibn-Mohammed al-Wazzan of Granada (1492–1526), was converted to Christianity and took the name of Leo Africanus after he had explored a great tract of the Niger basin and of the Sudan, had been captured by Christian pirates, and brought to the Pope in Rome, at whose hands he received honorable treatment. His description of Africa, which appeared in 1520, provided the Western world with one of its most important sources of knowledge about the Dark Continent.

Discovery, however, was only one of the minor activities of the Arabs in Africa. The great wave of Islamic conversionary zeal could not be halted by the great continent with its trackless forests. The faith of Mohammed forced its way into the heart of the continent, took root among the Negro tribes, and created new realms whose enmity to Christendom was, much later, to bar the passage of European explorers and even to cost them their lives. True, the Arabs kept their settlements mainly to the coastal areas, but their trade—chiefly in slaves and gold—took them deep into the wilderness. Later, deep in the tropical jungle, on the endless plains, and in the arid desert the white explorers continually met Arab traders willing to show them the way and help them with important information. So the secrets of the continent had been uncovered long before the white men came and began their more thorough exploration. But other questions—such as the course of the mighty African rivers—were not answered till in the nineteenth century a number of white explorers came to devote their energy, their health, and their lives to the final scientific clarification of geographical questions that had remained obscure in Europe for far too long a time.

Toward the end of the seventeenth century, Swift was still able to poke scorn at a new map of Africa in the lines:

> *Geographers in Africa maps*
> *With savage pictures fill the gaps,*
> *And over uninhabitable downs*
> *Place elephants, for want of towns.*

The new era of African exploration began in the year 1788 and was brought to its conclusion thanks to the great navigator James Cook. His voyages had awakened a keen interest in the exploration of foreign lands and so produced results that helped the promotion of a new venture; this was the British Association for Promoting the Exploration of the Interior of Africa, founded in 1788 and developed a couple of decades later into The Geographical Association of London. The founder and moving spirit of the British African Association, to use its shortened form, was Joseph Banks, who had accompanied Cook on his voyages as a naturalist. His organization adroitly combined scientific with practical ends—such as the search for fresh commercial possibilities—and so people began to unloose the purse strings, which are otherwise not so easy to undo.

The company, with intelligent consideration, always devoted its funds to the solution of some clear-cut problem and was diligent in selecting the most suitable men. After the failure of the first four expeditions whose task was to reach the Niger from Senegambia, a young Scottish doctor and botanist called Mungo Park (1771–1806) succeeded in carrying out this difficult mission.

When Park, with an interpreter and a Negro boy, a horse and two donkeys, some corals, amber, tobacco, a few things to barter, two fowling-pieces, two pairs of pistols, a compass, a pocket sextant, and a parasol, set out on his journey in 1795, the Niger was still thought to have mouths in Senegal and Gambia. When in 1797 he returned—sick and penniless—he had solved the riddle of the Niger, which flowed eastward and had nothing to do with the Senegal and Gambia rivers and their westerly courses. On his journey Park had marched through the vast forests of the Sene-gambian plain, passing through the desert lands between Wulli and Bondu, then through Bondu itself—he bought permission to cross it by giving the Negro king his best article of clothing, a blue suit. He was imprisoned in Kadjaage, and after his release wandered on to the city of Gungadi, with its great mosque. To his astonishment, Park found Mohammedan churches and schools everywhere in the western regions of Africa. Then he crossed the upper Zambezi, was stripped by robbers, deserted by his inter-preter, imprisoned again by the Arabs of Ludamar and spent months of suffering from heat and sandstorms, thirst and hunger. Later he made a desperate escape, found his way to the Niger and explored it, lay seriously ill for months in a native hut, and finally returned, marching with a great caravan of Negroes.

Two years later Mungo Park published a book about his ex-periences which sold beyond the average author's dreams. His account became such a best-seller that its figures topped those of that classic *Robinson Crusoe*. This gave a great stimulus to Afri-can exploration, which now headed toward the complete dis-covery, and so to the later mastery by Europeans, of the myste-rious continent.

It took innumerable explorers and travelers to complete this work. The names of many a successful one have remained un-revealed in the history of exploration; many another who came to grief on a solitary journey or who, as companion to a more famous traveler, never achieved prominence, found his grave in jungle, forest, or desert. A number of the explorers who achieved some measure of fame also paid with their lives for their incursions into that savage and somber tropical hell.

Among them were Major A. Gordon Laing (1794–1826), who reached Timbuktu from Tripoli and was killed on his way back near Arauan; the Englishman Davidson, struck down on his way across the western Sahara; and the wealthy Dutchwoman Alexine Tinne, who after an unhappy love affair gave her whole heart to Africa and carried out journeys of some significance to the upper Nile, but was murdered in the Sahara in 1869, at the early age of thirty, by Tuaregs who suspected that her steel water-container contained gold or money. The twenty-six-year-old theological student Friedrich Hornemann of Hildesheim got an introduction to Joseph Banks and was sent to Africa as early as 1798 on behalf of the African Association; there, disguised as a Mohammedan merchant, he accompanied a trading-caravan from Cairo to Fezzan, established the latitude of Murzuch, its capital, and so fixed a definite point in the terrible unknown back of beyond. He then visited Tripoli and made his way to the Niger, where he perished at some place unknown before he was even thirty. The young Leipzig astronomer Eduard Vogel (1829–1856), a man with the gentle face of a dreamer, went out into the heart of Africa to look for the explorer Heinrich Barth, who had disappeared in the Sudan, and found him—his obituary had already been published by the Berlin Society for World Exploration in their journal—living in the forest of Surrikolo, between Kano and Kuka. Vogel then tried to push on to Adamawa, but on reaching the Sultanate of Wadai was butchered by Moslem fanatics with ironbound clubs because he was writing with a magic wand (a pencil). Seven expeditions went out to rescue Vogel or to find out what had become of him; in the course of these the French doctor Biny was murdered in Kordofan and the German explorer Moritz von Beurmann lost his life. In 1849 that experienced explorer James Richardson led a British expedition that inaugurated the great days of exploration in the Sahara and the Sudan; among his companions were the geologist Adolf Overweg and the astronomer Heinrich Barth. Only Barth survived the five and a half years of wandering; Richardson died during the first month, Overweg after eighteen months, both falling victims to the climate.

Heinrich Barth (1821–1865) ventured into regions protected not only by nature's defenses, but by the fanatical enmity of their Mohammedan inhabitants toward any stranger; he achieved far greater successes than any white explorer of Africa before him, and brought back invaluable geographical, historical, anthropological, and philological material. It was through his researches that Europe obtained its first basic knowledge of the huge area lying between Tripolitania, the Benue, the upper Niger, and the land of Wadai. Barth mapped some twelve thousand miles, explored almost half of Africa—the western Sudan, the Sudan itself, and the Sahara—and provided a reliable account of the Berber and Negro tribes of the Sahara as well as of the many Mohammedan countries in the Sudan, already in their decline. While foreigners like C. G. Thompson, the English explorer, gratefully recognized Barth's achievements, the academic arrogance of German scientists accorded him a place of honor only in a very half-hearted way: in 1863 he was given a professorship (but only an honorary one) at the University of Berlin and lived to enjoy it for only two years, for he died at the age of forty-five.

His work was continued by the great explorers Gerhard Rohlfs (1831–1895) and Gustav Nachtigal (1834–1885). Rohlfs had been a go-getter from early youth on. He twice tried to escape from the confinement of the schoolroom; fought as a volunteer in the Schleswig-Holstein militia against the Danes; studied medicine, but did not take his examinations; became an Austrian soldier, deserted and joined the French Foreign Legion and served in Algeria for five years. For his African travels he adopted a method ideally suited to the conditions: he went over to Islam and, as a wandering doctor, traveled through the countries of Morocco, the Sahara, and the Sudan, from which Christians were barred. In spite of his garb, he twice came within an inch of losing his life. At the oasis of Kenatsa a sheik, who had seen the silver money he carried, attacked him in his sleep; Rohlfs lay two days and nights helpless in the desert, bleeding from nine wounds, with his upper arm shattered, till two passing pilgrims rescued him. Eighteen years later, in 1879, when he was on the point of moving on from the oases of Cufra (which no white man had reached before him) to Wadai, an ambush cost him the whole of his equipment and forced him to turn back. Rohlfs spent much longer in the heart of the continent than any of the other great

German explorers of Africa, and if his scientific results are on a lesser scale than theirs, he collected a mass of new information. He was the first to cross the continent from the Mediterranean to the Gulf of Guinea, in 1865–7, and during his six great journeys he visited many regions in which no white man was again to set foot for decades.

Like Rohlfs, Nachtigal, who first went to Africa because of a serious lung ailment, armed himself with a thorough knowledge of the Arabic tongue and mode of life. He distinguished himself as personal doctor to the Bey of Tunis, and in 1868, without asking any financial reward, fought a great epidemic of spotted fever. The Dark Continent had him in thrall; after meeting Rohlfs and taking on a mission to deliver presents from the King of Prussia to Sheik Omar, the ruler of the Sudan, he set out from Tripoli on February 18, 1869, with a caravan of five men and eight camels on a journey into the heart of Africa. This was to last five years, and it took him, continually plagued by thirst, through the wild hill country of the marauding Tibbu, across the central Sahara to Murzuch, and thence on to Bornu and Kuka, where he handed over his gifts to the Sultan. From that base he explored the country round Lake Chad for three years and obtained precise information about the central Sudan. When at last he started for home, he disguised himself as a Mohammedan sheriff and pilgrim in order to penetrate the forbidden secrets of the Wadai country. In this he succeeded and was thus able to establish the facts about the fate of the unfortunate Eduard Vogel, who had been murdered there seventeen years earlier. In January 1874 he traveled on by way of Darfur and Kordofan and reached the Nile at Khartoum. The Viceroy of Egypt sent a state vessel to fetch him in triumph to Cairo.

And so the empty spaces in the map of Africa were filled in piecemeal.

Among the many explorers who contributed were Sir Richard Francis Burton (1821–1890) and John Hanning Speke (1827–1864), who explored Abyssinia and East Africa together, discovering Lake Tanganyika and contributing much toward the solution of the problem of the Nile's sources, which had been a matter of controversy for thousands of years; after the two men had fallen out, Speke was able to go on alone and chart Lake Victoria and the river's upper reaches. Of the German travelers in Africa three are worthy of note: Theodor von Heuglin (1824–1876) in Abyssinia and the Nile basin, the over-modest Karl Mauch (1837–1875) in the gold-bearing areas of South Africa, and Georg Schweinfurth (1836–1925) on the upper Nile.

But while a vast number of Africa's riddles were thus solved by a host of devoted explorers, it was left to two men—of whom the second-named gave the decisive impulse to the economic development and to a revolutionary political reorientation of the whole continent—to explore the innermost heart of Africa, till then hardly penetrated even by the Arab slave-traders. They were Livingstone and Stanley.

"Dr. Livingstone, I presume?"

The question was asked by a man of ruthless energy, who had fought his way through the trackless wilds of Africa, as he raised his sun helmet and tried with all his might to stifle his raging excitement.

A lean, aging man in a red flannel jacket and worn-out gray trousers, his face deeply etched by grief and hardship, smiled wanly as he removed his gold-braided cloth cap and gave the answer:

"Yes."

The scene was a native village, far from civilization, with the ancient African name of Ujiji—a village noisy with the arrival of Stanley's caravan, headed by drums, and with the shrill cries of the excited inhabitants. Readers in America and Europe would soon be eagerly conning the reports of this meeting in their newspapers, for it produced one of the greatest sensations of the nineteenth century. Who were these two men who were now meeting in an inaccessible part of deepest Africa unseen by any white man before them?

David Livingstone, born in 1813, came of an old Scottish clan. His was a deeply religious nature; after studying medicine, he took holy orders and went to Africa to help the black man find the way to Christendom, and to combat the evil of the Arab slave trade.

He was twenty-seven years old when, at the Cape, he first stepped onto African soil. Nine years later he set out on the first of his great expeditions, which were to serve equally the cause of his missionary task and the exploration of vast tracts of central and southern Africa about which no map had anything to say. Livingstone dedicated thirty long years—half of his life—to unknown Africa.

Accompanied by his wife and children, he first crossed the Kalahari Desert to Lake Ngami. In 1851 he reached the upper Zambezi; from 1853 to 1856 he roved up and down the length of South Africa as far as Luanda and back to Quelimane; in so doing he discovered the Victoria Falls of the Zambezi. Then he sent his family home to England—Africa, the secret, unintelligible continent, had taken full possession of him. For six years, from 1858 to 1864, he explored the Zambezi basin, Lakes Nyassa and Chilwa, Lake Tanganyika, the River Luapula, Lakes Ngami, Merowe, Bangweulu. Constantly at war with and yet a devotee of the wilderness, always on good terms with the natives, he was a calm, peaceful man who, in spite of his aversion to publicity and limelight, was to win world-wide fame as the first European to cross Africa. Posterity had him to thank for its knowledge of the whole course of the Zambezi, the upper Congo reaches, and some of the great lakes at the heart of the continent.

By 1866 he was well enough known throughout the world for people to wonder what had become of him. Since the beginning of that year no particle of news of him had reached the world outside; uneasiness about his fate was growing, and the English press was constantly asking: "Where is Livingstone?" Gradually men became more and more convinced that he was dead. James Gordon Bennett, the young editor of the *New York Herald*, one of the most successful and resourceful newspapermen of the century, rightly sensed a scoop and in 1871 set Stanley, one of his best reporters, on Livingstone's trail.

Livingstone was alive, but in no position to communicate with the outer world. During the years of his disappearance—utterly in thrall of the magic of inner Africa—he was seeking the solution of a problem that stirred scientific minds as deeply as, in later years, the search for the North and South Poles was to grip their imagination. This was the source of the Nile, that majestic river which had played so important a part in the world's history over thousands of years. Livingstone was driven not by a desire for an explorer's fame, but simply by the irresistible urge to unravel the secret so long held by Africa's forests. His motive power was the urge to explore, combined with the force of the old legends, and possibly allied to a sense of religious martyrdom as well.

Livingstone risked his life as no other man ever did in order to get at the kernel of the African problem. He believed that the Lualaba River flowing northward in central Africa was the main upper feeder of the Nile, and therefore pressed on to the north in search of it, through the most inhospitable country, over the high plateau between Nyanza and Tanganyika. On his first two attempts his whole party—men and animals alike—perished. On the next essay his boat, built with so much difficulty and toil, sank on Lake Bangweulu, and the whole stock of barter materials—the only currency known to the savages—as well as all the medical equipment, were lost. Livingstone was thus absolutely unprotected against malaria. For months he wandered about with the remnants of his expedition, stripped of equipment and supplies, amid a tangle of unknown rivers, through plains and forests, sustained with food at the hands of friendly natives, till finally after an absence of two years he got back to his starting-point. The returned wanderer was as thin as a skeleton, completely toothless, starving and sick. Nonetheless, he continued his search. One wild goose chase followed another. Frightful African diseases kept him to his sickbed for long stretches and put him out of action. Before he was really fit, he started off again on the desperate, fruitless search for the Nile's sources—back to the Lualaba, back again to Ujiji. And now where to? It was impossible to reach the safety of the coast because hostile marauding tribes barred the way; the supply dumps were empty, there was no hope of supplies from anywhere. At that moment a totally unexpected savior turned up: Stanley.

The man who had penerated into this trackless waste in the hope of finding the recluse Converter of the Heathen, the lost "River-Seeker" (as the natives called him), was a very different man from the elderly, quiet Livingstone, worn out by his sufferings. Stanley was an active man, possessed of great energy, whom nothing could divert from his objective; a true explorer who in earlier days would have been a conqueror and a ruler; a descendant of the great race of venturers by land and sea who reigned in the golden age of discovery. Instead of being able to found an empire in the huge slice of Africa he was the first to open up, he was left no other course by the age in which he lived than to parcel out the news value of his achievements and win a glittering fame with his sensational articles in the press. His was a decisive part in the political partition of innermost Africa—but only as an agent, paid by a European state on a purely commercial basis.

John Rowlands (born in 1841) experienced all the bitterness of an illegitimate child's boyhood, spent without a glimmer of love in one of the notorious institutions that Victorian England provided for such cases. The boy grew up under the lash of a schoolmaster who was—a small matter noticed much too late—also a madman. After a terrible scene the lad ran away, took pitifully paid jobs as an errand boy, renewed his acquaintance with the lash, and tried to escape from his misery by absconding to sea: but all he found there was more lashes and more misery. At the first port of call, New Orleans, he sought refuge on land. There the fifteen-year-old homeless runaway found a post in the business of Henry Stanley, a rich merchant, the first human being to show him any kindness at all. Stanley adopted the young man, who took his name, but a few years later again found himself alone in the world without means, for his fatherly patron died without having made him his heir. Years of penury and privation followed; somehow he made his way successively as woodcutter, shop assistant, private soldier in the American Civil War, harvester, sailor, and world hobo, till in 1867 he succeeded in obtaining a reportership on the *Chicago Tribune* and *New York Herald*.

Now at last he was on the way up. Henry Morton Stanley lived according to the rule that a first-class man is distinguished from a fifth-rate man by the toughness he shows in getting over his failures and starting again. Stanley's toughness was rewarded: in a very few years he became a world-famous journalist and something more—a writer whom journalism elevated to a higher plane.

During his first few years he was able to save three thousand dollars. This money he risked to go at his own expense to report the British expedition in Abyssinia against the brutal, megalomaniac Emperor Theodore. After his articles had attracted considerable attention, he succeeded by great skill in being the first to send a dispatch to New York about Theodore's capitulation; he had the luck, into the bargain, of being the only one, for the cable between Alexandria and Malta broke down. At first everybody thought the *Herald*'s report was a sensational fabrication, but Stanley was soon justified, and from then on he began to obtain one important assignment after another. He was sent to Athens, Smyrna, Rhodes, Beirut, and Alexandria. Then came the chance of a lifetime: James Gordon Bennett sent him to find Livingstone—at all costs.

Stanley arrived in Zanzibar at the end of January 1871, after executing a rapid tour for his paper on the way. This took him up the Nile, to Jerusalem, Istanbul, the Crimea, Odessa, Trebizond, Tiflis, Persepolis, across to India, back to Mauritius, and only then to Zanzibar.

And there began a venture that bordered on lunacy: a search in the depths of African forests and wildernesses for a man about whom nobody knew anything—even whether he was alive or dead. A venture akin to looking for a needle in a haystack, and one that would bring success to Stanley only if he enjoyed a double stroke of luck—that is, if Livingstone was really still alive and if he actually succeeded in finding him.

Stanley for the first time in his life organized an expedition. There were 31 armed volunteers, 153 porters, 27 beasts of burden, 2 horses, and 3 white men as his special bodyguard. The party carried with it the means of barter in the interior: linen, calico, pearls (black for the Ugogo, white for the Ufipi, egg pearls for the

Uhoho, and so on), and wire, which was worth its weight in gold
in the heart of Africa.

On February 5, after a ten-hour crossing from Zanzibar, they
landed on the east coast of Africa and set out on the trying march
inland toward Lake Tanganyika, for it was from thereabouts that
the last news of Livingstone had come. There were no roads or
ways, no bridges over the broad, swampy rivers; thickets of rushes
and trailing plants barred all progress and had to be laboriously
cut away. The men's clothes were torn to shreds, their skin lacerated by the branches of the *Acacia horrida*, their flesh deeply
punctured by the thorns of a kind of aloe; a stinging plant, which
lashed their faces at every step, produced painful sores.

Stanley suffered from African fever from the very first day; he
had twenty-three attacks in thirteen months and was often deliri-
ous for days on end. The tropical disease was to rack and destroy
his body for another twenty-five years. Africa took savage toll of
the first man who tore apart the barriers to the untouched wilderness at the heart of the continent.

But Stanley drove his column relentlessly onward, heedless of
the swarms of insects—wasps with giant stings, fleas, grasshoppers,
all-devouring white ants—which attacked it; regardless too of the
shameless extortions by native chiefs who haggled over inflated
tolls for passage through their filthy villages. In spite of drenching
thunderstorms, pitiless heat, smallpox outbreaks and other ail-
ments among the porters; in spite of the rapid reduction of their
insufficient rations; in spite of the danger threatening from snakes
and wild animals; in spite of dying men who fell by the wayside,
still the march went on, deeper and deeper into the forest night,
into the uncanny, inscrutable heart of Africa.

At the beginning of June, Stanley wanted to make his way over
a high mountain range, to Unyanyembe, the "Land of the Moon,"
but the Arab traders whom he met from time to time—they were
the only people with exact knowledge of the interior of Africa—
advised him not to, for they knew nothing of the region. Although
the guides and the porters demurred, Stanley ordered them on
into the unknown country. When the column started, its head
moved off in a different direction, hoping that the white stranger

to this land would not notice. Stanley repeated his orders. The porters put down their loads, and a mutiny was clearly brewing. Stanley met fear with terror; he ordered the Wangwana warriors in his pay to shoot down any rebellious porters, then, with whip in hand, forced the leading porter to move on. The others followed like sheep, and the march went on.

This sort of thing happened several times—there was even an attempt on Stanley's life—before the last doubt about his inflexibility was dispelled.

On November 3, after months of bitter struggle against nature's savagery, they met a caravan of the Waguha, who lived near Lake Tanganyika, and among the answers to the usual questions learned from them that a white man, an ailing old man coming from the distant interior, had arrived at Ujiji.

Stanley hurried on by tremendous forced marches, urging the lagging porters forward by grants of extra pay. On November 10, pressing on ahead of the column, he caught sight of Lake Tanganyika's boundless, glittering silver shield, and a few hours later he was shaking hands with Livingstone.

They remained together four and a half months; they went on reconnaissances together, the younger man drinking in great drafts of the older's experiences, and as they talked unendingly, he became intrigued with the riddle of the Lualaba. Did that great river, flowing to the north, lead to the Nile? If not, where did it lead?

Livingstone refused to return to Europe with Stanley; he no longer found it possible to tear himself away from Africa. On March 12, 1872, Stanley took moving leave of the man who had become his friend and his shining example. Livingstone was to wander restlessly through the murderous wilderness, heedless of the distant world, driven on by his secret urge, seeking his rivers and the souls he meant to comfort, for another eighteen months till he died on the shores of Lake Bangweulu. Stanley, marching straight to the coast and reaching it in two months, quitted Africa, only to be met with cool skepticism by a world busy with its own troubles.

Of course his reports excited tremendous interest in his own country, but it was tempered by a mistrust that eventually blossomed into open attacks and disgusted him with Europe. For there the scientists and scholars simply would not concede that an American journalist, not one of themselves, had found Livingstone; they even cast doubts on the authenticity of the letters Livingstone had given him to bring back. Stanley had to appear before the Royal Geographical Society in London in the role of a defendant in order to clear his name. Even then a whispering campaign persisted, secretly pursuing him and embittering his whole life.

Eagerly Stanley accepted the first opportunity to return to Africa. He accompanied the British punitive expedition against the Ashanti tribes on the Gold Coast as a war correspondent, pressed on with them through jungle and poisonous swampland to the almost inaccessible capital, Kumasi, where after its capture he gazed aghast in the marketplace on the bodies of thousands of people the natives had slaughtered in sacrificial prayer to their gods to grant them victory.

On his way back Stanley learned of Livingstone's death—ten months after its occurrence—and now he could no longer bring himself to rest without completing his work by solving the riddle of the Lualaba. He managed to gain the backing of the *London Daily Telegraph* and of James Gordon Bennett for a new expedition. The western half of Africa was still a great white vacuum on the maps, Lake Victoria was hardly known; nobody knew whether it was joined to the Nile, or where the waters of Lake Tanganyika flowed to; there would be enough material of interest to educated people in the reports he would send back. As it was, Stanley's second expedition served not only to broaden the geographical knowledge of his time, but to open up a new field of activity for European power politics in that hitherto unexplored wilderness.

At the end of November 1874 began the largest and most important of Stanley's expeditions, based once again on Zanzibar: a new, bitter campaign against the inaccessible, against rocks and deserts, gigantic trees and trailing plants in the forests, against thundering cataracts and noisome marshes, against hunger and sickness, and against the wild men and beasts who peopled the wilderness. All his efforts to avoid bloodshed were vain; in the very first weeks there was a pitched battle when the natives surrounded his camp and tried to overrun it. He lost a quarter of his men before he succeeded in routing the attackers. He reached his first objective, Victoria Nyanza, after 104 days of laborious marching. Nobody was even sure about its shape—Captain Burton, McQueen, and other contemporary explorers believed it to be a chain of lakes; while Speke, who was killed by a bullet in an ambush while actually discussing the problem, was sure it was one great lake.

When Stanley launched the prefabricated cedarwood boat that had been brought along, none of the native porters dared to get into it, so overcome were they by superstitious dread at this unpredictable adventure. They all had excuses, but none of them gave the true reason—that they feared to leave solid earth and commit themselves to the unfamiliar element. In the end Stanley forced eleven terrified natives, their teeth chattering with fear, into the boat.

The journey along the shores of the lake lasted eight weeks and not several years, as the native interpreter, a man with a magnificent Struwelpeter shock of hair, had foretold. Stanley and his men were to encounter fierce exertions, fights with the truculent inhabitants of its shores and islands, an honorable reception by King Mtesa of Uganda, dangerous storms and fierce pangs of hunger, before they got back to camp. The secret of Lake Victoria was laid bare. The next task was to solve the riddle of the Lualaba —was it a tributary of the Nile, the Congo, or the Niger?

In the Uhombo district the column entered a region into which no white man had ever penetrated. The natives, who were more repulsively ugly than any other man Stanley had ever seen, were frantically excited; they were barbaric travesties of men, whose development had halted on a very low rung of human progress. It was not only their crude features, but their filthy bodies streaked with ocher and their hideous diet of the heads of mice, viper skins, and gorilla bones that horrified Stanley; while the savages on their part kept up a continuous loud screeching query whether the white man was really a human being, and seemed most unwilling to accept him as one of their own kind. It was almost as if the inhabitants of two different planets had met.

On the party went, two hundred and fifty toilsome, energy-sapping miles, to the banks of the Lualaba, which at this point was a magnificent river a mile wide, flowing from south to east, apparently toward the Indian Ocean. All the Arabs and natives could tell them was that it turned northward farther up its course and then flowed endlessly on and on till it reached the sea. But the country to the north was said to be so horrific that nobody could get through it alive; the native porters, beside themselves with fear of cannibals, snakes, leopards, and gorillas, wanted to turn back.

Stanley was faced with a difficult decision. Should he turn back to the Zambezi in the explored south or follow the problematic river northward, building canoes at some suitable spot and heading downstream in them till the expedition met the Nile, some great lake, the Congo, or the Atlantic? Stanley consulted Pocock, the last of his three white companions to survive thus far.

Pocock was greatly disconcerted by Stanley's brave idea of a boat journey. At last—after all, who could say which was the right course?—he suggested tossing a coin. Stanley agreed and took out a rupee. "Heads, northward and the Lualaba; tails south and the Zambezi." They spun the coin six times; six times it came down tails. Fate had spoken her clear verdict. Then Stanley gave his own: "North and the Lualaba!" Pocock agreed enthusiastically. "Don't worry about me," he said, "I'll stick by you, sir." And so he chose the road that was to lead him to his death.

Accompanied by an escort of armed slaves, whom Stanley had to hire from the Arab slave-dealer Tippu Tib at an extortionate price to prevent his porters from deserting, they went on into the horrid night of the tropical forest, where it was sometimes impossible to take consecutive steps. Painfully the column moved on, to the sound of hideous war signals and the hollow nerve-racking rhythm of the wooden drums with which the savages telegraphed all the news about the strangers through the jungle. Enemies lurked in the forest, crocodiles awaited their prey in the waters, poisoned arrows twanged from the undergrowth. Once the furious savages attacked desperately for three days on end, determined to destroy the caravan. In the end Stanley succeeded in buying twenty-three boats from the natives; the realization of his crazy plan was at hand and the expedition could really be continued on African waters. Just in time, for Tippu Tib and his slaves refused to stay with Stanley and turned back.

For sheer courage, Stanley's decision to commit himself to the totally unknown waters of a river running thousands of miles through a wilderness where at all hours of the day death, starvation, sickness, and murderous attack stalked their prey, can only be compared with Orellana's great venture down the Amazon. Had this adventurous seven-month navigation of a great river taken place in an earlier age, it would have been handed down as legendary; in our swift-moving days, though its details were published and read, it has lapsed into oblivion.

The small flotilla of frail craft paddled along between the dark, impenetrable forest walls on water that blazed like fire under the strong sun. At the end of ten days they came to a halt; the river, encountering a steep ridge, broke into raging eddies, flung itself over rocky cliffs—the Stanley Falls. The boats had to be dragged at the cost of unspeakable exertions through the jungle and over trackless heights until calm water was met again. During the months to come this happened repeatedly, for the river teemed with rock barriers, rapids, and falls.

Things grew even more difficult when the stream, narrowing to a sixth of its former width, raced madly downward through a number of separate channels. The natives on the banks flew into bloodthirsty rages at the sight of the boats: there were daily skirmishes and even miniature pitched battles. Every evening there were wounded to tend and dead to bury.

In the Ituka country the river turned westward away from the Nile; Livingstone's theory was at last discounted. At the same time, its surface broadened to mighty proportions, some three miles from shore to shore. Pleasant islands appeared, and the only things unchanged for the better were the worry about food and the fight against the savages. The black hordes attacked incessantly—cannibals, as their enemies' bones and skulls about their campfires proved only too well. They came in monstrous eighty-oared boats, making a fiendish din, with drums beating, trumpets braying, and war songs resounding; their heads were decorated with parrots' feathers, and they never ceased attacking till they were beaten. After which fresh swarms renewed the assault.

But one day everything changed. A great tributary, the Aruwimi, joined the river on whose course their journey had lain so long. There could no longer be the slightest doubt that the secret of the Lualaba was unmasked. They were on the Congo.

At the same time they found peace again. Here the natives were friendly, bringing fruit and flour. Privation was at an end, for the great majestic stream flowed through a land of wonderful fertility. Here they found date and oil palms, bananas, teak and mango, tamarinds, ferns, water lilies, ginger bushes, nux vomica, and dragon-blood trees, myrrh and odellium shrubs, rubber and cotton, glowing colors and sweet scents. It was a veritable paradise through which they now traveled; and though, toward the end of February, the many islands, bays, and backwaters sometimes made it difficult find the way, their deviations harbored no danger, for every island offered shelter and refreshment.

This idyllic passage, however, came to an end. The waters darkened, swarms of mosquitoes banished all hope of sleep, the distant war cries of the natives sounded again. Hills constricted the river's course till it raced down over lava reefs and rock barriers to hurl itself over the edge of huge terraces into the depths with a deafening roar. Then, after a succession of gigantic waterfalls, it flowed on again, a thousand feet lower down.

Once again they had to transport the boats overland; when the current allowed, they moved cautiously along the very edge of the river, but raging eddies took their toll whenever a crew got too far out from the bank. On one occasion three boats disappeared together into the abysses of a fall.

On reaching the Inkisi territory all hope of progress seemed to vanish, for the river narrowed to a single raging maelstrom between insurmountable rock walls. Stanley spent days in reconnoitering the ground; the river was impossible, the wilderness to the north and south unexplored and dangerous, but he certainly

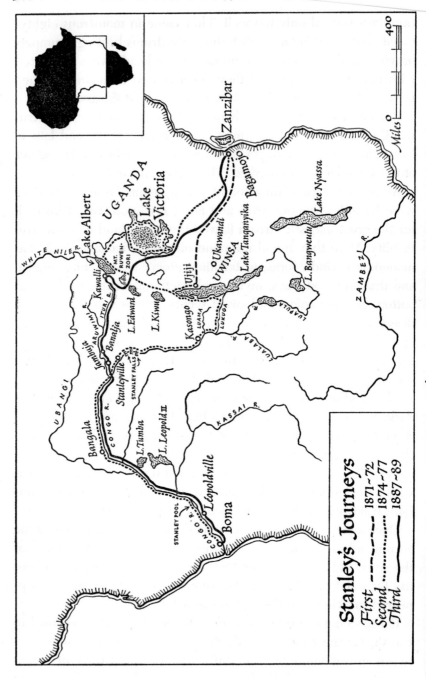

Stanley's Journeys

First — — — 1871~72
Second ·············· 1874~77
Third ———— 1887~89

could not stay where he was. There was nothing for it but to get the boats up the cliffs, over the plateau above them, and down again.

Straining every muscle, they lugged the boats inch by inch up the thirteen-hundred-foot precipice. Once on the plateau, a new sixty-foot boat had to be built of teak; rocks had to be blasted, a slipway laid through the jungle, a forge installed. Their bodies were enfeebled by an outbreak of dysentery, but Stanley's will of steel prevailed, and his tenacity won for him the respectful title of *Bula Matari,* "The Rockbreaker," from the natives.

There were still five sets of falls to be dealt with before they could reach the river's mouth. On July 3 when Pocock, the only white survivor in Stanley's company, was drowned in a whirlpool, utter despair fell upon the black retinue. They had just mastered the fearsome Massassa Falls and they were utterly exhausted. They could not face another step forward: all they craved was death itself. A greater menace than nature's savagery or that of the inhabitants faced the expedition.

Such crises are common to all great ventures of the kind. Alexander's soldiers forced him to turn back in India; Columbus would have failed had not land been sighted within the appointed time; the host of mariners and explorers who turned back too soon have remained nameless and unknown. It was only by dealing with this obstacle that Stanley could master his fate.

He assembled his men and addressed them: "You say you have no strength. And I have none, my friends, I assure you. I am as hungry as any of you. I am so tired and sorry that I could lie down smiling and die. If you all leave me, I am safe and there is no responsibility on me. I have my boat, and it is in the river. The current is swift, the fall is only a few yards off. My knife can cut the rope, and I shall then go to sleep forever. There are the beads; take them, do what you will. While you stay with me, I follow this river until I come to the point where it is known. If you don't stay with me, I will cling to the river and will die in it."

These simple words of a weary man still determined to carry out his mission, unheroic but intelligible to the simple minds of his black followers, were successful in improving their morale. The

expedition moved on again and disposed of one of the most difficult sectors of the route. It involved three miles of progress in
thirty days, at the cost of several more deaths in the raging waters.

In the rapids between the great falls they tied the boats together with ropes of reed fiber; on shore they scaled the cliffs on
rope ladders. At the Mbelo Falls, Stanley's boat was sucked into
a whirlpool and the lashings that held it to the others parted; it
seemed as if nothing could save him, yet he managed to reach the
shore. The blacks could scarcely believe their eyes and were so
impressed that they read into his recovery a sign from the gods
and no longer had any doubt about the expedition's ultimate
success.

On July 30 at Isangila Stanley learned the stupendous news that
the sea lay only five days away. In order to spare his men the
struggle with the remaining falls, he decided to march overland.
The column of starving, hollow-eyed, emaciated figures tottered
across the arid, scorching plain with only one thought in their
minds—the sea! Forty of them were sick men indeed; one went
out of his mind and rushed off into the wilds with his parrot on
his shoulders. It was on August 12, 1877, two and a half years after
setting out from the Indian Ocean, that Stanley reached Boma on
Africa's Atlantic coast. The sensational news was already going
out over the world's telegraphic network before he lay down to
take his first recuperative sleep.

Even now he gave himself no respite. Hardly had he discovered
the most important part of a continent, a river with surrounding
areas equal to the Mississippi's or the Amazon's, when he started
on the development of this vast area. He foresaw the immense
possibilities of trade and mutual economic advantage for Europe
and Africa, once the Congo could be used as a means of transpor-
tation. Moreover, he had learned at first hand the obstacles of
cataracts and whirlpools and that for a length of about three hundred miles roads and railways would have to be built. But he had
precise plans to put forward and, having paved the way with his
newspaper articles, he went straight to England to offer his native
land a matchless political opportunity to develop central Africa.

There he was to meet with a bitter, utterly unexpected disappointment. The man whose great vision was to conjure out of the white blank on the map, out of its inaccessible, inhospitable wildernesses, a flourishing economic empire, was forced to negotiate with shipowners, business houses, bankers, and ministers, to deliver lectures and addresses, without finding anyone ready to lift a finger on his behalf.

Among all the powerful men in Europe only one was farsighted enough to show any interest in the Congo—Leopold II of Belgium. He invited Stanley to see him, discussed the project thoroughly, and found the money to back it, after a last abortive attempt in England had resulted in a decisive final rejection.

Two years after leaving the mouth of the Congo, Stanley was back again bringing four small steam launches; with fourteen white men and two hundred blacks at his disposal, he set to work on opening up access to the interior.

The first year produced fifty miles of surfaced road as a result of endless negotiations with the natives, of marches totaling thirty-five hundred miles, of meticulous preparation and laborious construction work. Stanley lived day after day on goat flesh, cooked bones, and unripe bananas. On this diet he carried out the work of a surveyor, mechanical and constructional engineer, builder, diplomat, negotiator, geographer, officer, doctor, teacher, and governor. After laying down four stations—Vivi, Isangila, Manyanga, and Léopoldville—he obtained the rights to build a railway, and the work mounted to an immeasurable extent, involving negotiations with hundreds of minor chiefs and dissensions with the useless whites who had been sent to him from Europe. In the end he had to return to Europe to select suitable material, and while he was away everything he had started in Africa came to a standstill. Back in Africa again, he encountered fresh obstacles, further treating with the chiefs—who in the end conceded him sovereign rights over their territories and so laid the foundations for the Belgian Congo as a state—and further difficulties with his white assistants.

Once Stanley was able to show in practice that this area—almost eight thousand miles of navigable waterways and a river network some fifty-four thousand square miles in extent—was no longer hemmed in by an inaccessible, impassable frontier, the political consciousness of the great powers of Europe was stung into awareness. An international conference at Berlin agreed on definite spheres of influence, and where there had been nothing but an unexplored wilderness before Stanley's Congo journey, European colonies began to take shape. In 1885 Leopold founded the independent state of the Congo, to become in 1908 the Belgian Congo, an imposing area from the mouth of the Congo to Tanganyika and the source of the Lualaba, a vast tract entirely discovered by Stanley and yet one in whose immense wealth he had no share. In 1885, too, Portugal began to develop Angola, that coastal district of Africa which had been in her possession since the days of the great discoverers. England took over Bechuanaland as a protectorate.

There were no more great tracts in Africa for Stanley to discover; all that was left were a few individual problems to be cleared up. Boundaries were quickly established and there was no more scope. French Equatorial Africa appeared in 1879 and in 1881 France took Tunis into her protection, while Italy captured Eritrea and Somaliland. Great Britain had occupied Egypt in 1882; in 1884 Germany took over German Southwest Africa, the Cameroons, and Togoland; in 1886 Nigeria became a British colony, and British East Africa followed in 1887 as did Rhodesia in 1889; in 1890 Germany took into her keeping German East Africa, which Karl Peters had occupied in 1884.

Political developments afforded Stanley the opportunity for yet another world-shaking achievement. The revolt of the "Mahdi"—Mohammed Ahmed, a fanatical Moslem leader—broke out in the Sudan. An Egyptian force under Emin Pasha had to fall back before the rebels and withdraw some hundreds of miles into the wilderness of Wadelai, north of Lake Albert.

Emin Pasha was a German, whose real name was Dr. Eduard Schnitzer. His unstable character, the urge to explore, love of adventure, considerable gifts, and a streak of unreliability combined to produce a restless life, spent at first in southeastern Europe and later in Africa. He must certainly be given credit for his explorations of East Africa between 1876 and 1892; during these he traveled through Unjoro, Uganda, examined along the lower Bar el Jebel the causes of the Nile's arrested flow, sojourned with the Latuku and Obdo tribes in the Makrara territory, near Lake Albert, returned to Khartoum, disappeared again into the Mombuttu wildernesses, and finally served under General Gordon, who was murdered during the Mahdi rising.

The British press grew highly excited over events in the Sudan, and was daily concerned over the fate of Emin Pasha's column, which was encircled on the north by the Mahdi's followers, to the east by rebellious Uganda tribes, and to the south and west by the dread jungle of central Africa, which was held to be impassable.

A committee was formed to raise funds for an expedition to extricate Emin Pasha, to which the Egyptian government contributed heavily; and who was more suitable than Stanley to seek out a man whose very whereabouts in the wilds of Africa were not established and to bring him back if it meant crossing the continent itself?

So, with a carefully equipped expeditionary force of considerable strength, Stanley moved off from the mouth of the Congo on his third African journey, which was once again to take him across the continent. When in July 1887 he reached the middle of Africa at Jambuja, there was still an area 500 by 350 miles in extent between him and Emin Pasha—an area untrodden by the foot of man, if a few pygmy tribes are excepted. He left a supply dump behind him and hurried on for 160 days through forest, bush, and undergrowth, without once seeing daylight, losing seventy-one men through death or desertion on the way. At the end of those weeks of hardship and hunger, the rations had shrunk to a maximum of two bananas a day. For 336 more hours the starving column dragged itself onward; had it not come upon a settlement of the Manjema tribe, every man of them would have perished.

Stanley pushed on and found Emin Pasha near Lake Albert; then, seeing that his supplies had not come up, he fought his way back through the jungle to Jambuja in 60 days only to find that they had been treacherously done away with. Back again he went to Emin Pasha and finally led him and his six hundred soldiers out to safety in spite of continual difficulties raised by Emin, who was none too pleased to be rescued.

On December 3, 1889, they arrived at Bagamoyo on the Indian Ocean coast, two and three-quarter years after Stanley had left the mouth of the Congo. The intervening sufferings, battles, treacheries, adventures, and disappointments provided material for an epic second to none of the great classic chronicles. It is worth giving an example at this point of the effect the primeval nature of the forests, through which he moved to Emin's rescue, had upon him, and of his masterly ability to describe them when for once the hardships of his fight against them were not too overwhelmingly in his mind:

Imagine the whole of France and the Iberian Peninsula closely packed with trees varying from 20 to 180 feet high, whose crowns of foliage interlace and prevent any view of the sun, and each tree from a few inches to four feet in diameter. Then from tree to tree run cables from two inches to fifteen inches in diameter, up and down in loops and festoons and W's and badly formed M's; fold them round the trees in great tight coils, until they have run up the entire height, like endless anacondas; let them flower and leaf luxuriantly, and mix up above with the foliage of the trees to hide the sun, and then from the highest branches let fall the ends of the cables reaching near to the ground by hundreds with frayed extremities, for these represent the air roots of the Epiphytes; let slender cords hang down also in tassels with open-work thread-work at the ends. Work others through and through these as confusedly as possible, and pendent from branch to branch—with absolute disregard of material, and at every fork and on every horizontal branch plant cabbage like lichens of the largest kind, and broad spear-leaved plants—these would represent the elephant-eared plant—and orchids and clusters of vegetable marvels, and a drapery of delicate ferns which abound. Now cover tree, branch, twig and creeper with thick moss like a green fur. Where the forest is compact as described above, we may not do more than cover the ground closely with thick crop of phrynia, and amoma, and dwarf bush; but if the lightning, as frequently hap-

pens, has severed the crown of a proud tree, and let in the sun-light, or split a giant down to its roots, or scorched it dead, or a tornado has been uprooting a few trees, then the race for air and light has caused a multitude of baby trees to rush upward—crowded, crushing, and treading upon and strangling one another, until the whole is one impervious bush.

But the average forest is a mixture of these scenes. There will probably be groups of fifty trees standing like columns of a cathedral, grey and solemn in the twilight, and in the midst there will be a naked and proud patriarch, bleached white, and around it will have grown a young community, each tree clambering upward to become heir to the area of light and sunshine once occupied by the sire. The law of primogeniture reigns here also.

There is also death from wounds, sickness, decay, hereditary diseases and old age, and various accidents, thinning the forest, removing the unfit, the weakly, the unadaptable, as among humanity. Let us suppose a tall chief among the giants, like an insolent son of Anak. By a head he lifts himself above his fellows—the monarch of all he surveys; but his pride attracts the lightning, and he becomes shivered to the roots, he topples, he declines and wounds half a dozen other trees in his fall.

This is why we see so many tumourous excrescences, great goitrous swellings and deformed trunks. . . . Some have sickened by intense rivalry of other kinds and have perished at an immature age; some have grown with a deep crook in their stems, by a prostrate log which had fallen and pressed them obliquely. . . . Some have been gnawed by rodents, or have been sprained by elephants leaning on them to rub their prurient hides, and ants of all kinds have done infinite mischief. . . .

To complete the mental picture of this ruthless forest . . . Every mile or so there should be muddy streams, stagnant creeks and shallow pools, green with duckweed, leaves of lotus and lilies, and a greasy green scum composed of millions of finite growths.

Stanley lived on for another fifteen years, the African fever in his veins, a victim of the Black Continent's magic, even at a distance. Political and commercial negotiations, the precise delineation of the Congo state's boundaries, the colonization of the country around Lake Albert occupied him constantly, till in 1890, at the age of fifty, he married. His wife found distractions to keep him away from Africa: journeys to America, Australia, Paris, Switzerland, parliamentary activities, and finally a new life on his own small estate thirty miles from London. Stanley was famous, he wrote books, lectured, planned; but the ruling mood of his last years was one of melancholy.

"Civilisation never looks more attractive than in the wilds, the wilds never more attractive than from civilisation," he wrote. The malicious rumors that pursued him hurt him deeply. "What then was my reward? To appear in the eyes of mankind a forger, a liar, a romancer. African spears wounded me, European slanders struck deeper wounds. But a man must not let himself be diverted from his course, just because the dogs bark."

He died on May 5, 1904, an outcast to his dying day. The Dean of Westminster refused permission to bury him in the Abbey.

9

ASIA NEEDED NO DISCOVERERS

THE HIDEOUS roar of Vasco de Gama's ships' guns ushered in the last chapter in the history of Europe's fluctuating relations with Asia, a chapter that brought the final integration of the huge Asiatic land mass into the European's geographical world picture.

Asia did not need discovering, for it was that greatest of all continents, to which Europe was attached as an appendage. She did not need discovering because migrations, voyages, and trade communications had already established the unity of the plains from Vienna to China; the basic relationship between the Indo-German languages, from Sanskrit through Greek, Latin, and ancient high German right down to modern European tongues, points to there having been originally a single language throughout the vast spaces of Euro-Asia. In earliest historical times the great silk routes led across more than a quarter of the globe from the Pacific shores to those of the Mediterranean. For several centuries Persia played the role of contact and exchange point between East and West.

And yet Europe had continually to discover Asia anew. The Euro-Asian land block proved far too big to preserve its unity for any length of time: even within Asia itself the great states of India, China, Central Asia, and Siberia developed as separate entities. It was not only the immense distances, but also the natural barriers—mountains, rivers, deserts, steppes, and wildernesses, storms, ice, and burning sun—which limited exploration; and when, into the bargain, warlike Islam drove a wedge between Europe and Asia to effect a sharp division between them, far-off Asia soon disappeared over the European's horizon.

Much, but not all, of the old knowledge was forgotten. And when spices became scarce, when men began to seek Prester John as a possible ally against the Mohammedans, when they began to believe Marco Polo's stories, the old traditions started to come to life again. The fabulous treasures of India, China, and Japan enticed men out onto the stormy oceans and resulted in the discovery of America, the circumnavigation of Africa, and the opening up of the sea road to India.

THE KHAN PRESENTING A TABLET TO THE POLO BROTHERS.
FOURTEENTH-CENTURY MINIATURE

When the Portuguese navigators sighted the Indian coast, Asia was discovered for the last time and for all time. Not until access had been wrung from those foreign seas, till the dangers and hardships of the long sea voyages were rewarded by tangible results, till conquests and further advances into the unknown followed the discoveries, could Asia be gradually plotted correctly on European maps and charts; for too long a time had the imaginative efforts of mapmakers started at the coast of upper India. In spite of the existence of a natural but far too lengthy overland route, Asia had to be reached by sea before it could count in Western consciousness—and so in the first comprehensive world geography—as a sphere of European discovery and exploration.

This was no question of areas that had remained unexplored. On the contrary, Asia's culture was, for the time being, far ahead of Europe's, and its geographical knowledge was outstanding. That is true especially of China, where the compass had already been discovered about 1100 B.C. In the twelfth century B.C., when the West was still inhabited by savage or half-savage tribes, Chinese culture understood the making and use of maps: not merely small maps for the everyday use of pilots or entries in journals, but maps of the whole realm of China. With the fall of the Chou dynasty, in the centuries immediately after the birth of Christ the general recession of culture set in; but thanks to the work of learned men and specialists, the traditional geographical knowledge and activities were maintained.

Progress was restored when, from about A.D. 600 onward, the Chinese Empire broadened out under the T'ang dynasty, relations with India became closer, and Buddhist influence found its way into China. The fruitful alliance of two cultures is typified by such great explorers and thinkers as Hiuen Tsang, who between A.D. 629 and 644 undertook extensive journeys through the highlands of Asia, the whole of Turkistan, Afghanistan, and India. He explored the whole of central Asia and India, searching tirelessly for Sanskrit manuscripts, and devoted the rest of his life to translating into Chinese the works he found.

A number of wonderful geographical works of the time show how far ahead of all other cultural spheres China was: in A.D. 648 a sixty-volume work was completed containing descriptions and maps of the newly occupied regions in western China; in 799 the learned Chia Tan, who had earlier undertaken the detailed description of all the provinces of China, put the seal on six years of hard work with the publication of a 34-foot-by-31-foot map showing the whole of China and the adjoining parts of central Asia. The great Chinese Empire now grew into a monster area ten times the size of China itself; hordes of Mongolian horsemen swept across Asia, mowing down everything that dared to get in the way. In 1206 the merciless Temujin was proclaimed ruler, under the title of Genghis Khan, over the scattered Mongolian races and began an unparalleled series of victorious campaigns; there was no power in the world which could stand up to his swift, reckless, grim legions, courageous unto death. The Mongols had no trace of culture themselves, but they understood extremely well how to organize and put to use all the sciences and achievements of the people they subdued. So they possessed detailed knowledge of the Euro-Asian land mass, seeing that Genghis Khan's empire and that of his successors comprised almost the whole world; they ruled over Mongolia, China, Japan, India, Asia Minor, Russia, and everywhere else they pleased. Western history and culture would indeed have followed a very different course had not the Great Khan died in the distant Karakorum just at the moment when the small western European appendage was on the point of being overrun, and had not all the army commanders been compelled to return home under an unbreakable Mongolian law. The passing of the Mongolian tempest brought it very clearly to the European consciousness—and in this instance it was the Europeans who were being discovered—that there were immeasurable tracts in the far east which they must themselves learn to know.

At that time, too, the Arabs were far ahead of Europeans in knowledge of Asia; their great geographers, such as al-Idrisi (twelfth century) and ibn-Batuta (fourteenth century), the most important land-travelers of all time, had described the main regions of Asia; Arab trade dominated the Near East and India; religious fanaticism had pushed its strongholds forward to the borders of Turkistan.

Before the Mohammedan wedge was driven between the two continents, the natural limits of cultural exchange between Europe and Asia (bounded by the Black Sea and the mountain ranges between Persia and Mesopotamia) were crossed in many places at various times. The greatest explorer and discovered was Herodotus, who, between 484 and 408 B.C., penetrated through Persia to Turan and on into the neighborhood of the Caspian Sea. In the next century Alexander's famous campaigns into Asia combined conquest with discovery, and his short-lived empire spread over Asia Minor, Assyria, Media, and the lands of the Parthians and Bactrians far outward to the Indus.

The next European penetration of Asia was the great achievement of a brave and solitary explorer: in the first century B.C. the

Greek navigator Hippalus crossed the Indian Ocean and reached the coast of India. A few merchant voyagers later followed his example, and a number of traders also took the land route deep into upper Asia and even reached China. For hundreds of years the silk trade and missionary zeal (Nestorian Christians settled as far afield as northern China) were the main motives for these solitary excursions between Europe and Asia before communications were again interrupted.

MARCO POLO'S GALLEY

But the first real European insight into the heart of Asia came after A.D. 1300, when Franciscans and Dominicans were sent to the courts of the Mongol khans, who had graduated from cavalry leaders to administrators of the various lands they had plundered. Unlike the Mohammedans, they bore no hatred toward the Christians (they were tolerant in the religious sphere generally) and gave the European envoys plenty of freedom of movement. Because the might of the Mongolian hordes would constitute a deadly menace for Islam's empire, the idea was to win it as an ally for the Christian Crusaders. The diplomatic attempts to set the Beelzebub of Asia at grips with the Devil of Arabia failed; but the monks who had sojourned with the Mongolian rulers brought back to Europe much new and very valuable geographical knowledge.

If it were a question of the "discovery" of Asia, one would have to include the journeys and scientific records of these holy fathers, zealous and intelligent as they were. But Asia had no need of "discoverers," for it was well enough known—certainly to its rulers, administrators, and scientists. The West was in a position to make considerable discoveries, but, strangely enough, the new fund of knowledge at first made singularly little impact, however great might be the achievements of those who produced it.

In 1245 Europeans were seen for the first time at the court of the Great Khan: these constituted a Papal mission, led by Giovanni de Piano Carpini. They remained in central Asia for two years, long enough for Carpini to commit to paper his observations and exact descriptions of the landscape in scientific form. The next embassy was sent by Louis IX of France. The Franciscan monk Rubruk (Ruysbroeck) and his companion Bartholomaus traveled across the Crimea to the Volga, parted on the shores of the Caspian, and established, when they met on its farther side, that this was an inland sea. In central Asia they encountered a fearful sand- and snowstorm, being fortunate enough to escape with their lives, and at the end of 1254 reached the court of the Great Khan, Mangu. Their diplomatic mission was as unsuccessful as that of their predecessors; but while Bartholomaus was able to accomplish much spiritual guidance and to render other services among the Christians in Mongolia, eventually devoting himself entirely to these good works, Rubruk returned safely to Europe, where he was able to publish the first book to contain plentiful and well-based information about distant Asia.

Missionary work in India and China brought other monks to Asia, of whom Montecorvino and Pordenone are specially distinguished for their valuable scientific material on central Asia, China, and Tibet. In 1260 the Polo brothers entered the Mongol state of Kiptchak (then under the rule of the bloodthirsty Genghis's peaceable cousin Kublai Khan, a patron of the sciences). This region stretched from north of the Caspian Sea to the Urals and the Don and carried on a thriving trade with the Tatars in Turkistan. Soon after their return home they set out again for distant parts, taking with them this time their seventeen-year-old nephew Marco. In the following years the young man had more opportunities than any other European of getting to know the world. After the journey through Persian deserts, over the ranges of the Hindu Kush into the Pamirs, the provinces of China became his second home; later undertaking the important duty of accompanying a Mongol princess to her betrothed, the Crown Prince of Persia, he became the first European to visit Java and Sumatra, before returning home from Persia. His account, a broad "tale of discovery" embracing the whole of Asia, has since become the outstanding work in all geographical literature.

Relations between eastern Asia and Europe could not be maintained for more than a few decades after Marco Polo's time. In 1368 a nationalistic government, unfriendly to foreigners, came into power in China, and, as usual in such cases, a period of divorce from the outer world and a falling-off of cultural standards set in.

The result was that the next time Europeans met Chinese, the former, who had in the meantime experienced a great rebirth of knowledge and science, were in some matters now the more forward; the Jesuit missionaries who were active in China from the start of the seventeenth century brought with them advanced astronomic, geographic, and cartographic knowledge and activity. Thus began a period of fruitful co-operation between East and West. For instance, after the rise to power of the Manchu dynasty, the Jesuit Johann Adam Schall von Bell of Cologne was nominated president of the astronomic court and observatory. In the course of the next few decades Jesuit fathers, using Chinese material and their own surveys as a basis, produced numerous maps of the whole of China including modern Siberia; these were cut in wood and printed.

Yet this fresh "discovery" of the Far East remained almost unnoticed in the West, for it was only a quiet after-ripple of the great wave of events which had already produced closer relations between Europe and Asia, and which inevitably flowed from discoveries and conquests, trade and colonization: such linked events as the settlement of the Portuguese on the Indian coast, command of the sea passage thither, further penetration into Asia. After the capture of Malacca and the occupation of the Moluccas in 1518, Ceylon and the whole Malayan archipelago came under Portuguese control; the first Portuguese traders reached China in 1514, but were soon sent packing. In 1540, however, it proved possible to settle a sizable colony in Macao; two years later the sailor Mendes Pinto reached Japan in a Chinese pirate ship and reported a most friendly reception. In 1549, therefore, the missionary Francis Xavier went there and was highly successful in his activities (Japanese nobles, whom he converted to Christianity, did not shrink from the long voyage to Rome to visit the Pope); but a few years later a highly nationalistic, xenophobic regime took over in Japan too; the Christian missions were mercilessly hounded out, and all entry into the Japanese islands was forbidden to Portuguese and Spanish merchants.

A further period of broadening geographical knowledge began for the European countries when they started to fight each other about the Asiatic regions. Dutch traders had established themselves on Formosa in 1609 and started the foundations of factories in Japan, where they alone of Europeans were tolerated. The writings of Bernhard Varen (1649) and Engelbert Kämpfer (1700) gave detailed reports of these islands, whose secrets had remained so well kept. The development of Dutch and English trading-companies that undertook conquests and founded monopolies with their own resources brought not only a new source of political power, but a flood of geographical knowledge which the Portuguese and Spaniards would rather have kept to themselves.

The supremacy of Portugal (and of Spain, her successor) continually dwindled, and other European powers, whose influence in the continent was ever broadening, eventually forced the original overlords out of Asia. After the great naval power of the Dutch East India Company had defeated the Spanish-Portuguese combined fleet off Malacca, the Dutch took over the spice-bearing regions, making Batavia in Java the central point of their rich colonial empire in the Sunda Seas; and in 1641, under Van Diemen, they took from the Portuguese their last base in the area, Malacca.

JESUIT MAP OF THE CELESTIAL EMPIRE. FROM GONZALES DE MENDOZA, 1589.

The British East India Company was meanwhile establishing itself all over India.

The Portuguese had a system of bases along the coast, so after placing a first fortress at Madras in 1639, the British went deep into the country, while providing themselves with highly important exit ports in Bombay (1665) and on the mouths of the Ganges (1696). Their chief rivals were the French, whose East India Company had its headquarters in Madagascar. Just as in America, so here the struggle for dominion over the huge territories involved skirmishes and battles in which the various native tribes fought alongside the European soldiers. At last in 1757, with the Battle of Plassey, victory went to the British.

In the first half of the nineteenth century England was thus able to conquer the whole of India, while the French took command of Indochina.

Great as Asia might be, it gradually disappeared into the maw of European power politics. It is possible to extend this simile: the lower jaw closed on the rich regions of the south and southeast, the upper on the north. For at the same time that the Portuguese, Dutch, French, and British were fighting for the best part of Asia, the Russians were quietly annexing a surface of many thousands of square miles in the far north.

The new "discovery" started from this side in 1567, when Ivan the Terrible wanted to reconnoiter what was going on beyond the Ural Mountains. There lay the land of Mangaseja (between the Ob and the Yenisei), where dwelt the "Samoyeds," a heathen tribe of small stature with flat faces. They were good runners and bowmen, drove swift dogs and reindeer in harness, and were known to eat men. They did not bury their dead, but ate them, and when a guest arrived he was offered a tidbit of children roasted on the spit. Beyond them lived other races whose mouths were on top of their heads, and indeed some who had no heads at all.

But Ivan knew a good deal more about those regions than the stories people told. Above all, he knew about the priceless furs that abounded there, for the Stroganovs had made him rich gifts of them when they came to Moscow to report. This Stroganov family had become fabulously rich and influential from the Urals all over Russia, through their trade in salt and furs. When they reported to the Tsar on their expeditions to Mangaseja and suggested the development of that land, he gave them independent powers over the Permer land, lying close to the Urals, which offered the best base for preparing forays into Siberia.

Since then, Ivan's interest in the lands beyond the Urals had been very lively, and that was why he sent a reconnaissance out in that very year of 1567; it consisted of the Cossack chiefs Petrov and Jalytchev, with a few qualified geographers and a small Cossack force. The mission was splendidly carried out; the expedition worked its way through Siberia, Mongolia, and China to Peking and brought back much reliable material and exact descriptions of the lands, cities, and peoples they had encountered. The only task now was to take possession of as many of these strange places as possible.

It was not easy, for a warlike successor of Genghis Khan, Kuchum by name, had overthrown the Tatars, Ostjaks, Woguls, and Samoyeds and declared himself tsar of "Sibir." The Stroganovs suffered heavily from the inroads and campaigns of this self-styled tsar, and when they could bear it no longer, they decided to march into Siberia. They made submissions in Moscow for the necessary backing, and in 1574 Ivan generously gave them suzerain rights over the "Siberian Ukraine" (which did not belong to him)—the land of Mangaseja and the regions about the Tobol, its tributaries and lakes.

For the attack on "Tsar" Kuchum, the Stroganovs hired a swarm of Cossacks, a riffraff of pickpockets, river pirates, robbers, fugitives, peasants, and dagger men for whom things had got too hot in the Don country. Led by chief Ermak Timofeev, who contrived to turn this dismal rabble into a well-disciplined body of fighters, they reached the Urals in 1580, signed on as mercenaries, and moved into the field. Eight hundred strong, well supplied by the Stroganovs with provender but poorly with muskets, they entered Kuchum's kingdom across the Tura. Thus began a victorious march similar to Pizarro's—except that the Cossacks had neither horse nor cannon, and that their opponents were mounted Tatars and other tribes used to the arts of war.

At the River Tobol the Cossacks, thanks to the terrifying crackle of their musketry, won their first fight with Kuchum's auxiliaries, who were by no means willing vassals; but at the settlement of Badassan on the Tobol they lost an engagement against one of his field armies and fled down the river. Here they overcame a settlement of Tatars, plundered it, and ate themselves strong again on the booty. On October 1 they met by far the larger part of the enemy's main force near the river mouth. Ermak saw no way out but to attack, and the Cossacks won their first big battle.

They immediately moved against Kuchum's headquarters.

The threat of winter and the lack of women, who were to be got only by capturing them from the Tatars, drove the Cossacks to a desperate attack on the fortified camp—and they took it by storm. The engagement reduced their effective strength to five hundred, but the vital issue had been settled. Kuchum's vassals began to desert him and gradually joined the victors.

Siberia was subdued, but in the following year Kuchum managed to collect another army of Tatars. Ermak was again victorious, but for the last time: shortly afterward he was killed in an ambush. Reinforcements from Russia consolidated his conquest: each year they pressed farther forward without any major conflict and made the region safe with countless settlements.

In 1596 the Barbar Steppe was incorporated; in 1598 the whole of what had formerly been Khanat Sibir up to the Ob and Irtysh was in Russian hands—200,000 sables, 10,000 black foxes, and 500,000 squirrel pelts a year went to Moscow as tribute. In 1626 the Cossacks were on the Yenisei, in 1632 on the Lena, in 1638 on the Pacific coast—an average progress of seventy miles a year for ninety years, till all Siberia was Russian. Siberia, that tremendous region of buried treasure, of choice furs, of rivers that sometimes literally teem with fish, of vast cedar forests, and of the greatest prairie in the world, stretching five thousand miles from the Amur to the Caspian Sea.

In 1696 the Cossacks completed its subjection with the capture, under Atlasov, of the Kamchatkan Peninsula. He thereupon wrote a report that in the faithfulness of its facts can bear comparison with the works of the great geographers.

The Russian conquests had reached their limit at the Chinese border. From 1649 to 1653 Chabarov led bloody campaigns of eviction along the Amur, but the Russians could never establish themselves because they were repeatedly attacked from inside China. After various struggles and battles, an agreement was signed in 1689 at Nerchinsk between the Russians and a Chinese delegation, advised by Jesuit fathers, and the frontier between the two states was thus delineated. So the only direction left to move in was the central Asian area in which—forgotten by the outer world—dwelt Turko-Tatar tribes in the Khanates of Kokand, Bukhara, and Khiva.

These areas of steppe and desert at the foot of the central Asian highlands evidently did not seem very attractive, for it was not till 1839 that Russia's military advance began in earnest with the subjection of the Kirghiz; after 1861 Russia attacked in turn the Tashkent region, Bukhara, the province of Fergana on the upper waters of the Syr Darya, then the Pamir district and Khiva, till in the last decade of the century every central Asian state had been wiped out and Russia's frontiers marched with those of British India as well as China's.

But before all this a peaceful traveler, one of the world's great explorers, had come out of Russia to lend important services to the unveiling of Asia's unknown districts; this was Przhevalski, who was the first European to follow Marco Polo's routes, while pressing deep into the heart of Asia in five great journeys of exploration.

The first journey took him from the boundary of Mongolia and Siberia, by way of Peking, to the upper Hwang Ho and the Gobi Desert; the second from the Chinese frontier town of Kuldja along the Tarim through the deserts of eastern Turkistan and the basins of the rivers Kashgar, Yarkand, Khotan and Aksu. A third and still harder journey led over the difficult mountain tracks of the great Kunlun Range into hidden Tibet; the fourth and long-

est, from Siberia across the high plateau between the Hwang Ho
and the Yangtze Kiang, and across the Tien Shan mountains to the
Issyk Kul. From this journey Przhevalski was able to bring back
an enormous amount of observation at first hand; his studies,
quite apart from his descriptions of the landscapes through which
he passed, embraced the climate, flora, and fauna of all these
regions, which thus became known for the first time to the outer
world.

During his fifth journey, whose objective was Lhasa, the explorer died in a town near the Issyk Kul which has since borne
the name of Przhevalsk. This great man, who succumbed to the
exertions of an explorer's life, was—excepting only Stanley—the
last great land traveler whose observations can truly be described, from the European point of view, as discoveries.

Part III

The Adventure Goes On

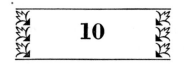

10

THE ATTACK ON THE NORTH POLE

Long before Marco Polo's days, the Greek Pytheas of Massilia (today's Marseille) had experienced a similar fate when his contemporaries refused to believe his reports about places he had seen. Pytheas, an outstanding astronomer, embarked in 325 B.C. on a voyage of exploration and trade in search of the places where tin and amber came from, which took him into the Atlantic Ocean. North of Britain he came upon an island in whose neighborhood fog and floating ice prevented further progress. This unpeopled sea, rich in storms and fogs, where the inhabitable world seemed to end, he named the "Lung of the Ocean," and to its breathing he attributed the ebb and flow of tides.

No ancient traveler made his way so far north as this adventurous Greek, whose reports certainly did not encourage further voyaging in that direction and so were soon forgotten. It was eleven hundred years later that ships first ventured again into northern waters, when Irish monks visited Iceland and Normans and Vikings—adventurers, fishermen, missionaries, and pirates—penetrated into the white sea to Iceland, Greenland, and America. According to all accounts handed down from the Middle Ages, the Arctic areas were highly unpleasant places; there was nothing to be found in them except ice and darkness, dread seas—the glutinous seas—swarming with monsters and, somewhere near Greenland, even an abyss into which plunged all the waters of the sea.

About A.D. 1040 a small fleet carrying Frisian nobles put to sea from Bremen to find out, in spite of such terrors, whether there was any truth in the story that if you sailed due north from the Weser you would find nothing but an endless, landless sea.

Canon Adam of Bremen, who lived in the eleventh century, wrote of these brave Frisians and their experiences:

After leaving behind Denmark on the one side and Britain on the other, they came to the Orcadian Islands, then leaving these behind and having Normannia on their right hand, a long voyage brought them to icy Iceland. Sailing on from this land toward the farthest Pole, they entrusted their brave venture and their further journey to Almighty God and St. Willehad, and came of a sudden into the dark mists, scarce penetrable by the human eye, of the Rigid Ocean. Lo, then a wave of the sea unstable between ebb and flow, which runs back to its unknown place of origin, drew the luckless mariners, despairing of their safety, into this Chaos. This, men say, is the bottomless Abyss into which, it is told, all oceans flow back and from which arises all ebb and flow. As they were entreating the mercy of God to take their souls to Him, the strength of the returning sea carried several ships along with it. Thus they were at the last moment, through God's help, saved from their great peril and were enabled by rowing with might and main to escape from the waves.

Escaped from this perilous Region, they were unexpectedly driven upon a certain Island, which was fortified like to a city by the very lofty cliffs which ringed it about. To visit the interior of which they went ashore and found the people therein stowed away in underground caves. Before their doors lay a great mass of vessels, finished in gold and similar metals which men prize for their rarity. After bearing away with them as many of these treasures as they could carry, the oarsmen hastened gladly to their ships. Of a sudden they perceived themselves followed by men of beyond ordinary stature, whom we call Cyclops and whose hounds of unaccustomed size ran before them. These did succeed in overtaking one of the crew, whom they did forthwith tear in pieces. The remainder safely reached their ships and were followed only by the loud outcry of the Giants.

After such perils the Frisian comrades returned to Bremen, where they did relate all in its true order to the Archbishop

Alebrand, and presently brought thank offerings for their happy
return to Christ and his true servant Willehad.

It can be reasonably established from this account that the
Frisian sailors tried to sail beyond Iceland to the North Pole—as
Adam has it: *"in ultimum septentrionis axem"* [1]—but found them-
selves in strong currents as the sea gradually froze over, till in the
end they managed to withdraw with the loss of only a few ships.
On their return voyage they managed to conjure away some
valuables from the lairs of the pirates in the Fåro or Shetland
Islands.

Even the Norman King Harald, whose northern voyage Adam
reports, had to turn back "beyond Thule" on account of fogs
and currents.

Once again much time elapsed before the next polar voyage.

When, in the sixteenth and seventeenth centuries, sailing-ships
ventured into the Arctic, it was not with intent to reach the Pole,
but in fulfillment of Sebastian Cabot's theory that to find the
northeast or northwest passage to Asia it was necessary to sail
ever farther northward. The English navigator Martin Frobisher
(1534–1594) followed Cabot's plan and sailed by way of Greenland to arctic North America. In so doing, he succeeded in making important discoveries, even if he failed to find the passage,
for he was the first after the Vikings to sight the south coast of
Greenland, and he discovered Baffin Land and Frobisher Bay.
There he met a quite unknown race of men who were clad entirely in furs, had broad faces with small, flat noses and slightly
slanting slits of eyes, and were able to master the sea's strongest
breakers in their handy skin boats—the Eskimos.

After the ventures of Frobisher, Hudson, Davis, and William
Baffin (1584–1622), voyages into these inhospitable regions
ceased because Baffin declared it an impossibility to sail round
the north of America. Following the decline in the power of Spain

[1] "To the extreme axis of the seven-starred constellation." The Seven Stars—the
Great Bear—served in the Middle Ages as the most notable constellation, always to
be seen, for astronomic and geographic orientation. The Greeks called it *Arktos*
("The Bear") and the point about which it and the whole firmament appear to
revolve, the Arctic Pole (now the Pole Star). And so the "Arctic" came to be the
designation for the earth's northern polar regions.

and Portugal, the southern routes round America and Africa gradually fell open to others and so the interest in the difficult northern route died away, to be reawakened only two centuries later when the British government offered the handsome prize of £20,000 for the discovery of the northwest passage. Thereafter the Arctic became the objective of numerous voyages of discovery, stimulated by genuine enthusiasm for exploration as well as by zeal to win the prize. A very important impetus was the effect of a book, *A Chronological History of Voyages into the Arctic Regions,* by the English geographer John Barrow, which came out in 1818 and provided a general spur to Arctic exploration. Barrow also used all his personal energy and initiative to promote the dispatch of various expeditions.

John Ross (1777–1856), the first man to find himself on the right course to the Pacific among the world of Arctic islands to the north of America, turned back—though advised against so doing by his lieutenant, Edward Parry (1790–1855)—in Baffin Bay, which he imagined, erroneously, to be an inland sea. In the following year (1819) Parry sailed onward with his own expedition to the strait that he named Barrow Strait, wintering on Melville Island and coming to the definite conclusion that the Pacific Ocean could be reached by way of it. Without knowing it, he had discovered and traversed the greater part of the northwest passage; by way of contrast, he tried vainly in later years to sail through to the Pacific from Hudson Bay and Lancaster Sound.

Just as Parry continued Ross's explorations, so did Ross at the age of fifty-two return the compliment. Accompanied by his nephew James Clark Ross (1800–1862), who had also been along on Parry's voyages, he made a successful advance into the Arctic. He discovered and named after the financier of the expedition the peninsula of Boothia Felix, where he was caught in the ice and spent two winters; in the course of sledge journeys among the neighboring islands his nephew James discovered the North Magnetic Pole. He was finally compelled to abandon his ice-bound ship and beat a laborious retreat to Prince Regent Strait, where he was able somehow to see a third winter through, thanks to supplies Parry had left behind. Subsequently, using sledges

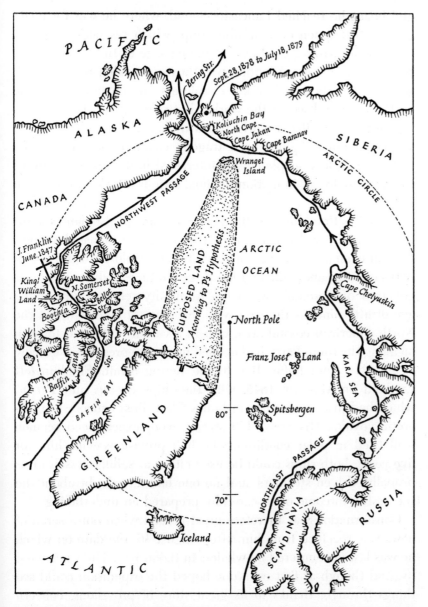

THE NORTHWEST AND NORTHEAST PASSAGES. THE MAP SHOWS PETER-
MANN'S FALSE CONCEPTION OF THE EXTENT OF GREENLAND, WHICH
HERE BLOCKS ACCESS TO THE NORTH POLE FROM AMERICA.

and boats, he reached Lancaster Sound, where he was fortunate enough to happen on a whaling-ship, which rescued the party.

The earlier romantic dream of the passage to India, which had haunted the great sea heroes, was thus superseded by the quiet, scientific efforts of a few keen explorers, driven into the Arctic by the urge to discover the world's last secrets. But the attention of the whole civilized world was switched at a single stroke to the north polar regions by a tragedy enacted there under the eyes of countless people closely interested in it. It was this event that eventually set in motion the final serious attack on the North Pole.

Sir John Franklin (1786–1847) was one of England's most famous sailors and had taken part in a number of naval actions. He had been a member of an expedition to explore Australia, and between 1818 and 1827 had led three Arctic expeditions; he was governor of Tasmania when the Admiralty selected him at the age of fifty-nine, as the man with the greatest knowledge of the North American coastal area, to lead a venture intended to push on along the route Parry had opened up and to press on as quickly as possible from Baffin Bay to the Bering Strait. Franklin left England on May 19, 1845, with the ships *Erebus* and *Terror*, which had just returned from James Clark Ross's successful Antarctic voyage. His crew, 129 strong, were experienced seamen well tried in polar conditions; he had provisions with him for five years; both ships could be used either as sailing-vessels or as propeller-driven steamers, and no one had any doubt about the successful outcome of so carefully prepared an undertaking.

Consternation was therefore great indeed when not a scrap of news was received from him after August 16, the date on which he was last encountered by whalers in Baffin Bay. The years went by, and though at first everyone hoped the expedition could see things through, thanks to its great store of provisions, concern mounted continually after an expedition led by John Rae, which had started out at the same time as Franklin, came back without having seen any sign of him.

In 1848 threefold rescue attempts were set in motion. James Clark Ross followed Franklin's route till ice compelled him to turn back; Henry Kellet and Moore tried to go to meet Franklin by way of the Bering Strait; Rae and John Richardson went over-land from the Mackenzie River to look for him.

Even John Ross, though now seventy-three years old, joined the search, but his efforts, in 1850–1, were of no avail. More than forty expeditions were sent out during the following years and the valiant rescue attempts cost lives as well as a great deal of money. In 1850 alone, sixteen ships of varying nationality combed the polar seas in every direction; they laid down supply dumps, erected beacons, marked rocky cliffs, burned flame signals, fired guns, launched hundreds of bottles and copper cylinders as a bottle post. They let loose thousands of gaily colored balloons with labels on them; they caught three hundred polar foxes, fitted them with little metal message boxes, and sent them out into unexplored wastes of ice. It was all in vain.

The Admiralty offered a reward of £100,000 for the rescue of Franklin and his men and half as much for definite news of them. Lady Franklin added a lesser sum from her own means; she also fitted out a ship to go in search of her husband at her own ex-pense. The tireless search inevitably broadened men's knowl-edge of the polar seas, and Robert McClure (1807–1873) actually took advantage of the opportunity to sail through to the Pacific on a dangerous voyage lasting several years, being finally com-pelled to leave his ship in the ice and complete the journey with sledges. By April 6, 1853, McClure had finally solved the riddle of the northwest passage, thereby proving that the northern sea route to the Pacific was practically useless. It was not till 1903–6 that a small motor yacht, the *Gjoa*, succeeded in forcing it—and then only by hugging the coast; her commander was Roald Amundsen. The complete passage from west to east (by Cook's intended route) was not made till 1940–2, when the eighty-ton Canadian police schooner *St. Roch* achieved the feat.

Neither McClure's nor any of the other search parties that set out to seek Franklin was able to throw any light on the fate of the lost expedition. So the government sent out a strong official fleet of six ships under the polar explorer and mariner Sir Edward Belcher (1799–1877), and named it the "Pride of England." But the grim strength of the Arctic was once again too much; Belcher lost one ship, the other five were frozen in beyond aid. He spent two successive winters in his icy prison. Twice he tried to blast a passage through the masses of pack ice—on one occasion he used eight hundred pounds of powder—but his vessels, held fast in the vice of the Wellington Channel, could not be worked clear. Threatened with a third winter, Belcher was forced to withdraw; abandoning his ships, he marched across the ice to Beechey Island, where he and his crew were picked up by transports and taken back to England.

Belcher brought back much information about the Arctic map, but not a grain of news about Franklin. He and his captains were court-martialed, charged with the loss of their ships, but were honorably acquitted. Belcher alone was given his sword back in silence to show that the court did not entirely agree with his conduct.

That was the last big expedition. Of the six ships it had cost, one, the *Resolute,* returned in most surprising fashion without captain or crew in 1855; she had been caught in the Arctic current and driven through the Barrow Strait, where an American whaler took her in tow. The *Resolute's* drift added important factors to the knowledge of the currents in the polar seas.

After nineteen costly government expeditions, embracing thirty-one ships in all, an Admiralty spokesman, Admiral Walcott, declared before the House of Commons on August 5, 1854: "I am of the opinion that every endeavor consistent with the honor of the country has been made and all practicable means exhausted in the search for Sir John Franklin and the enterprising officers and men who were his companions. I can only believe that the vessels forming the ill-fated expedition have foundered and that their crews perished."

There was only one person who did not give up the search— Lady Franklin. She risked the rest of her means to fit out the small screw steamer *Fox,* which Francis Leopold McClintock (1819–1907) volunteered to command; he had already taken part in the search parties of Ross, Austin, and Belcher and was the first white man who had learned from the Eskimos how to manage a dog sled. Lady Franklin was of the opinion that the searches had all taken place in the wrong region and was haunted by the grim thought that they ought to have looked for her husband in the neglected corner between the peninsula of Boothia Felix and the mouth of the Black River. As it happened, her wifely instinct was right; the Admiralty, the explorers, and the navigators had been looking for the lost voyager much too far north and had even believed him to have got through to Asia across the open polar ocean.

Lady Franklin was soon justified. In 1853 John Rae, while making a topographical survey for the Hudson's Bay Company, was the first to stumble on the right track. At Boothia he met some Eskimos who told him that a few years before about forty men had abandoned their ship, crushed in the ice, and gone southward in their boat in the direction of King William Island. They were in a very exhausted condition and later only about half of them were seen alive; the last few to survive had sustained life on the flesh of their comrades, and afterward no signs of life were seen any more. An old Eskimo woman also reported seeing men straggling across the ice toward Montreal Island. One after another they collapsed and died, and only one reached the island alive. "He sat on the shore, a great strong man. His head was in his hands, his elbows were supported on his knees. He sat there motionless as I approached him. He looked at me wearily and tried to speak. But as he opened his mouth to do so, his chin fell forward, his head sank on to his chest, and he was dead."

McClintock succeeded in clearing up the fate of the Franklin expedition. During 1857, the first winter of his voyage, he lay fast for 242 days in the ice of Baffin Bay. The next year he navigated through Lancaster Sound to the Bellot Strait, between Boothia Felix and North Somerset, and there carried out extensive sledge trips. During these he found skeletons and remains of the expedition on King William Island, among them a report, dated April 25, 1848, which contained the following information:

The *Erebus* and the *Terror* had been abandoned on April 22, five miles to the northwest, after being locked in the ice since September 12, 1846. The officers and crew, 105 men in all, had

landed, under Captain F. R. M. Crozier, in latitude 69° 37′ 42″
north and longitude 98° 41′ west. Franklin had died on June 11,
1847. Up to the date of writing, the expedition's casualties had
amounted to nine officers and fifteen men. It was the survivors'
intention to make for the Great Fish River the following day,
April 26.

The report was signed "James Fitzjames, Captain H.M.S. *Erebus*" and countersigned "F. R. M. Crozier, Captain H.M.S. *Terror*
and Senior Officer."

Franklin's tragedy had resulted in the exploration of further
regions of the Arctic and the solution of the mystery of the northwest passage. The observations made on the search for Franklin
also gave rise to a scientific hypothesis, unfortunately a very
false one, which stimulated further polar expeditions: this was the
possible existence in the farthest north of an "Open Polar Ocean,"
kept free of ice by a kind of Gulf Stream, and the further great
possibility of reaching the North Pole across it. In the next few
years Kane, Hayes, Hall, Nares, and Markham all pressed on toward the Pole by routes west of Greenland, without finding such
a tract of open water.

The lack of success of these Americans seemed to confirm the
theory of the German geographer August Petermann (1822–
1878) that America was cut off from this polar sea by Greenland,
to which he accorded far too great a length, and that it could be
reached only by passing to the east side of Greenland or from
Novaya Zemlya. Petermann was one of the best propagandists for
exploration. While active as a cartographer in England, he worked
hard in the cause of the search for Franklin; after taking over the
famous Geographical Academy in Gotha from Justus Perthes and
turning the little town into the world center of geographical research through his skill in attracting to it the greatest scientists,
he applied himself to setting in motion the African journeys of
Gerhard Rohlfs and Karl Mauch, as well as the expeditions that
went out to look for the missing explorer Eduard Vogel. He spent
fifteen years in advocating with great energy an attempt on the
North Pole by his prescribed route, and succeeded in launching
two German polar expeditions. These, however, proved his plan

Henry M. Stanley

David Livingstone, Missionary and Explorer of Rivers

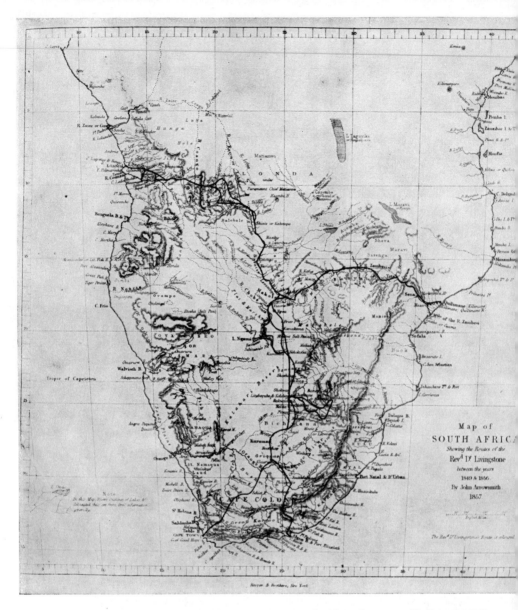

The Routes of Livingstone's Journeys in South Africa between 1849 and 1856

A Stormy Passage on the China Sea. From a Fifteenth-Century Ink Drawing by Sesshu

Portuguese Travelers in the Port of Sakai. From an Early Seventeenth-Century Japanese Scroll

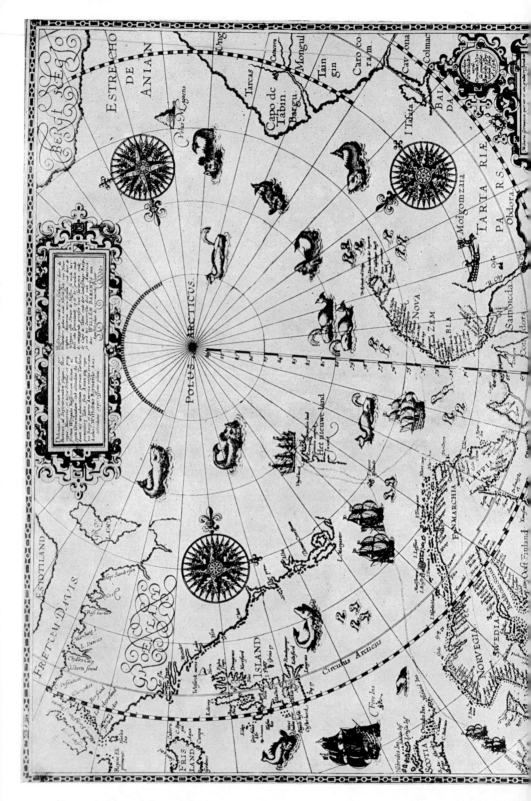

Barents's Map of the Arctic Regions, 1598. From Landschoten's *Navigatio ac Itinerarum*

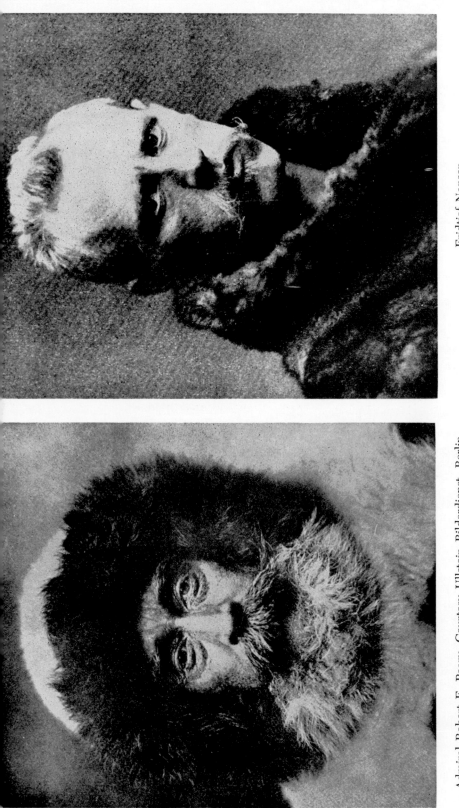

Admiral Robert E. Peary. Courtesy Ullstein Bilderdienst, Berlin

Fridtjof Nansen

South Georgia—Gateway to the Antarctic

Mount Erebus, the Antarctic Volcano Named after Ross's Ship

oald Amundsen,
irst to Reach the South Pole.
ourtesy Ullstein Bilderdienst,
erlin

cott Finds Amundsen's Tent at the Pole.
t the Left, Scott; Behind Him, Dr. Wilson; at the Right, Evans

Admiral Richard Byrd, Alone in the Antarctic. Courtesy U.S.-Amerika-Dienst, Berlin

Byrd and Members of His Party About To Set Out for the Antarctic.
Courtesy U.S.-Amerika-Dienst, Berlin

to be impracticable. Unfortunately the burden of his immense activities and domestic misfortunes so undermined his health in his later years that he took his own life.

In the sixteenth century there had already been voyages of discovery—resulting from Cabot's urge to seek a northeast passage —in the seas to the north of Europe along the route by which Petermann thought the North Pole could be reached. The most significant were those of Willem Barents (1550–1597), made at a time when the Dutch, who were achieving more and more independence and stature in their historic war against Spain for world power, were eagerly seeking a new, unmenaced line of communication with China and Japan.

In 1594 Barents reached the east and west coasts of Novaya Zemlya, and in the following year, with a new expedition, got stuck in the ice; in spite of this, he persuaded Dutch commercial circles to finance yet another venture. Accordingly, two ships left Amsterdam on May 10, 1596, captained by Corneliszoon Rijp and Jan van Heemskerk, but under the over-all command of Barents, who acted as chief navigator of the second ship.

On June 19 they discovered Bear Island, and on the 29th Spitsbergen, which had probably been sighted by the Norwegians in the twelfth century. The ships then separated, Rijp returning to Holland. Barents sailed on through the sea that now bears his name, rounding the north point of Novaya Zemlya and getting shut in by the ice on August 26 in a bay on the northeast corner of the island (Barents Ice Harbor). This, however, did not mean that the ship lay safe and snug; on the contrary, it was forced farther and farther out of the water. The sailors managed to get their provisions ashore in time and were able to build a solid house out of driftwood. In it they spent the whole of the polar winter under appalling conditions. While they were able to ensure life by eating polar-bear meat and fish, their sufferings from the cold were intense. When they tried to dry their wet clothes by the fire, the side away from it grew stiff with cold; when they wanted to sleep they had to lie on ice two inches thick. On November 3 they saw the sun for the last time before impenetrable gloom enveloped them for eighty-one polar nights of round-the-clock darkness. The house was buried in a thick shroud of snow, through which a way had to be dug whenever they wanted to get out.

When warmer temperatures eventually cleared the sea of ice, they dug out from under deep snow the two ships' boats of their lost vessel and set out for home on June 13. Barents, whose energy had kept the whole team going, was so sick with scurvy that he had to be carried to the boat. He died on June 30 while they were resting on an ice floe. After weeks of terrible journeying between floes, they at last encountered a Russian whaler, which took them to Kola. Twelve of the seventeen men who had spent the winter in Novaya Zemlya got back safely to Amsterdam in a Dutch merchantman. Two hundred and seventy-four years later Elling Carlsen, a Norwegian sea captain, found the hut in perfect condition and still bearing Barents's inscriptions.

After the death of the great Dutch navigator it was more than two hundred and fifty years before a European ship ventured on the northern route to Asia around the top of Europe. All the same, plenty of geographical information was collected in the interval, for reports from the rich whaling- and sealing-grounds attracted numerous Dutch and English catchers into the European Arctic Ocean, the Barents Sea, the Kara Sea, and as far as Spitsbergen. The hunters learned the secrets of these waters so well that they rejected spring and early summer in favor of the late summer and early autumn, the period between the melting of the old and the formation of the new ice, as the best time for their activities. A Stockholm professor of theology made such good use of this experience that he became the first man to circumnavigate Europe and Asia. His name was Adolf Erik Nordenskjöld (1832–1901).

During a number of polar reconnaissances this Swedish scientist established that the straits between Novaya Zemlya, the Island of Vaigach, and the mainland, where most of the attempts to force a passage had come to grief on impassable barriers of melting ice, was a less practicable route than the maligned Kara Sea, which the famous explorer Karl Ernst von Baer had dubbed "The North Pole's Ice Cellar," in spite of the fact that in the late summer only scattered ice floes were to be found floating there. Nordenskjöld started from Göteborg on July 4, 1878, in the *Vega*, a five-hundred-ton whaler with a sixty-horse-power engine. The finance of the venture had been shouldered by generous patrons.

Everything went smoothly till he reached the mouth of the Yenesei on August 6. Progress was then hampered both by fog and by ice fields, which caused towering jams. On August 19 he reached Cape Chelyuskin, the northernmost point of Siberia, which no European ship had ever reached by this route. In a continual race against the threat of being frozen in, he sailed past Cape Baranov, Cape Jakan, and the North Cape. The *Vega* drew nearer and nearer to the Bering Strait, but a few days' delay caused by pack ice proved decisive; Nordenskjöld was forced to a halt just short of the Bering Strait. On September 28 the ice pack, closing between Koliuchin Bay and Cape Serdze Kamen, finally hemmed him in. Only a few hours earlier the passage would have been possible.

The enforced hibernation lasted 295 days. It was June before the south winds brought a thaw with them, and July 18 before the ice started to move. They were sitting at lunch that day when the ship suddenly began to tremble gently. Nordenskjöld described it like this: "Captain Palander rushed on deck, saw the ice in motion, and immediately gave the order to get up steam. For a moment wild elation reigned on board. The crew embraced and kissed one another and wished each other success, joking and laughing. Not two hours later, at 3.30 p.m., the *Vega*, gaily dressed with bunting, was on her way to her destination under sail and steam."

Less than three weeks later they reached Cape Serdze Kamen and on July 20, the next day, sighted dark ranges on the horizon. "They were the tops of the eastern corner of Asia, the East Cape! At about 11 a.m. the *Vega* was in the middle of the channel that joins the Arctic and Pacific oceans. The ship hoisted flags and gave the Swedish salute to greet the Old and the New Worlds. We have made the Northeast Passage."

It had thus taken more than three hundred and fifty years to fulfill Sebastian Cabot's plans to find the way to Asia by way of the northwest and northeast passages. Times had altered out of all recognition, but the urge to sally forth into unknown parts of the world remained unchanged. The explorers now knew that there were no treasures awaiting them, no new lands or seas to be discovered, nothing to be gained but new geographical facts, and those at the risk of their lives. But the adventure had yet further to go. The last alluring goal was the Pole itself. Who would get there first?

While Nordenskjöld was sitting stuck in the ice and no news whatever came in, memories of the Franklin disaster awoke the gravest misgivings. Two ships went in search of the scientists, one fitted out by the Russian commercial magnate Alexander Sibirjakov, who had contributed important sums to the expedition, the other by James Gordon Bennett, the proprietor of the *New York Herald,* the man who had commissioned Stanley.

Bennett sent the steamer *Jeannette,* a ship specially built for polar work; a crew was carefully selected from thirteen hundred volunteer candidates and the command entrusted to George Washington De Long (1844–1881). His brief was not only to look for Nordenskjöld, but to get to the North Pole; the expedition was therefore provisioned for three years.

It was in 1879 that the *Jeannette* reached Koliuchin Bay after a difficult passage of the Bering Strait. Learning that Nordenskjöld had moved on safely from there, De Long made for the North Pole. In the neighborhood of Herald Island the ship was soon frozen in to drifting ice and became the powerless plaything of the winds and currents. At first she moved forward so slowly that it took five months to cover fifty miles; then she was carried north, then south, always in danger of being smashed to pieces by the large floes. In the end the ice tore a considerable hole in her, and from then on the pumps had to be manned day and night— for seventeen months!—to keep her afloat. They wintered twice (discovering the lonely islands Jeannette and Henriette during the second), but were powerless to save their ship, which, unable to bear the pressure of the ice any longer, filled with water under their very eyes and sank early on the morning of June 17, 1881, after drifting helplessly around for twenty-one months.

They saved part of the provisions, and with sleds and three boats the crew fought their way over the rough ice to the islands of New Siberia and toward the mouth of the Lena, in the erroneous hope of finding there some human habitation. De Long kept the worst news from them so as not to discourage them: the ice on which they were wandering was being steadily driven northwest away from the coast! On their terrible journey they discovered Bennett Island.

At last they succeeded in reaching open water, where they could use the three boats, but a great storm almost immediately scattered the small craft. One of them probably sank very soon. A second, under the leadership of G. W. Melville, managed, after 108 hours at sea, to reach the coast of the Lena delta, where, in spite of terrible privations on the way, they managed to struggle on to a Russian village. Almost as soon as they had reached safety, they started off again to look for their shipmates, but, utterly exhausted by a fight against heavy blizzards, they had to abandon the search.

The third boat, with De Long in it, also reached the mouth of the Lena, but this unfortunate party could nowhere discover a ship or a settlement. Only two German sailors, Nindermann and Noros, who had been sent on ahead, got through safely; the others died of the grisly cold and starvation. On a later search of the Lena delta, De Long's body was found, and by it one of the most moving documents of polar history, a diary he had kept almost to his last hour. This economically worded record revealed all the horrors of a forlorn struggle against the overmastering elements and laid bare the stature of a human spirit marching with open eyes toward death and meeting it with courage and unshakable resolution. A simple monument marks the site of the disaster.

Wreckage from the *Jeannette* was found on the south coast of Greenland, and the realization that it could only have drifted there across the polar cap revived Petermann's theory of 1852 that there was a current setting toward the North Pole to the north of Franz Josef Land. It was the intention of the Norwegian polar explorer Fridtjof Nansen (1861–1930) to exploit this current after he had first crossed Greenland and collected a mass of new information about the Arctic. Instead of coming to grief in pack ice as his predecessors had done, he planned to use the moving ice itself as his means of transport.

Important scientists and polar experts opposed this as a crazy undertaking, but Nansen was not deterred by that. He obtained funds from the Norwegian parliament to build a ship strong enough to withstand the ice pressure.

On June 24, 1893, Nansen set out in the *Fram* (*"Onward"*), whose hull was of such hardy construction and so armored with steel plates that it could be forced out of the water but never crushed by the ice, and whose interior was so buttressed with beams and props that a carpenter compared it to a spider's web. He made for the "Jeannette Drift" and on September 20, in latitude 77° 44′, allowed the ice to close in on him. Floes and blocks several feet thick crowded in on the ship and piled up into veritable towers of ice, cracking, thundering, grating, and groaning, but she held fast and was only forced upward. And then began the slow drift northwestward in crazy loops. Four seasons and a second winter passed; the *Fram* withstood a mass attack by ice thirty feet high, but she did not reach the Pole. And so she was swayed, backward, forward, hither, thither, under Arctic fogs or nights brilliant with clustering stars, with nothing to greet the eyes of her crew save snow and ice, above which often blazed magic displays of the colorful Northern Lights illuminating the sky with their glittering violets or their crimson serpents.

After his second winter Nansen decided he must move more quickly to his goal. Leaving the *Fram* in latitude 84° under her captain, Sverdrup, he and his lieutenant, Johansen, set out to march the three hundred miles separating them from the Pole. Their equipment consisted of three sleds, two kayaks, and twenty-eight dogs. When they started off on March 20 they hoped to cover the distance in thirty days and their supplies were based on that assumption.

In the teeth of northerly gales they pressed forward over bad ice. Again and again they had to carry the sleds hundreds of yards over piled-up floes and blocks; the way was barred by open crevasses, moraines of ice blocks, innumerable mounds of piled ice; their clothes were often frozen to the consistency of suits of armor. On April 17 they reached their most northerly point— farther north than anybody had ever gone before, but they had to admit that they should have been much farther on the way by then. Before them lay a chaos of ice blocks, but the worst was the realization that the ice beneath their northward-moving feet was drifting south; it was vain to continue a struggle whose end could be foretold with precision.

So back they turned toward Franz Josef Land. Their provisions shrank and shrank; one after another, the dogs had to be slaughtered, until they again found bears and seals to live on. In August they came upon open water, but fog and murk foretold the imminent approach of winter. As soon as they reached firm land, they built a hut of boulders, roofed it with walrus skins, went hunting and laid in provisions, and in it they spent the winter.

When the sun came out again, Nansen and Johansen went on, fighting their way through blizzards and drifts, from floe to floe, island to island, till in the middle of June they at last emerged from the chaos of ice into the open sea. They were now able to forge ahead freely in their kayaks in spite of strong winds and high waves. But when they landed on the foreshore of Cape Barents to spy out the land, a terrible thing happened. Nansen described it as follows:

As we stood up there, Johansen suddenly shouted: "Good God! There go the kayaks!" We rushed down like a whirlwind, but the kayaks were already well out from shore and drifting rapidly away—the ropes had broken! "Hold my watch!" I cried to Johansen as I threw off some of my clothes so that I could swim better: I dared not shed them all, for then I would too easily have got cramp. The next moment I was in the water; but the wind was blowing off the ice and the kayaks with their tall rigging offered a good hold and were already a long way out. The water was icy and it was devilish difficult to swim in one's clothes. The kayaks were still drifting out, often quicker than I could swim. Could I possibly catch up with them? All our hopes of survival were floating away with them; all our belongings were on board—we hadn't so much as a knife. It was Hobson's choice: to get cramp and be drowned or to reach shore again safe but without the kayaks. I struck out with the strength of desperation. When I got tired I swam on my back and saw Johansen running up and down along the water's edge; he told me later that those were the worst moments of his life. What could he do? He didn't believe I could reach the kayaks, and what good would it be if he plunged into the water too? When I turned over again, our boats seemed a little nearer to me; my spirits rose and I redoubled my exertions, but I could already feel my limbs stiffening. It couldn't last much longer. Yet, while my exertions were weakening, the distance was definitely decreasing. Perhaps I could reach them after all! So I swam on with my last reserves of strength. At the last gasp I was able to reach out a hand to grasp the snowshoe lying at right angles across the stern. I gripped it fast, pulled myself in to the kayak, and counted myself safe at last. But my body was by now so cold and stiff that I could not pull myself into the boat. Was it all up, even now: so near and yet so far from safety? I struggled like a madman and in the end managed to get one leg onto the rim of the sledge which lay on deck; gradually I succeeded in working my way aboard. Eventually I found myself sitting on deck. I could no longer feel anything. How could I paddle the kayaks, fastened, as they were, together? Before I got them loose I was frozen stiff. It was only by paddling with might and main that I got my blood into circulation again. I steered into the wind, and in my wet woollen shirt I could feel it going clean through me as I shivered there with rattling teeth. I threw off the torpor I could feel creeping over me, and stroke by stroke I slowly drew nearer to the rim of the ice. Then suddenly I saw something moving across my bows—two auks. We had little enough food, and the idea of bringing back our supper galvanized me. I picked up my gun and got both birds with one round. Johansen got into a terrible state, thinking, as he told me afterward, something frightful had happened and that I had gone out of my mind. At last I reached the edge of the ice and he rushed up and helped me out. I could scarcely stand upright. He tore my clothes off and dressed me in the few dry things we still had; then he spread my sleeping-bag on the ice, pushed me into it, and covered me with a sail and everything else he could lay hands on. It was a long time before I stopped shivering and warmth began to ebb back into my body. I fell asleep while Johansen was putting up the tent and preparing the two birds for supper; when I woke up the meal had been ready for some time and was warming over the fire. Hot soup and a decent hot meal soon got rid of the last ill-effects of my bathing-party.

Five days later, after paddling along the coast in their kayaks, they ran into two men in those icy wastes. They were members of the British Jackson expedition, which had spent the last year in exploring Franz Josef Land. Nansen and his friend were saved; the expedition's supply ship took them back to Vardö in Norway. And on the very day when Nansen was setting foot once more on Norwegian soil, far up in the northern seas the *Fram* was freed from her prison by much laborious sawing and blasting and some time afterward also reached home safe and sound.

One day in 1908 a man walked into the office of the *New York Herald,* where James Gordon Bennett had once given Stanley and De Long their assignments. At least 577 polar expeditions had gone out since 1800; none had reached the Pole, many had perished miserably. He wanted to undertake the 578th—after all, if it succeeded, the results would outweigh those of all the others put together.

Robert Edwin Peary (1856–1920) had for twenty-five years been advocating new methods of polar exploration. Most polar expeditions came to grief through cold and starvation. All right, who managed to live in the Arctic? The Eskimos, of course. So an Arctic explorer must live as they did.

Peary, whose life's aim was to reach the Pole, had not only succeeded in living like an Eskimo, but had taken his wife with him into the far north, and there, in latitude 77° north, where never a white man or woman had come into this world, his daughter was born.

Peary had already carried through four important expeditions. He had crossed Greenland several times and so confirmed its island status; he had tried eight times to reach the Pole, and twice, as the result of his meticulous preparations, in 1902 and 1906 had penetrated the polar sea with his dog sleds to points not far from the Pole before having to capitulate to the ice pack.

Nobody was better fitted to reach the Pole than this fearless, energetic, careful planner. Once again—and his quest of the Pole now found him more than fifty years old—he had made the most careful preparations; for him it was now or never. But, for all his merits and qualifications, one important item was missing: the necessary capital.

This was the moment to enlist once again the aid of William Reick, the *Herald's* financial manager, who had always been sympathetic.

Peary asked for an interview.

"Sorry, but Mr. Reick has left us. He's with the *New York Times* now."

It was an answer for which this man who was more at home in the Arctic than in an editor's office was not prepared. "Well, can I speak to Mr. Lincoln?"

Charles M. Lincoln, one of the paper's other editors, had previously attended negotiations with Peary.

"Sorry. Mr. Lincoln isn't with us either. He's gone to the *Times*, too."

This was a serious blow to Peary's hopes.

"Well, with whom can I speak?" he inquired. "Is the boss in?"

An editor Peary had never seen appeared and listened amiably while Peary explained that he had collected funds almost sufficient for an expedition and was now offering the sole journalistic rights to the *Herald*, as he had done before. But the editor took the view that readers had gradually grown tired of reports in which nobody quite got to the Pole, and he showed Peary out politely. "This time," he said, "we won't insist on exclusive rights. And if you do reach the Pole, we shall no doubt get the news through the normal channels. Thanks a lot, Commander."

Deeply disappointed, Peary left the office racking his brains.

Where could he find the money? With a heavy heart he went to the *Times*. Perhaps his old acquaintance Reick would—

On the seventh floor of the *Times* skyscraper he met with a very different reception. Very soon Peary was in conclave with the people who counted; inside an hour the contract was signed. Peary got eight thousand dollars in return for the sole rights of publication; the paper also undertook to market anything Peary might write afterward, on a royalty basis.

On July 6, 1908, Peary sailed from New York in the well-proven steamship *Roosevelt* and disappeared into the northern silences. A few letters came back from Newfoundland and Labrador, then no more news while Peary drove on from the north of Greenland toward the Pole along a chain of supply dumps he had laid, traveling by the light of a brilliant moon.

Then a very different kind of report arrived. On September 1, 1909, a cable from Shetland reached the Central Telegraph Office in New York. It read: "Here on board is the American explorer Dr. Cook, who reached the North Pole on April 21, 1908, while on a North Polar Expedition. Cook arrived in May 1909 at Upernavik from Cape North. The Eskimos confirm the truth of Cook's journey." The telegram was signed "Knud Rasmussen, Inspector of North Greenland," the title of a high Danish official.

Dr. Frederick A. Cook, of Brooklyn, was a fairly obscure man; all that was known about him was that he had been along on two of Peary's expeditions in 1891 and 1902, as well as on a Belgian polar attempt, as doctor. This news was doubly unwelcome to the *New York Times,* for the *Herald* had previously paid twenty-five thousand dollars for the exclusive rights to Cook's reports, and the *Times* was thus faced with the difficult business of laboriously collecting the news from secondhand sources.

Cook's report that he had taken only thirty-five days from Cape Columbus to the Pole, where he had discovered firm land and explored thirty thousand square miles of an unknown region, was received with some suspicion. The whole world was in a ferment, but the American Admiral G. W. Melville, who had taken part in the voyage of the unlucky *Jeannette*, stated that there was no smooth ice so far north, that the march would have had to take place in total darkness, and that the whole story was a fraud. On the other hand, when Cook arrived in Copenhagen on September 4 he was received with enthusiasm and given an audience by the King and by the scientific faculty. But a London journalist, Philip Gibbs, of the *Daily Chronicle*, asked such exacting questions that Cook became a little uncertain and answered that he had been accompanied on the last part of his journey only by Eskimos unversed in the sciences and that he did not have his records with him.

Almost immediately, on the night of September 6, Reick rushed into the office of the editor in chief of the *Times* waving a sheet of paper. It was a cipher telegram bearing the message: "Got O.P."—the old Pole—meaning that Peary had reached the North Pole.

In a trice the editorial offices became an anthill of activity. Reports and data about Peary were collated, two telegrams came from him in Labrador, a correspondent was sent to Copenhagen to interview Cook, whose reply was: "Two records are better than one." Then, on September 7, the *Times* felt itself in a position to publish its most sensational issue: three columns on the front page carried the "I have the Pole" story and five inside pages were devoted to the report of the discovery, to which it, of all the world's newspapers, had the exclusive rights.

This precipitated a newspaper war without parallel. Who had really got to the Pole, and who had been the first to discover it? Peary cabled: "Cook's story should not be taken too seriously. The Eskimos who accompanied him say he went no distance north and not out of sight of land. Tribe confirms."

The *Times* published a detailed account from Peary himself, which told how he started out on March 1 with his sleds after the most careful preparations and made excellent progress by a series of relays in a temperature of 59 degrees below zero. On April 2, in latitude 87° 47′, he separated from the main body and, accompanied only by his black servant, four Eskimos, and five sleds with the forty best dogs, made a dash for the Pole. Every ten hours they halted to rest, drink tea, and eat something: then they went off again.

The weather was overcast, and there was the same gray and shadowless light as on the march after Marvin had turned back. The sky was a colorless pall gradually deepening to almost black at the horizon, and the ice was a ghastly and chalky white, like that of the Greenland ice cap—just the colors which an imaginative artist would paint as a polar icescape. How different it seemed from the glittering fields, canopied with blue and lit by the sun and full moon, over which we had been traveling for the last four days.

The going was even better than before. There was hardly any snow on the hard granular surface of the old floes, and the sapphire-blue lakes were larger than ever. The temperature had risen to minus 15°, which, reducing the friction of the sledges, gave the dogs the appearance of having caught the high spirits of the party. Some of them even tossed their heads and barked and yelped as they traveled.

On April 6 they camped at a point in latitude 89° 57′.

Yet with the Pole actually in sight I was too weary to take the last few steps. The accumulated weariness of all those days and nights of forced marches and insufficient sleep, constant peril, and anxiety seemed to roll across me all at once. I was actually too exhausted to realize at the moment that my life's purpose had been achieved.

A little later he wrote:

The Pole at last. The prize of three centuries. My dream and goal for twenty years. Mine at last! I cannot bring myself to realize it. It seems all so simple and commonplace.

After covering the last lap to the Pole, Peary remained thirty hours on the ice cap and crossed it from side to side; soundings in a deep crevasse proved that the Pole was not on a land mass, but on a tremendously deep frozen basin of the sea.

Nearly everything in the circumstances which then surrounded us seemed too strange to be thoroughly realized, but one of the strangest of those circumstances seemed to me to be the fact that, in a march of only a few hours, I had passed from the western to the eastern hemisphere and had verified my position at the summit of the world. It was hard to realize that on the first miles of this brief march we had been traveling due north, while on the last few miles of the same march we had been traveling south, although we had all the time been traveling precisely in the same direction. . . .

East, west, and north had disappeared for us. Only one direction remained, and that was south. Every breeze which could possibly blow upon us, no matter from what point of the horizon, must be a south wind. Where we were, one day and one night constituted a year, a hundred such days and nights constituted a century. Had we stood in that spot during the six months of the Arctic winter night, we should have seen every star of the northern hemisphere circling the sky at the same distance from the horizon, with Polaris [the North Star] practically in the zenith.

It was not enough that Peary had reached the Pole—he still had to convince everybody that he had been the first to get there. The controversy about Cook and Peary raged furiously, but in the end a scientific commission, after carefully checking his submission, decided that Peary had without any shadow of doubt been to the Pole, whereas the University of Copenhagen, once it had studied the material somewhat hesitantly produced by Cook, declared that it was questionable and left in doubt whether Cook had really reached the Pole. After that, Cook's course took a swift downhill turn. A reporter discovered that Cook had been the first man to climb Mount McKinley in the Rockies; a second reporter was more adroit and was able to prove that this was a pure invention of Cook's. In the end, the man who had momentarily enjoyed the fame of having discovered the North Pole found his way into prison for embezzlement.

In the course of time the North Pole and its surroundings have become as familiar as any other part of the world. It has been approached by exploratory expeditions with ships, icebreakers, airships, airplanes, and even submarines; it has been ringed round by numerous weather stations. The depth of its waters, the hu-

midity of the air, the stratification of its bed have all been measured. Today, when the trans-polar route is already among those
flown by international airlines, full information is available about
the divisions between land and water in the polar regions, about
the temperature at which ice forms, the direction of the glacial
drifts, the climatic and biological conditions, thanks to the pains-
taking efforts of innumerable scientists.

Against this background, the sufferings of the early polar explorers, who paved the way for all that has happened since, have
gradually been forgotten. Modern technical methods have almost
obliterated all appreciation of the bitter fight they used to have
to wage against the cruelty of nature. In addition, nature herself,
as modern man finds her, has greatly changed; she is less harsh
and cold than she was in the days of Franklin and De Long. Recent measurements show clearly that the polar regions are growing warmer. The surface area of Siberian Russia which was in the
old days permanently icebound has retreated more than thirty
miles since 1850. Labrador and Canada enjoy warmer weather, as
is proved by the many types of birds which have migrated there
during the last thirty years; many, too, have migrated from the
continent of Europe northward to Greenland, Iceland, and the
Fåro Islands. And the International Ice Patrol, which was inaugurated after the *Titanic* disaster in 1912, has confirmed that
the danger from icebergs is steadily on the wane.

11

THE SIXTH CONTINENT

M ANKIND, when asked how many continents there are, has almost always given the wrong answer. At various times it was three, four, or five. Even today there is no general realization that the south polar continent, Antarctica, is at least as large as Europe and a good deal bigger than Australia, or that it commands valuable mineral resources and contains the greatest expanse of high tableland in the world, larger than the plateaus of the Andes or Greenland. In fact, only the Tibetan plateau is comparable in size.

Men's thoughts have been occupied for thousands of years with the idea of a great southern continent. There were fabulous rumors of its rioting flora and its exotic fauna—nor was this a foolish fairytale, for it is definitely known that in the world's early days the climate ruling in the south (and also north) polar region was subtropical and the area was rich in plants and thickly covered by forests.

In historical times, however, there has been nothing there but snow and ice. The approaches to this remote, lonely continent are guarded by an ocean whose fierce, icy hurricanes and driving fogs lash its waves to greater heights than have been encountered in any other seas. That intelligent, genial student of nature, Aristotle, rightly guessed that the Antarctic was a world of ice and predicted that if and when men penetrated into the far south, they would find landscapes and temperatures similar to those found in the extreme north.

Aristotle was far ahead of his times. Three hundred years later, in 43 B.C., Pomponius Mela still believed in a habitable continent, whose inhabitants he called "the Antipodes." A theory was developed and actually adopted by Ptolemæus that there was such a great land mass in the south and that it served to maintain the balance of the world. In the early Middle Ages, when it was thought that we lived on a flat planet, this idea was forgotten. But it was kept alive among Arab scientists, who were the heirs of classic science and culture, and after the Crusades it was passed back by them to the Christian civilization of the West. So the maps of the late Middle Ages again showed a great area of land to the south, *"Terra Australia Incognita"* or *"Brasilia Inferior."*

At first the southern continent was made to cut off the Indian Ocean at the bottom, turning it into an inland sea. After Vasco da Gama's voyage it disappeared from its position there and wandered farther south in the form of a great lump of land which shrank and shrank in direct proportion to the failure to discover it, till after Cook's voyage it vanished altogether.

But Cook at the same moment brought to a close a long era of inaccurate geographical presentation and opened a new chapter in geographical research. January 18, 1773, the day on which he became the first to cross the south polar circle, in fog and raging seas and constantly threatened by the huge icebergs that bore down on him, is the date when Antarctic exploration began—though Cook himself did not believe it possible to carry through such a venture. He attributed the existence of the terrific ice masses he encountered everywhere to the presence of a land mass lying entirely within the polar circle and utterly inaccessible. He wrote of the "indescribably horrid aspect" of this region, which nature had condemned never to feel the sun's warm rays; and he was convinced that, in face of such fearful dangers, no one would ever venture farther south than he himself had gone.

Indeed, for a very long time no explorer appeared prepared to visit and examine that deserted region of ice. Only whalers and seal-hunters were encouraged by Cook's reports to press farther south, and in the rich grounds off South Georgia they found rich rewards for their courage. At the same time they discovered fresh clusters of islands outside the polar circle, while the first islands to be found inside it were discovered by the Russian naval officer

Fabian Gottlieb von Bellingshausen when the Tsar sent him on a voyage of exploration. Later, whale-hunters like Weddell, Biscoe, Kemp, and Balleny drew nearer to the polar continent and sighted its coasts.

Their successes were the inspiration of further scientific expeditions. In 1840 Charles Wilkes, an American, sailed some 1,250 miles along the coast of the land that now bears his name, in search of the South Magnetic Pole. In the same year the French sailor Jules Dumont d'Urville, second only to Cook among explorers of the South Seas, discovered a stretch of land forming part of the Antarctic continent, to which he gave the name Adélie Land in honor of his wife. And in the same year two ships set out from England which were destined to reveal during their desperate voyage some of the most important secrets of the sixth continent.

After the German scientist Gauss had published his pioneering work on the earth's magnetism and men were engaged in producing the most precise magnetic maps possible, specially designed for use with compasses, it was realized that the lack of knowledge about conditions in the most southerly sea areas was a very inconvenient lacuna. Alexander von Humboldt addressed a memorandum to the Royal Society in London and so strongly advocated the necessity for south polar exploration that the committee set plans actively in motion for such an undertaking. They succeeded in impressing the government, which provided funds for an expedition and placed it in the charge of the successful discoverer of the North Magnetic Pole, James Clark Ross.

Two ships whose names were to be immemorially engraved on the pages of polar research were placed at Ross's disposal, each with a crew of sixty-four, commanded by Captain Crozier. They were the ex-warships *Erebus* and *Terror* (340 and 370 registered tons, respectively), which were later to disappear in the icy wastes of the far north with the ill-fated Franklin expedition.

The ships reached Hobart in August 1840, and there Ross met a man well known to him as a polar authority, Sir John Franklin, who was at that time governor of Tasmania. What he had to tell came as a bitter disappointment to Ross. The news of the recent

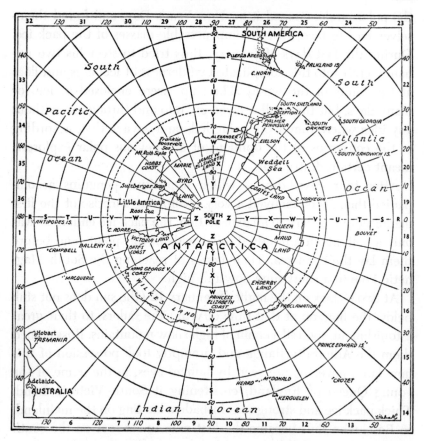

Map by Russell James Walrath. Reproduced by permission of Lillian L. Walrath.

ANTARCTICA—THE SIXTH CONTINENT

successes achieved by Wilkes and d'Urville left him with a strong impression that the grass had been mowed under his very feet.

He had arrived too late. What should he do? In a fury he jettisoned all the plans he had laid. He certainly did not propose to go home again, but he decided to sail south on an entirely different course, roughly along longitude 170 east—quite unaware that by so doing he was paving the way to a great personal triumph and, later, to the successful discovery of the South Pole.

The ships left Hobart on November 12 and sailed toward the ice. They fought their way through heavy December gales toward the polar circle, crossed it on New Year's Day, and found themselves face to face with the impenetrable masses of the pack ice. During the first days of January, Ross tried to steer his two unhandy craft into this complicated wilderness of icebergs and floes at the limits of the world. The ships were enclosed in ice for many days, but they still pressed on, into and through it, without any idea where they were being led, on a voyage that, according to the consensus of the opinions of all previous polar explorers, meant certain destruction.

After four days, during which inquisitive penguins accompanied them, they enjoyed a very comforting surprise of the first magnitude: contrary to all expectation, the pack ice ended—it was only a belt, about a hundred miles wide at this point—and before them lay the open sea. Their hopes of reaching the South Magnetic Pole in a short time now ran high.

At two o'clock on the night of January 12 (the sun does not sink below the horizon at that time of year) the sailors, to their great astonishment, sighted a chain of high snow mountains. Ross named them the Admiralty Range and promptly took possession of this new land, never before seen by human eyes, in the name of the young Queen of England, christening it South Victoria Land. Thick pack ice and strong seas forbade a landing on the mainland, so Ross, who thus became the first man to set foot on the south polar continent, held the symbolic occupation ceremony on a small island (Possession Island). After brief celebrations the party hastily quitted the islet, which stank pungently of guano and whose penguin population defended it fiercely with their sharp beaks.

During the succeeding days, with the sighting of new islands and coasts, it became increasingly clear that Ross had discovered, in its true extent and significance, the continent at whose existence Cook had hinted. Ross was thus chosen by destiny to reveal, by his exploration of the sea that bears his name, the very sector of the Antarctic from which it later proved possible to reach the Pole itself.

On January 27 they made another, but by no means their last, sensational discovery. Above a great mountain range that they were approaching they saw rising a thirteen-thousand-foot cone that was emitting smoke and flames. It was an active volcano. Ross described as unforgettable the sight of flames leaping from the summit, and the cloud of smoke, shot through with red reflections, that hung above it, in the midst of the endless white waste of snow. Close to this fiery peak they found a smaller volcano, this one extinct. The two mountains were named Erebus and Terror after the ships, and the island on which they stood, Ross Island.

The voyage continued satisfactorily till suddenly confronted with a new kind of obstacle to progress. An intriguing low white line, which seemingly had no end, grew steadily higher as they drew near to it, and finally revealed itself as a smooth, sheer ice wall about two hundred feet high; a wall which, though Ross sailed along it for a hundred miles searching for a crack, never offered the slightest sign of a cranny to breach it. So, with the southern summer drawing to its close, he was finally compelled to quit the Ross Barrier, whose surface is now known to be the size of France and to have an area of some two hundred thousand square miles, and sail back to Tasmania.

At the end of November 1841, as soon as the polar winter was over, Ross put out to sea again to find the end of the ice wall. But the wild Antarctic gales held the ships up, the fogs were denser than ever, and by January 18, when it had proved impossible to work a way through the belt of pack ice, a howling northwesterly hurricane came screaming down on the ships through the floes.

All our hawsers breaking in succession, we made sail on the ships and kept company during the thick fog by firing guns, and by means of the usual signals: under the shelter of a berg of nearly a mile in diameter, we dodged about during the whole day, waiting for clear weather, that we might select the best leads through the dispersing pack; but at 9 p.m. the wind suddenly freshened to a violent gale from the northward, compelling us to reduce our sails to a close-reefed main-top-sail and storm stay-sails: the sea quickly rising to a fearful height, breaking over the loftiest bergs, we were unable any longer to hold our ground, but were driven into the heavy pack under our lee. Soon after midnight our ships were involved in an ocean of rolling fragments of ice, hard as floating rocks of granite, which were dashed against them by the waves with so much violence that their masts quivered as if they would fall at every successive blow; and the destruction of the ships seemed inevitable from the tremendous shocks they received. By backing and filling the sails, we endeavoured to avoid collision with the larger masses; but this was not always possible: in the early part of the storm, the rudder of the Erebus *was so much damaged as to be no longer of any use: and about the same time I was informed by signal that the* Terror's *was completely destroyed, and nearly torn away from the stern-post.*

For forty-eight hours the tempest blew the ships helplessly around among the heavy masses of ice, sending them crashing into the floes, chasing broken bits of icebergs into one another, and hurling thundering sheets of water over everything. The sailors could only cling to whatever was handy.

We all watched with breathless anxiety the effect of each succeeding collision, and the vibrations of the tottering masts, expecting every moment to see them give way without our having the power to make an effort to save them.

Darkness fell and a heavy blizzard began which did not let up till midnight, when the wind changed and began gradually to moderate.

Although the shocks our ships still sustained were such that must have destroyed any ordinary vessel in less than five minutes, yet they were feeble compared with those to which we had been exposed, and our minds became more at ease for their ultimate safety.

When the sea had gone down, the necessary repairs took days; the *Terror* had to have a new rudder. Then Ross renewed the battle with the pack ice. When on February 2 he finally succeeded in breaking through, he had spent fifty-six perilous days in the attempt. Three weeks later he sighted the great barrier and again sailed along it, but failed to reach its eastern end on account of impenetrable ice, which in the end prevented his making further headway. He was only able to establish that the eastern sectors of this huge ice wall were not so high as those he had observed elsewhere. In latitude 79° 10′ he had to turn back; and this was his farthest point south in either voyage.

On the return voyage, too, he was pursued by bad weather, but on emerging from the polar circle he had every reason to hope that he had encountered the last of the gorgeous-looking but monstrous icebergs. His most perilous adventure was, however, still to come.

At noon on March 12, a foggy day, the wind freshened suddenly and violent squalls of snow set in. The sails of the *Erebus* had just been reefed when, without warning and with terrible suddenness, a gigantic monster of an iceberg loomed up close to her. Ross tried hard to miss it by trimming sail to leeward, but in the same instant the *Terror* bore down on him under full sail. This is his description of the result:

We instantly hove all aback to diminish the violence of the shock; but the concussion when she struck us was such as to throw almost every one off his feet; our bowsprit, topmast, and other smaller spars were carried away; and the ships hanging together, entangled by their rigging, and dashing against each other with fearful violence, were falling down upon the weather face of the lofty berg under our lee, against which the waves were breaking and foaming to near the summit of its perpendicular cliffs. Sometimes she rose high above us, almost exposing her keel to view, and again descended as we in our turn rose to the top of the wave, threatening to bury her beneath us, whilst the crashing of the breaking upperworks and boats increased the horror of the scene. Providentially they gradually forged past each other, and separated before we drifted down amongst the foaming breakers, and we had the gratification of seeing her clear the end of the berg, and of feeling that she was safe. But she left us completely disabled; the wreck of the spars so encumbered the lower yards that we were unable to make sail, so as to get headway on the ship; nor had we room to wear round, being by this time so close

*to the berg that the waves, when they struck against it, threw
back their sprays into the ship.*

Ross committed himself to a breakneck maneuver—backing.
This was a dangerous thing to do, for the masts of the sailing-
ships were built and made fast so as to withstand very little pressure from in front. The ship rolled heavily, her yards kept on
scraping against the berg, but:

*No sooner was the order given, than the daring spirit of the
British seaman manifested itself—the men ran up with the rigging
with as much alacrity as on any ordinary occasion; and although
more than once driven off the yard, they after a short time succeeded in loosing the sail. Amidst the roar of the wind and sea, it
was difficult both to hear and to execute the orders that were
given, so that it was three quarters of an hour before we could get
the yards braced bye, and the maintack hauled on board sharp
aback—an expedient that perhaps had never before been resorted
to by seamen in such weather: but it had the desired effect; the
ship gathered stern-way, plunging her stern into the sea, washing
away the gig and quarter boats, and with her lower yard-arms
scraping the rugged face of the berg, we in a few minutes reached
its western termination; the "under tow," as it is called, or the re-
action of the water from its vertical cliffs, alone preventing us
being driven to atoms against it. No sooner had we cleared it,
than another was seen directly astern of us, against which we
were running; and the difficulty now was to get the ship's head
turned round and pointed fairly through between the two bergs,
the breadth of the intervening space not exceeding three times her
own breadth; this, however, we happily accomplished; and in a
few minutes after getting before the wind, she dashed through
the narrow channel, between two perpendicular walls of ice, and
the foaming breakers which stretched across it, and the next
moment we were in smooth water under its lee.*

It proved possible to get the ships into some kind of order again
during the next few days. At the beginning of April, after a hundred and seventy days at sea, Ross made port in the Falkland Islands. In the course of the following polar summer he attempted

a third voyage, which began at the end of December, but unfavorable ice conditions forbade any major exploratory work. Ross returned home after an absence of nearly four years, to receive an enthusiastic welcome; he brought back with him an immense amount of fresh scientific material, but the cost at which it was obtained seemed to act as a deterrent, for no expedition ventured into those perilous waters for a long time to come. Their reconnaissance was, in fact, not renewed till George Nares (1831–1915), in the course of his famous voyage through the three great oceans in search of scientific marine data, visited the Antarctic and confirmed the existence of a south polar continent.

For a time it was again left to whalers, such as the Norwegian C. A. Larsen, who pressed on into the south polar ocean, to make discoveries there. It was on January 24, 1895, that the first man set foot on the mainland of the Antarctic continent: a sailor serving under Captain Bull went ashore on that Godforsaken icy coast to gather stones and mosses, not in the course of his duties as a sailor, but because he was in the first instance a natural-historian. His name was Carsten Borchgrevink (1864–1934). This Norwegian scientist did great service in the cause of Antarctic exploration; he established the presence of plant life in the region, spending the winter of 1899 and a whole year afterward in making weather observations which proved that scientific research was possible in the interior as well as along the coastal fringes of the south polar continent.

Another purely nautical expedition was that of the *Belgica,* commanded by Adrien de Gerlache: Amundsen took part in her voyage. The ship spent the winter of 1898 off the west coast of Graham Land, not intentionally, but because she was icebound. International geographical conventions in London (1895) and Berlin (1899) gave a strong impetus to south polar research; scientists of all countries united in the view that the southernmost point on earth must be reached and the answer provided to the question whether they really had to deal with a continuous land mass or whether the scantily explored continent would prove, on closer inspection, to be a group of islands.

So it came about that in the first five years of the new century five important expeditions sallied forth. One was British (R. F. Scott—the Ross Sea and South Victoria Land), one German (E. V. Drygalski—Kaiser Wilhelm II Land), one Swedish (Otto Nordenskjöld—Graham Land and Louis Philippe Land) and one French (Jean Charcot—Loubet Land). The results were considerable, but disappointing in relation to the heavy expenditure that launched each of these undertakings. Only Scott brought back information of a new kind; this resulted from the pioneering experiments he made on lengthy sled journeys through the wastes of snow. Although he had called on Nansen before starting south and sought his advice, only practical experience and harsh reverses taught the lessons of how to move about the Antarctic; the continual need to guard against crevasses and "sastrugis" (hard, glassy edges and ribs of snow, often hidden beneath the soft surface snow); what provisions were most suitable; the need for laying supply dumps along the route; the technique of cookery, camping, dog-management, and a hundred other details that might mean life or death in a crisis.

After some months of preparation, false starts, and training-runs, three men set out on the first great sledging-journey in the history of south polar exploration on November 2, 1901. They were Robert Falcon Scott (1868–1912), one of the most courageous and memorable discoverers of all time: Ernest Henry Shackleton (1874–1922), an enthusiast who was able to inspire enthusiasm in others, passionately devoted to the cause of research; and Dr. Edward A. Wilson (1868–1912), a gifted and versatile scientist and also an ideal companion—a man whose services have almost been forgotten since his day, though he exerted an undoubted spiritual leadership during both of Scott's expeditions.

The efforts of these three famous explorers suffered one setback after another. Most of the dogs died early on the trip, probably because their food went bad; the men themselves suffered acutely from hunger, owing to an underestimate of the rations required; and in the end they had to turn back on December 30, suffering from weakness and scurvy. Shackleton's condition deteriorated on the return journey to such an extent that it became a race with death. Later, when Shackleton lay on his sickbed in England after nearly dying in the Antarctic, he was already making plans for his next expedition. Polar fever had caught him in its grip, as the Africa fever had caught many another before him.

"Indeed the stark polar lands grip the hearts of the men who have lived on them in a manner that can hardly be understood by the people who have never got outside the pale of civilisation," he wrote. The moment he was fit again, this unknown reserve officer who had already been forced to withdraw from one expedition to the Pole set about collecting funds for his own expedition, sparing no effort in his attempt to scrape the money together.

Shackleton's toughness produced results, and on August 7, 1907, he sailed from England in the forty-year-old, slow, but immensely strong steamship *Nimrod*. The ship carried, besides members of the expedition, ten Siberian ponies, which Shackleton had selected with great care. He hoped to be able to move ahead much more quickly by using them, for they could haul a far heavier sled than the polar dogs. One of them had to be shot just before the crossing of the polar circle, because it was thrown onto its back in its box during a hurricane and it proved impossible to get it onto its feet again on the deck of a rolling ship continually awash with great breakers.

Shackleton had intended to pitch camp in Balloon Bay—so called because Scott had there employed captive balloons in order to get a view across the great ice wall—but to his amazement the landscape had altered drastically since Scott had been there; huge chunks of the wall had broken off and drifted away in the meantime. Now numerous whales were sporting in the resulting bay. A change of name to match the changed conditions seemed unavoidable, so it became the Bay of Whales. But Shackleton rejected the idea of trusting himself to so mercurial a floor as that of the barrier ice, preferring to have firm ground beneath him. Scott was later to assert the same preference. Amundsen was the only one who dared to pitch his camp on the ice of the Bay of Whales—a fact that earned him the discovery of the South Pole.

Shackleton set up his base near Cape Royds on Ross Island and sent out several expeditions. One of them climbed the 13,200-foot peak of Erebus, though none of the three men concerned had alpine experience or were previously acquainted with polar ground. A party under Professor David reached the South Magnetic Pole, covering fifteen hundred miles on the double journey. The main attempt on the Pole itself failed; it proved impossible to lay down supply dumps before the onset of the polar night because a wide stretch of water between the winter quarters and Hut Point hampered the movement of laden sledges. Shackleton's description of the arrival of the polar night is a splendid example of his artistic and literary powers:

The sunsets at the beginning of April were wonderful; arches of prismatic colours, crimson and golden-tinged clouds, hung in the heavens nearly all day, for time was going on and soon the sun would have deserted us. The days grew shorter and shorter, and the twilight longer. During these sunsets the western mountains stood out gloriously and the summit of Erebus was wrapped in crimson when the lower slopes had faded into grey. To Erebus and the western mountains our eyes turned when the end of the long night grew near in the month of August, for the mighty peaks are the first to catch up and tell the tale of the coming glory and the last to drop the crimson mantle from their high shoulders as night draws on. Tongue and pencil would sadly fail in attempting to describe the magic of the colouring in the days when the sun was leaving us. The very clouds at this time were iridescent with rainbow hues. The sunsets were poems. The change from twilight into night, sometimes lit by a crescent moon, was extraordinarily beautiful, for the white cliffs gave no part of their colour away, and the rocks beside them did not part with their blackness, so the effect of deepening night over these contrasts was singularly weird.

Spring began in August, and with it immediate preparations for the attack on the Pole. By dint of some weeks of work, two depots were laid at Hut Point and a hundred and twenty miles along the way to the Pole. The expedition set out on October 29; it consisted of Shackleton, Marshall, Wild, and Adams. The sleds were drawn by the four surviving ponies. The distance to the Pole was nearly nine hundred miles, over totally unknown ground —eighteen hundred miles there and back.

Even as early as the first week of November, Shackleton had to admit that they were making slower progress than expected. Snowstorms delayed them (the worst feature of each day's delay being that thirty-eight pounds of horse feed were consumed); hidden clefts and crevasses, into which the ponies kept on breaking through, barred the way. After some days of good progress over smoother surface, they found themselves on a high snow field through whose hard crust the ponies fell time and again. On November 21 they had to shoot the first to collapse from complete exhaustion; its flesh was added to their provisions.

On November 26 they passed the previous "farthest south," the point Scott, Shackleton, and Wilson had reached before. Shackleton wrote in his diary:

It falls to the lot of few men to view land not previously seen by human eyes, and it was with feelings of keen curiosity, not unmingled with awe, that we watched the new mountains rise from the great unknown that lay ahead of us. Mighty peaks they were, the eternal snows at their bases, and their rough-hewn forms rising high towards the sky. No man of us could tell what we would discover in our march south, what wonders might not be revealed to us, and our imaginations would take wings until a stumble in the snow, the sharp pangs of hunger, or the dull ache of physical weariness brought back our attention to the needs of the immediate present. As the days wore on, and mountain after mountain came into view, grimly majestic, the consciousness of our insignificance seemed to grow upon us. We were but tiny black specks crawling slowly and painfully across the white plain, and bending our puny strength to the task of wresting from nature secrets preserved inviolate through all the ages.

A few days later a second pony, reduced to a mere skeleton, had to be shot; the two others were almost done for. On December 1 it was the turn of Shackleton's favorite pony. On the 7th, Shackleton, Adams, and Marshall, hauling a heavy sledge, heard a sudden shout for help from the rear. Wild, who was following with the pony sledge, had fallen into a concealed crevasse. The sledge was still safely lodged on the lip of the crevasse, but the pony had disappeared for good. Wild had been fortunate enough to be able to cling to the lip of the crevasse at the last moment.

Progress was now noticeably slower, for the four men had to drag a load of a thousand pounds. This is Shackleton's record of December 12:

Our distance—three miles for the day—expresses more readily than I can write it the nature of the day's work. We started at 7.40 a.m. on the worst surface possible, sharp-edged blue ice full of chasms and crevasses, rising to hills and descending into gullies; in fact, a surface that could not be equalled in any polar work for difficulty in travelling. Our sledges are suffering greatly and it is a constant strain on us both to save the sledges from breaking or going down crevasses, and to save ourselves as well. We are a mass of bruises where we have fallen on the sharp ice, but, thank God, no one has even a sprain. It has been relay work to-day, for we could only take on one sledge at a time, two of us taking turns at pulling the sledge whilst the others steadied and held the sledge to keep it straight. Thus we would advance one mile, and then return over the crevasses and haul up the other sledge. By repeating this to-day for three miles we marched nine miles over a surface where many times a slip meant death.

It was in such conditions that they fought their way forward, up into the grim glacier world, with their rations growing shorter and shorter. They suffered from snow-blindness and mountain sickness, and their hopes were daily diminished of ever reaching the smooth plateau that beckoned to them from afar but revealed nothing but new precipices, abysses, and ridges as they drew nearer to it. On this terrible march they discovered the highest glacier on earth, the Beardmore, but what good was that to them? It was the Pole they wanted.

The fight became desperate as with their last remnants of strength and their last crumbs of food they battled against time and the blizzard that screamed down upon them. Often it was only the rope that saved them from falling to their death in the deep crevasses. Still they struggled on. But on January 6 the fury of the storm rose to such a pitch that they were unable to leave their tent and had to accept the bitter knowledge that they could not reach their goal. All during the 7th and 8th they remained imprisoned in the tent, suffering acutely from cramps:

Again all day in our bags, suffering considerably physically from cold hands and feet, and from hunger, but more mentally, for we cannot get on south, and we simply lie here shivering. Every now and then one of our party's feet go, and the unfortunate beggar has to take his leg out of the sleeping-bag and have his frozen foot nursed into life again by placing it inside the shirt, against the skin of his almost equally unfortunate neighbour. We must do something more to the south, even though the food is going, and we weaken lying in the cold, for with 72° of frost, the wind cuts through our thin tent, and even the drift is finding its way in and on to our bags, which are wet enough as it is. Cramp is not uncommon every now and then, and the drift all round the tent has made it so small that there is hardly room for us at all. The wind has been blowing hard all day; some of the gusts must be over seventy or eighty miles an hour. This evening it seems as though it were going to ease down, and directly it does we shall be up and away south for a rush. I feel that this march must be our limit.

When at one o'clock the next morning the hurricane began to abate, they got up at once and started on their last stage forward, half running, half walking. At nine o'clock they halted at their farthest point—88° 23′ south—hoisted the Union Jack, and declared the territory British. They looked longingly through their binoculars across the broad plateau on which lies the Pole—only a little more than a hundred miles away, but too far if they were to get back alive. Then four heartbroken men turned back.

The return march involved even worse exertions, for rations had now sunk below subsistence level, but they fought their weary way back and reached their base. Shackleton had proved that, with a little more luck, the Pole could be reached; success was now only a matter of time. His own failure so close to the objective was entirely due to unfavorable circumstances—the early death of the ponies, the blizzards, and the rest. At the same time he had shown a high sense of responsibility for his companions, sufficient to triumph over any craving for glory. If Shackleton had started from the ice of the Ross Barrier and so had in hand the 125 miles by which he fell short, he would have reached the Pole. As it was, the decision to turn back at the vital moment, with the goal so near, required a strength of character which cannot be measured in terms of success or failure.

Shackleton continued to devote the whole of his life to Antarctic exploration. In 1914–17 he was able to lead another expedition into the Weddell Sea, and during it he discovered the Caird Coast. As he was setting out in 1921 to circumnavigate the whole polar region, he fell sick and died, worn out by his restless zeal and exertions.

"Am going south. Amundsen."

This was the telegraphic message received by Robert Falcon Scott as in October 1910 he and his expedition were making the final preparations for their dash into the Antarctic on a journey designed to reach the Pole—quite apart from other scientific considerations. He had selected the sixty-five best men out of eight thousand enthusiastic volunteers; he had been able to equip the expedition splendidly, with the financial help of Great Britain, Australia, and New Zealand.

Scott immediately took account of the sportsmanlike communication sent by Amundsen, but he had no means of assessing its full import. He could not know that the ambitious Amundsen was staking everything on this journey, having spent all his personal means on exploring the Arctic and forcing the northwest passage; he had then raised funds from government and commercial sources in Norway and been given command of Nansen's famous *Fram* for the purpose of exploring the unknown regions round the North Pole, in the hope of reaching the Pole itself. Nor could Scott know that when Peary's successful journey to the

Pole took away Amundsen's appetite for that particular fare, the Norwegian had laid secret plans for the conquest of the South Pole instead, had used up all his resources by the time the *Fram* reached Buenos Aires, down to the last penny, and that in order to avoid recriminations and disgrace he must bring this last fling to a successful conclusion.

Roald Amundsen (1872–1928) once wrote the significant sentence: "Fortune is like a lovely, much-coveted woman; the man who really wants her mustn't sing serenades under her window, he must climb through the window and abduct her." Fortune smiled on Amundsen, but only because he prepared and fortified himself so well that in the end everything ran smoothly and according to plan. When he was setting out the details of all his arrangements in 1909, he wrote: "The men will return from their march to the South Pole on January 25, 1912." That proved to be the precise day on which he returned to base.

There were three special reasons for Amundsen's success. The first was the use he made of very carefully selected and trained Eskimo dogs; though the dogs pulled smaller loads than ponies could, they were much handier on difficult ground, they broke through the snow crust into holes and crevasses much less frequently, they ate less, and could, in any case, be kept well nourished, being carnivorous, on the flesh of other dogs that had died. Other special factors in Amundsen's favor were a remarkable scientific choice of equipment and supplies, and the mastery of ski technique which the Norwegians alone possessed at that time.

Scott had arrived in the Ross Sea during January 1911 and, intending to follow Shackleton's known route to the Pole, made his base on the west coast of Ross Island. It was planned to put a small detachment ashore on King Edward VII Land, but they failed to achieve a landing and the ship brought them back to Ross Island. On the way back through the Bay of Whales they met with an unpleasant surprise in the shape of another vessel sailing through those deserted wastes of ice: as they approached, they recognized the famous *Fram*.

They stayed some days with the Norwegians—all of them handy individuals, well used to privations, who made an excellent impression—before bringing Scott the unwelcome tidings. He wrote in his diary that all recent events seemed to pale against the almost unbelievable news that his men had run up against Amundsen in the Bay of Whales. His companions wanted to start at once for the Pole—supply dumps had already been laid—but common sense triumphed over excitement and Scott decided not to alter his arrangements.

But an entirely new situation had arisen, and the whole world was following with feverish tension this unique race in the remote Antarctic. Who would get to the Pole first? Amundsen, who was only just organizing his base, but whose route from the ice of the Bay of Whales was straight and nearly a hundred miles shorter, and who could start earlier because he was using dogs? Or Scott, who was better equipped, knew his route at first hand, but had to wait for the more favorable conditions of the polar spring because of his ponies?

On training-runs during the preparation of his base, Amundsen found that stretches of about seventy miles a day could be covered in good weather, but that progress was slow indeed on foggy and windy days. Then the polar winter set in. Amundsen started the moment it was over.

It was September 8. The thermometer during the days that followed fell to fifty-five degrees below zero, several of the dogs died, and finally Amundsen had to turn back. He had, however, made the vital discovery that his party must be sensibly reduced.

On October 10, 1911, he was off again, with only four companions—Olaf Olavson Bjaaland, Helmer Hanssen, Sverre H. Hassel, and Oscar Wisting. The weather was kind and everything went smoothly; it was not till October 22 that they entered the danger zone and met with an accident, Bjaaland's sledge disappearing into a deep crevasse. Luckily he was able to save himself; the sledge was hanging some yards down the rift and one of the men had to be lowered on a rope to bring the load up to the surface literally piecemeal. Then at last it proved possible to retrieve the sledge itself.

They met with a few more mishaps before reaching easier ground. The dogs ran at full stretch; the men, on their skis, had fastened themselves to the sledges, and about four hundred miles were covered in excellent time. Then the pace slowed a little while Amundsen, with great forethought, insisted on a careful marking of the route. Altogether, they set up a hundred and fifty snow pillars six feet high; to do so they had to hack out of the solid ice no fewer than nine thousand blocks of snow.

The weather remained good, even after they left the last depot behind on November 7, but a week later the easy traveling ended with high mountains rising skyward. The Ross Barrier, over whose ice their route had led, ended here; now they had to scale the coast proper of the continent and gain the plateau on the other side of the mountain range. In order to facilitate this, Amundsen left everything that could be spared behind him in a new dump. It was still 350 miles to the Pole—700 there and back—and he now calculated the exact amount of food men and dogs would need and apportioned the lease of life of the respective animals. He reckoned that forty-two dogs would be needed to reach the plateau, twenty-four of which could be slaughtered up above; that would leave eighteen dogs for three sledges. Along the rest of the route they would probably have to kill six more, but it was essential to keep twelve for the return journey, which could safely be made with two sledges.

They started up the difficult ascent on November 17, and Amundsen was fortunate enough to find a good approach route into the great complex of mountains on the very next day: a lengthy glacier tongue affording a much better route, however serious its difficulties, than if they had found it necessary to climb the rugged, snow-and-ice-covered mountains themselves.

For days the route went steeply upward, between cracks and abysses, until at last they reached an altitude of 10,500 feet above sea level. This was the bad moment when the dogs had to be slaughtered. Amundsen retired to his tent and tried to drown the cracking of the rifles by pumping the primus stoves till they roared so loudly that he could not hear the shots. In spite of the successful mastery of the ascent, there was no rejoicing in camp that night. "There was an oppressive note of sadness in the air," wrote Amundsen. "We were all devoted to our dogs."

The party was tied to the spot for some days by an icy storm, and when they did get on the move again their progress was still hindered by it. The plateau remained level, but soon became glacier ice again. Then began the most laborious stage of the march. They had to feel their way forward, through thick fog, over ground resembling a frozen lake; at times they seemed to be moving over empty barrels, so hollow was the ringing of their feet. Although they occasionally broke through thin ice, they crossed this difficult ground, which they christened "The Devil's Dance-Floor," without a serious accident.

After December 2, when they reached a height of 10,800 feet, they found stretching before them a level plain broken only occasionally by moderate-sized crevasses and eminently suitable for skiing. Nearer and nearer they moved to the Pole. They laid a last supply depot on the height to which Shackleton had pushed forward by his different route, at 88° 25'. Mindful of that achievement, Amundsen recorded: "Ernest Shackleton's name will always remain written in flaming letters on the history of the South Pole. I can think of no man who affords a better example of those qualities—courage and strength of purpose—which are able to achieve miracles." Then, turning his thoughts to the immediate future: "What will greet our eyes at the Pole? A great, endless plain unseen before by the eye of man, untrodden by his foot? Or—but surely that is the only possibility? We have come so quickly that there surely can be no doubt that we shall be the first to reach the goal!"

On the evening of December 14 they were close to the Pole, and their mood was almost one of Christmas Eve festivity. On the morning of the 15th they hurried on. At three in the afternoon the command to halt rang out. They were at the Pole. There was no doubt about it, for the sledge-leaders checked the readings carefully with their instruments. This was definitely the Pole, and it lay on dry land at an altitude of 9,500 feet.

There followed the most joyous moment of the expedition as the Norwegian flag was hoisted aloft.

Amundsen wrote:

Affection and pride shone from five pairs of eyes as the flag un-
folded in the fresh breeze and fluttered out over the Pole. I had
insisted that this historic act of striking the flag should be carried
out by all of us together. The honor belonged to the whole party,
not to any one member alone, for each man had risked his life in
this struggle and we had all stood together through thick and
thin. This was the only way I had of expressing my gratitude to
my comrades in that deserted place. I also felt that they under-
stood my gesture. Five raw, frost-damaged fists gripped the
sledge-runner, hoisted the flapping flag, and planted it—the first
ever to stand on the geographic South Pole. And so we raised our
beloved flag and gave the name of King Haakon VII Land to the
plain in which lies the Pole.

Every man of us who stood there will remember that moment
for the rest of his life. But the polar regions are not exactly suitable
for long ceremonies and one's next thought is: "The shorter, the
better."

Amundsen reminded himself how odd was the journey by
which he had come there:

Probably no one has ever reached a goal so exactly the opposite
to his first intentions. The north polar regions—nay, the North
Pole itself—had been my only dream since childhood's days. And
here I was standing at the South Pole. Was there ever such a
paradox?

They crossed the whole immediate polar region from end to
end and put up a tent on the pole itself. For safety's sake, Amundsen left in it a letter addressed to the Norwegian king with a
short report of his journey, and also a second letter for Scott.

The march back to base, during which Amundsen discovered
the high range of the Queen Maud Mountains, prospered beyond
all expectations. They were able to follow their old tracks for
part of the way, their markings made it easier to find the route,
and the following wind speeded the tempo till it was at times almost a gallop. They arrived at their base, "Framheim," after

ninety-nine days of absence, to be greeted with frantic enthusiasm.

In the meantime, Scott had also started out for the Pole, but his
expedition was under an unlucky star from the very beginning.
Even before reaching the Beardmore Glacier his motor tractor
was ditched and his ponies were dead. In spite of all, the party
marched on, dragging their sledges themselves, fighting their way
forward daily in the face of fierce blizzards.

At 87° 32′ south their last escorts turned back. It had been decided to make the final dash for the Pole with a small selected
party of the greatest possible strength. This consisted of Scott
himself; Dr. Edward Adrian Wilson, the scientist; Captain Lawrence Oates, of the Inniskilling Dragoons; Henry Bowers, another
officer; and Marine Sergeant Edgar Evans.

The ensuing drama at the world's southern pole can only be re-
enacted in the economical words that Scott, in spite of the crip-
pling cold and all the hardship and exhaustion that beset him,
entered daily in his diary.

*January 11th, 1912. I never had such pulling: all the time the
sledge rasps and creaks. We have covered 6 miles, but at fearful
cost to ourselves. . . . About 74 miles from the Pole—can we keep
this up for seven days? . . . None of us have ever had such hard
work before.*

*January 16th. The worst has happened, or nearly the worst. We
marched well in the morning and covered 7½ miles. Noon sight
showed us in latitude 89° 42′ S., and we started off in high spirits
in the afternoon, feeling that tomorrow would see us at our destination. About the second hour of the march Bowers' sharp eyes
detected what he thought was a cairn: he was uneasy about it,
but argued that it must be a sastrugus. Half an hour later he
detected a black speck ahead. Soon we knew that this could not
be a natural snow feature. We marched on, found that it was a
black flag tied to a sledge bearer; near by the remains of a camp;
sledge tracks going and coming and the clear trace of dogs' paws—
many dogs. This told us the whole story. The Norwegians have
forestalled us and are first at the Pole. It is a terrible disappoint-*

ment and I am very sorry for my loyal companions. Many thoughts come and much discussion have we had. Tomorrow we must march on to the Pole and then hasten home with all the speed we can compass. All the day dreams must go; it will be a wearisome return.

January 17th. The Pole. Yes, but under very different circumstances from those expected. We have had a horrible day—add to our disappointment a head wind of 4 to 5, with a temperature of −22°, and companions labouring on with cold feet and hands. We started at 7.30, none of us having slept much after the shock of our discovery. . . . The wind is blowing hard, and there is that curious damp, cold feeling in the air which chills one to the bone in no time. . . . Great God! This is an awful place and terrible enough for us to have laboured to it without the reward of priority. Well, it is something to have got here, and the wind may be our friend tomorrow.

From this ghastly disappointment, to which there is probably no human parallel, the men were never able to recover. The strength and energy bred of triumph were wanting later on at the very time they needed them most desperately. Their strength deteriorated in alarming fashion. The pitiful ration on which they lived—nothing, of course, was known in those days of vitamins or calories—proved deficient at the critical point. The weather was exceptionally cold and bad: as a result, ice crystals formed, producing a sandlike texture of the snow, so that the exhausted men could often hardly keep the sledges moving. From January 24 onward Oates and Evans showed signs of developing frostbite.

On February 7 they reached their depot at the top of the Beardmore and began the descent of the world's greatest glacier.

February 14th. There is no getting away from the fact that we are not going strong. Probably none of us: Wilson's leg still troubles him and he doesn't like to trust himself on ski; but the worst case is Evans, who is giving us serious anxiety.

Evans, whom Scott had described as a pillar of strength, had undergone a terrible transformation. With his intense devotion and admiration for his leader, he was probably the one who found fate's cruel stroke the hardest to get over. By now he was no longer quite accountable for his actions, and twice he lagged behind inexplicably. His companions, when they went out to look for him, found him at last, a distraught being, on his knees, his clothes disarranged, his gloves cast off, his hands frozen. He regained consciousness, but could not remember what had happened; then he went off into a faint. Somehow they managed to get him back to the tent. At half past twelve he died.

It is a terrible thing to lose a companion in this way, but calm reflection shows that there could not have been a better ending to the terrible anxieties of the past week. Discussion of the situation at lunch yesterday shows us what a desperate pass we were in with a sick man on our hands at such a distance from home.

On March 2 they reached the big supply dump on the barrier ice. But here they met with three further disasters. The oil ration they collected was far too small to enable them to reach the next depot, seventy miles away; Oates's feet were now frozen; and the weather took a turn for the worse, with the temperatures down to seventy-two degrees below zero at night. The next morning it took them an hour and a half just to put their boots on.

March 3rd. After 4¼ hours things so bad that we camped, having covered 4½ miles. One cannot consider this a fault of our own—certainly we were pulling hard this morning—it was more than three parts surface which held us back—the wind at strongest, powerless to move the sledge. . . . God help us, we can't keep up this pulling, that is certain. Amongst ourselves we are unendingly cheerful, but what each man feels in his heart I can only guess.

On March 4 they covered only three miles in a four and a half hours' grim battle with the sandlike snow. Next day their condition deteriorated from hour to hour. Oates was at the limit of his endurance.

March 5th. We mean to see the game through with a proper spirit, but it's tough work to be pulling harder than we ever pulled in our lives for long hours, and to feel that the progress is so slow.

On March 11 Scott ordered Wilson

to hand over the means of ending our troubles to us, so that any one of us may know how to do so. Wilson had no choice between doing so and our ransacking the medicine case. We have 30 opium tablets apiece and he is left with a tube of morphine. So far the tragical side of our story.

On the 14th one of Scott's entries reads: "It must be near the end, but a pretty merciful end. . . ."

March 16th or 17th. Lost track of dates but think the last correct. Tragedy all along the line. At lunch, the day before yesterday, poor Titus Oates said he couldn't go on; but he proposed we should leave him in his sleeping bag. That we could not do and induced him to come on, on the afternoon march. In spite of its awful nature for him, he struggled on and we made a few miles. At night he was worse and we knew the end had come.

Should this be found I want these facts recorded. Oates's last thoughts were of his Mother, but immediately before he took pride in thinking that his regiment would be pleased with the bold way in which he met his death. We can testify to this bravery. He has borne intense suffering for weeks without complaint, and to the very last was able and willing to discuss outside subjects. He did not—would not—give up hope to the very end. He was a brave soul. This was the end. He slept through the night before last, hoping not to wake; but he woke in the morning—yesterday. It was blowing a blizzard. He said, "I am just going outside and may be some time." He went out into the blizzard and we have not seen him since.

I take this opportunity of saying that we have stuck to our sick companions to the last. In the case of Edgar Evans, when absolutely out of food and he lay insensible, the safety of the remainder seemed to demand his abandonment, but Providence mercifully removed him at this critical moment. He died a natural death, and we did not leave him till two hours after his death. We knew that poor Oates was walking to his death, but though we tried to dissuade him, we knew it was the act of a brave man and an

English gentleman. We all hope to meet the end with a similar spirit, and assuredly the end is not far.

On the 18th Scott's right foot froze. They used the last of the gasoline; only a little fuel was left with which to prepare food and some liquid to drink. But they were getting nearer and nearer to the next supply dump, a sizable one where they would find a plentiful measure of everything. Only one more day of normal marching now and they would be safe.

Monday the 19th March. Today we started in the usual drag-ging manner. Sledge dreadfully heavy. We are 15½ miles from the depot and ought to get there in three days. What progress! We have two days' food but barely a day's fuel. All our feet are getting bad—Wilson's best, my right foot worst, left all right. There is no chance to nurse one's feet till we can get hot food into us. Amputation is the least I can hope for now, but will the trouble spread? That is the serious question. The weather doesn't give us a chance—the wind from N. to N.W. and −40° temp. today.

March 21st. Got within 11 miles of depot Monday night; had to lay up all yesterday in severe blizzard. Today forlorn hope, Wilson and Bowers going to depot for fuel.

March 22nd and 23rd. Blizzard bad as ever—Wilson and Bowers unable to start—tomorrow last chance—no fuel and only one or two [rations?] of food left—must be near the end. Have decided it shall be natural—we shall march for the depot with or without our effects and die in our tracks.

March 29th. Since the 21st we have had a continuous gale from W.S.W. and S.W. We had fuel to make two cups of tea apiece and bare food for two days on the 20th. Every day we have been ready to start for our depot 11 miles away, but outside the door of the tent it remains a scene of whirling drift. I do not think we can hope for any better things now. We shall stick it out to the end, but we are getting weaker, of course, and the end cannot be far.

It seems a pity, but I do not think I can write more.

R. Scott

It was on November 12 that a search party found the tent, snowed in to its apex, with the three bodies in it. Scott lay in the middle with his left hand resting on Wilson, his dearest friend. They found, too, diaries, notes, some films, a meteorological journal kept up to March 13, and one or two last letters in which Scott asked that their dependents might be cared for: his wife and son, Wilson's wife, and Edgar Evans's widow.

The searchers buried the dead and raised a great hillock of snow over their grave; on top they erected skis in the form of a cross. They searched several days for Oates's body, but in vain.

After discovering the South Pole, Scott's more fortunate rival still longed to get to the North. In 1918 he attempted to repeat Nansen's drift on a northern course that he hoped would bring him to the Pole, but after spending two winters on the Siberian coast he had to give up the effort. In 1923 he intended to fly to the Pole, but his machine was damaged during trials in Alaska. In 1925 he joined the American explorer Lincoln Ellsworth in a second attempt, but they were forced to crash-land a hundred and fifty miles short of the Pole and were able to start back again only after weeks of tremendous effort. In the following year Amundsen at last succeeded in flying over the Pole, again in Ellsworth's company, in the rickety airship built by the Italian Nobile. But this time, just as he had once forestalled Scott, another was ahead of him by a short margin, as will be seen later. In June 1928 Amundsen tried to go to the rescue of Nobile, whose airship had come to grief on a second attempt to reach the Pole. This act of comradeship and readiness to help cost him his life. He perished on the flight from Norway to Spitsbergen.

Parents are fated to meet with all sorts of surprises about their children; but few can have experienced such an exciting shock as a pair in Winchester, Virginia, whose eleven-year-old son suddenly disappeared. The boy was known for his wild, adventurous nature, but his parents can hardly have expected that their son would turn up in the Philippines in a sailing-boat which he had managed in some unexplained way to acquire. If they had not apprehended him, he might even have carried out his intention to sail round the world.

The name of this practical youngster was Richard E. Byrd (born on October 25, 1888). His urge to do things did not only spend itself in adventure, but also drove him to an energetic study of mathematics and natural history, for he meant to become a sailor. So well did he pursue his studies that he got into the Naval Academy when he was only fifteen. There, as later in his service in the Navy, he distinguished himself both by his practical keenness and his scientific interests. After the First World War a new passion seized Byrd in its grip—the passion for flying—and he was one of the first to fly across the Atlantic. His energy in pursuit of science in no way lagged behind. When he began to be preoccupied with polar exploration, he took up twenty-two branches of science which have a bearing on it. In his accounts of his expeditions he revealed a gift of expression far beyond that of any other polar explorer, and one worthy of a great author.

In April 1926 hasty preparations were under way in Spitsbergen for an undertaking that had attracted a great deal of attention: the ambitious Italian Nobile wanted to be the first man to fly over the North Pole in an airship. With the experienced assistance of Amundsen and Ellsworth, he was eventually to succeed in making the first flight over the Pole to Alaska.

The start was timed for May. The airship, the *Norge*, had not yet arrived when on April 29 an American vessel unexpectedly entered the harbor of Kings Bay and decanted the airmen Byrd and Floyd Bennett with a rickety Fokker aircraft only forty feet long and with a wing span of sixty feet. Byrd had learned of Nobile's intention; when on May 7 the *Norge* landed, Nobile knew to his discomfiture that he had a competitor who had every intention of flying first to the Pole.

Both parties pushed ahead with their preparations at top pressure. The luckless Andrée and two companions had perished in an attempt, made in 1897, to reach the Pole in a balloon; their diaries and photographs (still in good enough condition to be processed) were found on Vito near Spitsbergen thirty-three years later. And now, after an interval of decades, the question of who would be the first to fly over the North Pole was to be decided in the next few days.

Byrd's first attempt ended in a snowdrift. His aircraft, the *Josephine,* was fitted with skids, and a snow runway such as is used for ski-jumping was prepared to make sure of a good start. In order to take advantage of the snow at its hardest, the flight to the Pole was timed to begin at the coldest time of the night. Byrd's pronouncement on the subject was that the *Josephine* would either fly straight off into the air or fly into pieces.

At the second attempt, on May 10 at five minutes to two in the morning, the machine took the air. About five p.m., when Nobile and his companion were sitting at a meal, an Italian workman rushed in shouting: "There's the drone of an engine!"

They all rushed out. The *Josephine* came into view and the whole improvised airdrome was full of excited people. The aircraft had to make two circuits before the runway was clear enough for it to come down. Byrd and Bennett climbed out, winners of the North Pole air stakes. They had been airborne for fifteen hours and had taken the prize off the very toes of the Italian with his big airship.

That evening Byrd was celebrating his triumph with Amundsen and Ellsworth, those resounding names in the story of exploration, when Amundsen laughingly inquired: "Well, Byrd, what next?"

"The South Pole," answered Byrd, half serious, half in jest.

The two men talked it over. Amundsen promised his full support, practical and advisory, and from that moment Byrd devoted himself wholeheartedly to the project.

It took him two and a half years to make the preparations for his expedition, all in the greatest secrecy. After the outstanding debt from the North Pole venture had been cleared off by serious efforts, fresh financial problems of a much more difficult kind had to be overcome.

Byrd once wrote with characteristic humor that science has to become a businesswoman when she is looking for a means to a dedicated end. "Even Columbus traveled on a profit-sharing basis." The assembly of the equipment presented a series of headaches. Every detail had to be thought out, for the failure of a single spare part later on could spell disaster.

Byrd put to sea in the Norwegian whaler *C. A. Larsen* on October 8, 1928. For his attempt on the South Pole, he followed Amundsen's advice exactly; he also took the very course by which his predecessor had reached the Antarctic. The passage through the ice pack began on December 15, with the *Larsen,* which acted as the flagship, towing the *City.* The method of forcing a way through the ice pack was for the ship to charge the ice under full steam, thereby lifting herself and breaking the ice beneath her. She then backed away, preparatory to another attack. The crew were thus heavily knocked about, and all the time they had to keep the *City,* which was being towed, from running into the *Larsen* and ramming from astern. Sometimes a dozen of these nerve-racking crashes broke away only a few yards of the ice, and both ships were constantly in danger of being frozen in.

A few weeks later, after the most strenuous efforts, they reached the open water of the Ross Sea. There the captain of the *Larsen,* intent on whaling, left the Byrd expedition for fourteen months.

They came to the Ross Barrier next day. It was now essential to reckon with the capricious perils of the ice, which changed and moved from one moment to the next. Great masses the size of skyscrapers broke away daily from the barrier, compelling the ship to stand a mile offshore. A few weeks later, when the ship had been laid alongside, the whole "quay," an ice platform they were using to unload her, broke off, and shortly afterward a second ship belonging to the expedition was hit by a gigantic block of ice just as she was arriving. Fortunately, nobody was killed by either of these accidents. Byrd, who was continually consulting the books of his predecessors Scott, Shackleton, Mawson, and Amundsen, searched in vain for the site of "Framheim" and eventually chose a sheltered bay for the settlement he proposed to build and name "Little America."

It was January 15, 1929, before the single-engined Fairchild aircraft could take the air on a reconnaissance flight. A new era in polar exploration dawned that day. Instead of the laborious struggle with dog sledges, it was now possible, though still not without mortal peril, to photograph and map an area of twelve hundred square miles in the course of a few hours.

But reconnaissance was not carried out only from the air; they also used a motor boat. Byrd narrowly escaped disaster when huge killer whales surfaced close to the boat, compelling the explorers to race ashore and wait there till the dangerous creatures disappeared.

At last the two vessels were unloaded and left Byrd and his party encamped on the icy continent. The base "Little America" had been completed by dint of tremendous efforts during the two short months of the polar summer; it consisted of two main buildings and some huts, all interconnected by underground passages, a radio station, and an airdrome. Two more reconnaissances had been flown in the meantime; on one of these the aircraft crash-landed and Byrd had to go out and rescue the crew—Gould and three others—from the ice wastes in which, after a search, he found them.

Even during those "summer months" the fierce cold and the knife-edged icy wind, which seemed to cut clean through ordinary clothes, had made life difficult enough. Now the polar winter set in. The slightest activity, such as the development of the photographs taken from the aircraft, became a fight against innumerable difficulties, for water in a liquid state was as rare as nectar. Water in any container that was not kept permanently heated immediately turned to ice.

Notwithstanding, thanks to modern technical methods, it was in these icebound huts that polar exploration took giant strides forward, such as no earlier explorer could ever have imagined in his wildest dreams. For he would have had to travel for months through snow and ice, making thousands of isolated observations, in order to produce a single map of the kind that was now being issued in endless succession; for error-free maps can be made from aerial photographs, once position, focal distance, and angle of inclination are known.

The most important operation being prepared in Little America was the flight to the South Pole in the triple-engined Fokker aircraft *Floyd Bennett*. It was impossible to carry sufficient petrol for the seventeen-hundred-mile round trip, so it was decided after considerable thought to lay down a petrol dump at the foot of the Queen Mauds and to let the plane land and refuel there.

A party set out under Gould to break a trail to the foot of the mountains, but Byrd emphasized that their geological researches were to take precedence over the flight aspects.

When Byrd brought the supplies for the dump by air, he flew over his comrades, who were painfully fighting their way over the ice yard by yard, and he could then see for himself the tremendous contrast between the old and the new methods of exploration. The airmen were stunned by the revelation.

On the return flight they had to force-land, and this might well have been a disaster. They were saved, however, by the wireless, thanks to which the smaller Fairchild aircraft landed next to them with the necessary fuel less than four hours later.

On November 28 the weather was so favorable that it was possible to attempt the polar flight. At 3:29 p.m. the man who had been the first to fly over the North Pole started his flight to the opposite end of the world.

The aircraft carried a fifteen-thousand-pound load. While he was racing toward the Pole at a hundred miles per hour, Byrd thought of Amundsen, who, eighteen years earlier, had traveled the same way on the icy surface and had considered himself lucky if he covered twenty-five miles in a whole day. At 8:15 they flew over the Queen Maud dump, just before the critical part of the flight—the crossing of the great range that guards the high polar plateau with its grim barrier.

Amundsen's crossing had been at 10,500 feet. Would the aircraft be able to get over it? Would the saddle be too narrow, or would vicious air currents perhaps force the heavily laden plane too far downward?

At the last moment Byrd chose a route along the Liv Glacier instead of the Axel Heiberg Glacier, by which Amundsen had traveled. The aircraft reached an altitude of 10,000 feet, but, in spite of every effort, refused to climb any higher; every time it rose a little, it dropped again in a very short time. There was nothing left but to open the gasoline tank; in two minutes five hundred gallons of precious fuel had gone streaming down through thin air. "Get rid of another two hundred pounds!" A sack of provisions went hurtling overboard. The plane spun in the grip of downward eddies. While the crew expected at any moment to be smashed to the ground, another two hundred and forty pounds of provisions—enough to keep the four of them alive for a month in case of an emergency landing—went overboard.

These costly sacrifices won them a bumpy few hundred feet of height—enough to make the vital difference. The plane lurched through a tiny gap between the Ruth Gade Glacier and the black walls of 13,240-foot Mount Nansen, clearing the nearest summits by a bare five hundred feet.

That left three hundred and fifty miles to go. At 1:14 on the morning of November 29, 1929, the aircraft reached the Pole and circled round it for ten minutes. Byrd threw out a memorial banner of Floyd Bennett's and thought of Amundsen and Scott. Then, with a strong wind at their tail, they turned for home. They tanked up at the Queen Maud dump, and eighteen hours after their start the plane landed without mishap at Little America.

This triumph was followed by three other missions: the geological research of the Queen Mauds; the completion of a plane-table survey of the Bay of Whales; and a closer reconnaissance of new country discovered to the east, which Byrd named Marie Byrd Land after his wife. In February 1930 they started for home.

Four years later Byrd undertook his second south polar expedition. When in January 1934 two ships re-entered the Bay of Whales, the whole lie of the land had changed completely owing to the "calving" of the ice. The coastline was unrecognizable, valleys were filled up, slopes had disappeared, the sea had bitten four miles farther into the bay. Sixty tons of the precious supplies they had been compelled to leave behind four years earlier had simply vanished.

They had to build a track eight miles long between cracks, abysses, and ice jams in order to manhandle fifty tons of cargo into the settlement—working with feverish haste, for every hour of the polar summer counts.

At the end of February the ships left the Bay of Whales, and then the sufferings of a polar winter started all over again. Byrd handed over his command to Dr. Poulter in March and himself occupied an advanced post. There he achieved one of the most memorable performances in polar history by spending several months entirely alone in the utter solitude of the advanced Bolling weather-observation station.

A man of Byrd's make-up, in comparing his own achievements with those of Amundsen, Scott, and Shackleton, could not avoid a sense of inferiority because he knew that the scientific equipment at his disposal was immeasurably superior to theirs. Looking back, he wrote:

Now I had been to both Poles. In prospect, this had promised to be a satisfying achievement. And in a large sense it has been—principally because the Poles had been the means of enabling me to enlist public support for the full-scale scientific program which was my real interest. . . . But for me there was little sense of true achievement. Rather, when I finished the stocktaking, I was conscious of a certain aimlessness.

His sojourn in the advanced post was to provide a unique achievement. His brave effort was devoted to the solution of an important scientific question: do the Poles influence weather conditions on the rest of the earth's surface, and if so, how? In risking his life to read thermometers, observe clouds, air currents, snow drift, and wind speeds, to service barographs, wind gauges, pressure gauges, and hygrometers day after day, he was responsible for the crossing of a new frontier. As long as weather forecasts depended on observations made in the central sectors of the world only, they could not be absolutely reliable. The extension of those observations to the whole of the planet's surface can in time ensure the provision of weather maps predicting conditions for some days ahead with reasonable certitude.

In a temperature of 52 degrees below zero Byrd, isolated by a hundred miles from Little America, began his vigil through the long polar night. The space he lived in was roughly twelve by nine feet. The meaning of solitary existence in the loneliness of the icy wastes; the problems of being left completely alone, such as how to avoid losing all sense of direction when out of doors (indeed, on one occasion Byrd found himself standing hopelessly at a loss in the white desert); how to cook without a cookbook (he had forgotten to bring one); his worries about the fortunes of the whole expedition and its other members; the introspections of a solitary being cut off from all human companionship—all this is to be found in Byrd's masterly book *Alone*, which has to be read if one is to have any real comprehension of his state of mind and body during that time.

While his companions were making a number of reconnaissances into the continent, Byrd was fighting a lonely battle for life itself. After June he began to suffer from severe headaches. Then he gradually noticed that he woke up later and later. At last he discovered the cause: fumes from the heating-system were poisoning him. As he continued to lose weight he tried desperately to escape death. He dared not raise enough heat to finish him off, but had to have enough warmth to prevent his freezing to death. Even in temperatures of fifty and sixty degrees below zero, he slept with his door open; his breath turned to frost on his blanket, but nobody knew of his plight, because he did not want to endanger the lives of his comrades by an S.O.S.

Dr. Poulter, however, began to worry about Byrd, whose radio messages were becoming more and more scrappy. The fact was that his transmitter had become defective and he was forced to use a hand dynamo to send messages; he was now so weak that he hardly had the strength to turn the handle. In reply to an inquiry of Poulter's, Byrd spelled out letter by letter in dreadfully slow time: "Don't ask me to go on turning. I am O.K." That didn't sound very satisfactory to Poulter. As his special-observation duties were directed to the showers of shooting stars, he conceived the idea of observations somewhat nearer to the Pole on a nocturnal journey. Byrd had given orders that he was not to be relieved till a month after the sun's return above the horizon, but Poulter succeeded, after persistent pressure, in obtaining leave to take this opportunity of looking him up. He fought his way through to the weather station with two companions and arrived just in time to rescue Byrd, who was only a shadow of his former self. They had to nurse the Admiral for two months before he was fit enough to be flown back to base in the aircraft on October 12; till then the four men managed to exist in that pitifully small space.

On January 19, 1935, the ship that was to take them all home appeared in the Bay of Whales to be greeted with loud cheers, and after everythng had been packed they started on their homeward journey.

Byrd's expeditions produced an incomparably greater mass of results than any previous explorer had ever been in a position to assemble in the same time. The first expedition achieved the polar flight, the geological exploration of the Queen Mauds, and survey work and geological discoveries in newly discovered Marie Byrd Land (during which Gould's expedition covered fifteen hundred miles), as well as much cartographic work. The second resulted in further discoveries, embracing the measurement of 440,000 square miles of land and sea, as well as scientific researches sufficient to fill several volumes, all indicative that a continuous continent existed around the Pole which had originally nourished a luxuriating flora similar to that of Australia, New Zealand, and South America and was now rich in coal and mineral deposits.

Yet only about a ninth of this continent—which, with its five million square miles, is about the size of Europe—was as yet known. In 1939 Byrd undertook a third expedition, during which a second base besides Little America was set up in Marguerite Bay, on the Antarctic coast of the Indian Ocean. In November 1940 the exploration of the Eternity Range was begun from this point, and during the same expedition Graham Land was explored and a mountain massif, as high as Mont Blanc but completely surrounded by open water, was discovered. The war forced the premature abandonment of the venture, and the explorers returned to the United States at the beginning of 1941.

During the war Admiral Byrd held a headquarters appointment in the American Fleet Air Arm. When it was over, he was able to devote himself to the preparation of a gigantic expedition that, by applying every means of modern invention to polar exploration, began a new chapter in its history.

Between December 2 and 10, 1946, a complete fleet left three North American harbors: Byrd's flagship, *Mount Olympus,* freighters, icebreakers, tankers, two destroyers, two aircraft-carriers, and a submarine—twelve ships in all, with crews amounting to four thousand men.

On the basis of his great experience and by using every modern form of equipment, Byrd had succeeded in developing an entirely new method of polar exploration. The hardships of wintering could now be avoided, for there were appliances that could be left at the weather stations quite unattended to record temperature, humidity, and wind direction. So these automatic stations could be set up during the polar summer and their statistics radioed to other weather stations staffed by experts. The other results of the researches undertaken during the short summer could be worked out by using larger parties of scientists in co-operation. Where in the old days exhausting transport and loading work had occupied the whole summer, now aircraft ferried men and machines between the Bay of Whales and Little America in the space of minutes. Electrically heated tents replaced underground diggings; radar facilitated unheard-of research work; and the old clumsy tractors were replaced by amphibians whose use had already been amply proven during the war's many landing-operations.

Even before Byrd's army went ashore, the aircraft were out on reconnaissance flights. Right at the outset it was shown that, in spite of the finest organization possible, the dangers of the Antarctic had not been entirely dealt with. The aircraft *Martin Mariner* had taken off from a carrier operating two hundred miles east of Little America out in the Roosevelt Sea. After two hours and forty minutes the plane radioed that it had run into a heavy blizzard; then all communications ceased suddenly.

In the howling snowstorm, above which the note of engines was no longer audible, the aircraft's crew heard a crash like thunder. The machine had flown straight into the ice. Only two of the crew escaped injury; two were slightly and two others seriously hurt, and three were dead. Just as the survivors were seeking protection in the wreckage, a gust laid hold of the aircraft and whirled it around like a plaything, putting the radio out of action.

Luckily, the storm abated next day. The victims of the crash collected provisions and a tent out of the wreckage, but found only enough to keep them alive for a week at the most. For several days fog prevented all attempts at a search. The unfortunate men eked out a bare existence from New Year's Day till January 11; then they were awakened by the most wonderful noise in the world—the sound of aircraft engines! Numerous aircraft belonging to the expedition had been searching the endless wastes of ice for a week. The difficulty for the men on the ground was to get themselves noticed, and this they did by the method used since time immemorial by all shipwrecked mariners: smoke signals. They hastily rolled a rubber keg out of the wreck, drenched it in gasoline, and set it alight. A column of black smoke rose into the sky, the aircraft swept low over them once, then circled several times, while those of the icebound party who were fit to do so danced for joy. Soon afterward a helicopter rescued them, and a little while later the world's newsreels were showing pictures of their safe arrival aboard the aircraft-carrier.

The landing at Little America began at the end of January 1947. They dug the old settlement out of snow many feet deep, and the provisions left there were found to be in good refrigerated condition. That deserted spot had been left far behind the times; pages out of newspapers, the print still clear on them, told of Hitler's latest victories in 1941. Like ancient newspapers all the world over, they served a useful purpose as fire-lighting material.

The results brought back by this highly organized undertaking were as important as they were numerous. The month of February was devoted to an immense operation by the aircraft, which flew over the whole continent and photographed it from the air, using a new type of triple camera which instantaneously took a color motion picture, a colored "still," and a black-and-white photograph. These pictures enabled the geologists to draw definite conclusions about types of rock and ore from the color and stratification of the rocks of which the mountains were composed. On February 16 Byrd himself flew to the Pole a second time, and during the course of this expedition the whole continent was circumnavigated for the first time.

When it came to evaluating the first results of these flights—a total of eighty-four flights covered nine hundred thousand square miles—Byrd had to admit that all existing maps of the coast of Victoria Land and Wilkes Land had become utterly worthless. Thanks to the new facts revealed, it proved possible not only to complete them but to redraw them entirely. A million square miles of previously unknown country were surveyed from the air; two thousand miles of coastline charted, nine large new bays, twenty-six islands, a 9,500-foot-high plateau in Wilkes Land, eight new mountain ranges, and three great peninsulas were discovered in this way. Near the Knox Coast they discovered extinct volcanoes and lakes whose temperature was warmer than that of any other in the whole Antarctic. Thanks to the new observations, places hitherto held to be mountains were revealed as bays, seas as giant peaks, land as inland seas; seventy thousand square miles previously thought to be land were identified as sea. Information about the variation of the Magnetic Pole was also collected. The meteorologists pin-pointed two areas where storms originate.

At the beginning of March the huge expedition arrived home. The data it brought home provided material for a long period of scientific appraisal and pointed clearly to future developments: global weather-forecasting, the mining and transport of invaluable ores. What will the Antarctic contribute to the future of mankind? Perhaps the digging up of colossal treasures of the earth, comparable to the great era of colonial exploitation, only with this difference: this time there will be no natives to suffer from its consequences. And what about the warm lakes, presumably fed from subterranean sources, and the snowless tracts that one American airman thought he saw? Maybe one day they will be the site of luxury hotels, or military airfields, or perhaps, as Byrd hoped, vast prairies of growing corn.

12

INTO SPACE

THE BIG white patches about which nothing was known have disappeared from the maps; the 200,000,000 square miles of our earth's surface are all known—at least in theory. Actually, in spite of all the voyages of exploration in ancient and modern times, there remain quite a few stretches of land in Asia, Africa, the Antarctic, Canada, and the Yemen which have never yet been trodden by man's foot and where men of action and inquisitive mind can still find a new field for their activities.

But the great all-compelling adventure is no longer to be found on this globe, which offers no more frontiers or barriers to be crossed. The horizon, the boundary line that man now longs to transcend, lies not before his eyes but above his head—above the atmosphere in the outer darkness of space. Man's imagination has, of course, been preoccupied with space travel for a very long time: H. G. Wells with his unforgettable *Time Machine*, and other novelists such as Jules Verne, Kurd Lasswitz, and, in more recent days, a horde of writers who, blending sheer fantasy with scientific fact, harrow us with brutal pictures of horror sufficient to quench in us any desire to go rushing about in space. At the same time, prophets, cranks, dreamers, scientists, and dilettantes are revealing the genuine possibilities of a thrust forward into the universe.

The greatest barrier to man's exploration of the world has always been the sea. Man is a being who belongs on land; he had to discover means of living and moving about on water. In the course of long ages he succeeded so well that what were once the perilous seas have yielded comparatively friendly traffic lanes.

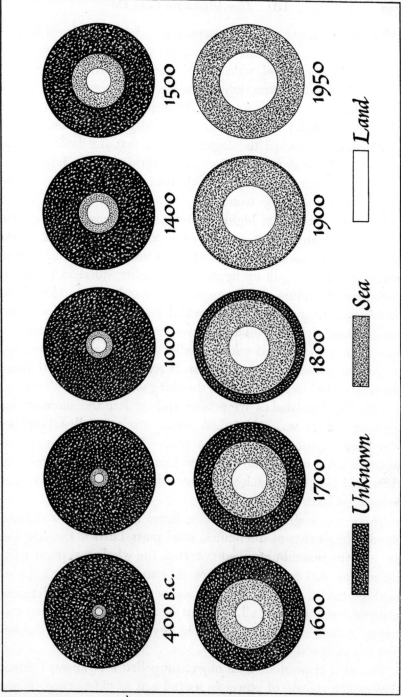

THE GROWTH OF MAN'S KNOWLEDGE OF THE GLOBE FROM 400 B.C. TO
THE MID-TWENTIETH CENTURY. BASED ON CALCULATIONS OF PROFES-
SOR W. BEHRMANN

After the conquest of one element, water, he had to learn how to travel in another—the air. But in order to realize his courageous dream of space travel, man has to learn to overcome the great force of the earth's attraction and he has also to command a source of propulsion sufficient to allow his means of transport to leave the earth behind. Only a quarter of a century ago a famous mathematician put forward the logical theory that the basic laws of nature made the development of such a form of power impossible.

On December 21, 1932, a bitterly cold night, a few men in the depths of a small pine woods only twenty miles south of Berlin were busy with their highly secret preparations. After a long period of planning they were on the point of trying out a new principle of propulsion—jet power. On a test bench for liquid-fuel rocket power units, lit up by two searchlights, stood an eighteen-inch-long aluminum rocket combustion chamber, its orifice—from which was to gush forth a powerful jet, engendered by liquid oxygen and alcohol—pointing downward. In a near-by observation chamber crammed with a medley of pipes, valves, shutters, and cocks, numerous instruments were ready to register with great precision what happened when the thing was released.

The last handshakes were over and at last the moment for lighting the jet was at hand. A young student called Wernher von Braun approached it with a twelve-foot rod, to the end of which a basin of gasoline had been fixed. He lit the gasoline and then held his giant match-stick under the jet nozzle of the rocket propulsion unit.

There was a great crack, and a flame shot high into the air. Planks, fragments of aluminum, steel parts hurtled through the air, and the searchlights went out; then the whole test plant went up roaring and reeking in flames. A sorry heap of wreckage, of bent pieces of iron, smoldering rubber, and pulverized measuring-instruments was all that was left after the explosion; fortunately, no human beings came to any harm. That was the beginning of space travel.

The idea of producing an object propelled in a forward direction by the release of power in its tail was as old as time. Thousands of years ago the Chinese had already used powder rockets;

it was in the twentieth century that the notion was born of sub-
stituting liquids to obtain a far higher content of energy and so
propelling rockets into space. Wild theories could not be converted into sober practice, however, until technical progress began
to provide a variety of new materials in great quantities: light
metal alloys, liquid oxygen capable of storage, and the many
products of electrical precision engineering. Also, from the outset
there were financial and organizational difficulties beyond the
power of private individuals to deal with. In the second decade of
the twentieth century plenty of individuals started experimenting
with rockets, but in spite of all their enthusiasm and many casualties, the most that could be achieved was an occasional partial
success and isolated contributions to the general development of
rocket propulsion. That pursuit was, in the end, left in very different hands—which is the saddest and ugliest feature of the
whole story.

The armaments branch of the German army was exploring the
possibilities of developing secret weapons and was particularly
interested in the production of rockets; their aim was to construct
a completely new kind of liquid-powered rocket with jet propulsion. In 1930 the relevant section was joined by Lieutenant of
Artillery Walter Dornberger in the capacity of an assistant; he had
previously acquired a diploma at the Technical High School in
Berlin. Under the army's wing, continuous developments in this
special field were now made possible; it was Dornberger who assumed the important responsibility for this work and eventually
installed and directed the Army Experimental Station at Peenemünde.

His work began with one final object in view: the production of
rockets which could be directed at level targets by a trajectory
ending in a vertical fall and which could carry the highest possible
explosive load—Dornberger himself described this as the "effective
load." He collected about him a team of brilliant assistants and
was especially lucky in his selection of Wernher von Braun. Even
as a schoolboy Braun had dreamed of flying to the moon one day
and had occupied himself with astronomy and other technical
studies; then he began to study at the Technical High School and

at the age of nineteen was working with all the possessed fury of a pioneer in the office of a private enterprise that maintained a "rocket airfield" at the Berlin suburb of Reinickendorf as long as its capital lasted.

Dornberger started by banishing the space fantasies from the mind of his young collaborator and set him to work on steady, sound research and development. The abortive test of December 1932 was soon followed by others that revealed new data and fresh difficulties; optimism and despair succeeded one another; results were achieved and were immediately followed by serious setbacks. The work on high explosives claimed its victims—as long ago as 1930 the inventor Max Valier, who had built a racing-car with liquid rocket propulsion, had been killed in a test run. In March 1934 four technicians of the Army Experimental Station lost their lives in an explosion that destroyed the whole test installation.

The more Hitler armed Germany, the easier it became for Dornberger to get funds for his costly weapon program. By the end of 1937 the first attempts at firing the missiles had already taken place. There were frequent snags and failures to be overcome, but on October 3, 1942, after two abortive attempts on June 13 and August 26, everything was ready. A gigantic rocket equipped with every kind of gadget—later to become the V2—stood there, with all its thirteen and a half tons of weight, waiting to be released. Then came the order:

"Ignition!"

The jet spat clouds of vapor. Sparks began to fly.

"First step!"

The operating engineer threw the second switch. The shower of sparks grew to a streak of flame, surrounded by smoke. The release cable fell away from the rocket.

"Take off!"

The last governing switch went over. Terrific forces of energy roared in a jet from the rocket as it quietly lifted and disappeared with increasing speed into the heights above—a metal cylinder, shining brilliantly in the sun, its sharp end uppermost, with a huge scarf of flame shooting down vertically below it. And then came its thunderous roar, whose swelling sound revealed the force of the combustion processes that had dispatched it. The burning gases were bursting out of the orifice of the jet at a speed of more than a mile per second and at a temperature of 2800° Centigrade.

By now the rocket had attained a speed of about three hundred and fifty yards a second and was approaching a barrier—the speed of sound—across which lay unknown and menacing dangers. The flight went on; the rocket burst through the barrier and reached a speed exceeding that of sound. It held together without bursting —and in that instant a new piece of knowledge was won which could only be gained by the results of this test.

On and on upward went the rocket, traveling at more than a thousand meters per second, racing toward space, approaching a new frontier—the last layers of the atmosphere. Then the fuel ran out, and the flame died away. The flight went on under the force of the rocket's own velocity of a mile a second.

At a record height of fifty-five miles the rocket turned back toward the earth. Would it be able to stand the conditions when its hull was plunged back into the denser atmospheric layers—the check, caused by air pressure, from fifteen hundred meters per second to eight hundred, which would cause heating of the outer casing to 680° Centigrade? The rocket did not disintegrate; it survived its return to the earth's atmosphere and fell, after its speed had been precisely measured by electrical instruments, with a terrifying and incredible return thrust of 192,000,000 meter-kilograms, into the sea.

Dornberger celebrated the proving of this marvelous new weapon of war in an address in which he did not forget to stress the possibilities in relation to space-penetration.

After this successful trial, naturally, more funds were provided than ever before. And yet the mass production of these weapons and their use in an attack on England never really got going because Germany was engaged in a war that transcended her means and her available resources. The various branches of war production had to wrangle for raw materials, skilled personnel, and building-licenses like hungry dogs about a gnawed bone. The V2 could have prospered only if it had been placed at the top of the priority list; that was not done because Hitler had seen in his dreams that no V2 would ever reach England.

At last, however, things took a turn the other way and the station at Peenemünde was given pride of place in the whole German arms program, while Hitler now screamed: "I want annihilation—total annihilation!" But it was too late; it was already July 1944 and the course of the war was already set for its inevitable end, with unavoidable defeat drawing ever nearer.

While the blind fury of the rocket attack on English cities rightly brought discredit on the names of the technicians who shared in the concept, there was one faint ray of light on this dark chapter in the history of invention. In March 1944, at a time when numerous failures were again afflicting the rocket trials, von Braun and two of his assistants were arrested for "sabotage" and placed in custody at Stettin.

Dornberger's efforts succeeded in getting the prisoners released. The interesting feature in this event, which was powerfully affected by internal strife among the Nazis about Peenemünde, was the ground on which the arrest was based. The "sabotage" alleged was that von Braun and the two other technicians had allowed a free rein to their ideas about space travel and had consequently failed to devote their entire energy to the perfection of the V2 as a war weapon.

After the defeat of Germany the experts continued their work, more or less voluntarily, in different countries. Nothing much is known about further developments in Soviet Russia: we have only heard that methodical progress has been made with V2 rockets and that they have produced a three-phase rocket said to have a range of over two thousand miles. At the end of 1952 the Russian periodical *Ogonek* predicted that the Russian flag would be planted on the moon within the next fifty years.

More details are available from America, where since 1945, with the collaboration of Wernher von Braun, rockets that reach an average height of a hundred miles, fully equipped with measuring-instruments and cameras, are being fired from the White Sands testing-grounds in New Mexico; and we know that

they return to earth undamaged, bringing invaluable observations
and data with them.

The German origin of rocket technique is perpetuated in the
use by American technicians of such terms as the *Meilerwagen*
(a special method of rocket transport evolved at Peenemünde)
and the *Mischgerat* (a part of the power unit). American research
has added many new developments. It is hardly possible for
rockets to fly off their track, for they have in the meantime
acquired precision electric "nerves" and "cells" of the highest
order, by which they can be steered with a great degree of
exactitude from the ground. This remote-control system has produced an astonishing range of miniature technical appliances:
radio valves the size of peas, transformers half the size of a ciga-
rette, and ten-valve assemblies small enough to go into a match-
box.

Conditions in the higher strata of the world's atmosphere are
becoming better known every day. This is the result not only of
the exact data obtained from pressure gauges, Geiger counters,
cloud chambers, spectographs, and similar automatic devices, but
from even more precise facts revealed by registration balloons,
which can remain in the air and have already reached a height of
twenty-one miles above the earth. True, that is no great altitude
for a rocket. The heights and speeds attained by the old V2's were
long ago exceeded when the idea of packing one rocket on top
of another was adopted, with the result that, the moment the
parent rocket reaches its maximum speed, another in its head
begins to function; in this way the velocity already attained is
added to the speed of the second rocket as it starts. On February 24, 1949, a two-phase rocket of this kind called "WAC Corporal" reached a height of two hundred and fifty miles and so
became the first object manufactured by man to fly into space—
for our atmosphere ends about a hundred and twenty-five miles
above the earth.

The present world's height records are, for the time being,
accredited not to men but to animals sent up for test purposes.
White mice that were filmed during the process apparently took
no notice of the changed conditions; a parrot scolded like any

other parrot when he came back to earth. The record-holder is a monkey that has been up to an altitude of eighty miles and come down safe and sound; as far as can be established on this planet of ours, he represents the highest form of life to have ventured so far out into space.

But men have also achieved performances in flight which may be regarded as steps toward journeys in space. Until 1947 the view was held that rocket aircraft could not exceed a speed of 670 miles per hour—the dreaded Sound Barrier—because the lifting-surfaces would disintegrate. This boundary, like the others, was crossed in a test flight; Major Charles Yaeger of the United States Air Force flew in a test aircraft at a speed of 1,000 miles per hour—well beyond the speed of sound.

That made it possible to undertake further trial flights, and it was not long before one took place which was certainly a signpost on the way to space-penetration. A young American test pilot, William Bridgeman, in the "Skyrocket," a needle-sharp thirty-eight-foot jet plane, reached a height of fifteen miles and attained—because he had left ninety-six per cent of the heavy air and ozone layers below him—a speed almost twice that of sound. The exact data of that flight have never been published,[1] but the experts reckon that for fully fifty seconds pilot and aircraft attained a state of complete loss of gravity—a condition which could in no circumstances be produced in a pressure chamber here on earth and of which experience is absolutely nil, but which is that normally ruling in space. On the basis of the available data, a test plane is being built in America capable of climbing to forty miles and achieving a speed of seventeen hundred miles per hour.

The fantastic dreams and calculations of technicians and space fiends have of course gone far beyond such levels. They are no longer thinking in terms of single- or double-phase rockets, but of triple-phase machines that will be able to carry crews into space and will make possible vast extensions, taking off from the moon or even from an artifical satellite. For, once clear of the earth's atmosphere, there is no difficulty about continuing into pressure-

---

[1] According to later reports, the altitude reached was twenty-six miles and the speed 2,125 miles per hour.

less space, and now that the basic hindrances have been overcome, men are considering the next stages of the journey.

By taking into consideration the orbits of the planets and conditions in the field of gravitation, the course space ships will have to take can be calculated, and also the planets they can circle and still get safely back to Earth. Mars and Venus are surrounded by atmosphere whose resistance will act as a brake on the speed of space ships, and it is quite reasonable to think of landing on these planets. Others are less alluring because of their intense heat, their bitter cold, their size—resulting in a greater force of attraction which might prevent getting away again—or because of poisonous gases.

As it will not be feasible to populate the strange shores of our solar system at once, it will be necessary to alter nature as manifested there. It has already been proposed, so far as the moon is concerned, to erect great halls of Plexiglass which the colonists can fill with an atmosphere suitable to their constitutions; then they will put up hothouses in the perpetual sunshine there, obtain metals and oxygen from the rocks, and end up by living far more comfortably than on Earth. The astronomer Fritz Wicky has developed even more far-reaching plans to use atomic energy to alter the natural conditions on the planets and, where possible, to switch the constellations on to more favorable tracks.

Planning becomes more difficult when penetration into the depths of space is involved. Even using the best space ships, which will have a speed of fifty thousand miles per hour in the solar system, the vast distances of the cosmos cannot be covered in the span of time allotted to a human being. It would require a few thousand years to reach one of the nearer stars. Plans to conquer this little difficulty vary considerably. The soundest method is that of "natural reproduction"; you send a space ship off on the journey with a crew of men and women, who reproduce themselves under a strict system of birth control and pass their knowledge on undiminished to their progeny. The 140,000th generation will arrive at the destination, the Pleiades, and will then have time to think about what it intends to do there.

Other planners, who find the above arrangements too meticulous, cling to the theory of relativity. If the space ship travels at about the speed of light, the actual time taken by the vehicle is greatly reduced. In this way the passengers could, like a ray of light, travel around for thousands of terrestrial years without losing more than a few weeks of actual time; so that when they return to Earth, what they count as "the present," together with their friends and relations, will long ago have disappeared in the gray mists of the past—at least so far as the generation then populating the world is concerned. (If the reader finds this passage lacking in clarity, will he please place the blame not on the author, but on the theory of relativity and the difficulties of presenting its ideas.)

Still others attempt to solve the problem by different flights of the intellect. Human intelligence, they say, cannot yet comprehend the fourth dimension, but one day it will break through that barrier, too, and then it will require only a jerk in order to turn up in a completely different part of the cosmos which today appears to be situated millions of light years away.

Such visions are too remote for present reality: let us content ourselves with the pronouncement of a rocket specialist that in order to compass such things mankind first needs some entirely revolutionary discovery so novel as to be comparable to Faraday's discovery of electromagnetic waves. If by such a step forward it became possible to achieve the speed of light by the use of cosmic or atomic particles, the doors would be opening on journeys into distant space. At the moment nobody has the faintest idea how or whether they can be achieved. All the same, the possibilities already revealed are sufficiently exciting.

Wernher von Braun, now only just over forty, is pushing on toward the fulfillment of space-ship travel with as much enthusiasm as when he was a boy. He is one of the few who have to their credit proven successes with the construction of novel types of rockets, and the very detailed plans he has worked out must therefore be given very serious attention. The pace von Braun would like to set is inclined to make the other experts feel slighty giddy. They doubt that his space rockets will stand more than one journey. They think of the labor that goes to the maintenance of a single rocket power unit, and reel backward at the notion of the fifty-one rocket ignition chambers that von Braun's space ship would require, remembering that a single irregularity in one of the fire-spitting jets could be the certain cause of a catastrophe: they recall that even the "WAC Corporal" returned to earth with partially fused steel plates. Specialists are always producing objections from their own particular spheres of study, and doubtless there will be considerable changes in von Braun's basic plans. But it is equally without doubt that any journey through space will have to take those plans into consideration or even incorporate them wholly; and in trying to conceive what the first leap into space will look like, it is essential to occupy one's mind with the thoughts von Braun has published in various places.

The greatest obstacle is the elimination of Earth's attraction. If it proves possible for man to construct a base outside Earth's atmosphere, it will be comparatively easy to start out into space from it, for there would be neither gravity nor atmospheric pressure to contend with as brakes on velocity. That is why von Braun has occupied his mind particularly with this problem. This is what he has written: "The development of the space station is as inevitable as tomorrow's sunrise; man has poked his nose into space and won't withdraw it."

There is a natural law that makes it possible to construct an artificial moon—in fact, the same law that keeps the real moon on its course around Earth. All you have to do is to keep the forward speed of the satellite and Earth's attraction constantly balanced, so that the artificial moon, just like the real one, would be continually rushing Earthward and at the same time be dragged away from Earth by its forward momentum. The best place for the balanced orbit of an artificial satellite of this kind is, according to von Braun's calculations, at a height of just under eleven hundred miles; there the station would have a speed of 15,750 miles per hour and would thus circle Earth every two hours. Having once reached that speed, no further driving-power is necessary, for there is no atmospheric friction; moreover, the men on the station would have no sensation of great speed, though circling Earth in two hours.

The emptiness of space is the ideal realm for the use of rocket power, for it contains the most suitable liquids, among them a mixture of nitrogen and hydrogen, called "hydrazin," and nitric acid, which von Braun declares to be exceptional sources of power.

His three-phase rocket ship is 250 feet high—about the height of a twenty-four-story skyscraper—and weighs 6,400 tons, or about the same as a light cruiser. This monster can lift a crew and load of more than 30 tons into space.

At the very start the fifty-one rocket chambers in the base section (the first "step") release their jets. Within 84 seconds three million pounds of fuel are consumed, resulting in a thrust of 12,800 tons. With a thunderous roar the monster, fully equipped with automatic steering, lifts very slowly—only fifteen feet in the first second—gains speed, and steers away in a flat trajectory, for this rocket cannot fly straight or even diagonally to its destination, but instead must circle half of Earth between starting and arriving.

Twenty-five miles up, it has already attained a speed of 5,300 miles per hour. The thrust of the first "step" gets throttled back to zero and the thirty-four combustion chambers of the second start to function, producing an additional thrust of 1,600 tons and using up during their 124 seconds of activity seven hundred tons of fuel. At the same time the base section is cast off and falls into the ocean; a hundred and fifty feet above the surface, ten rockets reduce the rate of fall, so that the body falls fairly gently into the water and can be salvaged by ships. Meanwhile, the rocket ship has climbed to a height of forty miles and achieved a velocity of 15,000 miles per hour; it then sheds the middle section, which is also retrieved later. Now the head flies on alone and 84 seconds later has achieved a speed of 17,130 miles per hour and a height of seventy-five miles. At this point, power can be turned off, for friction has ceased to exert its force, and the space ship arrives by its own momentum at the intended level of the "two-hour track" where the satellite is to be built.

With the assistance of a few maneuvers—a short burst from the jets and an automatic orientation—the ship swings onto the track and itself starts to play the part of an artificial satellite, circling the earth at a constant height—1,080 miles—at a constant speed. The crew will have the impression that the ship is motionless while Earth rotates once every two hours below. The journey will have taken fifty-six minutes, of which only five will have been made under jet power.

Now the crew of the space ship, clad in special space outfits, begin to build the station. The work will not be very hard, as everything will be happening in soundless, gravity-less space, where even the biggest pieces of equipment need only be tipped out; nothing can fall, be it man or object, for everything, obedient to the law of satellites, floats without weight in space. The only thing to be guarded against is being carried away; but small applications of rocket power can soon bring one back to the right place.

Since the cargo of one space ship is insufficient to build a space station, a supply line is necessary. Other space ships follow and lie alongside the building-site. After twelve flights the station is complete. Von Braun has even calculated the cost of the whole operation—four billion dollars—and if work were started today, we could see the artificial satellite circling our planet as a visible star within ten years.

Even the size and power of the space station have been worked out down to the last detail—such as its circular shape, rotation, ventilation, water supply, and engines powered by the sun. Being free from surrounding atmospheres, it would provide novel possibilities for the exploration and observation both of space and of Earth's surface, every corner of which would be closely watched through special optical instruments, thus putting an end to the age of Iron Curtains and secret military preparations. The station could even be of military value by threatening every point on Earth's surface with annihilation by atomic bombs, so that the builders of the first space station could either have complete control over the globe or enforce the peaceful co-operation of all nations.

But having succeeded in reaching the requisite height for a space station, there still remains the problem of how to get back:

a problem not of thrust but of braking-power. The space ship (the third component of the rocket) leaves the two-hour track and reduces its speed to 1,025 miles per hour, but as it nears Earth it starts to dive and acquires a velocity of 18,750 miles per hour. This is where the skill of the pilot comes in, for he must now allow the ship to circle the earth at a height of fifty miles. Atmospheric pressure gradually puts a brake on speed, during which process the outer casing of the ship's hull reaches a temperature of 700° Centigrade and becomes red-hot. During this gliding flight the craft gradually loses height and speed, till at fifteen miles above the earth it is traveling at only the speed of sound and can then circle down to the ground like a conventional aircraft.

The great space station will serve, among many other purposes, as the starting-place for journeys into space; once it is in being, the first flights to the moon will soon follow. As von Braun says, that is "a comparatively easy undertaking" because it will not be necessary to build a new space ship and the whole journey there and back will take only ten days. The moon ship will be put together on the space station and will consist of the power plant of the head (the third component) of the space rocket, which will be mounted on a light fabrication of aluminum supports. A few fuel tanks with the fuel in them, a few controls, and a cabin are all the moon ship will require, and it will not be rocket-shaped as in the best of thrillers—for there is no air pressure to counteract in space—but a strange polyglobal contraption.

The moon ship will leave the station with the considerable velocity already imparted by it, and, after a short two-minute burst of rocket power, will then hurtle on an exact course to the moon at 22,000 miles per hour. After an unpowered flight of five days the continual drag of Earth's attraction will bring it to a halt precisely fifty miles above the surface of the moon's reverse side. No power is necessary for the return journey, which will be effected by the attractive power of Earth; the moon's attractive power is too weak to influence the ship. During its "Earthward fall" the moon ship gradually regains its velocity of 22,000 miles per hour, checks it with a two-minute power burst, and rejoins the two-hour track at the space station. Landing and taking-off tests on the actual surface of the moon will follow on later flights.

Oddly enough, flights to Venus and Mars, which are also within the realm of possibility, would not need much more fuel than a moon flight because a lower velocity would be required to reach a point outside the sphere of Earth's attraction. Thence, the space ship (obviously a better-constructed vessel than the moon ship) would fly unpowered through the firmament under the influence of the sun's attraction, just like a stone thrown by somebody. But the ship's course would have to be computed with meticulous exactitude in this case.

The journey to Mars—or, more precisely, to a circular track about Mars or to one of its satellites—would have to be very thoroughly prepared on a national or international basis. In order to assemble all the material for such an expedition, 950 space-rocket flights to the space station would be necessary, and these preliminaries alone would eat up 5,320,000 tons of fuel. After hundreds of tons of provisions, water, oxygen, instruments, and the rest have been ferried there, the fleet of ten ships in close convoy could start: it would be madness to undertake such a flight with only one space ship. Seven of these would be principally engaged in carrying passengers; the other three would be transports, to be left behind on Mars. Seventy people, all experts in the most varied branches of science who had undergone a year's training with this flight in view, would be engaged in the venture.

After a flight in space lasting 260 days—on an elliptical, not a straight, course to the objective—the space ships would pick up a course 625 miles above the surface of Mars and would circle as regularly as the space station circles Earth. There would then be plenty of time for observations and landing-attempts in special small space boats, for not until 449 days later would the relative position of Mars and Earth be such that a return journey could be begun, having due regard to the courses of the planets. The journey back to old Earth would take another 260 days, so that those space travelers who had come through it all alive would have been two and a half years away from home by the time they got back.

The technical means for penetration into space are either available now or can be provided in a reasonably short time. It will be possible to develop, for the first landings on strange stars, remote-controlled robots that will be able, with the aid of electronic brains, to do all sorts of work. But in the long run man himself will have to share in the desperately risky business of space travel, and he is the weakest link in the performance of this great adventure, for his development has been achieved in conditions diametrically opposite to those ruling in space and on the other starry bodies. The first space adventurers must be tough, highly trained men of action with nerves of iron, prepared to risk their very necks. It will not be difficult to get volunteers for the venture. Plenty of volunteers offer themselves even now for rocket experiments at the American rocket centers, and a year or two ago, when the Hayden Planetarium in New York jokingly offered reservations for trips to the moon and other planets, twenty-five thousand people from all over the world, most of whom were quite prepared to travel through space, made interested inquiries.

In the days of the great mariners a handful of reckless men dared the perils of unknown horrors inflated by fairytale repetition. Today's space pioneers have precise knowledge of the perils to which they will be exposed. These are incomparably more terrifying than anything that has ever menaced all the irrepressible adventurers in the world's history.

The very ascent of the rocket subjects men to forces that nature has not equipped them to withstand. The lightning-like acceleration increases Earth's drag fourfold. When a car starts violently, it is easy to observe that a human body resists every acceleration as a result of its inertia. What is a gentle pressure in a car becomes a shattering force in a rocket. The space traveler immediately feels as if several people were lying on him; forty seconds after the start he weighs the equivalent of a marble statue of his own body, and a few seconds later he has acquired the weight of a monument of solid iron. This is not the result of the terrific speed of the vessel; it is due to the acceleration alone, which, just before the first and second components are shed, for a few seconds reaches eight or nine times the force of gravity and so increases the passenger's weight eight- or ninefold. It has been revealed during aero-medical tests in centrifuges that a man in a sitting position collapses when the force of gravity is raised from five to six times. Space travelers will lie on beds made to fit their bodies to an inch; lying on their backs, men have already stood a seven-fold weight increase for as long as two minutes during tests. It is therefore assumed that strong specimens with a healthy circulation can stand a rocket start with no worse effects than blackout and exhaustion.

The next unusual condition the space traveler will have to get used to is just the opposite: loss of gravity. It may be amusing to picture men floating around while the morsel they want to eat jumps off the spoon and the milk refuses to pour out of the bottle but spurts out of it like a fountain at the slightest agitation. But the feelings of a man exposed to that state would in actual fact be far from amusing, for with his loss of gravity every means of sensing direction would also disappear: he would have the feeling that the floor had been removed from under his feet and that he was involved in a never-ending fall. After many painful experiences and after bumping himself black and blue all over, he will eventually get adjusted to these conditions, and his life will have been brightened during his sojourn on the space station by a slight increase of gravity artificially furnished by its rotary motion.

Space offers man nothing but perils; he will have to summon up all his inventive skill in order to counter them. The problem of oxygen supply will have to be solved. The walls of the ship will, we hope, give enough protection against the sun's ultra-violet rays, which, in the absence of mitigating atmosphere, would roast human beings alive in no time. There is no knowledge yet whether they can stand up to the cosmic rays in space over a period. The windows of the ship and of the station will have shutters that will be opened only for observation purposes, for the "unearthly" aspect of the sky will be insupportable—a knife-like contrast between the white-hot sun and the Stygian darkness of space. So the first men to leave Earth's atmosphere and approach the sun will have to live in artificial lighting.

The absence of cushioning atmosphere will also allow the sun's heat so powerful an effect that outside walls will have to be specially treated with preparations like magnesium oxide, in order to deflect the rays and keep the interior cool.

On the journeys to other planets the perils increase in a ratio that cannot be foreseen. The greatest danger of all is that one of the many artificial means man needs to maintain himself in space may fail, or that unpredictable external accidents will result in his annihilation. A most serious menace will be that of meteors hurtling about space; in Earth's atmosphere these are checked and worn down, but in the cosmos they go whirling around at a velocity of hundreds of thousands of miles per hour, and if they were only the size of a grain of sand they would go clean through the wall of a space ship. Protection can no doubt be evolved against the very small ones, but nobody knows how a space ship is to survive a collision with one of the larger meteors. And even if safety measures such as ejector cabins can be evolved against all kinds of disaster, the fact remains that if man is exposed without protection or artificial assistance to a single one of the conditions obtaining in space, in that instant he dies. He is suffocated for want of oxygen, or the lack of atmospheric pressure brings his blood to boiling-point, or the temperature murders him—everything is fatal to him.

However ghastly the dangers pictured beforehand by the sailors who ventured in the ships of Columbus or Magellan, they are nothing in comparison to the perils that the space traveler of the future can already gauge with such nice precision. If it ever really proves possible to burst through the sky above us, it will be only because the spirit that has always spurred the great explorers on to cross the horizon is still at work. So while the external circumstances and the technical factors allow of no comparison, tomorrow's discoverer can find in yesterday's the pattern of energy, intelligence, courage, depth of character, and readiness to die. He will also find plenty of discouraging examples of human weakness, error, and vice. And one of the greatest lessons history can pass on to the explorer of the future is the realization that exploration is not just a mere matter of discovering; he will also have to be able to take all that discovery implies and demands.

BIBLIOGRAPHY

American Geographical Society of New York: *Problems of Polar Research.* New York, 1928.

Amundsen, R. E. G.: *First Crossing of the Polar Sea.* New York, 1927.

——: *My Life as an Explorer.* New York, 1927.

Arciniegas, G.: *Amerigo and the New World.* New York, 1955.

Bakeless, J. E.: *Lewis and Clark, Partners in Discovery.* New York, 1947.

Baker, J. N. L.: *A History of Geographical Discovery and Exploration.* London, 1937.

Beaglehole, J. C.: *The Exploration of the Pacific.* London, 1934.

Beazley, Sir Raymond: *The Dawn of Modern Geography.* 3 vols. Oxford, 1897–1906.

——: *Prince Henry the Navigator.* London, 1895.

Belcher, Sir Edward: *The Last of the Arctic Voyages.* London, 1855.

Berens, S. L. (comp.): *The Fram Expedition.* Philadelphia, 1897.

Biggar, H. P.: *Precursors of Jacques Cartier.* Ottawa, 1911.

Bishop, M.: *Champlain: the Life of Fortitude.* New York, 1948.

Bolton, H. E.: *Coronado, Knight of Pueblos and Plains.* New York, 1949.

Bourne, E. G.: *Narratives of the Career of Hernando de Soto.* 2 vols. New York, 1922.

Brainard, D. L.: *Six Came Back: the Arctic Adventures of David L. Brainard,* edited by Bessie Rowland James. Indianapolis, 1940.

Brebner, J. B.: *The Explorers of North America, 1492–1806.* London, 1933.

Brown, L.: *The Story of Maps.* Boston, 1949.

Byrd, R. E.: *Discovery: the Story of the Second Byrd Antarctic Expedition.* New York, 1935.

——: *Little America; Aerial Exploration in the Antarctic; the Flight to the South Pole.* New York, 1930.

Cartier, Jacques: *The Voyages of Jacques Cartier,* edited by H. P. Biggar. Ottawa, 1924.

Cary, M. and Warmington, E. H.: *The Ancient Explorers.* London, 1929.

Chatterton, E. K.: *Captain John Smith.* New York, 1927.

Cherry-Garrard, A.: *The Worst Journey in the World; Antarctic 1910–1913.* London, 1937.

Christie, E. W. H.: *The Antarctic Problem.* London, 1951.

Clowes, G. S. L.: *Sailing Ships: Their History and Development.* 2 pts. London, Science Museum, 1931–1936.

Cook, F. A.: *My Attainment of the Pole.* New York, 1912.

Cook, J.: *Captain Cook's Voyages of Discovery,* edited by John Barrow. London, 1944.

Coupland, Sir Reginald: *Livingstone's Last Journey.* London, 1945.

Crouse, H. M.: *In Quest of the Western Ocean.* New York, 1925.

DeLong, G. W.: *The Voyage of the Jeannette.* Boston, 1884.

De Soto, Hernando: *The Discovery and Conquest of Terra Florida*, edited by W. B. Rye. London, 1851.

Díaz del Castillo, Bernal: *The True History of the Conquest of New Spain*, edited and translated by A. P. Mandslay. 5 vols. London, 1908–1916.

Dornberger, W.: *V-2*. New York, 1954.

Franklin, Sir John: *Narrative of a Journey to the Shores of the Polar Sea in the Years 1819–1820–1821–1822*. London, 1910.

Gilfillan, S. C.: *Inventing the Ship*. Chicago, 1935.

Goldner, F. A.: *Bering's Voyages*. 2 vols. New York, 1922–1925.

——: *Russian Expansion in the Pacific, 1641–1850*. Cleveland, 1914.

Guillemard, F. H. H.: *The Life of Ferdinand Magellan and the First Circumnavigation of the Globe*. London, 1890.

Gwynn, S. L.: *Mungo Park and the Conquest of the Niger*. London, 1934.

Hakluyt, R.: *The Principal Navigations, Traffiques and Discoveries of the English Nation*. 8 vols. London, 1913.

Hart, H. H.: *Sea Road to the Indies*. New York, 1950.

Heawood, E.: *A History of Geographical Discovery in the 17th and 18th Centuries*. Cambridge, 1912.

Henry, T. R.: *The White Continent*. New York, 1950.

Hulbert, A. B. (ed.): *The Crown Collection of Photographs of American Maps*. 5 vols. Cleveland, 1904–1928.

Humboldt, A. von: *Personal Narrative of Travels to the Equinoctial Regions of America During the Years 1799–1804*. London, 1852.

Jane, C. (ed.): *Select Documents Illustrating the Four Voyages of Columbus*. 2 vols. London, 1930–1933.

Joerg, W. L. G.: *Brief History of Polar Exploration Since the Introduction of Flying*. New York, 1930.

Johnston, Sir Harry Hamilton: *A History of the Colonization of Africa by Alien Races*. Cambridge, 1913.

Kamal, Prince Youssouf: *Monumenta Cartographica Africæ et Ægypti*. Cairo, 1926– (in course of publication).

Kimble, G. H. T.: *Geography in the Middle Ages*. London, 1938.

Kirkpatrick, F. A.: *The Spanish Conquistadores*. London, 1934.

La Condamine, C. M. de: *Histoire des pyramides*. Paris, 1751.

——: *Journal du voyage fait par ordre du Roi a l'équateur*. Paris, 1751.

——: *Mesure des trois premiers degrés du méridien*. Paris, 1751.

Levermore, C. H. (ed.): *Forerunners and Competitors of the Pilgrims and Puritans*. 2 vols. Brooklyn, 1912.

Ley, C. D.: *Portuguese Voyages, 1498–1663*. London, 1947.

Ley, W.: *Rockets, Missiles and Space Travel*. New York, 1952.

Livingstone, D.: *Missionary Travels and Researches in South Africa*. New York, 1860.

——: *Some Letters from Livingstone 1840–1872*, edited by David Chamberlin. London, 1940.

Lorant, S.: *The New World*. New York, 1946.

Markham, Sir Clements: *The Journal of Christopher Columbus and Documents relating to John Cabot and Gaspar Corte Real*. London, 1893.

——: *The Lands of Silence.* Cambridge, 1921.

——: *The Letters of Amerigo Vespucci.* London, 1894.

Means, P. A.: *Fall of the Inca Empire, and Spanish Rule in Peru 1530–1780.* New York, 1932.

Mill, H. R.: *The Siege of the South Pole.* London, 1905.

Mirsky, J.: *To the Arctic.* New York, 1948.

Morison, S. E.: *Admiral of the Ocean Sea.* 2 vols. Boston, 1942.

Murphy, R. G.: *Logbook for Grace.* New York, 1947.

Nansen, F.: *Farthest North.* New York, 1897.

——: *In Northern Mists.* 2 vols. New York, 1911.

Newton, A. P.: *The European Nations in the West Indies 1493–1688.* London, 1933.

——(ed.): *The Great Age of Discovery.* London, 1932.

——(ed.): *Travel and Travellers of the Middle Ages.* London, 1930.

Nordenskiöld, A. E.: *Facsimile-Atlas to the Early History of Cartography with Reproductions of the Most Important Maps Printed in the XV and XVI Centuries.* Stockholm, 1889.

——: *Periplus: an Essay on the Early History of Charts and Sailing Directions.* Stockholm, 1897.

Nordenskiöld, Otto: *The Geography of the Polar Regions.* New York, 1928.

Nunn, G. E.: *The Geographical Conceptions of Columbus.* New York, 1924.

Owen, R.: *The Antarctic Ocean.* New York, 1941.

Park, M.: *The Travels of Mungo Park.* London, 1910.

Parkman, F.: *The Jesuits in North America.* Boston, 1882.

——: *La Salle and the Discovery of the Great West.* Boston, 1942.

——: *Pioneers of France in the New World.* Boston, 1882.

Parks, G. B.: *Richard Hakluyt and the English Voyages.* New York, 1930.

Parry, Sir William: *Three Voyages for the Discovery of a Northwest Passage from the Atlantic to the Pacific.* New York, 1840.

Peary, R. E.: *The Discovery of the North Pole.* New York, 1910.

Penrose, B.: *Travel and Discovery in the Renaissance 1420–1620.* Cambridge, Mass., 1952.

Pizarro, Pedro: *Relation of the Discovery of the Kingdoms of Peru,* translated and edited by P. A. Means. 2 vols. New York, 1921.

Pohl, F. J.: *Amerigo Vespucci: Pilot Major.* New York, 1944.

Polo, Marco: *The Book of Ser Marco Polo,* edited by Sir Henry Yule and Henry Cordier. 2 vols. London, 1921.

Prescott, W. H.: *History of the Conquest of Mexico and Peru.* New York, 1936.

Prestage, E.: *The Portuguese Pioneers.* London, 1932.

Ravenstein, E. G.: *Martin Behaim: His Life and His Globe.* London, 1908.

Ronne, F.: *Antarctic Conquest: the Story of the Ronne Expedition 1946–1948.* New York, 1949.

Ruge, S.: *Geschichte des Zeitalters der Entdeckungen.* Berlin, 1881.

Sanceau, E.: *The Land of Prester John, a Chronicle of Portuguese Exploration.* New York, 1944.

Scott, R. F.: *Scott's Last Expedition.* 2 vols. New York, 1913.

Scott, R. F.: *The Voyage of the Discovery*. 2 vols. New York, 1905.

Shackleton, Sir Ernest Henry: *The Heart of the Antarctic; being the Story of the British Antarctic Expedition 1907–1909*. 2 vols. Philadelphia, 1909.

Smith, J.: *The Generall Historie of Virginia, New England and the Summer Isles, Together with the True Travels, Adventures and Observations, and a Sea Grammar* . . . 2 vols. Glasgow, 1907.

Sörensen, J.: *The Saga of Fridtjof Nansen*. New York, 1932.

Spruce, R.: *Notes of a Botanist on the Amazon and the Andes*. 2 vols. London, 1908.

Stanley, D. (ed.): *The Autobiography of Sir Henry M. Stanley*. Boston, 1909.

Stanley, H. M.: *In Darkest Africa*. 2 vols. London, 1890.

Stefansson, V.: *The Friendly Arctic*. New York, 1921.

——: *Great Adventures and Explorations*. New York, 1947.

Stevenson, E. L.: *Terrestrial and Celestial Globes*. 2 vols. New Haven, 1921.

Sykes, Sir Percy: *A History of Exploration*. London, 1950.

Taylor, E. G. R.: *Late Tudor and Early Stuart Geography 1583–1650*. London, 1934.

——: *Tudor Geography 1485–1583*. London, 1930.

Thwaites, R. G.: *Original Journals of the Lewis and Clark Expedition 1804–1806*. 7 vols. New York, 1905.

Tschudi, J. J.: *Travels in Peru*. New York, 1847.

Vaillant, G. C.: *Aztecs of Mexico: Origin, Rise and Fall of the Aztec Nation*. New York, 1941.

Von Hagen, V. W.: *South America Called Them*. New York, 1945.

Wagner, H. R.: *Sir Francis Drake's Voyage Around the World: Its Aims and Achievements*. San Francisco, 1926.

Whymper, E.: *Travels Among the Great Andes of Ecuador*. London, 1892.

Wieder, F. D. (ed.): *Monumenta Cartographica: Reproductions of Unique and Rare Maps, Plans and Views in the Actual Size of the Originals; Accompanied by Cartographical Monographs*. 5 vols. The Hague, 1925–1933.

Williamson, J. A.: *The Age of Drake*. London, 1938.

——: *Hawkins of Plymouth*. London, 1949.

——: *The Voyages of the Cabots*. London, 1929.

Winsor, J.: *Christopher Columbus*. Boston, 1891.

—— (ed.): *Narrative and Critical History of America*. 8 vols. Boston, 1884–1889.

Wolf, A.: *History of Science, Technology and Philosophy in the 16th and 17th Centuries*. London, 1935.

——: *History of Science, Technology and Philosophy in the 18th Century*. London, 1939.

Wright, J. K.: *The Geographical Lore of the Time of the Crusades: a Study in the History of Medieval Science and Tradition in Western Europe*. New York, 1925.

Zim, H. S.: *Rockets and Jets*. New York, 1945.

INDEX

A NOTE ON THE TYPE
IN WHICH THIS BOOK IS SET

The text of this book is set in Caledonia, *a Linotype face that belongs to the family of printing types called "modern face" by printers—a term used to mark the change in style of type-letters that occurred about 1800. Caledonia borders on the general design of Scotch Modern, but is more freely drawn than that letter.*

The book was composed, printed, and bound by Kingsport Press, Inc., Kingsport, Tennessee. The typography and binding design are based on originals by W. A. Dwiggins.